# FIVE HUNDRED FEET
# TO GO

He tried momentarily to trace the source of
the leak, but the constant slopping of the
rising pool of water in the sphere made this
impossible. The immediate danger was that
the submersible would come to a stop sooner
rather than later and begin to sink back into
the deep, the mounting pressure of water
accelerating it beyond his control, trapping
and drowning him in the plummeting
bubble.

Now he felt the grip of chill through the
survival suit, which, though it protected him
against sudden hypothermia, would do
nothing to stave off the bone-twisting pain
and death from the bends.

# DEEP
# CHILL

D0595681

# DEEP CHILL

## IAN SLATER

# W🌐RLDWIDE®

TORONTO · NEW YORK · LONDON · PARIS
AMSTERDAM · STOCKHOLM · HAMBURG
ATHENS · MILAN · TOKYO · SYDNEY

For my brother, Robert

**DEEP CHILL**

A Worldwide Library Book/June 1989

ISBN 0-373-97104-4

# ACKNOWLEDGMENT

I would like to thank Dr. Noel Boston, a friend from my oceanographic days who is now Executive Vice President of Bennett Environmental Consultants, Vancouver. I also extend my gratitude to my friend, Professor Charles Slonecker, for his help. Most of all, I am indebted to my wife, Marian, whose patience, typing and editorial skills continue to give me invaluable support in my work.

"You can't get enough of it', can you?" she added happily, her soft auburn hair streaming out on the hard sea breeze

# 1

FRANK AND GLORIA were enjoying a relaxing walk—until they heard the screams.

Standing on the high vantage point of Oregon's windswept Ecola Point fifteen miles south of the Columbia River's mouth, with the vast Pacific blue stretching westward before them, Frank Hall and Gloria Bernardi were looking out at the lonely, deserted lighthouse. It looked the size and shape of a square wedding cake, atop the jagged coal-black fist of Tillamook Rock, punching out of the sea more than a mile offshore. He told Gloria about the great storm of October 1934, when hundred-mile-per-hour winds drove waves so huge that they threw fifty-pound boulders more than 130 feet into the air, smashing the lantern's prism and extinguishing the light that warned sailors of the danger that lay in wait off the great, brooding mass that was Tillamook Headland. Despite the lighthouse—and the brave keepers who manned it for more than seventy years until a modern automatic beacon was installed in 1957—scores of ships and their crews had perished, and no doubt more would perish, off the rugged, surf-pounded coast.

"What a cheery soul you are," said Gloria playfully. "I would have thought you of all people would have had enough of storms." She was referring to the storm that had assailed both the *Petrel*, the oceanographic research ship Hall had been on, and the island where she had been banding and studying seabird rookeries for her graduate degree at the University of Oregon. She and Hall had come close to perishing then themselves.

"You can't get enough of it, can you?" she added happily, her soft auburn hair streaming out on the hard sea breeze.

"I refuse to answer that question," he answered, grinning, "on the grounds that it may incriminate me."

"The *sea*," she replied. "I meant the sea—not sex."

His boyish smile made him look younger than his thirty-seven years; his blue eyes were highlighted against his sea tan and his brown shock of hair parted by the wind.

They continued up the narrow path, following the spine of the cliff, passing wind-sculptured spruce and pine that swept up the mountainside behind them.

Pausing at the summit to take in the southern vista of forest, cliff and sea that had so moved Clark at the end of his and Lewis's crossing of the continent in 1806, Hall recalled Clark's description of the view as one of "the grandest and most pleasing prospects which my eyes ever surveyed." Sweeping south beneath them was the surf-laced curve of Crescent Beach, and Haystack Rock, enwreathed in gossamer mist so that the monolith sparkled jewel-like in the morning sun. Seabirds crowded about the rock. A few brave surfing types, black dots in their rubber wet suits, were paddling out from it and the cluster of smaller rocks surrounding it at the foot of the coastal mountains that swept majestically back from the sea in a wave of green forest. The forest extended as far as Cape Falcon and the unmistakable bulk of Neahkahnie Mountain, which looked out of the distant spray.

What Gloria had said was true, and he knew it. Despite all the dangers he'd experienced in salvage work and in searching for sea gold—the metalliferous, or metal-rich, muds that came jetting up from the ocean floor where volcanic-fed vents had ruptured into the sea bottom—Hall loved it; he loved everything to do with the sea. He took such pleasure in explaining to her how superheated water travelled thousands of miles below the earthen crust, leaching out vitally needed minerals such as cobalt and nickel, and then suddenly spurted forth in the ice-cold of the deep seas, often when the great sea plates had buckled against each other. Where minerals separated out, there were formed the much sought-after mounds of extraordinarily rich mineral deposits; also, by chemosynthesis in the warmth and nutrient-rich environment of the superheated vents, an astonishing profusion of sea life often existed where it had been thought impossible for anything to live. Gloria knew that, as beautiful and rich as the deposits were, they were extremely difficult to locate, and that only those with an expert knowledge of the deep seas, like Frank, stood any chance of finding them. The name Haystack Rock reminded her of the nature of his profession—looking for the proverbial needle in the haystack. The areas to search in the deep oceans were so vast, the competition so fierce and unscrupulous and the danger of the sea so formidable that more than once he had been involved in a battle for his very survival. Still, he told her, he loved the sea, even though his most recent search for sea gold off the coast of Oregon had not yielded a single test tube of the stuff, not even a core barrel sample.

Rather it had brought him afoul of a highly unsavory member of Swiss financial circles, Herr Klaus, the owner of the multinational giant SRP—Swiss Rhine Petrochemicals. In an effort to have the North American scarce-mineral market all to himself, Klaus had involved the Soviet government, which had marked Hall as an oceanographer to be watched—the kind of fearless American who would challenge a rival head-on, a modern man who exhibited, as Moscow had put on file, that "curious old-fashioned capitalistic trait" that Americans described as "putting everything on the line." Frank was a cowboy, Moscow had decided, his weapons not the horse or six-gun or the lariat, of course, but the modern research ship and the know-how to probe the deepest reaches of the sea.

Hall had broken records working in the new ADS—Atmospheric Diving Suit—going where no man had ever gone before, with nothing but a tether line connecting him to a ship, inside the ADS's suit an oxygen tank and carbon dioxide scrubber. At a pressure of one thousand pounds per square inch the slightest rupture would have meant instant death. But for Frank Hall, life itself was a risk. You did what you could to minimize the risk, but the only constant at sea was the unexpected, which could hit you at any time. You shoved the fear away from you and got on with the job—whether it was checking out a telephone cable in two hundred feet of water on the eastern seaboard's continental shelf or retrieving a torpedo that had gone haywire in one of the Navy testing ranges in the Straits of Juan de Fuca off the Canada-U.S. border, or locating and helping to retrieve artifacts for the British Museum off Andros Island in the Caribbean.

In all that time Hall had learned only two things for certain: that working in the deep sea was much tougher than working in space, which was one of the reasons NASA trained their astronauts underwater first; and that while the first mistake you make in most businesses won't ruin you, in deep sea it can kill you. He had already attended the funerals of a half-dozen friends—scuba and hard hats alike.

The danger was the thing he knew that Gloria worried about most; though she hadn't told him yet, it was the one thing that still held her back from saying yes, she'd marry him. She loved him, but she wasn't sure she could live with the constant knowledge that whenever he was called out in an emergency, or even just instructing a group of would-be treasure hunters in a tank, something as simple yet unpredictable as an appendicitis attack might occur, something that could safely be put right ashore but that could kill you fifty feet under. Every time he'd go out to dive she'd be left worrying about whether he'd come back. She wondered whether she'd get used to it after a while, like the spouses of airline pilots or police officers. And what kind of life would that be? One thing she was determined not to do was to marry him and try to turn him away from the danger. If the deep sea was where he wanted to work, then that was what would make him happiest, and therefore both of them happiest.

"Do you ever get used to it?" she had once asked the wife of another diver.

"No."

"Does it get better—I mean as they get older?"

"No. They have to make enough money before they get too old to do the job—so the older they get, the harder they push themselves. The risks keep going up. You ever see the insurance rates for an old diver, honey? By 'old' I'm talking forty, forty-five."

Gloria was thinking about that now, as she looked over at Frank. She had sat down on a rock, but he still stood gazing out to sea, watching a school of jellyfish, their translucent blue bells all but invisible except for the sun glinting off them as they washed in with the tide. "Thought you might be getting tired of it all," she said, despite her resolve. "Have you ever thought of teaching, Frank—I mean starting up a school for oceanographic—"

"We know so little about it," he said, sitting down next to her.

"*You* say that?" she said. "You know more about the sea than anyone I know, and practical, everyday stuff."

Frank shrugged, with an old-fashioned modesty that Gloria liked. "We've only dipped our toes in," he explained. "Three-quarters of our world is covered in water, and we still know so little." She could see he was getting excited again. "You know," he went on, oblivious to the smile on her lips, "that sea washing in a couple of hundred feet below us could well be the same sea that washed these shores a million years ago, the same water that rose, became snow, melted, formed the rivers that flowed into... well, the saline solution in our mothers' wombs is almost exactly the same as that of the sea and that—"

"Frank!"

He stopped. "What?"

She reached out and stroked his muscular forearm. "Let's go back to the cabin."

He looked down at her then, and reaching for her, forgot all about oceanography. "We don't have to go back to the cabin." He began kissing her neck.

"Someone'll see us here," she said.

He lifted her chin. "Are you serious?" He nodded toward Cannon Beach, a mile or so south down the trail through the long bracken and fern. "Look," he said, "not a soul within miles." He turned to the sweep of the mountain behind them and, cupping his hands, shouted, "Is anybody there? Bird watchers? Perverts?"

"You nut!" She laughed. "Someone might come up the trail."

"Then," he said, doing a bad Groucho Marx imitation, "we'll lurk in the bushes, m'dear. Entertain the woodland critters."

"I love you," she said.

He held her close and they kissed deeply, longingly.

"Let's go to the cabin," she repeated.

"It's a mile and a half," he said. "I'll never last! You're driving me crazy—you know that?"

"Uh-huh," she said blissfully. "Let's go to the cabin." She tried to get up but he pulled her back, her breasts against his face. She pushed him off. "The cabin!" She started off toward the track's summit, then down the trail toward the beach. He took off after her as she disappeared from view.

Then they heard the screams.

# 2

RUNNING AT PERISCOPE DEPTH, her radio whip up for the quick, twice-weekly, top-secret CLS—coded location signal— the USS *New York* approached the shallow waters of the Bering Strait that led to the Chukchi Sea. The eighteen-thousand-ton leviathan, a Trident nuclear ballistic-missile submarine SSBN 921, took a "search" periscope fix on the projection of Fairway Island several miles off her port side. Then, retracting her whip aerial, the *New York* swung away from the Alaskan "door" to the ice-cold Chukchi Sea, turning instead toward the western or Siberian "door." There she took another fix, this time on the Russian island of Big Diomede and the American island of Little Diomede, the jagged Siberian coast looming in the background. At last she zigzagged again, turning southward into the Bering Sea. Her secret mission was to run for four days and nights, listening for enemy activity while running close to but not crossing the ocean border between Russia and the United States that had been agreed to in 1867. After her mission the *New York* would head east for her home base in Bangor near Seattle, in Washington State.

Captain Wain was glad to be leaving the narrow fifty-mile strait between Alaska and Siberia. A scant hundred and twenty feet deep, it was too shallow for his sub to run safely submerged much below her periscope depth. He was worried, too, about the Soviet microphone arrays running on the sea bottom parallel to Siberia's Kamchatka Peninsula, where a squadron of the Soviet Pacific hunter/killer subs were based.

And in the heavily silted strait between Russia and Alaska the rafted ice floes coming down from the Chukchi Sea often penetrated thirty, sometimes fifty, feet below the surface before melting and depositing their detritus. They could trap the six-hundred-foot-long, forty-two-foot-wide and thirty-six-foot-high Trident between ice and the bottom like a beached whale. The *New York* needed deeper water, where she could run at flank speed if necessary.

The sight of a bearded crew member reminded the captain of an order he'd been intending to give, and temporarily distracted him from his worries. "Take it off," said Captain Wain, "all of it," his tone good-natured but serious.

"Gee, Captain," replied submariner Jenkins, one of the *New York*'s reactor crew. "I've kind of gotten used to it."

"I know—and it keeps you warm whenever you're topside on watch. Well, the Russkies know that, too, Jenkins, and I don't want any of them peering through their binoculars at us as we head up Hood Canal and seeing a bunch of scuzzballs. That's a dead giveaway that we've been on Arctic patrol. So shave it off, sailor."

"Yes, sir," said Jenkins, leaving the sub's command and control center directly below the twenty-five-foot-high sail. He made his way aft along the narrow gangway through "Sherwood Forest," the twenty-four seven-foot-wide and forty-five-feet-high missile tubes, to the reactor room where the "fire," or controlled nuclear fission, generated the enormous heat that boiled the water to drive the huge steam turbines. Jenkins was easygoing. The old man's orders that everyone's face had to be "as clean as a baby's bottom," by the time they reached the base at Bangor, Washington, elicited a grin amid the salt-and-pepper beard that would soon be a memory for him. It was typical of the skipper to have thought of everything days in advance. Hell, Jenkins told himself, they were only now about to start the really important part of their patrol, and it would be at least three or four days before they were clear of the Bering Sea and on their way back to Bangor and the happy lights of Seattle.

The sub was rigged for red, so that in the unwanted event that they had to surface, the eyes of the OOD—officer of the deck—and the two lookouts on the sail's bridge would be able to adjust more quickly to the darkness. In the redded-out condition of the sub Jenkins's face took on the look of a lascivious satyr. At the entrance to the reactor compartment he put on the yellow rubber bootees used to cover the operators' shoes to prevent any radioactive dust particles from being transported throughout the sub.

What, Jenkins wondered, was the skipper going to do about the Good Doctor—the name they had given to the civilian sonar expert aboard from the University of Washington. He had a beard, and what was more, Jenkins reminded his shipmates on watch in the reactor room, he had had it when he came aboard.

"You donkey, Jenkins," one of the other men told him. "The doc won't be on deck when we go past the MSF." He was talking about the special magnetic silencing facility set up on the shore of Hood Canal, which wiped off a sub's magnetic signature as it left port so that the Russians' microphone arrays throughout the Bering Sea and elsewhere couldn't readily identify a particular sub either as an SSN—nuclear attack submarine—or SSBN—a nuclear ballistic missile submarine—and so guess its assigned mission or targets.

"I forgot about that," said Jenkins. "Hey—the skipper kept him below checking out that sonar ball when we were on our way out." He nodded to himself, watching the bank of steam pressure gauges. "The skipper's a smart cookie. Too bad, though. I got a girl in Seattle who's crazy about beards."

"That's 'cause it covers your ugly face," a yeoman called Knead said sourly. "Take that fuzz off and you'll frighten the crap out of her."

"Hear that, Chief?" asked Jenkins, turning to one of the reactor room's petty officers. "Is that nice talk?"

"Never mind," said the chief. "I'll still love you."

"Aw, shit. Thanks, Chiefie."

Up forward in sonar control, his straw-colored hair bisected by the black spring of a headset, the Good Doctor, William Dyer, was listening intently along with the three other watch-standers. The tall twenty-four-year-old sonar specialist kept switching channels, each one representing a different direction of possible attack. The sounds came in on the BQQ-5 multi-purpose sonar from both the bow arrays and those trailing from the pods mounted on the stern's twin twenty-foot-high vertical stabilizer fins, which controlled the trim of the most powerful nuclear ballistic-missile submarine in the world. The *New York*'s UYK-7 computer and Mk-98 missile control systems were capable of launching its twenty-four Trident II ICBMs in less than twelve minutes. Each missile was topped with eight one-hundred-kiloton warheads, and their range was more than four thousand miles.

The *New York* was running at nowhere near her unofficial flank speed of thirty knots, having slowed down so as to reduce extraneous noise on the sonar channels. There was none of the pinging sound so often associated with submarines, for the *New York*, like the rest of her Trident K-class, was essentially a listening submarine, her heaviest reliance being on her electronically enhanced passive sonar arrays, which needed only half a watt of electricity to detect anything moving miles ahead of her. This capability, together with the streamlining of her forty-foot diameter and six-hundred-foot-long zeppelin-shaped superstructure, made the Trident the quietest SSBN in the seas. It was her greatest asset, and for the Russian hunter/killer subs their greatest danger. Unless they were lucky enough to get directly behind her, in the blind zone behind the prop, screening themselves from the pickup capability of the *New York*'s TACTAS, or tow-assisted sonar arrays, then the *New York* would always know where they were before they knew where she was. In Moscow the American submarine's advantage was unacceptable, providing a decisive edge in any nuclear engagement, one that could win a war. But so long as U.S. technology had the edge there wasn't much the Politburo or the Soviet Ministry of Defense could do about it.

"What's that?" asked one of the sonar watchstanders, pointing to a pronounced green hiccup on the round twelve-inch-diameter screen.

Dr. Dyer didn't respond right away. His face serious as usual, concentration furrowing his forehead, he looked older than his twenty-four years. He hadn't mentioned to the crew why he always looked so worried of late: his wife, Margaret, was expecting their first baby any day now. If the patrol along the U.S./Russian ocean border was completed as scheduled—in the next five or six days at most—he would be home in time. He didn't talk much about his private life, for he was a shy person, and the constant talk about sex and booze embarrassed him, some of the jokes frankly making him blush. He knew a lot about electronics but not a great deal about the world, and so mistook the sailors' preoccupation with sex as a sign of insensitivity rather than their habitual way of passing the hours off watch—and, depending on who was the officer of the deck, *on* watch, as well. Besides, despite all his scientific training, Dyer harbored the superstition that if you talked about a thing before it happened, then it wouldn't happen the way you wanted it to; some awful catastrophe would occur to punish you for your pride. Accordingly, he kept his personal concerns to himself.

Dyer held the headphone closer to his ear. The sound in question wasn't so much a surging type as much as a wide scatter, but with more intensity than that usually emitted by distant turbulence, internal waves or even the mixing of water layers of different salinity. He checked the depth gauge: two hundred and twenty feet. It could be a deep scattering layer of the kind that had perplexed so many sailors in World War II—a wide layer of plankton, the microscopic forms of life in such profusion that, rising toward the surface after sunset and falling during the day, they dispersed sonar beams; instead of reflecting a clear signal as did metal objects such as other ships, the layer gave off a "frying pan" static that had confused sonar operators and fathometers until they discovered what was causing it. That was the kind of sound Dyer was hearing now, but it was more intense, almost as if several scattering layers were stacked on one another.

"Ever heard anything like it before?" Dyer asked the other watchstanders.

No one had, but soon it increased so much that one of the men told Dyer it reminded him of fat "in the fire."

Then, above the fierce crackling, they could hear the faint throb of an engine. Dyer fed the engine's signature, faint though it was, into the computer for a matchup and identification from the master list of all known enemy subs, diesel-electric as well as nuclear—giving priority to hunter/killers in the Soviet Pacific fleet, whose SOSUS—sound surveillance system hydrophones arrays—the *New York* had been sent specifically to test and "rate according to NATO specifications."

"No Matchup" flashed on the computer screen.

"Maybe a new sub?" Captain Wain suggested over the intercom. "An Alfa?"

In the control room one of the watchstanders exchanged glances with a buddy who was sitting on watch at the ballast/control board. No one wanted to be ID'd by an Alfa. A hunter/killer, the thirty-five-hundred-ton Alfa was much smaller and harder to detect than the Soviets' monstrous thirty-thousand-ton Typhoon. At forty-two knots submerged, the Alfa was also faster than the bigger, much quieter Trident and had a titanium-alloy pressure hull, enabling it to submerge twice as deep to three thousand feet.

Dyer instructed the computer to check all Alfa subs, including those reportedly still on the ways in Leningrad's Sudomekh Yard. Three new Alfas showed up on the screen, but none was supposed to have been launched.

Nevertheless, Wain decided to play it safe. Besides, he had authority from Washington to test Trident's anti-hunter/killer tactics in an open-sea "war patrol" situation to see if it duplicated the tests carried out in the torpedo acceptance trials on the range off Keyport, Rhode Island.

"Torpedo tube report?" he barked.

"One and three, Mark 48s," was the immediate response. "Two and four, MOSS 70s."

"Very well. Sonar bearing?"

"Zero five three."

"Range?" asked the captain.

"Ten thousand yards and closing."

"Ten degrees left rudder," ordered Wain.

"Ten degrees left rudder," came the confirmation.

"Range?"

"Steady at ten thousand."

"Because we're turning?" asked Wain.

"Yes, sir." The reply came from one of the sonar watchstanders who had quietly replaced Dyer in the operator's chair now that they were in combat mode.

Wain turned to the "fairweather" or bow planesman sitting in the pilot's seat on the right side of the command and control room. The man's eyes were riveted to the depth gauges and continuous compass readouts as he eased the steering column back and forth. Immediately to Wain's left the copilot, or stern planesman, sat at an identical control column, monitoring and correcting the angle of dive and rise. The diving officer stood behind them, his khaki officer's uniform a different hue in the redded-out control room from the darker shades of the other ranks' blue denim uniforms. "Turn five degrees left rudder," Wain ordered.

"Five degrees left rudder."

Next Wain looked toward the sonar console located just forward of the control center and the thirty-five-foot sail above him. There Dyer was looking worried as he cupped a headphone to one ear, his free hand gripping the side of the console.

"Range?" Wain asked.

"Ten thousand yards and steady, sir."

"Bearing?"

"Zero four eight."

"Shoot!"

"Set."

"Fire two!"

"Fire two!" the executive officer repeated.

Wain then ordered the sub farther around on a port tack. "Fire four!"

"Fire four. Number two fired and running, sir."

The sub shuddered as the MOSS—mobile submarine simulators—streaked out, the two of them forming a V thirty-five degrees apart.

"Slow ahead. Silent running."

Their bait was cast. The two decoys emitted signals simulating a Trident. Ideally the opposition would think there were two Tridents, the second one sailing in the sound shadow of the other.

But Dyer was still looking worried. "Noise is still there," he said to no one in particular. "Sounds a bit like a . . . could be a diesel-electric running near the surface. . . ."

"Or there could be something wrong with our array," Wain suggested.

"Possible," said young Dyer, who had not been at sea for nearly as long as the captain but long enough to know that Murphy's Law—anything that can go wrong will go wrong—was even more applicable at sea than on land. He was looking at the printout from the rush of incoming sound from the two decoys. The signatures of both MOSS 70s were distinct, at least to the trained eye, but so was that of the unidentified vessel. "Darn it!" said Dyer in an uncharacteristic show of frustration. "It's still there."

The captain was more annoyed than perplexed. A MOSS was an expensive ultrasophisticated piece of equipment; it was supposed to confuse the *enemy*. It certainly wasn't meant to be ignored by them.

Wain looked across at his executive officer, who was fresh from an underwater detection course at the naval school at Monterey. "They cover this one at Monterey, Sloane?"

"No, sir. But I've got a possible explanation."

"Let's have it."

"Maybe their captain's just dumb—or he's never seen a MOSS running before."

Dyer glanced up, about to respond, but then his hand shot up to the right earphone, pressing the headset to his ear as if trying to pick up a fainter signature coming in via the *New York*'s passive array. "Moving away," he said, though this wasn't registering on the UKY-computer as it should. But he could definitely hear it, he said. Whatever the noise was, it was definitely receding.

"Unless," Sloane suggested, "they're trying to pull a fast one...somehow muffling it. Making it seem as if they're pulling out of the area."

"How would they do that?" Dyer cut in, concerned that his professional competence was being challenged.

"Don't know, Doc," answered the exec, which only worried Dyer more.

As the *New York* proceeded, the EWO—electronics warfare officer—kept checking the readouts from the hull's inbuilt sensors, which took continuous measurements of water temperature, current flow and salinity. The computers constantly compared these with the figures on the oceanographic charts, for the Trident, ever cautious about compromising its greatest asset, its quietness, felt its way through the seas using the known oceanographic data rather than risking any noise emission itself by using the narrow-beam active sonar in its belly to ascertain depth of sea. No matter how narrow the active beam or how briefly it was used, a matter of seconds even, its sound was nevertheless dispersed underwater much more quickly than in air and was capable of being heard by the Soviets' passive arrays located either on the sea's bottom or aboard the hunter/killers sniffing through the depths like predatory sharks.

Suddenly Dyer began to laugh, taking everyone in the control room by surprise. "It's not a sub at all," he announced, immediately relieved for himself, his pregnant wife, his as yet unborn child and the more than one hundred submariners aboard.

Wain was just as relieved but not nearly as happy. The Good Doctor's initial suspicion that the noise might be coming from a Soviet sub had just caused Wain to fire off a half million dollars' worth of electronic decoys for no good reason—which would have to be explained to superiors, not by Dr. Dyer but by Captain J. D. Wain.

"Are you sure it isn't a sub?" Wain pressed.

Dyer was ignorant of how little it took to ruin a naval career. "Oh, yes," he answered the captain, his self-confidence restored, growing with every increasing pulse coming in over the passive array. "There's more than one now... must be half a dozen or more."

"More what?" Wain asked coldly.

"Fishing boats probably. Diesel, of course. That's why we thought the first one was maybe a diesel sub running near or on the surface."

Even in the red light of the control room Wain's face could be seen to become a deeper shade of red at Dyer's use of *we*.

"You mean *your* sonar is working properly now, after giving us a screwed-up readout?"

Dyer didn't notice the intentional jab; he was too struck by his own brilliance. "No," he conceded graciously. "Oh, something could be malfunctioning in the sonar sphere, all right, but I can tell through the headsets. That frying noise—"

"What about it?" asked Wain.

"I think it's fishing boats as well as plankton."

"What kind of fishing boats?" asked the exec, not from any real interest but out of loyalty to his commanding officer.

"Don't know," replied Dyer. "I'm not an expert in that area, but the frequency suggests quite a few."

IN FACT there were more than fifteen hundred of them, mostly from Japan, spread over the immense stretches of the North Pacific. Another ship could go for days and not see or hear them, given the dense fogs that plague the Bering Sea. Even when the weather was relatively clear the squid and other fishing boats from the Asian fleets, primarily Korean and Taiwanese, and those from Poland, Canada and Russia were difficult for the most modern of submarines to distinguish from one another. What the general public believed to be the quiet depths of the deep ocean was, in fact, an astonishingly noisy place, where thousands of different sounds created the din of a living sea—from the stupendous grinding and, at times, explosions along the ever-changing borders of the massive oceanic plates that lay beneath the unexplored three-quarters of the planet, to the deafening crackle of the tons of microscopic organisms devoured by the great whales.

Lying in wait amid this ocean of noise, the drift net fleets bobbed up and down as they ran north and south of the Aleutian chain, using their devastatingly effective strategy to trap the massive schools of steelhead, sockeye, chum and chinook salmon that migrated through the northern Pacific during the summer months, often in the nutrient-rich upwellings from sea bottom vents, and the abundant squid so prized as a delicacy in the Asian markets. In all, the drift nets stretched out in June or July to cover more than eighteen thousand miles—enough net to extend halfway around the world—a deadly curtain of twenty-nine to sixty-six mesh per yard nylon over twenty-five feet deep, suspended beneath an endless line of bladder floats, as more than fifteen hundred drifters lay in wait for the vast schools of fish. The more the fish swarms panicked, rushing blindly at the net, the more fish ended up on the tables of the world.

But there was a huge unseen cost, a cost not tolerated in the Atlantic—but then the Atlantic, for all its fury, was much smaller and easier to police, a mere lake compared to the Pacific. The cost of using drifters was called "bycatch" or "incidental catch." A lot of fish that weren't wanted—including tens of thousands of mammals, among them whales, seals, dolphins, sea lions and porpoises—inadvertently got caught in the monofilament nets. The environmentalists protested; the fishermen said they didn't want to trap the incidental species. But what they liked even less was to lose their drift nets, which became wrapped around the mammals, particularly the beaked whales and the diving seabirds. Thousands of red-billed puffins, murres and terrified shearwaters, all fighting desperately to disentangle themselves from each vessel's twenty-mile-long net, often tangled themselves so badly that the net was dragged down by the sheer weight and fury of the life-and-death struggle. Thousands of miles of the near invisible net, the fishermen complained, were lost each summer, sinking sometimes slowly, sometimes quickly with the currents, in what the fleets with unintentional irony called a ball-up, a huge bale of net that, if it ever hit a submarine—which would probably mistake it for what it was in part, a great school of fish—could very easily entangle the sub, snagging especially about the long diving planes that extended sixteen feet from either side of the vessel's thirty-five-foot-high sail.

ONE SECOND the *New York* was gliding along at twenty-five knots at five hundred feet, the next she was plunging toward the bottom, dropping like a stone in a vortex of negative buoyancy, caught in a clash of different-density layers where a huge internal wave of warmer and therefore less dense water sucked her down. The highly trained crew reacted immediately. Speed was not reduced, for that would only have made the sub act even heavier in the hard dive mode she was unexpectedly in, her sail's two sixteen-foot diving planes jammed.

"Blow all tanks!" Wain ordered.

The chief of the watch, to the left of Wain, didn't hesitate. A great rush of air sounded throughout the sub as the compressed air from the boat's storage flasks surged out to the ballast tanks, forcing out water in an attempt to regain positive buoyancy, and giving the sub a desperately needed up angle. The diving planes moved slightly but not enough for an up angle. The high pressure air manifold could be heard screaming, a leak bleeding off precious air intended to pump up buoyancy in the flank tanks.

Wain ordered reduced speed, trying to prevent the sub from driving into the bottom at over a hundred miles per hour as increasing water pressure accelerated the dive. The planesman, sweat streaming from his face, pulled back hard on the steering column. He managed to gain an up angle, but the diving planes were still jammed. With ballast tanks not completely blown, they were still in negative buoyancy when they passed one thousand feet—fifteen feet more than their test depth and still falling.

The stern planesman tried to trim the *New York*'s level, but there were strong currents in the less dense water column. Wain was reminded of the near miss he'd had three years before off the mouth of the Amazon River when the mighty river's effluence caught another sub unawares and nearly drove her down.

At fifteen hundred feet, the *New York*'s collapse depth, a small half-inch pipe burst. With more than seven hundred and fifty pounds of pressure per square inch on the hull, the leak became a torrential downpour in the control room, men and instrument panels hidden from one another by the spray, electronic circuitry sparking and shorting out. In less than thirty seconds the leak was found and sealed, but by then the *New York* was beyond seventeen hundred feet and still going down. The only thing that might save them, Wain knew, was the safety factor built into the subs. Though not officially acknowledged, it was one and a half times the test depth. Officially the Trident's "test" depth was one thousand feet, but he knew it was actually nearer fifteen hundred, which meant collapse depth was nearer two thousand two hundred and fifty feet.

According to the salinity and temperature readouts, the bottom here was supposedly no more than three thousand feet. Wain prayed the instruments were right, for if they went beyond crush depth a sudden implosion would reduce the sub to no more than scattered debris—their bodies would be smashed to bloody pulp in pressures of over twelve hundred psi.

In the sudden plunge, before the stern planesman regained some lateral control, there was utter chaos, especially in the forward section where no amount of training had prepared the men for the effects of the dive: jet-force sprays erupting from even the tiniest leak, men crashing into one another as they tried to secure the bulkheads, banks of red emergency lights flashing, pressure on the hull doubling every hundred feet.

During the eight seconds of the dive the worst hit was the galley, forward and below the control room, though not a drop of water had penetrated its pressure cylinder. Only moments before, during the third sitting of the long Arctic day's fourth and last meal, two cooks, relaxed in their immaculate white uniforms, bakers' aprons and red kerchiefs, had been kidding several of the crew, who had been bitching about the smell of onions "stinking up the whole damn boat."

"Stinking?" one cook had said. "I'll tell you about stinking." And he proceeded to tell how bad it was in the old World War II diesel subs, when fresh water was so rationed that only the cook and the oiler were allowed to shower every day. "For no more than three minutes," he added. "Not even the old man could shower. You want to know about stink!"

"That's the truth," confirmed one of the four quartermasters on board. "This here's the world's finest piece of space age technology—inner space technology, which poses a damn sight tougher questions than all that outer space crap. Hell, our reactor produces so much water and oxygen we have to jettison some. You baby-faced lot spend seven weeks at school in New London, then come on here and moan about goddamn onions. I gotta feed you bums for less than five bucks per man per day. Wanna know how I do that?"

"Onions!"

"You got it!"

Everyone was taking the discussion in good spirits. That was in part why they'd been chosen—for their ability to live harmoniously at close quarters. Despite its enormous size, the Trident was still a fighting ship; first consideration had to be given to how much extra equipment, especially electronic, could be accommodated.

"That true, Quartermaster? Or you jus' jivin' me?" asked a third class torpedoman's mate. "About that five-dollar bullshit!"

"No, Hennessy, you're right. It's not five bucks, it's four fifty-seven."

"Now I believe you, man. I've never heard the Navy come up with a round figure yet." The torpedoman's mate disposed of the remains of his meal and started to walk away.

"Hennessy?" the quartermaster called.

"Yeah?"

"Where the hell's your dosimeter?"

Hennessy looked down at his denim shirt as if expecting to find dandruff. All he could see was the Navy Eagle and his one dark blue stripe. The quartermaster was right—the thermal-luminescent radiation indicator was missing. "Must've dropped the darn thing."

"Better find it before Brady sees it's missing."

"Brady's an asshole."

"Yeah, well, he's also officer of the deck today. He finds out you don't have a dosimeter on he'll have your ass."

"Shoot, I get more rads in Seattle in half an hour than I get from this tub in a month."

"Suit yourself," said the quartermaster. "But you know, Hennessy, too many of those rads and your pecker falls off."

"My pecker ain't fallin' off. I got a girl in—"

"Hey, you guys!" quipped a sonarman, taking a seat for the fourth sitting. "You hear that? Hennessy's got a girl and she's alive!"

"Lucky bastard!" said another, putting down his tray. "Some guys have all the fun. Where is this live one, Hennessy?"

"In Bremerton—only a few miles from the base. Anyway, she asks me one time if I might be radiated."

"What did you tell her?"

"I asked her what if I was? So she says—"

Hennessy didn't finish. In the next second the sub's nose dropped like a rock, the angle so sharp that two vats of boiling vegetable oil spewed out from the french fry tubs, hitting three men and scalding them even as they leaped up from the tables. One man, falling, took a red-and-white-checkered tablecloth with him, banging against the bulkhead to add to the racket of men shouting and cutlery, broken dishes and cooking pots crashing to the deck. The oil became a mass of flame, setting four men on fire.

Ironically the modern age that had placed these men on the most efficient fighting weapon the world has ever known made them pay in unexpected horror. Their clothing—the best, most up-to-date the Navy could produce—caught fire and, being synthetic, unlike the wool and cotton of yesteryear, stuck to them like melting plastic wrap. The victims raced about the mess, screaming, unable to keep their footing, unable even to lie on the sharply inclined floor.

Their shipmates grabbed hold of whatever they could, two of them snatching carbon dioxide extinguishers from the wall. But they were unable to aim the extinguishers accurately as the sub yawed violently, and the clouds of carbon dioxide gas and powder froze anything they contacted, including one man's eyes. Amid the slipping, sliding debris of the galley and mess, and to a lesser extent in the narrow passageways, as fire crews pursued the half-crazed men to douse them, the ill-aimed extinguishers doused as well the vital lithium hydroxide and reactivated charcoal scrubbers that were supposed to rid the air of poisonous carbon monoxide fumes or carbon dioxide. They were rendered completely ineffectual or their regenerating or scrubbing capacity was seriously damaged, greatly reducing their usefulness for extracting poisonous gases from the air.

Meanwhile, her prop thrusting full astern to act as a brake, the sixteen-thousand-ton *New York*, now under two thousand feet of water and incapable of regaining positive buoyancy, skidded along the sea bottom like some great injured whale, unable to rise. She was trapped at the southern extremity of the Aleutian basin on a slope that the executive officer estimated, from the incline of the missile deck, aft of the sail, to be on the safe side of forty-five degrees. From the most recent NAV-STAR plot he put their position at about a hundred miles south-southwest of Attu, the westernmost island of the crescent-shaped Aleutian chain that stretched in an east-west arc for over a thousand miles between Alaska and Siberia. The remote Attu, he knew, was the closest in the chain to the U.S./Russian sea border, which ran almost parallel with the north-south international date line that cut through the Bering Sea.

Wain called for damage reports, moving forward from the stern's machinery rooms, which housed the auxiliary diesel electric engines, to the turbine room, reactor room, Sherwood Forest, forward to the control center and sonar room and from the other two levels below data processing, in crew's quarters and the torpedo room. The reports came in from each of the pressure cylinders that, welded together, made up the foot-long pressure hull that lay beneath the more vulnerable six-hundred-foot-long streamlined superstructure or external hull of the sub.

Two of the sailors had died immediately, if not outright from suffocation in the fire then from the deadly freezing vapor from the carbon dioxide extinguishers. Minor leaks were being secured, but one that had penetrated the main ballast area in the stern, well aft of the reactor and turbine room and forward of the three-story prop, was so severe that one of the aft machinery rooms had had to be immediately sealed off with a watertight door and abandoned so that the bulkhead wouldn't give way. Four men were trapped inside. The others who had made it out in time could hear nothing from the next compartment but the rushing sound of water.

Despite the loss of thirteen men already out of the crew of a hundred and fifty—a hundred and fifty-one, counting the civilian, Dyer—Wain knew that the worst thing short of outright implosion that could threaten all of them would be something wrong with the reactor. The "coffee grinder," as it was affectionately called, had been designed not only to drive a submerged sub at high speed for years on end—the duration of a patrol was theoretically limited only by food supplies—but to go on providing the power to generate more fresh air than was required. But now a second report was coming in from the reactor room. The men's dosimeters, Wain was told, and the rad counters in the room itself were indicating high levels of radiation.

"Where's the leak?" asked Wain.

"Haven't found out yet, sir."

"What level are you at now?"

"Eighty rads."

"Well, Charlie, shut 'er down, secure the room and get everyone the hell out of there."

Lieutenant Charles B. Lane, the *New York*'s reactor officer, ordered the reactor crew out. Then, still inside, he spun the wheel on the door of the polyethylene-shielded pressure hull that was the reactor room. Lane knew more about the reactor than anyone aboard, including the captain. He figured that if he could find the hairline fracture in the titanium alloy shield encasing the core, he might be able to seal it with lead epoxy. They could then restart the reactor, using the diesel-auxiliary during the four hours required for reactor start-up after it has been shut down. He could even tap some emergency battery power, and although it was always risky to go onto emergency power, once the reactor was restarted there would be no need of the batteries, anyway. Lane calculated that this attempt was a risk worth taking, for with most of the scrubbers gone he estimated they would last only four to five days at the most, stuck on the bottom.

He put his case to the captain, who wanted to order him out of the reactor but who also saw the logic in Lane's brave proposal. The deciding factor for Wain was that it had been some time since the *New York* had risen to periscope depth to emit a quick location burst signal. The Pentagon, of course, knew the sub's approximate heading, but it would be a race against time to locate her exactly unless the reactor leak could be found and sealed. Then a terrible but very real possibility assailed Wain. Even if the radiation leak was found and could be sealed, generating fresh air and water and enabling them to last as long as the food supply, it would be pointless in the end if the Pentagon couldn't find them. Search parties by land and air could search for weeks over rugged terrain, failing to find the survivors of, say, an aircraft. But in the vastness of the Pacific Ocean... As a submariner Wain was well aware that even if the Pentagon knew exactly where they were—which it didn't—rescue wouldn't be guaranteed. It would be like looking for a needle in a haystack, he conceded to Lane, except that here there was the added problem of the haystack being covered by two thousand feet of water. Everyone aboard knew that in all the annals of sea rescue *no one* had ever been rescued alive from a submarine at this depth.

They were trapped and alone.

In fact, until now Wain and those of his crew who had survived the *New York*'s precipitous plunge hadn't realized the irony of their predicament, namely that the very qualities that were the pride of the *New York*—her ability to dive so deep and her ability to hide unseen and unheard—were now her arch enemies.

And there was something else: those crewmen aft of the four-story-high missile section were complaining of the heat, the temperature climbing, even though at the bottom of the ice-cold North Pacific it should have been getting cooler. Perhaps, Sloane suggested to Wain, the lagging around the still-hot pipes leading from the reactor to the turbines and other machinery in the sub had been shaken loose by the impact. If that was the case, there was danger of another fire. Wain ordered the executive officer to take a party and check the lagging throughout the sub and report back.

# 3

ON ADAK ISLAND, four hundred and twenty-five miles east of Attu, the officer commanding the U.S. naval antisubmarine base knew he had to make one of the most important decisions of his life. He was just as certain that he didn't want to make it.

The second of SSBN 921's twice-weekly radio contacts with the base's ECX jet hadn't come through. The pilot reported he had circled the scheduled rendezvous area for as long as security allowed but then had had to break off and return to Adak.

If the Adak CO was to go by the book, he would have to encode a message concerning the failed contact and send it higher up. But everyone knew communications with subs were notoriously bad, especially in the Arctic, and the CO knew that if he raised what turned out to be an unnecessary alarm, he ran the risk of being labeled a "panic merchant" by his highly competitive colleagues. Yet for him to delay too long might put the lives of the men aboard the *New York* in jeopardy if something had happened to her.

A nuclear sub was capable of staying down a long time, months, in fact, if its reactor wasn't damaged, and if the sub was lost, had gone below her crush depth, there would be no hope for the men, anyway. Still, if he didn't report the matter quickly enough and there was an inquiry, even though his delay might have made no difference—if the sub and its crew were already done for—he might suffer the fate of the officer aboard the surface ship who, in 1963, had delayed sending a loss-of-contact advisory when the underwater phone link was broken with the USS *Thresher*. That officer had been named a "party" before the naval court. "Party" sounded innocuous enough, and it had been made perfectly clear that the court in no way held the officer responsible for the sinking of the nuclear sub, but the officer had been duly advised of his right to "counsel." And the reality was that being party to an inquiry could sound the death knell of a career.

Using the scrambler phone, the Adak CO contacted Cobra Dane, the phased-array radar station on Shemya Island three hundred and eighty miles to the west of him, only forty miles east of Attu and one of the Aleutian's TECHNINT, technical intelligence gathering and monitoring stations. Perhaps the *New York*, against all her normal running procedures, had surfaced and broken radio silence after failing to make her scheduled location report to the ECX jet. Or again, against all orders, she might have sent out the pings of an active sonar pulse for possible pickup on the hydrophone arrays the U.S. itself had planted at various strategic places along the ocean boundary of the U.S.S.R., in an attempt to report her downed position—though if she was sitting on a bottom consisting of mud, the active signal might well be absorbed by the sedimentary layers.

Cobra Dane station at Shemya Island Air Base reported to the Adak CO that they had received a loud pop from their plug-in to the SOSUS—the hydrophone sound surveillance system on the U.S./U.S.S.R. ocean border—but the signal had been too scrambled by a steady fumble of turbidity currents to identify either the source of the noise or its exact position. Cobra Dane added that for several days now there had been 3.6 Richter Scale volcanic disturbances in the twenty-thousand-foot Aleutian deep. They had swept westward from Amchitka Island past Attu toward the general area of where the *New York* should be, according to Adak's projected track of the sub's patrol course from her last contact in the Bering Strait.

"Well," asked the Adak CO, "what do you guys think this 'pop' was?"

"No idea, sir."

"Think it could have been a sub—at crush depth?"

"Don't know, sir. We might have been able to tell if we'd gotten a signature from props, but this volcanic activity around here smothers damn near everything else. Course, we wouldn't have got any prop sig anyway if her turbines were shut down and her prop wasn't spinning."

"Guess not, but you think it was a sub?"

"Possible, sir. Could have been a bogie."

Christ, that's all I need, he thought, the operators at Shemya playing noncommittal, covering their ass with a possible bogie, a Soviet HUK—hunter/killer.

The Adak CO was in the biggest bind of his career. Should he send the message about the sub's failure to report, or not? The machinery of search-and-rescue was enormously expensive for any ship, but for a nuclear sub it ran into millions of dollars the first day.

"Can you give me approximate coordinates of this pop of yours?"

"Affirmative," answered Cobra Dane. "Parameters as follows: longitude 169 to 172 degrees east, latitude 52 degrees 10 minutes to 53 degrees 12 minutes north."

The Adak CO hung up, traced the area on the computer's 1:1 million chart of the Bering Sea and was appalled. If the *New York* was the pop Cobra Dane had heard, the search would be in a little-known area around the Aleutian Trench. It would cover an area of more than three thousand square miles in the southwest Bering Sea, sprawling between the Aleutian Basin in the north, Emperor Seamount Ridge to the south, and Russia's two Komandorsky Islands one hundred and thirty-five miles west-northwest of Attu. No one who hadn't been to sea could fully understand what it meant to carry out a search over an area seventy-two miles by forty miles, over submerged mountain ranges in seas that suddenly shifted from the shallows of sea mounts, or undersea volcanoes, to the darkness of deeps so deep that they could swallow the Rockies and still have thousands of feet of water to spare. Another small detail, he told himself sardonically, was that you would have to do it all in some of the worst weather in the world. But was the sub lost or was Cobra Dane correct in the cautious suggestion that the *New York* might well be involved in one of those dangerous cat-and-mouse games that the two superpowers engaged in to keep their first strike capability razor-sharp in an area where—unbeknownst to the public—their outer garrisons faced each other within what Commander of Submarines Pacific called America's "front porch" and what the enlisted men at Adak called "Ivan's shithouse."

The Adak CO walked out of his prefab command hut and surveyed his wild domain. By the calendar it was summer, but the barren hills were covered with a white mange of snow. The seaweed-green dune rippled in the constant north wind, which howled in from the cloudy green sea over the flatland of the base and the dozens of huts housing most of the island's five thousand inhabitants. Up here with little else to do than watch videos, stand watch and go see the Stellar sea lions breeding against the black lava beaches, it was easy for the best of officers to "jump the gun" merely because the Soviets were so close.

Pulling up the fur collar of his parka, he gazed out at the sea, lost for a moment in thoughts of having been born too late, trying to imagine the sense of excitement that must have attended the great American armada in the summer of 1943 when the U.S. force of over thirty thousand assembled for the invasion of Kiska Island east of Adak against the Japanese forces there. He recalled, too, that it had turned out to be a lot of fuss over nothing, for despite the fierce battles that had raged on other islands in the chain during World War II, the garrison at Kiska had been evacuated by the time the American invasion force arrived.

The Adak CO finally decided to wait a little longer, to give the *New York* time to send out a signal. It wasn't as if the nuclear subs were unprepared for emergencies. She could do a number of things to attract attention if she was down. The Navy spent a lot of time preparing crews for any eventuality.

Then he hit upon a brilliant cover-your-ass plan for either contingency, whether she had gone down or not. He would draft a message immediately, and if he hadn't heard anything in another half an hour he'd send it. If the half-hour delay was ever questioned, it could readily be explained away by his having had the message encoded. Anyway, thirty minutes wouldn't make any difference for a nuclear sub with seventy-five days' supply of food and water.

He could have no idea how wrong he was.

WHILE THE COMMANDING OFFICER of Adak station waited for the thirty minutes to expire, six hundred miles away to the northwest Lieutenant Yuri Vasyutin was on watch at the Mednyy station, the southernmost of the two Komandorsky, or Commander, Islands on the Soviet side of the U.S./Soviet ocean boundary and two hundred and fifteen miles northwest of Attu. Vasyutin was in contact with Moscow, relaying the latest coordinates of a missile test that had originated in Plesetsk, situated in the peat bogs and forests around the Yemtsa River five hundred miles north of Moscow. The dummy warhead from the test was to have come down in the sea off Kamchatka Peninsula, which it had, but ten miles from the designated target. This margin of error was satisfactory for a strike against American cities but unacceptable for surgical strikes against super-hardened military targets.

This evening, however, Lieutenant Vasyutin wasn't so much concerned with reporting another *brak*, or dud, as with reporting a scramble of signals he had received from the volcanic activity in the Aleutian chain. It wasn't unusual, but amid all the other signals, fishing boat chatter and the like, there had been the sine wave of a popping noise, a sound like the distant uncorking of a champagne bottle. For the split second it appeared on his screen, Vasyutin had thought it looked like a pressure hull bursting or, more accurately, imploding under enormous pressure.

The lieutenant's job had been made easier ever since the KGB American spy Walker had sold Moscow the location of all the U.S.'s SOUSS underwater listening grids along with the Americans' supersecret KL-47 cryptographic machine. Nevertheless Vasyutin took pride in the fact that it was his feel for the work, his ability to distinguish what to the ordinary electronics warfare officer might seem nothing more than an unexplained anomaly in the cacophony of sound coming from the sea, that made him one of the best operators the Soviet navy had. Of course he was aware that his opposite number six hundred miles to the east on Adak Island would also have heard the noise, but the pop, he thought, wouldn't have been nearly as distinguishable as a possible hull implosion because the volcanic rumble that had cloaked the sound would be much stronger in the East Bering Sea near Adak than in the west, near the Komandorskys. The difference, he explained to Moscow HQ, wasn't unlike that of two neighbors listening to their radios when someone in the neighborhood, or in the same apartment block, starts up an electric drill. Though both radios crackle and sputter with static, the one closer to the disturbance will usually have its signals scrambled much more. In this case, the Komandorsky Islands had been on the clearer side.

Vasyutin's superior in the Kremlin, a naval commander, accepted the astute lieutenant's point, with one reservation. "You're sure the Americans wouldn't have picked it up?"

"No, sir, I think they will have heard it. But with the bulk of interference occurring on their side of the Aleutian chain, I think they might not be one hundred percent sure."

"You are?"

"Almost, sir."

"Enough to contact Khabarovsk?" The headquarters of the Far Eastern military theater, the Soviet equivalent of the U.S. Chief of Naval Operations, was located in Khabarovsk.

"Yes, sir."

"Yes, it's all very well for you tucked away out there, Comrade. Nothing but bird shit to fall on you."

The lieutenant would hardly have used *tucked away* to describe his posting on the godforsaken island at the windblown extremity of the Motherland's eastern approaches. Still, he understood his superior's reluctance to act. If he was wrong, the displeasure of Naval HQ and, if it went that far, the Politburo would crash about the commander. Next thing he would be minesweeping in the Persian Gulf, with strict observance of the nonalcoholic dictates of the Arab hosts. Life without vodka would be hell itself.

"Are you *positive*, Comrade," pressed the commander, "that it isn't one of our submarines off course?"

"Please stand by, sir," Vasyutin replied, moving the cursor on the screen of his IBM clone manufactured in East Germany and instructing the computer to give a graphic display of all Soviet Pacific Fleet dispositions. All subs, sixty-five diesel-electric and forty-five nuclear, were accounted for, including those in dock. "Yes, sir," affirmed Lieutenant Vasyutin. "It was definitely an American submarine."

"Size?"

"Can't say for sure, sir, but they don't send toys into that area. It's too close to the line. From the sine wave, though, I would say a Trident."

"So you heard a hull pop. What depth?"

"About seven hundred meters."

"Location?"

"Between longitude 169 degrees east and latitude 52 degrees 50 minutes north."

"Will the American operators have the same coordinates if they heard this pop at all?"

"Approximately, sir, depending on the sub's last contact. But this is only an assumption."

And, thought the commander, feeling relieved, if Vasyutin was correct, if it was a hull popping, then all the Americans would be dead along with the shattered remains of their submarine. That would reduce the pressure on him to report Vasyutin's suspicions to the Politburo. The sub would be scattered all over the bottom, just as the *Thresher* and several Soviet subs had been when, for whatever reason, they had been forced below their crush depth. Then he recalled the depth. "Vasyutin, you said seven hundred meters?"

"Yes, sir."

"But that isn't below crush depth for a Trident. We estimate that it's considerably more than seven hundred meters. It couldn't have been a Trident or any other American—"

"Sir," Vasyutin cut in immediately, seeing the problem—that his superior thought he had a good reason for not reporting Vasyutin's hypothesis. "The popping sound wasn't necessarily a pressure hull imploding."

"Then what in hell—"

"A Trident's sonar is housed in a sphere beyond its pressure hull—in a nose housing. Otherwise its sensitive listening devices couldn't—"

"Yes, yes," interrupted the commander, as if he had known this all along. "Well, thank you, Vasyutin."

Yes, Vasyutin thought when he signed off on the secure phone and turned to the operator next to him. "But will the bastard pass it upstairs, eh?"

"Is there gold in it?" the other man asked, meaning were there gold epaulets, a promotion, to be had for the commander if he did pass it on.

"Are you serious, Comrade?" asked Vasyutin. "An American submarine—they'd kick everyone else out and make him admiral."

"So what do you think will happen, Comrade?" asked the operator.

But Vasyutin just changed the subject, to the difficulty of finding a good lay on the three-mile-wide, thirty-seven-mile-long island of Mednyy. No amount of hardship bonus could compensate for the lack of good beddable women, he said. He knew it was a lot safer talking about sex than speculating on what the higher-ups in Moscow might do, especially when there had to be at least one KGB man on each watch observing you.

One thing was certain: now that the commander understood that the pop was probably the sub's sonar and that therefore the sub and its missiles weren't destroyed, he would be breaking the Kremlin record for the bureaucratic hundred-meter dash. If he didn't report the presence of a crippled American sub with more explosive power in its twenty-four missiles than all the explosives used in the Great Patriotic War of '41-'45, including the A-bombs dropped on Japan, the commander would join the other comrades in Gorky or some other equally frigid clime—without hardship bonuses and with KGB on every hectare.

# 4

RACING ACROSS RED SQUARE, the shiny black ZIL contrasted sharply against the dull red brick of the Kremlin walls. A policeman halted a babushka, who quickly grabbed her grandson's hand, pulling the small boy away from the path of the limousine as it flashed past toward the Spassky, or Savior's, Gate. Proudly the grandmother pointed to the man dimly visible through the gray velour curtains of the fleeting car, but the young boy was so excited by the fact it was the premier that he saw nothing but a blur.

"Why is he in such a hurry?" asked the boy.

"Because he has important business," the old woman replied. "He is the most important man in the world."

"WHAT DOES THIS MEAN?" asked the premier. "Gray lady down."

"It's the American Navy's term for a submarine that's gone down, Premier. When that phrase goes out everyone at the Pentagon scrambles."

"When did we intercept it?"

"Forty minutes ago, sir."

"Then you'd better give it to POD."

"Yes, sir."

Within minutes the dispatch was en route via motorcycle courier to the Pacific Ocean Department that had been established by Gorbachev.

IN HAWAII the trade winds had the coconut palms swaying sensuously, their shadows playing feverishly over the turquoise pool like darting squid. His mai-tai tasted so good that Admiral John Clayton, Jr., COMSUBPAC, Commander of Submarines Pacific, disdaining the short straws provided, lifted the short, wide cocktail from his poolside table and tipped it high until the ice cubes tumbled forward.

"John. Don't be so uncouth."

"Off duty, May," Clayton replied to his wife good-naturedly, winking at his aide.

"You sound like a walrus," May retorted, but her comment was made with such good grace and taken by Clayton in the same spirit, with such lack of asperity that the admiral's aide, Lieutenant Commander Freeman, could have guessed the two had been married a long time, even if he hadn't already known.

"Well, we won't have too many mai-tais in that NATO posting, May," the admiral reminded her.

"A small price to pay," interjected Freeman amiably.

"True," the admiral answered, turning toward the aide, squinting in the harsh noon sun that bounced off the immaculate white summer dress uniform he'd worn over to Kauai to inspect the outer island's radio and communications post. "A man always welcomes a promotion, eh, Freeman?"

"Yes, sir."

"Mind you, I'm not saying I won't miss this."

"In that case, sir, I'd better order another round."

"And you, Commander?" asked Mrs. Clayton. "Will you miss Hawaii?"

"No, ma'am."

"Hell," interjected the admiral, "it's a promotion for him, too, May. Those who stay together get promoted together."

"That's awful repartee," said May. "You'll have to do better than that in Europe, dear."

"Oh..." The admiral hesitated. "Bananas! Old George Patton wasn't an egghead and he got along just fine in Europe. Didn't he, Freeman?"

"Yes, dear," May returned, "but old George Patton spoke French."

"Well, that's Free's job." He pointed at his aide. "He can order all the wines and give me a printout of good jokes and I'll make damn sure we know where all the Russkie subs are. That's *my* job."

"And I know you'll do it very well, dear," said May, and she squeezed his arm.

The admiral grunted, looking up at the swaying palm fronds, their pale green etched sharply against the blue sky. He closed his eyes and took in a deep breath, savoring the warm, perfumed air of the islands, listening to the surf hissing unseen beyond a high fringe of coarse beach grass acting as a windbreak, protecting a riot of hibiscus, orchids and plumeria that grew about the pool. He could hear a parrot squawking in the open foyer of the hotel behind the pool and, opening his eyes, he could see the bird moving mechanically back and forth on his perch from one leg to the other, his blood-red crest occasionally fluffing in peaks of curiosity during the arrival of new guests who were often startled by the parrot's plea, "Have a heart, Dundee. Give us a Foster's. Have a heart."

"Someone told me," said Freeman, "that the Australian brewery has trained hundreds of parrots for the big hotel chains."

"Unfounded rumor," commented the admiral. "First of all, the quarantine laws in most countries—"

He was interrupted by Lieutenant Commander Freeman's beeper going off. The commander's hand slid into his pocket as he rose and, excusing himself, walked across the manicured lawn and down the hot crazy pink stone stairway to the admiral's waiting limousine, its pennant fluttering stiffly in the breeze.

"Another rumor?" said May, looking after the aide.

"What?"

"The rumor," answered May, "that you were off duty. I hope we have more time with your NATO posting than we've had here."

"Ah," he replied. "Don't worry. Probably some congressman calling Pearl to tell 'em he's changed his flight. Freeman has to meet them at the airport—he likes our PR people to be one hop ahead of Congress."

When he reached the limousine Freeman got in the spacious back seat. The bulletproof glass between himself and the driver and the closed laser-safe windows secured the car as an effective command post receiver. The lieutenant commander watched the message coming in on the pullout IBM laserwrite. Groups of eight numbers to be decoded on a one-time pad, a new pad each day. He tore off the message. His guess was the same as the admiral's, that Pearl Harbor had probably just received information that one of the congressmen, most likely on the important Naval Appropriations Committee, was coming in earlier than expected; Admiral Clayton, therefore, would have to fly back as soon as possible from Kauai for the reception. In an age of terrorism congressmen often altered flight schedules as one of the simplest ways to confuse an enemy.

Through the intercom Freeman asked the driver to leave the car. The driver, of course, had been cleared to top secret, but in Freeman's view there was no point in taking any risk. Besides, the Navy had never quite gotten over the shock of the Walker family spy ring in the early eighties, when a father, his son and his brother had sold the Russians a mass of vital information and classified operational procedures from the carrier USS *Nimitz* and the most secret U.S. naval codes from several of the first American nuclear submarines.

As he looked back at the limousine, the driver saw Freeman pull out the sliding desk from its front seat recess and begin decoding from a one-time pad. The lieutenant commander was shaking his head and appeared to be swearing. Well, thought the driver, there goes my date this evening with the lovely wahine at Poipu Beach.

When he finished decoding, Lieutenant Commander Freeman called Lihue Airport, telling them the admiral would be boarding his plane for the twenty-minute flight to Pearl. He walked back across the immaculate green lawn through the plumeria-perfumed air toward the admiral and his wife, past the flaming branches of the coral tree, feeling the warm caress of the trade winds and taking in the salty air, the turquoise clarity of the sea as it burst in pure white on the coral strand. He understood once again why they called these islands a paradise, thought of how lucky he was to be alive there, and how bad news seemed so out of place.

THE ARCH OF PINES overhead flashed by as the admiral's limousine, between two security cars, sped from Poipu Beach toward Lihue. Mrs. Clayton wasn't in the car, having preferred to stay on overnight at the hotel. The yellow sheet of paper in the admiral's hand fluttered frantically in the air conditioner's cold blast.

"Turn that thing off!"

"Yes, sir."

In the suddenly still, humid air the message now hung limply like a dead thing. The admiral read the decoded message again, more slowly this time:

NO COMMUNICATION FROM SSBN NEW YORK SINCE 0945. TACAMO REPEATED VLF SIGNAL AT ONE ZERO ZERO FIVE AND ONE ONE FOUR FIVE. NO RESPONSE. COBRA DANE REPORTS POSSIBLE EXPLOSION IN AREA. LONG 169 TO 172 E. LAT 52 10 TO 53 12 N. EXPLOSION UNCONFIRMED DUE TO VOLCANIC ACTIVITY IN AREA.

Admiral Clayton said no more until they reached the airport and he was buckled up in the Lear jet. Then he turned to Lieutenant Commander Freeman. "Free!"

"Yes, Admiral?"

"I want that NATO command. I don't want any more goddamn suntans. Too much of that stuff'll give you cancer."

"Yes, sir."

It was the admiral's offhand way of telling Freeman, as the security men entered the plane after them, that he didn't want any screwups that would deny him the congressionally approved appointment as supreme head of all NATO forces. Which meant if the damn sub was down they had to get it up. And fast.

"Let's get the DSRVs," Clayton said to Freeman, then frowned when Freeman told him that one of the U.S. Navy's forty-nine-by-eight-foot, cigar-shaped deep sea rescue vehicles was stripped right down in San Diego dry dock.

"It's out for at least two months, sir."

"Where's the other one then, damn it?"

"Tongue of the ocean test areas."

"The Bahamas! Well, maybe we can airlift it to the nearest base up there—Attu, isn't it?"

"Yes, sir, but, ah, the Bahamas vehicle is having problems. O-ring corrosion. They have to be replaced."

"Goddamn it! Those things are touchier than jet fighters. How long before it's operational?"

"Two or three weeks."

The admiral said it was a damn disgrace. "A country like ours and only two of them." Turning his attention to the map of the Bering Sea, he asked, "What's the depth?"

"Two to three thousand feet, though Pearl tells me oceanographic charts show the area is heavily ravined. A lot of it's much deeper—it plunges to seven thousand and more in places in the Aleutian Trench area."

"If we got a DSRV operational, could it bring her up, if she's not below crush depth?"

Freeman shifted uncomfortably in his seat, fingers drumming the heap of files in his lap. "Yes, sir. But the trouble is, before a DSRV's belly hatch can lock onto the sub's escape hatch we have to find the sub. The coordinates, depth and location we've been given are only approximate. We're looking at around three thousand square miles. And the sub may not be in two to three thousand feet anymore. By now it could have slipped into one of the ravines."

The admiral looked from the map to his aide. "Jesus, I thought I was the pessimistic one. How about all her flares and her messenger-sonobuoy? Any sign of them?"

"Attu Island hasn't picked up any signal yet, Admiral. Besides, being practically on the Russian/U.S. border and less than a hundred and fifty miles from the Komandorskys, the skipper's not likely to let the Russians know where he is if he can help it."

"Then no signal could be a good sign. Then again, there won't be anything for us to find if they've sprung a leak."

Freeman nodded gravely, but now he felt compelled to counter the admiral's growing pessimism. "Yes, sir, I know. But if she's still intact and not in one of the ravines, she could be holding out."

"Something's got to be seriously wrong, Free—otherwise the goddamn thing wouldn't be down there."

"I agree, Admiral, but those watertight sections are welded so tight it's possible to have two or three ruptured without damaging the integrity of the others. And the carbon dioxide scrubbers should be good for months."

Sighing deeply, the admiral sat back in the seat, still studying the map of the northern Pacific. It was only natural for both of them to want to focus on the optimistic side, but as

COMSUBPAC he knew he had to consider the darkest possibilities. "And if the scrubbers screw up?" Before Freeman could answer, the admiral went on. "They have, you know."

"I realize that, sir," said Freeman, then, sidestepping the potential catastrophe as adroitly as possible, he continued, "but first we need to locate her if we can. Then find out whether they're still alive."

"Right," Clayton agreed. His eyes moved down the map from the arc of the Aleutians to the far-off Olympic Peninsula in the lush green corner of America's northwest to Bangor, home base for the USS *New York*. "Well, we've given Washington the names of all the whiz kids in our files. We'd better find out who they finally settle on. Whoever it is better be damn good."

Freeman had wondered for a while if the admiral was more concerned about securing his NATO post than rescuing the hundred and fifty men aboard the downed sub. As if reading his aide's mind, the admiral said, "We'd better get a surface ship up there right away, ready for overall control of the operation. Do we have any in the general area?"

"A fast frigate—FFG 218, the *Boise*. She's off Attu. She's on test runs after repairs to her prop in dry dock. Another frigate, two hundred miles east at Kiska. And a cruiser—but she's a long way off between here and the Aleutians."

"All right. Have the *Boise* go into search pattern. Order the Kiska frigate and the cruiser into the area off Attu. Maximum speed."

"The *Boise* might be a bit dicey. She's probably running a bit rough after dry dock. She had to have some work done on the prop."

"I don't give a damn if they've got scurvy on board. Get her into a search mode."

"Yes, sir."

"Free?"

"Sir?"

"These Bering Sea patrols—running close to the Soviet lines. Were any authorized by my predecessor?"

"No, sir. You authorized all of them."

"Hmm," mumbled the admiral. "Then it's our asses on the line, Freeman."

"Yes, sir."

"All right, contact Washington. Top secret. Give 'em the sitrep as we see it and ask for instructions. And, Free?"

"Yes, sir?"

"Stress we need the best man in the country—and we need him fast."

# 5

AT FIRST REAR ADMIRAL James Gill, Chief of Naval Operations or CNO, welcomed the appearance of the special messenger on the fringe of the White House reception for the king of Saudi Arabia. Gill saw it as a welcome break in a night otherwise filled with unimportant chatter, polite jokes and fruit juice only, in deference to the Islamic code. But Gill, the man ultimately responsible to the President for authorizing the "snoop" patrols to see how far the Americans could penetrate the Bering Sea before Soviet SOUSS arrays picked them up, soon wished himself back in the shallow anonymity of the White House reception.

Following Gill into the ground-level study, which some presidents since Carter preferred to the Oval Office, was Gill's immediate subordinate, the DUW—Director of Undersea Warfare. He was voicing his most vital concern—whether the submarine *New York* was retrievable, not only for the sake of the 150 men aboard but, more important, he believed, for the lives of countless others. His major worry, he told Gill, was whether the *secrets* of the *New York* were retrievable. Gill sat down at the desk, feeling presidential, the black sheen of the mahogany softened by the peach glow of the desk lamp. The DUW closed the door to the study and elaborated on his worst fear. "Even if the sub's destroyed, if the Soviets get there first they'll bring up a lot more than debris. Decoder rotors, silent running baffles, full-strike contingency plans—the whole lot!"

Admiral Gill pulled out a scratch pad from the desk drawer. "Let's deal with our side first. Who's COMSUBPAC recommending?"

The DUW glanced down at the decoded situation report from Hawaii. "First of all, Clayton's boys say that given the ruggedness of bottom terrain and the usual surface turbulence around the Aleutians it would be near impossible to bring the sub up."

"You're telling me they haven't got anyone?"

"No, sir. They say if it's impossible there's only one man for the job—an oceanographer-cum-salvage type, name of Frank Hall. Works out of Astoria. Has his own company, Sea Gold, Inc. Must say I agree with them, Admiral."

"He's worked for us before?"

"Yes, sir—Eagle Island."

"Oh, *that* Hall."

"Yes, sir. When everything hit the fan with the Soviets. But he's done other work for us as well—torpedo retrieval on the Juan de Fuca Range off Washington State."

"Security rating?"

"No problem, sir," said the DUW. "Top clearance. He received a Presidential citation for the Eagle Island job."

"If he's so good," said the CNO, "why don't we have him, period?"

"Well, sir," answered the DUW, "he's...a little...unorthodox."

"A fairy?" said the admiral.

"No, sir. He's an original. Good at pulling rabbits out of hats but works by his own rules."

"Charles," said Admiral Gill, uncharacteristically dropping formality in his determination to get the job done, or at least attempt it as soon as possible, "I don't want a magician. I want someone who can bring up a sub if there's anything left to bring up. *Before*, as you point out, the Russians get to it."

"Well, if anyone can do it, sir, Hall can. But..." The DUW hesitated. "There is a problem...."

The DUW was interrupted by a knock on the door. His aide handed him the file and latest up-to-the-minute information on Frank Hall of Sea Gold, Inc., Astoria, Oregon. The aide had attached the yellow telex to a five-by-seven color photo, a waist-up shot of the five-foot-eight-inch Hall. His shock of brown hair and his china-blue eyes were his most arresting features.

"Go on," urged the admiral.

"First," the DUW continued, "we'll have to give him special authority for the attempt. He understands there have to be rules and he'll follow them, but the second they don't make any sense he'll break all of them."

"All right, I'll back him all the way."

"Ah, I wouldn't do that, sir," said the DUW, looking down at the message.

"Why?"

"It might be better to leave yourself an out in case he gets too unorthodox."

"All right. Tell him all major decisions have to get final okay from me."

"The other problem, sir, is the newspapers. We don't want the Russians to get the jump on us. They may not even know about this yet."

"You want a gag order?"

"If possible, yes, sir."

Admiral Gill looked concerned. It wasn't that protecting national security went against his democratic impulse; he knew that, contrary to public knowledge, gag orders had been used often enough in the American press in war and peace, from Roosevelt's undeclared war on the German U-boats long before Pearl Harbor to Howard Hughes's CIA mission, under cover of the Summa Corporation, to salvage a Soviet Golf class sub that went down in the sixties. But this was more difficult—a hundred and fifty men missing, presumably still alive. The pressure for information about them and, more important, the possibility of leaks of highly classified information would need careful handling.

"Any gag order would have to come from the President," said the admiral. "There's no way the press would take it from Joint C in Cs. Write up a draft of one for the President, pointing out the crucial need for silence in the interests of national security and—"

He looked up for a second as a Navy special messenger, long white gloves tucked smartly under his left arm, came into the study accompanied by one of the DUW's aides, then continued, "Point out that any delay or complication in rescue efforts caused by the media could seriously threaten national security as well as the lives of the men aboard. Better reverse that—say it could seriously *endanger* the lives of the men aboard as well as national security. That sounds better. Don't mention anything about the codes aboard or the decoder. Let them think of that themselves. Works better that way. Tell them we'll give them all the info later, as soon as national security items are secure—if we get her up. That way it doesn't sound like a gag order, only a delay. They can live with that.''

"Ah, sir . . .''

"Yes?"

"It seems there is another problem.''

"What?"

The DUW handed Gill the message he'd just received, his facial muscles tightening, readying himself for a salvo. It came, full force.

"My God! He's on a sex charge!" Gill read the message again. "Jesus Christ, Commander. How in God's name can we use him now?" Gill looked up, eyes bright with anger, thrusting the message at the DUW. "You didn't tell me he was a pervert! He's on a goddamn sex charge!"

Thunderstruck by his bad luck, the admiral read out the text of the message, which shocked even his sailor's knowledge of human depravity. Smacking the paper with one hand, he glowered at the DUW. "It says here he was seen by at least six witnesses. *Six!*" He looked down again at the message. "On a goddamn beach—Cannon Beach. With his girlfriend! Jesus Christ, Charlie, you said this guy was all right, and it turns out he's flashing his pecker on a goddamn public beach, pissing all over. . . .''

The DUW, beet-red with embarrassment, could only offer the suggestion that there must have been "some mistake.''

"You're damn right there's a mistake. And *we* almost made it. His name is—'' the admiral looked at the message sheet again, "—Hall, right? Frank Hall?"

"Yes, sir, but—"

"Frank Hall? Sea Gold, Inc., Astoria. Am I right?"

"Yes, sir, that sounds—"

"Well, you've seen it. He's in jail." Gill dropped the yellow sheet of paper onto the desk, shaking his head. "We can't use him, Commander.''

"I . . . I can't believe it, sir. I'm sure there must have been a mix-up. The cable doesn't say anything about...I mean, about Hall having anything to say?"

The admiral reluctantly returned to the crumpled message. His voice was lower, becoming more dispirited by the second. "It gets worse. 'Arresting officer upon approaching the suspect, a male Caucasian...saw the suspect standing over the victim. Suspect resisted arrest, telling the arresting officer he had been trying—'" the admiral turned to the DUW with an expression of disbelief and disgust "'—to resuscitate the victim, after he'd knocked her down. While reading the suspect his Miranda rights, the arresting officer noted that the suspect was joined by a Gloria Bernardi, who subsequently advised the suspect, Hall, not to say anything until they had access to an attorney.... The suspect is now in Clatsop County Jail.'" The admiral glanced up. "That's Astoria, apparently. Commander—" Gill stopped, but the DUW knew from the admiral's tone, from the whole atmosphere of the meeting, that he was as close to an official reprimand as any commander, officer or rating ever wanted to come.

"Admiral," said the DUW, "give me an hour."

"To do what?"

"To call Astoria. I can't . . . Let me check it through, Admiral. We've got more than a hundred men trapped down there. And he's still the best chance we've got to—"

"*Half* an hour," said Gill sharply, and walked out. He headed back to the reception, grateful to be once again among Arabs.

# 6

"HOW'S THE GIRL?" Hall asked, massaging his wrists after the removal of the too-tight handcuffs he'd been forced to wear on the ride from Cannon Beach to Astoria.

"I haven't heard," Gloria replied, relieved that Frank had finally been released from police custody. Apparently the Navy was trying to get in touch with him and had convinced the police to let him go.

After they heard the screams, everything had happened so fast that Gloria had difficulty remembering the exact sequence of events. Frank had passed her a minute or so before she reached the base of the cliff at the end of the trail. Then she had fallen, tumbling onto the beach, where a pretty brunette, screaming wildly, was beating her fists against Frank. He finally caught the woman with a short right hook, and she stumbled backward, her arms hanging loose, her body crumpling to the sand. A moment later a wide-bellied khaki figure came running toward them, waving in a frantic plowing way as if he was charging through deep powder snow. As he neared the base of the cliff, he drew his gun and fired a warning shot in the air.

"Frank—" Gloria had begun, but by then there was pandemonium. A dozen or so other people arrived at the scene, some of them youths, who looked as if they wanted to beat Frank up. A siren sounded as an ambulance approached along the hard, sandy beach from the direction of the Lighthouse Motel; the moment it stopped, two attendants, one with a folded stretcher, ran awkwardly through the squeaky dry sand toward the body of the woman. The man in khaki, who it turned out was the sheriff, read the Miranda to Frank: "Anything you say may be taken down..." Meanwhile, the young bucks tried to outshout everybody, including a bevy of outraged women from the Cannon Beach Conference Center, who had been out on the beach for a stroll, wearing big buttons proclaiming they were members of WAR—Women Against Rape.

Arms splayed, Frank had been shoved against one of the washed-up logs by the surf's edge. Breathless, he said nothing as the deputy frisked, then cuffed him, but began to object to the deliberate tightening of the cuffs. The growing crowd, incensed that he had the gall to say anything at all in his defense, surged forward threateningly, and as Frank was dragged away, Gloria fought desperately but unsuccessfully to break through the ring of angry spectators to reach the police car parked above the beach. By then the ambulance, the woman inside, was on its way to the nearest hospital.

By the time the sheriff and his partner got Frank up the high wooden stairs near the Lighthouse Motel, the crowd had grown and spread, milling around the waiting squad car like flotsam surging around a rock. One man, who lived in a beachfront cottage, said it was the biggest crowd he'd ever seen in Cannon Beach. The sheriff's car moved off slowly. "We've got to get the son of a bitch to the lockup as soon as we can," said the sheriff, "before something uglier happens."

The crowd thinned out a little as the squad car, with Frank behind the grate, crawled down Beach Avenue to the main street and turned left. But then the sheriff, seeing the fuel gauge near empty, told the deputy to pull into the gas station by the conference center. By the time the tank was half-filled, fists were pounding up and down the car, hostile faces pressing against the glass.

Inside, Frank Hall watched the fish faces mouthing obscenities as if through aquarium glass. He said nothing, not even acknowledging Gloria's brave wave to him, not wanting anyone in the increasingly ugly crowd to know that he and she were somehow connected. He knew Gloria would believe his account of the events on the beach, but even to her it wasn't something you could explain in two or three minutes.

"You fucking creep!" a young surfer spit, his face twisted grotesquely against the rear window.

One of the WAR women, pressing up against the windshield, swore at him violently, her false teeth slipping now and then in her fury. The deputy waved her away as the sheriff signed the credit card slip, pushing the tray out to the attendant through a thin slit at the top of the passenger's window. The WAR woman was pressing hard against the sheriff's window, her face twitching in a frenzy of hate as the car started to inch away from the gas pumps. Hall smiled and blew her a kiss. There was a shriek, as if someone had fallen off a cliff, and the woman seemed thrown back from the car by an electric shock. The crowd's attention shifted to her as the car turned toward the conference center, then crossed the bridge, gaining speed, traveling toward Pacific 101 to head north to Astoria.

"What the hell'd you do?" demanded the sheriff, turning around, sweat trickling down behind his ears. It was confusing; Hall thought the sheriff was asking about the woman he'd

knocked out and urinated on. "I saved her life," he answered.
"But there's no way with that crowd that I could—"

"I mean that lady back there at the gas station."

"Oh, her," said Hall. "I smiled at her. Thought it might
cheer her up."

"Never mind the comedy, Bud. You're in big trouble."

"No," said Hall, looking out at the mist, which was being
burned off by the sun and seeking refuge in the rolling green
folds of hills that swept down to the sea. When he turned back
to face the grate, he saw the sheriff was holding a pocket-size
tape recorder in plain view.

"As long as you know it's turned on—okay?" said the sheriff.

"Okay," Hall answered easily. "Let's hear the playback."

"You haven't said anything yet."

Hall nodded. "All right. This year El Niño, the warm current from South America—"

"Hey, I know about that," the deputy piped up. "El Niño—
it means the Little Christ, right?"

"Shut up, Duane," said the sheriff, turning back to face
Frank. Jesus, he cursed silently, didn't Duane know anything?
Once you got them talking you were halfway to a confession.
"What about El Niño?" pressed the sheriff.

Hall shrugged, causing the handcuff chain to rattle, as if
considering how best to begin. "Some years El Niño and the
Davis Current run farther north than usual. That means the
water is a few degrees warmer, not enough that *we'd* notice it,
but a world of difference for sea creatures."

"So?"

"This year we got more of the phylum Cnidaria—a flash
name for the invertebrates including jellyfish—coming up north
from California in the warm water. All kinds. You must have
noticed more jellies than usual."

"So?" the sheriff said again noncommittally. His eyes nar-
rowed; he figured he could see a con coming a mile away. "All
you've told me is there's a lot more jellyfish around this year."

"Yes, particularly Portuguese man-of-wars," Hall continued. "They look like small blue saddles with long, trailing tentacles with stingers. What we—"

"Who's *we*?"

"Oceanographers," explained Hall.

"Go on."

"Well, the long tentacles contain millions of microscopic nematocysts—stinging cells. They inject their toxins through their barbs into their victims in a few milliseconds. In Australia the box jelly kills a person in less than three minutes. Jellyfish toxin poisons the brain, ruptures red blood cells and interferes with the flow of calcium through the myocardial membrane—that's the membrane surrounding the heart—which can cause the heart to stop. Causes kidney failure. Different people react differently. Some I've seen at sea just get big red welts and feel a little sick and that's all there is to it. Others, like that woman on the beach I heard screaming—she'd already been stung before I got to her—go into anaphylactic shock. She..." Hall saw the sheriff frowning and decided to use a new tack. "You allergic to anything, Sheriff?"

"Ragweed."

"Well, what I'm talking about here is severe respiratory shock caused by allergic reaction. That's why I did what I did. Vinegar works just as well as urine, but it's not something you carry around with you, right? So that was the best I could do in the few seconds I had. Uric acid acts just like vinegar, you see. Inhibits the nematocysts—stops the stingers from firing. But—" Hall looked worried "—the trouble is, even though I started mouth-to-mouth right after that, I could see how badly she'd been stung. I mean, I think she might have been too far gone before I got to her. Poor kid."

The deputy looked across at the sheriff, who sat pressing the recorder against the grate and staring at Hall. No one spoke for a minute. Finally the sheriff switched off the recorder, extinguishing its red eye. "Bullshit!"

"No," said Hall evenly, "it's true. You sometimes have a couple of drownings, kids most likely, but what it really was was jellyfish stings—they always affect young kids more. They go belly-up in the water, get washed up against the rocks, and everyone thinks they've been drowned. Course there should be marks—red welts that swell up, even get filled with pus. They can leave a permanent scar. But people with allergies sometimes need only a small dose of whatever they're allergic to—a bee sting, for example—to send them into shock, and it can leave hardly any mark at all.''

Hall fumbled awkwardly in his top pocket and pulled out one of his cards, poking it through the square-inch mesh of the grille. "Sea Gold, Inc., in Astoria. But you don't have to believe me. Contact Oregon State U, Washington State or Scripps Institute in California, near La Jolla, if you like. Ask any of them to have a look at the woman I fished out. She'll have welts on her, all right. And they're not from me.''

He sat back, his head leaning on the hot leather, and looked out at the sandy strip flashing by in a long, endless ribbon. ''I only hope I did some good.''

The sheriff half believed him by then, but he didn't phone any of the places Frank Hall had suggested. Instead, he called the D.A.'s office in Portland and got them to check out Frank and his story with Oregon State U. Everything he'd said was confirmed, but the D.A. told the sheriff to hang on to him anyway until the fingerprint check had been run with the FBI. Finally, the call came from the D.A., telling the sheriff to let Hall go; the last thing they needed was to have the victim's family suing the department if she didn't survive on the grounds of having thwarted the oceanographer's quick-thinking first aid. On top of that, the D.A. said, they had the Department of Navy at the Pentagon breathing down their neck, asking the sheriff for the name of any reporter who inquired about the incident.

THREE HOURS LATER everyone in the Navy who knew about the submarine's situation was breathing more easily. Nothing further had happened. Not one newspaper had mentioned the story, which attested to the power of the gag order. In the end, the reporters hadn't wanted to forfeit the good, hard information on the Russian sub they hoped to get later on. Also, it struck the much-relieved Director of Undersea Warfare—who pointed it out to the CNO, letting the rear admiral think it was his own idea—that only one man in a million would have known what to do with the woman who had been so badly stung by one of the migrating swarms of Portuguese man-of-wars.

"Balls!" said Hall when the CNO complimented him on being a man in a million. "Anyone who knows anything about jellyfish could have told you that."

"Maybe," said the CNO. "But very few would have had the guts to do something about it."

Hall mumbled something. He was in a bad mood. The young woman, a mother of two, had died despite his efforts. Gloria kept telling him that it wasn't his fault, that he'd done what he could. He knew that, but still felt badly about it.

The CNO asked him if he'd try to help them save a hundred and fifty men who were also victims of the sea. The surface ship in charge of the overall operation would be the USS *Boise*. "You can fly to Attu," said the CNO. "From there I'll have another fast frigate take you and your equipment out to join her."

They told Hall that if he agreed to help, he was not to tell anyone besides his fiancée and his business partner, a marine mechanic, where he was going. They wanted to give the Russians as little advantage as possible in the event that the Soviets had picked up the *New York*'s sinking from their listening post on the Komandorsky Islands.

# 7

AT THE FOREIGN MINISTRY in Moscow, whose huge, forbidding tower looked as if its base had been dipped in muddy water, its remainder creamy white in comparison, Comrade Ilya Skolensky sat ensconced in his twentieth-floor office, surrounded by files. Skolensky was the newly appointed director for POD, Pacific Ocean Department. His large, temporary side table by the window was piled so high with bulging manila folders, some dusty, some brand-new, that they obscured his view of the river.

With Europe a military standoff, the Politburo under Gorbachev had increasingly turned its attention to the vast Pacific theater, in a movement to outflank the NATO powers. This newfound interest in the Pacific was encouraged by such de-

elopments as the declared South Pacific nuclear-free zone, a
think in the American defense perimeter that Moscow quickly
enetrated with protestations of fraternal relationships be-
ween the "peoples of the South Pacific" and the Soviet Union.

The Politburo had directed Skolensky to act swiftly yet at the
ame time cautiously to get access to the American submarine
ecrets. His first problem was to find out exactly where the
ubmarine was. Thus Admiral Litov, Commander of FE-
VD—Far East Theater of Operations—had been summoned
om Vladivostok.

"Comrade Director, finding a downed Trident would be ex-
emely difficult," Litov now told him. "It is as if you were
top the Toronto tower...." The reference to the CN—Cana-
ian National—Tower in Toronto, the highest free-standing
ructure in the world, was Admiral Litov's way of letting the
irector know he had done his homework, that he knew the
irector had once been assistant head of the Institute for Ca-
adian and U.S. Studies.

"It is as if, Director, you had a cotton thread attached to a
ebble and were lowering it from the CN Tower—trying to
wer it to an ant. First, you wouldn't even be able to see the
nt. Then there would be the air currents, of differing strength
nd direction every few feet, like different salinity layers in the
cean. And finally, you'd be trying to do it in the pitch-dark."

The extreme difficulty of the task came as a shock to Sko-
nsky. He had predicated the entire program of entry, of ac-
ually going aboard the downed U.S. sub and getting at its
ecrets, upon being able to find it before the Americans. "Are
ou telling me it *cannot* be found?"

Admiral Litov looked around the office. He would have
referred to be aboard his flagship, the U.S.S.R. cruiser
*Novograd*. His silence conveyed an unspoken question to the
irector of the Pacific Ocean department.

The director understood and shook his head. "No one in the
olitburo told me how difficult it would be to find the subma-
ne." He paused, then smiled. "Of course, some of them aren't
o bright at the best of times!"

Convinced now that the office wasn't bugged, Litov visibly
laxed.

"Well," asked the director impatiently, "how do we find it?"

"We don't, Comrade. It is an area so precipitous we have no idea exactly where it is. We could be so close, yet so far. We simply wouldn't know. It's a job for the best Deep Sonar Pro-filing in the world—in which our country lags badly, due to the allocation of what should have been naval funds to outer space research. So we do what we have being doing for years. We let the Americans do it for us."

"Can they?"

"Our Siglint, Signal Intelligence, trawlers have intercepted unusually heavy radio traffic between Washington, D.C., the American COMSUBPAC in Hawaii and the Trident base in Washington State. Also there's been Pentagon traffic to Ore-gon, to a town called Astoria. Have you seen the Eagle Island file, Comrade?"

Skolensky nodded, moving uncomfortably in his seat as if he'd been bitten. Everyone in his young, eager department considered the Eagle Island file mandatory reading—a classic lesson on how a highly coordinated, major Soviet strategy plan centered on the windswept heights of an island off the Oregon coast, had been detected and utterly wrecked by *one* man, an American oceanographer of outstanding courage and highly unorthodox methods. "Hall!" he said. "They're going to use Hall again?"

"No," said the admiral. "*We're* going to use him."

Skolensky leaned back in his soft calfskin chair, a symbol of his high office. "Follow him, you mean?" he asked, the fin-gers of both hands meeting to form a cathedral spire, or, if you were a party member, a tent.

"Yes, Comrade," answered Admiral Litov, permitting a faint smile to crease his rough, weather-worn face. "He's an expert in deep water sonar. For years he's used it looking for wrecks, rich metalliferous mud deposits, lost practice torpe-does. You name it."

"Hmm. And if he finds the submarine we move in."

"Yes," said the admiral. "But there is one difficulty I should mention, Comrade."

"Go on."

"The Americans will know we are following them, and they could begin countermeasures. Signal jamming, that kind of thing. Sending in what they call AVs—auxiliary vessels—intelligence-gathering ships, to scramble our communications."

Skolensky's index fingers were now pressing hard into the bridge of his nose, stopping the flow of blood, turning his nose white as he concentrated. When he removed his fingers he instantly felt relief from the pressure point. "Why," he asked, "do we have to play the American game, Admiral, allowing them to possibly put us off the scent?" He continued before the admiral had time to respond. "I think we should be allowed to join the hunt, as the Americans say, from the word go."

"You have a suggestion, Comrade?"

"Oh," said Skolensky, "better than that, Admiral. I have the solution."

THE FLASHING LIGHTS SLOWED the tourist traffic heading south on Pacific 101. The police cruiser weaved through the double lanes, its siren a relentless wail, heading south from Astoria toward the Clatsop County airport. It turned off 101 onto a lonelier narrow road, passed repair work, where pebbles clattered against the chassis and the loamy dust rose smokily into the purple twilight.

"No hard feelings?" asked the sheriff, his tone somewhere between "I apologize" and "I was just doing my job."

"None at all," Hall replied good-naturedly, watching a big cumulonimbus pile up ominously, rolling down from Cape Disappointment over on the far side of the mile-wide delta. Beyond the wide flatland of the Columbia's delta, sea and sky merged into an indeterminate zone devoid of horizon, unsettling to the eye. To the west Hall could see the faint dots of birds spiraling high over the salt marshes, silhouetted against the sunset, which was now streaked with vermilion. Soon it would be pitch-dark, and the night birds, the hunters, would be out for the kill.

Gloria had been silent all the way from the county lockup. She wasn't so willing to forgive the police for the hasty arrest, and was anxious, even resentful, that Frank had so willingly agreed to leave her at the Pentagon's request and to fly off so quickly into God only knew what, without consulting her. During the little time they had had together that day, Frank had been busy telephoning his mechanic, Bill Reid, at Sea Gold's machine shop in Astoria, arranging to have the *Serena I*—Sea Gold's two-man submersible—thoroughly checked and flown up, courtesy of the Navy, to Attu Island as soon as possible, hopefully within six hours of Frank's departure. Whether it would be needed, Frank had no way of knowing until he had a better picture of exactly what the situation was off the Aleutians.

As disappointed as she was at not having more time with him, Gloria admitted to herself that if Frank had been one of the men aboard the *New York*, she'd want someone to go quickly to try to rescue him. Still, she was upset. She had told him she wanted to go with him, but he'd refused point-blank. "Too dangerous," he'd told her as he'd left the jail. "It's no place for a woman." That had infuriated her. She liked Frank's old-fashioned manners, his protective instincts, but with them came what she viewed as all the old-fashioned assumptions about what women could and couldn't do.

His hand found hers now in the cozy darkness of the squad car and squeezed gently. "Still mad at me?" he asked quietly.

"Yes."

"I'd love to have you with me, but with all those sailors aboard the support ship I'd be worried you might fall for one of them." He nudged her. "I'm not going to risk that."

"Soft soap," she said, though pleased by the implied compliment. "I just want to be with you," she answered.

"I know. There's nothing I'd like better, but there's bound to be heavy seas up there. Satellite photos show a string of lows from the Aleutians to the Pole. It'll be Seasick Alley. You're better off working on your thesis."

"I'm nearly finished now."

"You're a biologist," he said. "There's nothing you can do up there. Besides, it'll be freezing cold—you know how much you like that. Finish your magnum opus on the Oregon seabirds. You'll be a lot more comfortable, believe me. There's another reason, too. The Navy doesn't like women aboard their ships. You know how chauvinist they are."

"Rubbish," she retorted. "They have them at sea now."

"On supply ships. Not war ships."

"War ships? Are they expecting trouble?"

"Five years ago I was on a job for the Navy in the North Atlantic. They wanted a two-man submersible to go down and fix a listening pod. When we got there, at the exact spot, we found two Russian cruisers, two destroyers, and the *Kiev*—one of their latest guided missile carriers, loaded with fighters. And on sonar we picked up two of their Echo class subs. Washington ordered us to withdraw."

"What's that got to do with me wanting to go with you?"

"Listen, it meant the Russians knew exactly where we were going. They didn't just *happen* to find us out there in the middle of the ocean. They knew where and when. It wasn't until later that they got the Walker spy ring. The old man, his son and his brother had all had highly sensitive jobs in the Navy. The son was a radio operator on the *Nimitz*. His father was on a nuclear sub. As radiomen they had access to war contingency plans . . . the lot. The Navy has tried to overhaul everything, but that's impossible. There's always the danger that something is missed."

"You're telling me the Russians could know already about the submarine being down?"

"Yes."

"I was with you on Eagle Island," she answered, returning to the subject uppermost in her mind—her desire to go with Frank. "That was a little dangerous, wouldn't you say?"

"Yes, and you nearly got killed."

"And I suppose *you'll* be safe and sound?"

"It's my job."

"What—getting killed?"

He didn't answer but held her close, hugging her against him.

She knew he was right, and he knew she understood, but more than a hundred men were trapped deeper than any sub had gone before without breaking up, or else they were already dead. Either way someone had to go down and find out.

# 8

INSIDE the *New York*'s increasingly stuffy mess there was a long groan, as if some monstrous creature was turning in its sleep, followed by a yawing noise throughout the sub like that of an ancient sailing ship straining to be free of its moorings. The sounds were somehow more disconcerting in the dim light that resulted from attempts to save power. The submariners knew the noise was caused by the strain of over a thousand pounds per square inch on the hull, the ocean reminding them of their precarious position.

To the average person, who sees in a photograph only the outer casing of a nuclear sub, it appears streamlined, and so it is if one considers only the superstructure. But beneath this is a structure much more cumbersome and vulnerable. Its series of pressure hulls are like peas in a pod, each by design separate, isolated from the rest by watertight doors should the metal skin of one give way. Each man aboard the *New York* knew the sub had already passed its test depth and was approaching its crush depth, and was wondering whether one or all of the hulls would soon give way if an envelope of colder and denser water descended about them. Then there was the added anxiety over the fissure in the reactor room.

Martin Knead, a tall, gaunt-looking crewman from the reactor room, tried to contain his irritation with Smythe, machinist's mate first class. For the third time in a row Smythe had held aces while sighing and acting as if he had been dealt the worst hand of cards in history, suckering everyone else into making higher bids. Now Knead owed Smythe three hundred dollars, not much to the world beyond the submarine but a packet for a submariner. Gambling was forbidden aboard the sub and the rule was strictly enforced by Captain Wain and his officers; next to women and drink nothing caused more problems, Wain believed, than money owed. Yet the gambling went on, the *New York* crewmen no different in this from any other sailor, using anything, toothpicks, cigarettes, as chips for money.

Knead slammed his cards down in disgust. "I'm out. Can't beat this kind of luck." He said *luck* with an edge to his voice that bordered on accusation, but Smythe simply slipped a small red notepad out of his blue denim pocket and after pointedly licking an indelible pencil he kept for such victorious occasions, he carefully wrote down the new amount owed by the reactor crewman. Next, he began shuffling the cards. His technique was a thing of beauty admired by his shipmates. He spun a full fan, reversed it and drew one hand away from the other like an accordion player, the cards streaming in a soft white arc flashing here and there with red and black as it concertinaed into a solid deck before he dealt the cards deftly. Knead had left the table, his place taken by an off-duty torpedo man.

"We should send up the down-haul," said one of the other players, a sonar operator.

"That's what I said," added Knead, taking out his loss on the captain's decision not to send up the orange messenger sonobuoy, with the down-haul, or what was in effect a lift-up rescue cable, attached.

"If he did that," said Smythe, spreading his cards in a curved fan close to his chest, "the Russkies would know just where we are, wouldn't they?"

"How do you know, smartass?" pressed Knead. "Could be our guys are looking for us, too."

"Sure they are," answered the yeoman, still trying to decide what to discard. "Trouble is, we're in Ivan's backyard. They've got a head start. Got to give our guys time to get here."

"Yeah, but their sonar's not as good as ours," put in the cook's assistant, one of the other players.

Smythe dumped a card.

"Don't matter, Cookie. Brigelow, the sonar guy, says we're below the scattering layer here. They put down a signal into that, all they get back is mush."

"So?" pressed Knead. "If the scatter's gonna fuck up the signals, all the more reason to send up the buoy. Right? So our guys can see *something*."

"I told you," said Smythe calmly. "The Russkies'd see the buoy first. We're so close to the U.S./Soviet line they'd send down a homer, and you'd get to the surface real quick. Only trouble is, you'd be dead."

"Bullshit, Smythe! The Russkies want to see what we've got in this boomer more'n they want us dead."

"Which is another reason," continued the machinist's mate imperturbably, still studying his cards, "why the old man doesn't want to send up the cable. If they latch on to us and pull us up intact, they've got our coffee grinder intact. Codes. The whole shebang."

"I thought that son of a bitch Walker and his gang sold the Russkies all that stuff about the K47 rotors?" Knead was talking about the cryptographic machine, the most secret in the U.S. Navy. Smythe was tapping a card thoughtfully, or was it a bluff? Knead wondered.

"He did sell it to 'em," Smythe conceded. "Gave them the circuitry of the rotors, so the Navy's had to change all the circuitry. Makes it a whole new ball game. The Russkies must want that real bad."

Knead was busy computing in his head how long it was going to take to pay Smythe the gambling debt. Three months, he figured, unless he could wipe it out—double or nothing—in another game. If he was going to do that, though, there wasn't any point in getting Smythe teed off at him. On the other hand, if the machinist's mate lost his cool, there was a better chance of winning back what he'd lost, and making more. Besides, he didn't like Smythe; he was the kind of guy who had answers to everything—the kind women liked, the kind women left their husbands for.

"Yeah," said Knead, restoking the argument. "What if our boys are in the area and they spot the buoy first and bring us up? Then we're out of it and the Russkies are up Shit Creek without a paddle."

Smythe raised his bet, watching Cookie frown in bitter disappointment. But who was bluffing? "Look," said Smythe impatiently. "Seeing the old man doesn't know who'd spot the buoy first, *if* anyone did, he won't take the chance, will he? Least not until he gives our guys time to reach the area."

"You forgetting about the radiation leak, Einstein?" pressed Knead. "If that gets worse, we'll have no choice but to release the fucking buoy, right?"

"Hey, that's right," said Cookie, his freckled face raised in alarm.

"That's wrong," said Smythe.

"Smythe's right," interjected the third player, an off-duty reactor room crewman.

Smythe looked up at Knead. "What's the matter with you, Knead? You work in there. If it's a bad radioactive leak and it's a choice between keeping us down or taking us and the leak topside where the radiation would contaminate every gob on the rescue ships, the old man'll keep us down."

"Oh, well, if you're so smartass sure, then why aren't *you* the fucking captain?"

"Same reason you aren't," retorted Smythe, returning his attention to the game. "Not smart enough. So stop tugging yourself off about releasing the buoy. The old man'll do it when he's good and ready."

"Hey, shitface, *I'm* ready—" Knead's arm shot out, his index finger only inches from Smythe's head "—to take your fucking head off!"

"Cool it, you two!" It was the chief of the boat, Bill Ryman, a short, broad red-faced man coming into the mess from control room watch to pour himself a coffee. "Knead, aren't you due to go back on duty?"

"We're on standby," said Knead. "RRO says no one goes in till he finds out where the leak is—how big the fracture is."

"If it is a fracture," cut in the other reactor torpedo man.

"That's what I fucking meant," Knead shot back.

"Okay," said the chief, pouring in too much creamer. "Better get fitted up in your gear, just in case."

Sullenly Knead turned to go.

"Don't forget to do up your booties," said Smythe, throwing out a card and picking up another.

Knead glowered back, opened his mouth to speak, saw the chief's warning scowl and went out, ducking his head before passing through and securing the watertight hatch.

"How much is he down?" asked the chief, slowly stirring his coffee.

Smythe, feigning puzzlement, looked at the other players. "What do you mean, Chief?"

"All right," asked the chief wearily. "Then how many *toothpicks* has he lost?"

"I think it's around three hundred. That right, guys?" Smythe asked the others. There was a murmur of assent.

Chief Ryman nodded, saying nothing for a moment, sipping his coffee until the others had resumed playing. There were no toothpicks visible. No cigarettes.

"I wouldn't let it get much higher than three hundred," he said.

Smythe turned to answer but stopped as the sub, shifting slightly in the turbidity currents, emitted a groan of protest throughout its entire length, steel flexing against steel as if about to buckle. Cookie's face paled, highlighting his freckles more as he stared above him, saw the bulkhead sweating. He lowered his hand, and Smythe glimpsed the queen of hearts and the grotesque joker.

"Go on, Smythe," said the chief as if nothing out of the ordinary had happened. "You were going to say something?"

"I figure it's good for morale, Chief," said Smythe.

"I just don't want anyone owing anybody else money."

"Money?" said Smythe.

"All right," said the chief, "toothpicks." Throwing the rest of the coffee into the sink, he added, "Maybe go a bit easy on him. Get it?"

"Got it," said Smythe.

"Good."

After leaving the mess, the chief reported to Sloane who, as executive officer, had sent him through the sub to check out morale. Ryman told him things weren't too bad.

"Be specific, Chief."

"Well, they're grumbling about the air—it's pretty foul in the torpedo room with the scrubbers out. And there's some debate about what the old man should do: send up the down-haul or wait. The waiting wouldn't bother the crew so much if it wasn't for the radiation leak. That's their main concern, sir. They don't know how bad it is." The chief's tone was as much one of inquiry as of report.

"I'd tell you how bad the leak was if I knew myself, Chief. But not even the reactor room officer knows yet. He's still back there aft in his hot suit." They called it "hot" not because it was necessarily radioactive but because walking about in the protective plastic suits and yellow plastic booties with the Vel-

cro soles—especially with the temperature continuing to rise—
was like being in a sauna.

"What else are the men doing?" asked Sloane. "Apart from
trying to outguess the captain."

"Gambling."

"I hope you sat on that smartly. The old man won't tolerate
any kind of—"

"Begging your pardon, sir, but I decided to let it run for a
bit."

"How do you figure that? Diversion?"

"More than that, sir. As long as they're worried about losing money and winning it back, it means they've still got hope
of getting out of hcrc."

The executive officer nodded and picked up the CASREP—
the list of casualty reports, material and personnel. Thirteen
dead, eleven men injured by the impact, four of those with
broken legs, one with a severe concussion and the others suffering from minor fractures. The smaller injuries weren't much
to worry about in themselves but enough to make the men,
most of them assigned to the control center, useless in manning consoles where split-second timing was critical. Under the
section for "morale" Sloane jotted down, "some grumbling
but Chief reports all in hand." The executive officer spoke
while still writing, the silver tip of his pen taking on a rosy hue
from the rectangular red light in his cabin. "Well done, Chief."

"Thank you, sir."

"Ever thought of officer school?"

"Hell, sir, I'm over forty."

"Never too late, Chief."

"For this pig boat it is, sir."

"And it's only subs you like?"

"Yes, sir. Cozy down here."

The executive closed the CASREP book. "If you change
your mind, let me know. I could recommend you, soon as we
get back to Bangor."

"I'll think about it, sir."

"Good man."

It was part real, part playacting, by Sloane, and they both
knew it. Everything hinged on the *New York*'s crew being res-

cued, and that depended on being found in the vastness off the Aleutian arc.

"Any idea how long the RRO will take to check out the leak?" asked Ryman.

"Nope, but we could wait out here for months, as long as we get the reactor fired up again. Use its steam to run the distillation equipment and fresh air compressors. But if the reactor has to stay shut down, we can run on the batteries. We'd be set for weeks. Food supply is good for months. It'd get a bit monotonous—cold chow to save power—still—"

"Jesus!" The chief grimaced. "By then Knead will have lost his shirt to Smythe."

The executive officer smiled. "Is it fair dealing, Chief? We can have one hell of a lot of trouble if—"

"Yes, sir, I don't think there's any cheating. It's just that Smythe is so good at sucking the others in. He never shows what he's thinking. Just sits there, the same expression on his face all the time. It drives the others nuts."

"Well, I'll back you if the old man finds out, but don't let it get out of hand."

The chief readily agreed. "If it looks like it will, sir, I'll just change the watch roster. That way I can keep—"

He was cut short by the silent, heart-stopping red flashing of "Battle stations! Battle stations!" throughout the sub.

IN THE CONTROL ROOM the two sonar operators were in a sweat at their consoles by the control center, receiving their signals from the now stationary passive array a half mile behind the sub.

There was nothing coming from the sonar bulb up front in the nose, it having been cracked or, more properly, imploded or popped as the sub passed its test crush depth. The microphones in the hydrophone aft of the sub were picking up rush so marked that its blip was the biggest thing either sonarman had ever seen on the high resolution display, their nudge keys and tracking balls being palmed deftly in their sockets, maintaining constant vectors between the unknown target and the *New York*.

"Not a boomer," said one of the sonar operators. "Big, all right, but smaller than us."

"Bogey?" asked Sloane as OOD. "Hunter/killer," he explained to Dyer, the civilian standing nervously nearby, as perplexed as the operators by the incoming signals.

"Possibly a bogey," the second operator answered, simultaneously pressing the keys for an EMA—matchup of all known enemy subs.

"Diesel or nuclear?" asked Captain Wain, who had just entered the control room, his face heavy with fatigue and little sleep. He was watching the shape of the tangerine blip from the attack center girding the periscope island, but not interfering with Sloane's orders.

"Pretty quiet," reported the first operator. "I'd say nuclear."

The matchup searching for "sound" signatures as well as three-dimensional shape recognition stopped at HUK—hunter/killer type subs, possible Victor (7) class, but the amber bar above the computer screen kept flashing "Unlikely," for the Victor class hunter/killers at 4600 tons—5680 submerged—were bigger than the blip. It was merely the nearest comparison of speed to sizes the computer could come up with.

"Moving fast," said sonarman one. "Speed thirty knots."

"Identification signal?"

"None."

"Target bearing?" asked Sloane.

"Three three five degrees."

"Range?"

"Three thousand yards. Closing."

"Torpedo tubes ready?"

"Torpedo tubes aligned two zero two degrees for after tubes. Twenty-two degrees for forward."

Whatever it was, was coming at them at an oblique angle. A contact torpedo would be no good.

"Target bearing?"

"Still three three five and closing. Two thousand yards."

"Very well. Homing torpedo. Tube three ready."

"Homing torpedo tube three ready, sir."

If he fired, the concussion could implode the *New York*—it would certainly reveal his position to Russian or American searchers. But was the signal Russian or American?

"Whales?" suggested Wain quietly. "Squawking to one another?"

The operators were doubtful. "Sounds too full. A very sharp echo, Captain. Whales usually have ancillary noise as well. A lot of—"

"Range one thousand yards and closing."

Matchup was still confused.

"Torpedo three ready, sir," repeated the torpedo officer.

"Hold your fire."

"Five hundred yards and closing."

"Four hundred yards and closing."

Now the hydrophones were receiving multiple echoes.

"Two hundred yards and closing."

Wain said nothing, legs and arms akimbo. It was up to Sloane.

"One hundred yards and closing."

"Sir—" The torpedo officer was anxious for the order to fire.

"Fifty yards and closing."

The sonar operator turned down the volume, his face a mask of pain as an enormous scratching sound came in at more than one hundred decibels.

"On us!"

Sloane, face shiny with perspiration, took the earphone. There was no sound of props. Not a trace.

"Passing . . . seventy-five yards. One hundred yards . . . withdrawing."

All the men in the redded-out control room were still tense, but as the potential target withdrew, the sounds of men shifting in the bucket seats along the baffled runners, sighing as they finally let out their breath, signaled the end of the crisis.

"Probably whales, sir," said one of the operators. "But I can't figure it out. Usually it's such a muffled echo, but this was so sharp, so strong, it sure felt like it was coming off metal earlier."

The other sonarman concurred.

Sloane had held off firing because he didn't believe the Russians would blow up the *New York*—at least not unless it became apparent that she couldn't be taken intact. And as yet there'd been no human contact from outside. Still, when it came right down to it, it had been a hunch. He knew Wain behind him knew that, and he felt the calf muscle in his left leg going into brief but uncontrollable spasm.

Soon confirmation came from both sonar operators. "A school of humpbacks, probably," one of them told Sloane.

"Barnacles," Dyer cut in, listening on the extra set of phones. "Whales get covered with barnacles. Hard as ceramic. Whales' sound bounces off their mates' calls like a metal deflector, back and forth. That's why we didn't get a sound of ship's engines."

Wain looked at the control room clock. It was near the end of the watch. Sloane looked as if he could do with a rest. "I'll take over now, Mr. Sloane."

"Yes, sir." With that he started to make his way forward toward his cabin. But he had only just left the control center when he received a call from the reactor damage control station. Lieutenant Lane had found the fissure—a hairline fracture only an inch or so long, and was patching it. Within a half hour, the radioactive reading of eighty rads dropped rapidly.

An hour after that the reactor control officer rang the captain in central. The radioactive reading had risen again, to ninety rads. Between one hundred and one hundred and fifty rads, nausea, vomiting and diarrhea would occur.

# 9

"ARE THEY MOWING the lawn?" Hall asked as the C-130 Hercules banked westward, away from the North American coast toward Attu Island, where the American searchers would be less than two hundred and fifty miles from the nearest Russian territory on the Komandorskys.

"What's that?" asked the U.S. Navy lieutenant in charge of liaison between the Navy and Hall.

"Mowing the lawn?" Hall shouted over the shaking crescendo of noise that was the Hercules's four engines. "Are they doing a side scan of the area? Regular depth sounders aren't any good near the serrated edges of a trench. It's like flying over flatland one minute, and jagged foothills the next. All you get is a lot of fuzz from multiple echoes. You need a good side scanner that can override the bounce-back and fan out to get a nice wide track. That's why we call it 'mowing the lawn'—get a swath of the bottom's profile instead of just a narrow, confused trace. The latest side scanners will give you a mile-wide swath in minutes. Still photography, on the other hand, means you have to take more than forty-five thousand exposures."

The Navy lieutenant, Michael C. Bremmer, Jr., shrugged. "Don't know what they've been using." He glanced at his Rolex.

Hall's sharp eye noticed the watch, and it struck him as unusual, a Rolex on a Navy lieutenant's pay. Well, it was reportedly a new Navy now, better paid, more efficient, one that hadn't lost a sub in more than twenty years. Until now.

Bremmer slipped his shirtsleeve neatly over the Rolex so that just the right amount of cuff would be showing under the gold-ringed, dark blue jacket sleeve. "By my reckoning, the search ships won't be in the general area yet. I'd say about another six, maybe seven hours. Around dawn."

"Find out if they've got a wide-track scanner or not."

"Will do," said Bremmer, unhooking his seat belt to make his way forward through the shaking, cavernous interior of the Hercules, its khaki cargo slings and nets draped against its inner skin where they were shivering in time to the constant vibration of the engines. The emptiness of the cargo bay stretching behind Hall reminded him of some of the caves on Eagle Island. The memory gave him a momentary shiver, not so much because of his own danger then or the unknown dangers he might face on this mission, but because of how vulnerable Gloria had been, of how they almost hadn't made it, of how lonely she would be now that he was thousands of miles away at the westernmost extremity of the United States.

When Bremmer returned, the news wasn't good: the U.S. Navy had the best sonar in the world, but they didn't have the latest wide scan transponder. Towed behind a ship, that latest state-of-the-art "fish" pulsated so powerfully—its pulse caused by the deliberate buckling of what was in effect a twenty-inch-diameter metal sandwich—that its signals fanned out to sweep an area a mile wide. It could cut search time to less than half what it used to be, reduce months to weeks and weeks to days.

"All right," said Hall, "then you'd better find out where the *Petrel* is."

"The oceanographic ship?"

"That's the one."

"But it's a government research ship," said Bremmer, as if there was something inherently distasteful about going to any branch of the government for help except the Navy.

"You're government, too, Lieutenant, aren't you? Or has the Navy been sold to a Japanese subsidiary?"

Bremmer grinned. "Well, have these people worked for us before? For the Navy, I mean?"

Hall could hardly suppress a smile, but of course he knew that what had happened at Eagle Island was still under wraps to all but the President, those who had been there, and a handful of need-to-know admirals immediately under the Chief of Naval Operations.

"Have they ever been in a situation like this before?" Bremmer went on. "I mean this isn't research. It could involve a bit of nasty stuff with the Soviets. It'll be tricky."

"Tricky's their business, Lieutenant. Tricky's their stock-in-trade, and we'd better find out where they are pronto. I know they'll be somewhere off the West Coast. They do a lot of seismic work for Alaska State U, Washington State and Oregon. This being summer, my guess is they'll be off Alaska."

"Yes, but what if they are? It'll still take them a good day or two to reach the search area. What do you propose we do in the meantime?"

"The best we can do with what we've got. First law of the sea."

"What's the second?"

"Improvise."

Bremmer looked at the man who they said was one of the best all-rounders on the high seas. In Washington Bremmer had been told that if Moscow knew about the USS *New York*, she couldn't be salvaged before the Soviets got to her. This time it wasn't simply a matter of technology, as when the Americans, more than twenty years before, had managed to retrieve a broken-off section of an Echo class Russian sub that had gone down in the Pacific. This time not only did the Russians have improved technology, but, more important, they had the sub somewhere in their own backyard. Bremmer agreed. Even if both countries' signal intelligence ships had logged the sound of the sonar hull collapsing under pressure at precisely the same time, the Soviets had the enormous advantage of proximity.

"What'll you do if the Russkies beat us to the area?"

"They have to find it first," replied Hall.

There was a thud on the fuselage, another, then another. As the two men peered out moisture-streaked windows, they could see nothing in the India-ink night except black smears across the panes where birds had just smashed into the aircraft traveling at more than three hundred miles per hour. Lieutenant Bremmer remarked it was creepy, suddenly running into stuff like that.

"Well," said Hall, "if two or three of those get sucked through the intake you won't have to worry about the Russians—or anything else."

"You're a cheerful son of a bitch!" said Bremmer.

"Realistic," replied Hall.

As Bremmer made his way back toward the Hercules's radio bay to find out the *Petrel*'s position, he wondered about Hall. He had heard that the oceanographer had a hard nose and a soft heart. But did he have enough know-how to deal with the Russians? Why in hell was he asking about a government oceanographic ship that, Bremmer recalled, was only a piddling hundred and fifty feet long, a midget compared to the big warships the Russians were sure to send out if they got wind of the Trident being down; a research ship that, despite its relatively high speed of twenty knots, would most probably be at least a thousand miles away and so couldn't possibly reach the search area off the Aleutians for at least fifty hours.

IT WAS OFFICIALLY summer, but this far north it was still cold and Alexander Androvich Kornon pulled up the high collar of his greatcoat to protect his ears from the harsh, biting wind

sweeping east of the Urals through his village beyond the outskirts of Ulan Ude. The thin spire atop an ancient church's cu-
pola pierced the unusually cold, copper-red sunset as he trudged
toward home, or rather toward the small, dilapidated, slatted-
board bungalow that had become a house of exile for him, his
wife and their teenage daughter, Tanya.

Oh, the locals had been kind enough three years ago when
they first arrived in this provincial city of three hundred thousand in the BASSR—the Buryat Autonomous Soviet Socialist
Republic. The minor official who met him at the station had
even brought an offering of *saga*, the traditional Buryat greeting of sweet yoghurt, and *urme*, a dry-tasting cream cheese beloved by the Northern Mongols, twelve percent of whom made
up the population of Ulan Ude, barely two hundred miles north
of the Chinese Mongolian-Russian border.

The minor official from the Ministry of Internal Affairs had
immediately informed Kornon that he had not really been sent
to Siberia, that in fact Siberia was only what Muscovites called
any territory east of them. "We are really in the Transbaikal,"
the official had explained proudly, as if that made any difference to an exile. The fact was, as the general's wife was quick
to point out to the official when he paid a duty visit to them in
their new home, that Alexander Androvich Kornon and his
family had been *ordered* to this godforsaken place. "And," she
had continued, "after he has given the best years of his life to
the country. To the Party. After—"

"Quiet, Natasha," Kornon had told her. "What's done is
done."

"Yes," she had replied bitterly. "Done for good."

"Enough!"

He had known then what she was about to say: the same
thing she had been saying ever since they moved into the shack
the Buryats called a house—that he had been a fool to stick his
neck out, to try to distinguish himself in hopes of speeding up
his move from alternate membership of the Politburo to full
voting membership. Kornon had tried to explain to her that he
wasn't as much to blame as was the captain of the Polish
mother ship he had sent out to Eagle Island, or as was Saburov, the Stalinlike, steely-eyed KGB political officer who had
been in charge of carrying out Kornon's plan to turn the Pa-

cific into a Russian-dominated naval zone. Beyond telling Natasha the names of the two men who had failed him as he had failed the Party, Kornon hadn't gone into any more detail except to name the American, the man who had ruined it all for them. That was enough for Natasha, and she was as determined as he was that he shouldn't tell her more. The secrecy had less to do with any concern on her part for state security than with concern for her own protection and that of their daughter.

All Tanya knew was that for some reason her father was in disgrace, that at school in Moscow other students began avoiding her, except her boyfriend at ballet where she had once been a star pupil. She had advanced in her dancing not, she knew, because she was a general's daughter. Parental status helped get you into the best schools, but there was no favoritism in the classes themselves. You progressed through merit or you fell by the wayside, one of the legions of discards that fluttered like autumn leaves in the great forests of beech, catching the sun's light for only a second before falling to hard mother earth—just as her father had fallen from grace with the Party.

Yet, unlike her mother, she noticed, her father was angry less with the Party than with himself; no matter that he'd been posted to the outskirts of Ulan Ude where in winter the temperatures plummeted to minus forty and where his sole responsibility was to act as assistant physical culture director for retired workers in the region. Her father had told her that the Party was always right, that it was nothing less than "correct treatment" he was receiving because he had greatly underestimated the American's strength. For a long time during the first twelve months of their disgrace, Tanya had thought he meant many Americans—Americans in general. It was only one cold November day in the second winter that she had found out the truth, or as much of it as anyone was going to tell her.

She had come home from school in Ulan Ude, where, despite the inferior teaching, she was keeping up her ballet, and had asked where her father was. Her mother told her he had gone on his daily grueling cross-country skiing exercise earlier than usual in order to reach home in time for a local committee meeting where once more he would be obliged to give a full account of his "self-reeducation" program to local Party officials, who would in turn give a full report to Moscow's Interior Ministry. From there, if Kornon proved satisfactorily contrite, the report would be forwarded to Dzerzhinsky Square for perusal by the KGB—which hardly seemed necessary, given the fact that the family was already under constant surveillance by local plainclothes KGB from Ulan Ude. In fact, Tanya's father had become quite friendly with one of the agents, and on one occasion had loaned him a pencil when the officer's ballpoint pen had frozen so solid he couldn't make the necessary entries in his surveillance book.

Tanya had gone skiing, too, that day in hopes of catching up with her father. Breaking out of a copse of beech trees, she had seen him stopped ahead, looking exhausted and leaning on his poles like an old man stooping on two walking sticks. His attention was apparently riveted on something at his feet, his breath coming out in short, rapid bursts like that of a frightened animal caught in some sudden danger. A strong wind had come up, whipping the snow into high drifts so that now and then the bent figure of her father disappeared, the snow blinding her as effectively as it muffled the sound of her approach. When she was almost upon him he looked around, and for a second she saw in the burning hatred of his eyes and the distorted features of his face, at once terrifying and terrified, a man she'd never known.

"Papa!" she called involuntarily, as if to stop something horrible from happening—what, she didn't know, only that the man before her wasn't her father but a figure so frightening that it instantly took her back to a never-forgotten experience as a small child—the terrifying sight of a swirling dancer in the mask of the mad monk Rasputin in an early ballet set before the Revolution. The monk was a black-capped monster, his arms outstretched for help and plunder, his presence filling the entire stage against a background of pristine snow.

Her father's right arm extended forward, jabbing quickly at the snow as he saw her coming up to him. She just glimpsed the letters *ZAL*—the moment before the sharp points of the ski poles turned what had been there to nothing but scratch marks in the snow.

"Papa!" Half alarmed, half afraid, she came to a stop. "What—what's the matter?"

She saw that he had been weeping—not tears of sorrow but of an all-consuming, impotent rage that his hopes for greatness had ended in the windswept vastness of the Transbaikal, in "a frozen hell" as a poet had once called it, not east of Eden but east of Lake Baikal "where souls disappeared in eternal ice!"

"Are you all right, Papa?" she asked, knowing that he wasn't, yet at a loss to know what else to say or do.

"Yes," he muttered, his cheek muscles flexing, sniffing harshly like some angry bear. "Of course I'm all right. Why do you bother me with such stupid questions? I'm as all right as this stupid wind lets me be. It makes my eyes water like crazy— should have worn my goggles. I—"

"Have mine, Papa."

"Don't be stupid. Go ahead, girl, you can be a windbreak for me. I'll follow you. Go on!"

Tanya did as she was told, but she was hurt that he had spoken to her so roughly, as a much older, crotchety man might have, as if he were jealous of youth and opportunity, afraid of getting old despite the fact that he was in remarkable health for a man in his fifties. It had surprised her. He had seemed to be taking seriously the rehabilitation assignments in his political exile, whereas most men in his position, she knew, would have been sulking and drinking, bemoaning their fate, merely waiting until times got better, or worse, expecting nothing, grateful only for being still alive. But her father had worked at keeping fit—that is, he had until this day, when something in him had finally snapped, a hatred of something he had written in the snow, of something that had possessed him and that he knew he must exorcise, kill, if ever he was to find himself again—not in the winter wastes of the Transbaikal but in the only place on earth that mattered: back in power, in the halls of the Kremlin.

That evening before her father came home tired and dejected from the long committee meeting in Ulan Ude, Tanya asked her mother what the word *Zal* meant to her father.

Her mother looked up quickly from her mending. "It is an English name," she answered. "A very common name. An unimportant name—a corridor—a hall. It's nothing.'' Just then her mother's hand flew up from her work to her mouth where she sucked the blood from where she had pricked herself, and she uttered a peasant oath so vulgar that Tanya was shocked that her mother even knew such a word.

Tanya was in bed asleep when Kornon finally got home from the meeting. He was in a foul mood and lay awake unable to sleep as the cold Arctic wind howled about the eaves of the clapboard house, creating phantom drafts that sought out every crack and hounded him like malevolent spirits. He told Natasha that the Ulan Ude committee had just told him that Moscow wasn't satisfied with his progress. He had been warned that if the American Navy substantially reinforced any of its Pacific stations as a result of the Eagle Island failure, he would face even more serious charges, for which the penalty was more severe than being exiled in the Transbaikal.

Now, six months later, it had happened. The Ulan Ude committee meeting, he told Natasha when he arrived home, had sounded exactly the same as the one he'd been through the previous winter, right up until their bombshell, which they kept to the last. They had told him he must go to Moscow to answer certain charges.

That night, as they lay together in bed, unable to sleep, she asked, ''How long will you be gone?''

He got out of bed and went to stand by the window, pulling on his greatcoat. Despite its being summer he felt cold and stood staring out at the dark expanse of forest bathed in silver moonlight. It had a beauty all its own, but there was, he felt nothing soft about it, nothing inviting. Even the moonlight looked hard. He talked to her about the beech forest he had skied through in winter, of how when they first came to Ulan Ude he had wondered why the bark of the trees wasn't all white as it should be but black for several feet up from the base of the trunks. ''Do you know why?'' he asked without turning around.

''Come back to bed,'' she said. ''You'll need all your strength for the journey. I suppose they aren't sending a plane. It will be the train.''

''The trunks are black,'' he continued, ''because in the worst winters when the snow was too deep for the deer to dig through and reach the grass, they had to eat the bark." There was a long silence and once more, talking to no one in particular, he said, "They ate the bark. To survive."

"You'll confess then?"

"If I have to. To survive."

Natasha said nothing; there was nothing to say. Her father had been shot in *yezhovshchina*, the worst of the Stalin purges. All she could do was hold out her arms to him as he turned back to the bed, to comfort him, to curse his enemies in silence lest the very mention of them fill him with such rage again that he wouldn't sleep. If she could kill the American, Hall, she would do it with her bare hands, for though she didn't know the details, above all it was he who had turned the Party's wrath against her husband, who had brought Kornon down.

In the distance she could hear the eerie baying of a timber wolf, then a little while later the crunching of heavy boots on the gravel outside, sounding as if they were coming toward the house.

"Alexander?" she said, shaking him. "Alexander, are you awake?"

He didn't move.

# 10

MARTIN KNEAD SLIPPED into protective yellow booties and sat outside the reactor room. He was uncomfortably hot inside the clear plastic suit, waiting morosely for his twelve-to-four watch to begin, still thinking about the money he had lost to Smythe. He thought of how much else he had lost, of time lost in the Navy. In fact, he blamed the Navy for the biggest loss of all; his wife, who at twenty-six was three years younger than he, had had a brief affair six months ago. She'd confessed, begged his forgiveness and promised it would never happen again. He had had suspicions, but had decided to give her the benefit of the doubt. It wasn't magnanimity on his part; it was simply easier to put in your time on a seventy-five-day patrol if you weren't dwelling on suspicion. It had occurred to him now and then, however, that she might fool around with another Navy man, although he had never thought it would be someone on the same boat, from one of the other crews.

But then, something had occurred just before this cruise began, which confirmed his nagging doubts. He had said his goodbyes and she had seemed particularly sorry to see him leave, which, he knew now, should have tipped him off straightaway. They had left port and the control rods had been "pulled" in the reactor, which had started the sub cooking to "critical," the normal operating mode. Then, as they had passed through Hood Canal on their way out from their Bangor, Washington, base, going through the 1,371 checks that had to be made, a leak had shown up on a sea gauge, the result of a faulty silver brazing. Captain Wain had immediately ordered, "Secure the one gauge. Use number two."

Two gauge began to dribble, and Wain ordered her back to Bangor for the yard "birds" to rebraze and to chew out some ass among the civilian contractors. The poor brazing wasn't an uncommon occurrence, given the thousands of soldered joints that had to be made on pipes that penetrated the pressure hull, and the problem persisted, despite ultrasound inspection of the joints where silver solder, stronger than the lead kind, was used. Just one such leak imperiled a sub.

After the *New York* returned to port and docked in the sub pen, Knead and most of the others in the crew had been given eight hours' shore leave while the yard birds worked overtime to fix the brazing. He hitched a ride outside the base to his apartment in Bremerton. The moment he was about to insert the key into the lock he heard laughter, and it was then that he realized just how suspicious he'd been all along.

He opened the door quickly to find Joanne, slim, with hazel eyes and a figure all his friends envied. She was still in her robe, laughing on the phone. She looked up quickly, surprised to see him, and waved affectionately, putting her hand over the mouthpiece, calling out to him. "What's up, hon?"

"We're back alongside—minor screwup. Got eight hours."

"Terrific!" she said, taking her hand off the mouthpiece. "Liz, Marty's home...uh-huh...something wrong with the boat. You and Teddy want to come over—have a beer? Uh-huh, okay, some other time. Uh-huh. What? You're wicked!'' She laughed again and hung up the phone.

Facing two and a half months away from her and with eight more hours of unexpected shore leave, Marty had just one thing on his mind.

After six years of marriage to Joanne, he knew her well enough to recognize, the moment he entered her, that she was sore, and they hadn't been at it enough that week, even with him going away, for her to be sore. She tried to cover it with a lot of Oohing and ''Give it to me, honey!'' She deserved an Academy Award for her gasping and thrusting, but no amount of faking, he knew, could cover the raw, hot stinging and tortured spasm. He glimpsed her face as he approached climax, saw her bite her lip, desperately trying to keep herself from crying in pain. And the more she tried, the more he rammed it into her. Finally he came crashing down on her, rolled off and asked, in a barely audible grunt, what was the matter.

''I don't know, a little tender. You're too big,'' she said, forcing a smile.

He wanted to ask her who he was, but he was too drained; he was seeing double in his temporary depletion. The thing he wanted to say, the fact he wanted to confront her with, was that he had just seen Liz Turner down on Washington Avenue on her way to the base to pick up her husband, a machinist's mate and one of his fellow crewmen. There was no way she could have been yakking away to Liz on the phone when he came in.

The rage rose in him again. He wanted to smash her, to knock her off the bed flat on her ass. How come she was so damn sore? Hell, she had always been open about telling him it was her period, or she wasn't feeling up to it, or whatever. Why had she let him have her if she was so damn sore? Worse still, why had she felt it necessary to put on such an act? There could only be one answer: to cover up the truth that she had a lover.

Knead reached over and pulled a cigarette out of his jacket pocket, lit it and inhaled so deeply that when he exhaled she joked that he looked as if he was on fire.

''That a fact?'' he said, staring icily at her.

''Damn you, Marty. You've got that goddamn hurt look again. You think I've been fooling around, don't you?''

"Yes!"

"You're paranoid!"

"Sure I am. Who is it? The fucking postman?"

"Listen, Marty. You've no right to—"

"I've no *right*? I've got every—"

"No, Marty. Just because I made a mistake once is no reason to think—"

"Once a whore, always a whore!"

She pulled on a pair of acid-washed jeans, slipped on a pullover, quickly brushed her long blond hair, then began rummaging in the bottom of the closet for a pair of runners.

"Where the hell are you going?" he shouted as she walked quickly out into the kitchen.

"Out!" she answered. He heard a door being opened, knowing from the sound it wasn't the door to the apartment but the door underneath the sink. She was yanking out the plastic garbage container. Why the hell was she worrying about taking out the garbage?

"Good riddance!" he shouted after her. "Bitch!"

For a second or two he remained sitting on the edge of the bed smoking, then suddenly he stood up. The garbage! It was just a hunch. He knew she wouldn't risk clogging the toilet, not with plumbers getting a million dollars an hour.

As Marty reached the kitchenette, a sickly combination of smells of rotting vegetables and violets assaulted his nostrils, the perfume bringing back the memory of the day he had first met her in the waterfront saloon in Seattle. But as she reached the door of the apartment it was the stench of the garbage that overwhelmed all else. "What the hell are you doing?" he asked.

"I told you. I'm going out."

"With the garbage?"

"Well, *you* take it out for a change. What's the matter? You jealous of rotting lettuce now?" Despite her sarcasm there was something defensive in her tone that gave her away, he thought. Or was it because he was so mad at her that anything she did would seem suspicious? He knew his rage at the mere thought that she might be even just *seeing* another man put him at a disadvantage in dealing with her. The Lord knew he'd made a fool of himself over her often enough already.

"You're goddamn paranoid, you know that, Marty?" she said, arms folded defiantly.

He kicked over the olive-green plastic container and turned it upside down, the trash spilling in a fetid pile on the imitation-tile floor. A putrid cucumber slid out of a punctured Baggie, its puslike slime oozing over crumpled-up coupons for Swanson TV Dinners, a pledge card for the PBS channel, some leftover ground beef with a green furry mold on it. And there it was, the wrapper gone, but the condom itself plainly visible, the open end tied in a knot like the neck of a deflated balloon.

Joanne made for the door, but one of her heels slipped on a Baggie and he had her by her long blond hair, the sweet smell of violets washing back over him, almost willful, it seemed, in its power to evoke all the sweetness of their first days together. He pulled her back, taking a turn in her hair as one would a rope. "Christ!" he said softly, hoarsely. "Not even my fucking brand... Get it?" he asked her. "'Fucking brand.'" He started to laugh in a strangled, choking way as if he couldn't quite get a full breath.

She swung her head around toward him, hurting and having to strain to see his face because of the way he was now twisting her hair. "I..." she began, "I love you, Mar—" He jerked her head back, her left cheek hard into his chest, and she could smell nicotine.

"Shut your mouth," he gasped, his breathing becoming more strained. "Shut your garbage mouth, you whore." He jerked her head harder. "You promised, Jo... you promised me. Now who was it, eh?" His voice suddenly rose and he swung her back hard against the sink, ends of her hair turning a dirty brown as they dangled in a puddle of water at the edge of the Formica.

"Don't worry, I'm not going to hurt you." He laughed hollowly. "But I need to know who it is, Jo.... C'mon, honey, tell me. Who's been dipping their wick in old Jo Knead, eh? Who is it?"

"You're gone too long, Marty," she sobbed. "I get lonely for you. I can't stand—"

"Sure you do. You get so lonely you have to have a bit of cock." Then he was screaming, bashing her against the wall, swinging her out, slamming her into the corner. "You're so lonely you have to have it before I'm out of harbor. Hey...hey...that right, Jo? That right?''

She tried to speak.

"Shut your mouth," Knead screamed. "Shut your garbage mouth, you slut!" Then just as suddenly he was in tears. He let go of her. "You told me you'd...you promised me, Jo."

"Marty..." she began, her face bruised. She stretched one hand toward him, the other gripping the doorknob for support. "Marty, you have to believe me...I never wanted to hurt you.... I don't know, I just have this thing...whenever..."

"Oh, Christ," he said mournfully, lifting his fist as if to strike her, then lowering it. Then his hands were on her throat, pressing slowly, and she felt so soft and hard at the same time and beautiful and ugly and all he could smell was stinking garbage and a sickly, clammy smell of violets, swearing that if he ever found out who it was he'd kill him and if she ever did it again he'd kill her and he threw her back hard against the wall as if finished with her forever.

KNEAD SAT WAITING to go into the reactor room, unaware that a second leak had been found, the level of radiation now almost a hundred rads, and that the order had been given that no one but the reactor officer still inside the room would be allowed entry. Even with the protective suits there was danger, for the shielded changing room encased within the larger reactor room itself could be so dense radioactively that simply getting out of the suit before reentering the rest of the sub would pose a severe problem; the normal decontamination sprays weren't up to full pressure due to the main feed pipe's having become dented when the sub hit the bottom.

"Knead?"

When he looked up at the boat's chief, Knead was wearing an expression of utter defeat, his depression so obvious the bosun had felt constrained to pause on his rounds of the boat.

"Listen, Knead, if you can't afford to lose you shouldn't gamble."

"What...?"

It was obvious to the chief that Knead didn't know what he was referring to. He wondered if the man was on something that was scrambling his brain, but he couldn't smell any liquor or any of the other cover smells from parsley to mints that were traditionally used to disguise the breaking of the Navy's absolute "dry ship" rule. "What the hell kind of junk are you smokin', sailor? Or are you swallowin' it?"

Knead didn't answer. Whether or not the reactor crewman, whose job was one of the most important aboard, was on anything, the chief didn't expect an answer; he only hoped that the question itself might shock Knead out of the gloom and doom he was carrying around. That kind of down-at-the-mouth crap, the chief knew only too well, could spread through a ship, especially a pig boat, quicker than clap in a brothel.

"Not on anything," Knead grunted finally, his tone matter-of-fact, a take-it-or-leave-it response that angered the chief.

"Okay, boy, but I know you've been gambling, and that's as bad as booze or any other shit once it's got you by the balls."

The reference to "balls" elicited a quick, penetrating glance from Knead, but the moment he saw the chief was only using it as a figure of speech he looked sullenly back at the gray steel floor, its mirrored finish distorting his reflection—his body appeared enormous, his head minuscule, the booties absurd. To escape the grotesque image, he sat back against the bulkhead, which was surprisingly warm, and gazed ahead at the peach-colored wall. Then, in a sudden and totally unexpected shift of mood, he reminded the chief how the Navy brass had had the sub's interior painted in pastel shades because they were said to be more conducive to an "airy, bright workplace environment" than dull, utilitarian colors. Knead wondered aloud how the hell pastels could make being trapped on the bottom, below crush depth with a reactor leak, a "bright environment."

Not expecting Knead's apparent return to the present, the chief was nevertheless quick to seize the opportunity of dealing with something that was at least understandable and that was probably behind Knead's odd mood shift as well as his aggressive behavior in the crew's mess. "Well..." the chief began, trying to remember, as every boat chief should, what the first initial on Knead's ID tag stood for. "Well, hell, Morgan."

"Morgan? Marty."

"Oh, yeah, sorry. Well, look, Marty. You know what these yard birds are like. It's not their boat. They hire some frappin' whiz kid from one of those Ivy League schools in the east. Degree in psychology or some other ology and he thinks paintin' the bulkheads like a goddamn whorehouse'll buck up the boys in blue. Shit, what we need now, boyo, is a couple of whores down here. Now *that* would improve the workplace. Only trouble with that is there'd be no work done and—"

Knead was on his feet, his face flushed almost purple, only a breath away from the boat chief. "Hey... hey! You got anything to say to me, say it. Right? I mean up front, man. Chief or not fucking chief. Okay? Got it? Up front or stow it. Right?"

Acting on intuition instead of naval discipline, the chief nodded slowly, accommodatingly. "Fine, that's fine, Marty. I understand. I got it. Anything I want to say to you'll be up front. A hundred percent."

"Right!" said Knead, turning as if to sit down but stopping, frowning, looking about him so intently that he almost had the chief convinced someone else was in the space outside the reactor room. "No codes," said Knead. "Don't want any..." He paused for several seconds, then continued. "That's a fact, isn't it, Chiefie?"

"What's that?" asked the chief tentatively, looking around to see if somebody else had slipped by. There was no one, only the sound of an ominous, slow drip from one of the overhead steam pipes, the lagging sodden through.

"Those college farts," said Knead, carrying on the conversation as if it had never been interrupted, "think they know everything. Isn't that a fact?" He looked up at the chief. "That Dyer... electronics whiz... knows nothing about a pig boat, huh? Way he blushes at a joke I figure his wife's got one in the oven... now he thinks he's Mr. Cock!"

The chief, for all the obscenities he was used to aboard ship, found Knead's reference to Dyer thoroughly offensive, and downright odd—sick more than simply pornographic. Knead seemed a damn sight more than depressed; he seemed unhinged, even given the leeway normally accorded the eccentricities of men who had to live in close quarters for up to two and a half months at a time.

The only thing the chief could put it down to was that it might be the only way Knead had of dealing with the undeniable and increasing danger that, because of bad air, rising temperature and damaged scrubbers, all of them might be dead within days. There was also the added worry of the loss of generating power if the reactor had to stay shut down, and the Navy's difficulty in searching for the sub while keeping its predicament secret from the Russians.

Despite the pressure of such overwhelming dangers, Chief Ryman knew part of his duty was to keep the morale of the crew as high as possible—to lie, if need be, to those who might otherwise crack. One thing the chief had decided to do was to double the maintenance watches, provided the exec approved, as this would help to keep every able man busy. For their entertainment during their off hours the forty-eight movie videos would be allowed to run practically nonstop, though each man would be required, under threat of court-martial, to use the plug-in earpiece on the multiple soundboard connected to the TV. The last thing they needed was a blast from the speakers alerting Russian searchers. On the other hand, though, he wondered if it would be better to ration the videos, create an air of expectation, something to look forward to.

Knead was still carrying on about Dyer. What Knead had against the electronics Ph.D. the chief didn't know and didn't much care. He was probably nothing more than a focus for Knead's fear. The chief had seen it often enough before; someone got mad at something or frightened, and next thing you knew there they were taking it out on someone else.

"Listen, Marty," the chief said before he turned to continue his inspection of the boat. "We're going to get out of this mess. I know it seems like the odds are stacked against us right now." Even as he was talking, the chief noticed it was becoming more difficult than usual to breathe. The air felt heavy. "But believe me, sailor, we're going to beat it. We're going home."

Knead stared up at the chief through the protective plastic mask that was fogging up now because of the rise in temperature. He lifted the face guard. He was pale, sweat trickling down his forehead, his expression apathetic, tired.

The chief wasn't sure he'd heard. "I mean it," he repeated. "We're gonna get out of this."

"I know *that*!" said Knead. He sounded so definite, so certain, that it was only at that moment, with Knead so sure, that the chief really understood for the first time how great the odds against them really were.

# 11

KORNON'S WIFE SAID she thought it was pure vindictiveness on the part of the Moscow chairman to have sent a man in the middle of the night, frightening the life out of them, ordering Kornon to be at the Ulan Ude station very early in the morning to catch the Trans-Siberian for the more than three-thousand-mile journey back to the capital. Everyone—at least everyone in Ulan Ude—knew that the only Trans-Siberian train that came through in the morning was the one going even farther east to the port of Nakhoda. Kornon, however, bitter as he had become about his exile, believed the time of the order was not the result of petty vindictiveness but of bureaucratic fumbling. The simple truth, he told Natasha, was probably that the clerks in Moscow hadn't bothered to check any changes in train schedule from winter to summer. "You know how everyone is in Moscow," he went on. "They think anything east of the Urals is frozen in Moscow time—or ought to be. They probably forgot to add the five hours difference."

"*Forgot*, nothing," countered Natasha. "Aren't you the one who's always telling me that the Party plans everything down to the last detail?"

She was right. The Party had planned everything, but that fact wasn't apparent until the Trans-Siberian came roaring through the hard, dirty yards of Ulan Ude. The long train was maroon with yellow trim, the Moscow-Vladivostok sign on each carriage, and the bold hammer and sickle crest beneath the star and CCCP's crossed hammer and wrench becoming visible as it slowed and came to a hissing stop, spumes of silvery-white vapor rising into the pristine air. Kornon, Natasha by his side, noticed the faces of people aboard were muffled in scarves, despite the fact that it was summer. Children were peering out through the thick condensation that had accumulated on the inside of the windows during the five-thousand-mile journey to the Soviet's Far Eastern republics. The station was engulfed in a mixture of smells: nauseating diesel exhaust, the mouth-watering aroma of warm, freshly baked bread and *pirozhki*—deep fried meat pastries—pierced now and then by a cool Siberian wind that moaned down from the Arctic to the wide reaches of the Amur River, which marked the southern boundary between Russia and China.

Kornon and his wife, in her peasant black except for a saffron scarf tied tightly about her head, waited, watching passengers who were about to disembark, seeing their frantic faces through the steamy windows, the joy of recognition, the plain agony of those who, in growing panic or disappointment, began walking quickly, then running up and down the train as the whistle signaled imminent departure. There was a tap on Kornon's shoulder. As he turned, he saw the face of a young colonel, an Aide to General Borgach. Kornon had discussed with Borgach his ill-fated plan to seek Soviet dominance in the Pacific; when the plan collapsed, Borgach declared, as he had said he would, that he had known nothing of it, had never heard of the misguided scheme.

It wasn't that Borgach had disliked Kornon. On the contrary, Alexander Androvich Kornon had been one of the brightest stars in the general's constellation, destined to move from alternate membership to full member of the Politburo—until Kornon involved himself with Eagle Island. Anyone remotely associated with that episode had fallen from favor. Even Borgach had, in spite of his care, been affected; on his retirement he hadn't been given as grand a dacha outside Moscow as he had hoped for, and permits for the foreign travel he had long planned weren't forthcoming—the price of having been a friend of Kornon.

His aide, Colonel Ustenko, too, had paid a price, his chances of further promotion unofficially understood to have been thwarted because of his indirect association with Kornon through Borgach. In fact, Kornon and Ustenko had never liked each other—a case of two ambitious and risk-taking men clashing with each other, like temperament repulsing like. Kornon was all the more astonished, then, to see Ustenko appear out of nowhere at the station at Ulan Ude.

"General, Mrs. Kornon." Ustenko inclined his head as far as Party deference allowed and no farther, but Kornon instantly saw that he was more cordial then he'd ever been—the kind of forced, official cordiality expected of lower Party officials when they were about to deliver a body blow. "Compliments," the colonel said, "from the Central Committee and General Borgach."

Natasha said nothing, her broad Slavic face imperturbable and inscrutable to the colonel, her peasant garb her sole act of defiance against the "progressives" of the Party, who had exiled her husband and his family.

Kornon nodded his acknowledgment but instinctively straightened to face whatever charge Moscow was about to make. No doubt this unsavory and perhaps final errand on the colonel's part was Ustenko's own act of contrition before he could be brought back into the "holy hierarchy" whose infinite wisdom guided all the peoples of the Republics. Kornon saw very well that Ustenko was the perfect choice for any such dirty work, almost guaranteed to get Kornon's back up—an acid test of whether the general's exile had really taught him humility. Instantly on guard, Kornon thanked the colonel for the Party's esteemed greeting and asked what was required of him.

Uncharacteristically Ustenko held up his hands in a gesture of perplexed innocence. "This I do not know, Comrade General. All I've been told is to bring you, I should say 'escort' you, to a preliminary hearing in Vladivostok and then to Moscow. The Ulan Ude committee has been notified."

Natasha looked at the train, whose doors were banging shut.

Ustenko smiled at her. "It won't leave without me."

Natasha looked at this colonel who had the power to hold up the Trans-Siberian. Then it *was* serious. "Don't go with him!" she said to her husband. "They won't let you come back. They're not taking you to Moscow!"

Kornon turned to her and smiled, not because he thought that she was mistaken, or that she was weaker than he and needed his courage to steel herself, but rather because in all the time they had been married, thirty-one years in December, he had never known her to speak so directly in front of a Party official. He needed her courage. Only Colonel Saburov, the political officer in charge of executing Kornon's Eagle Island plan, had received her disapprobation so forcefully, when she had told her husband in Saburov's presence that the colonel was one of the most evil men she had ever met. Kornon had ignored her then, too, but he had also known, as he knew now, that—as much as she loved him, as much as a woman could love, and as much as she was correct about Saburov, as much as she might be right about Ustenko—she didn't understand the Party.

The Party sometimes needed ruthless men, and when it ordered you to accompany Ustenko to Vladivostok, you went. Orders must be obeyed; he had always insisted upon that in his own command. He couldn't expect less of himself. And sometimes, he believed, men had to be ruthless. The Revolution would have died without such men. Besides, in his time, he had been as ruthless as any of them. That was life.

"Goodbye," he said, and kissed her.

DIVERTED NORTHEASTWARD because of a storm moving in fast across the Sea of Japan toward the North American continent, the Hercules with Frank Hall aboard flew a direct line along longitude 165 degrees to a point west of the Alaskan peninsula, near the western tip of Unimak Island. The plane then swung around, skirting the northern flank of the storm system.

The lights of Dutch Harbor glistened like diamonds, a tiny enclave of civilization tucked away to the north beneath the brooding mass of the seven-thousand-foot-high Makushin Volcano. Hall recalled the summer he had spent there years ago as a teenager, working as a packer in what had then been one of a dozen or so fish canneries when that industry had been thriving and when Dutch Harbor had been the most prosperous fishing port in the United States. There were so many crab pots in those days, he told Bremmer, that at the end of the autumn season the stored-up, two-man-size traps almost completely covered the old abandoned wartime Army depots, so that from the air it had looked as if you were passing over fields of rust.

Then the boom had burst. The Bering Sea, often called the most abundant fishery in the world because of the great migrations of so many species, was being overfished. Suddenly the days when it wasn't unusual for some of the best men to make over a hundred thousand dollars a week on crab alone were ended. Arguments among the scientists and fishermen raged as to the reasons behind the collapse. Was it the result of overfishing? Or had rising temperatures in the seas around the Aleutian chain, caused by deep-sea thermal activity and eruptions of the kind that had given birth to islands like Surtsey off Iceland virtually overnight, killed off millions of fish? Local Aleuts in the village of Unalaska near Dutch Harbor, some of whom were descendants of the original inhabitants of the islands, blamed the underground atomic bomb tests carried out on the island of Amchitka some six hundred miles westward in the chain. Hall wondered what they would do now if they knew that a sub lay somewhere on the bottom halfway between Attu and the Komandorskys, not only a submarine containing more explosive power than all the wars in history but one in which each missile was much more powerful than the tests carried out on Amchitka.

From the records he'd seen since those days, collected by both Canadian and U.S. oceanographic ships like the *Petrel*, he told Bremmer, he was convinced that the truth lay in a combination of factors, one being the increased temperatures due to the thermal activity between the Pacific and North Atlantic plates moving and pulling apart below the seas along the full extent of the deep Aleutian Trench, and another the proliferation of predatory fish stocks such as cod who ate the young crab. The sea, Frank said, had its own laws, its own idiosyncrasies, often more savage and more hidden than most people realized.

There was a crackle in Hall's headset as Bremmer, who had been summoned forward by the copilot, checked his map under the cone of the side light and reported, "That's Umnak Island down on your left. All that stuff that looks like clouds is steam from a volcano on the island."

Hall was about to tell Bremmer that it wasn't a volcano but rather a series of fumaroles, or vents, through which hot sulfurous and other gases were escaping from thermal activity beneath Partov's Cove. The cove was located on the narrow neck between Umnak's smoldering Okmok Caldera, and Mount Vsevidof, the latter named from the time of Russian ownership of the Aleutians, before the United States more than a hundred years ago bought Alaska, including the Aleutians, for a million dollars. But Hall said nothing; he knew that Mike Bremmer, as liaison officer, was trying his best to be helpful. Besides, Hall thought, no one likes a smartass. He might need Bremmer as the vital link between himself and the surface ships during any attempt to rescue the men in the trapped sub—if the Navy found it. Hall waved his thanks to Bremmer for the lieutenant's well-intentioned, if inaccurate information about the fumaroles on Umnak Island, now swallowed by rain-swept darkness.

"We should reach Attu around dawn," Bremmer went on, checking his clipboard, as he made his way back from the cockpit.

"Not in this williwaw," said Hall, feeling more at home by the second as they headed for the remote westernmost island in the far-flung chain. His love for the wild places of the earth had been rekindled by the sight of Okmok Caldera sending up its strange and elusive vapors, blown helter-skelter high into the blustery night like the smoke signals of some subterranean tribe that had inhabited the mysterious earth since time immemorial.

"A willy what?" asked Bremmer.

"Williwaw," said Hall. "It's a very powerful wind up here that can reach a hundred and twenty miles an hour. I don't just mean airspeed but on the ground. It blows across the Aleutians so hard that it often drives the rain horizontally. The islands have virtually no vegetation to speak of except wild grasses, so the wind just roars on through. There's no really big land mass to stop it before it hits the islands full blast."

"Thanks, Professor." Bremmer forced a smile. If there was one thing he couldn't stand, it was a smartass. Well, Hall had better know all about willy whores and then some if he was going to get the *New York* up from the bottom of the sea—that

is, if anybody could find it after they'd—what had Hall said?—
mown the grass.

Shrouded in fog, the rugged, snow-veined peaks of Attu
looked ominously unwelcoming when the Hercules finally
banked to begin its decent, relying more on its instruments than
on ground control either from the air base on Shemya Island
thirty miles east or on Attu Island.

"Can't see a damn thing," remarked Bremmer, his tone be-
traying the apprehension of a man much more comfortable in
the wardroom of a destroyer than flying blind over unseen
peaks that he knew climbed to more than three thousand feet
above the forty-three-mile-long island. The Hercules came in
on a crosswind that buffeted the huge plane as if it was a glider.
The tearing of the wind combined with the reverse thrust of the
engines so that every part of the plane seemed about to fly apart
in the throes of an uncontrollable shuddering. A sudden skid
on the rain-slicked tarmac did nothing for Bremmer's anxiety.

Glancing across at Hall, he marvelled at how disgustingly
cool the oceanographer was under the circumstances. To his
further astonishment, he noticed Hall was reading a book,
some oceanographic report or other to do with tectonics, the
action of the huge plates of the earth's crust that, grinding
against each other, caused everything from earthquakes to the
tsunamis that, as Hall had told him on the way up, were often
mistakenly called tidal waves. Trying to adopt the cool demeanor of the oceanographic all-rounder he'd heard Hall was,
Bremmer forced himself, though white-knuckling it, to lean
over casually, feigning interest in the book. "Any good?" he
asked nonchalantly.

"Information's all right," replied Hall. "The trouble is only
about one academic in ten can write anything without having
verbal diarrhea." Hall paused. "Like calling a big wind a williwaw."

Bremmer grinned, despite his nervousness about flying blind.
Hall was okay.

The engines were still in the high scream of reverse thrust.
"Yeah," shouted Bremmer, "I see what you mean." He
paused. "Listen, are you as cool as all that?"

"As what?"

"I mean sitting back there reading and...I mean, doesn't this stuff..." He gestured to the impenetrable rain whose persistent roar joined the cacophony of sound about the Hercules. "I mean, the pilot told me that up here you can't even trust the instruments—that magnetics in the high north play all kind of tricks on you like wrong direction, and these winds—the old molly whores you were talking about, I guess—foul up the airspeed indicators. How can you relax, man?"

"I don't," said Hall easily. "Flying in zero visibility's not my idea of whooping it up."

"No shit?" said Bremmer, the relief visible as he sat back, still gripping his seat as if he was in the electric chair. "You don't enjoy it?"

"No," Hall replied. "Anyone who's not afraid of flying through pea soup is an idiot. And," Hall went on as the Hercules planed and skidded in the rain, "damned if I'd want him as liaison officer. Same thing on a submersible. You need a bit of fear, otherwise you get too complacent. You start to believe all the dials and gauges instead of your own gauges—your head and gut instinct."

Suddenly Bremmer's relief was displaced by a much starker fear than flying blind. "Yeah...I see what you mean, Frank. But, ah...ah...listen, what's this about submersibles? I mean I'm strictly public relations. Hell, all my training's in signals and then PR. I'm only along to translate your requests to the Navy brass until we get to an on-scene surface ship in the area. I know squat about submersibles."

"Doesn't bother me. That's what the Navy's hired me for. What I need is someone down there with me, so that when we go to the surface and I have to leave you there to get something made in a hurry you'll know exactly what I want. You will have seen it. I can't waste time overseeing improvised construction on deck. That'll be your job."

"You mean you'll want me to go *down* with you?"

"Right. You can translate all the williwaws," said Hall, smiling as the plane's engines subsided and the steady pouring of the rain became louder. "Unless," he continued, "you'd rather not. We could go over a lot of the submersible stuff you'll need to know between here and the search area. Otherwise, I'd have to start all over again with someone else when we get there. By then those boys on the sub could be running out of time.''

Hall knew he was putting pressure on the younger man, but the pressure on the one hundred and fifty aboard the *New York* was, if they were still alive, bound to be a lot worse.

"Sure, okay," said Bremmer gamely. "I'll go down if you like."

"Good," said Hall. "If they've found where she is, we'll probably need only one trip." He didn't bother mentioning that below a thousand feet, about half way to the sub's test depth, the translucent to inky-blue light would give way to pitch-black, or that, if anything went wrong over a jagged bottom, their landing in the Hercules on Attu would seem like a Sunday drive by comparison. And then there were the Russians. With his knowledge of underwater acoustics, of the sound layer, for example, which could transmit a noise halfway around the world, Hall simply couldn't believe that the Soviet listening stations hadn't picked up the *New York* going down.

# 12

WHEN THE HERCULES finally landed on Attu, neither the U.S. Navy loran station there nor the Air Force station on Shemya, fifty-odd miles to the east, had good news. Despite long-range air patrols rendezvousing, waiting for radio signals during the *New York*'s prearranged time slots, and despite sonar runs by three U.S. Navy surface ships ordered into the area by Admiral Clayton in Hawaii—two fast frigates, guided missile type, one of them the USS *Boise*, and a cruiser—no one had come up with an image of the *New York*, despite several early claims that they might have found her.

Hall understood, knowing how it was during a search. Watching a sonar trace was like looking for someone you knew in a crowd; if anything in the distance bore the slightest resemblance to what you were searching for, your mind could easily turn expectation into what you thought was reality. And having regular Navy types searching for something on the sea bottom, over two thousand feet below the surface, was like asking a regular photographer to read an X-ray. Hall knew he'd have to see the sonar traces himself. For one thing, depending on the angle of approach of the surface ship and its speed, a sharp peak looking like a conning tower on the trace might well be nothing more than a slight hump on the bottom/water interface.

Right now he was thinking about the fast frigate here in Attu to take him and the *Serena I* to the search area. "What's its speed?" he asked the CO.

"Twenty-eight knots."

Hall automatically added another seven knots to the official speed to get the more likely, if classified, figure of thirty-five knots. The problem was that with the storms that had forced the Hercules to swing farther east than anticipated and that were still coming on strong from the west along the line of the Kuro Siwo—the black current—the frigate's speed would be cut in half, at best. This would mean that by the time she rendezvoused with the USS *Boise* in the search area and transferred the *Serena I* another six to ten hours would be lost—more lead time for what Frank was sure would be a Russian move. He had thought of going out with Bremmer in the standard LAMPS— light airborne multipurpose helicopter—aboard the frigate, but it would be too light for the storm line; that was always the trouble with them. When he had more time he planned to ask Bremmer what a light *non*airborne multipurpose helicopter would be doing on a ship. "How about your long-range aircraft based on Shemya?" he asked the Attu CO.

"Out on long-range patrol right now—looking and listening for her, Mr. Hall."

"What are they listening for?" asked Hall. Before Attu's commanding officer could answer, Hall went on. "I hope they don't think they're going to hear a sonobuoy—or see one, for that matter. If the sub is in the general area north of the Emperor Seamounts, then it'll be closer to Russia than to Attu— which means that if it's still intact and the skipper releases a sonobuoy, it'll alert the Russians sooner than it'll alert us."

"Well, there could be an oil slick if she's gone down," responded the CO, miffed at the oceanographer's suggestion that he hadn't thought the problem through before asking Shemya to put up every available aircraft.

"Could be an oil slick anyway," said Hall, "whether she's gone down or not. That would be the smartest move."

Bremmer couldn't help but admire Hall's quickness of mind; he had seen immediately, for example, how an oil slick could be one of the best signals of all, if some malfunction was preventing radio communication. It wouldn't involve any noise that might alert the Russians. And even with the storm it was something that the superior American TEMPSATS, temperature-sensitive satellites, could pick up amid differences in surface temperature photography.

"Still," Hall added, "if the Russians have put up long-range aircraft with temperature-sensitive photography, too, that could put us neck and neck."

"Then what do you suggest we do?" pressed Attu's CO, an edge to his voice. "You're the expert."

"None of us is *the* expert," Hall responded. "Otherwise we'd know exactly where to go, Captain. I'm as much in the dark as you are here. But I'm just as worried about Ivan cashing in on this as I am about where the *New York* is."

"Surely the men are more important than the damn sub?" said the captain.

"The point is, Captain, the Russians only care about our coding equipment and our codes, and if those bastards in the Kremlin find out precisely where she is before we do, they won't give a fish's tit about our boys down there—if they're not shark food already."

"If the sub's below test depth, there won't be much coding equipment, codes or anything else to see, will there? The depths in that general area are deeper than the *New York*'s test depth—over fifteen hundred feet."

"Then the Russians know something you don't," said Hall.

"What's that?"

"That test depth is only two-thirds of the crush depth. The *New York* could have a couple of hundred feet to go before she starts to break up."

"If she's not already flatter than a pancake," the CO responded.

"We can only try," countered Hall. "And I'd appreciate anything you can do." His tone was conciliatory. He understood why the Navy man was more worried about saving the men than the codes.

"Hell, he was right, wasn't he?" asked Bremmer when the Attu CO left. The Navy could always change a code, but it couldn't bring back a dead crew of 150 men. "Why wait?" Bremmer pressed. "Why wouldn't the skipper release a sonobuoy, let everyone within monitoring distance know where he was, including the Russians, if it meant even the slightest possibility of rescue?"

"Because," Hall explained to Bremmer, "you'd risk killing a lot more men than that in any future Soviet-American punch-up, if the Russians get a good look at that Trident reactor as well as the sonar nose, crushed or not. Anyway, our problem right now is how to get there."

"Where?" asked Bremmer, looking nonplussed.

"To the search area," Hall answered.

"But the CO just told you. We're going on the frigate."

"No. Too slow, Mike."

Bremmer didn't like it, being suddenly called by his first name. Not that he didn't like the oceanographer being friendly. But it was Hall's easy tone that did it, like an arm around the shoulder when you're being asked, ever so politely, to do something you'd rather not do, like fly blind again in the Hercules.

Bremmer was wrong. It was something much worse.


ONCE HE AND COLONEL USTENKO boarded the train, Ustenko surprised Kornon by not leading him into a "soft" carriage, what Westerners would have called first class and in which officers normally traveled on the Trans-Siberian. Instead Ustenko, clearly under orders to deny himself and the general the comforts of normal Party status, made for one of the much more crowded "hard" carriages. There the air was filled with dense, pungent, bluish-gray smoke, the snores of sleepers, the chatter of old, scarf-clad babushkas and of men in the favored dark-colored sweat suits, and the raucous laughter of several Buryat men playing Preference. The Buryats tie strings dangled from the earflaps of their Chinese-style summer caps; the weathered, leathery lines of their faces were a striking contrast to the paler ones of passengers like Ustenko and Kornon, from the western republics.

For Kornon, the ambience was foreign, only serving to reemphasize his sense of exclusion from the "real" Russia west of the Urals, the Russia that he and other Muscovites feelingly called home. For a moment he thought that he might well have been in China, just across the border, and he felt the ancient hostility between Russians and Chinese, a deep-seated, almost pathological fear and distrust that in the sixties and seventies had caused bloodshed in the border disputes around the Amur River.

He and Ustenko weaved their way through the swaying, overcrowded carriages, some with more than sixty people squashed into a perspiring press of humanity. Kornon found it oppressive and claustrophobic after the vastness of the birch forests outside Ulan Ude. Although he had hated every day of banishment from Moscow, the crush of bodies around him now filled him suddenly with a revulsion and—what was more frightening—with a rising apprehension that he might not be so grateful after all to leave the forlorn wastes of the Transbaikal for the unexpected chance to reenter, however briefly, the crowded world of Moscow.

He was wondering, too, whether despite his assiduous efforts to keep up with what had happened in his field since his exile he might be unable to carry on a normal conversation with anyone about anything, after being out of personal contact for so long. It was true, he told himself, that his expulsion had steeled his instinct for survival wherever he was, but he felt like an athlete barred from the real games, the shadow practice he had kept up for survival lacking the conviction of a man who must play for real each day if he is to keep his talents truly honed.

"What more do they want?" he pressed Ustenko again. "Even if you don't know the details, Colonel, you must sense what they expect of me."

Ustenko sat down in an aisle seat and, by outstaring a peasant, got her to move away so he could take a window seat. He took off his coat, for the carriage was overheated, and loosened his collar and tie. Kornon, still standing, also took off his coat. His uniform was beautifully pressed. He knew, because he'd served on disciplinary committees himself, that the first thing they looked for was whether you had bothered to keep up your appearance. You had no chance of getting out of the doghouse if you showed signs of a lack of self-discipline, or self-respect.

As far as self-respect was concerned, he decided he'd be damned if he'd lower himself to ask Ustenko any more questions. It was a bad sign if Ustenko was too contemptuous to answer him, a colonel no longer wary of offending a general, even an exiled one. Either that, thought Kornon, or the insolent bastard really didn't know what they wanted. If he didn't know, then why didn't he say so? Perhaps the Chinese had breached the Amur again, or a U.S. ship had penetrated Soviet sovereignty. It was a common enough ploy, a high Party official blaming someone already in exile for something they didn't want to take responsibility for. He'd done it himself. But like an adulterer who suddenly discovers that he's the one being cuckolded, the fact that he'd done something to others often enough didn't make it any easier for him to accept that someone might be doing it to him.

Ustenko called the concession woman over to order a glass of Baikal—a herb-flavored cola. He asked Kornon uninterestedly if he would like a glass.

"A vodka," said the general. "Stolichnaya." If Ustenko wasn't going to tell him anything, then the hell with him! Make him pay for the most expensive, eighty percent proof! And to hell with the cola and its "medicinal" Siberian herbs. And to hell with Siberia. Forever.

"Vodka?" the woman asked.

"Yes," said Kornon. "Vodka. Something with guts in it!"

Ustenko smiled and ordered two colas, giving her the money and waving her away.

Handing Kornon a cola, Ustenko kept smiling and said quietly, "You have been away, General." He raised the oily glass for a toast.

Kornon sat in silence, his body caught in the rhythm of the train, trying to work out the problem. The colonel loosened his tie a little more, slumped slightly, his legs sprawling—all the signs preparatory to a long journey. Birch forests slipped by as the train gained momentum on a downhill grade. After a few minutes, Ustenko pointed out the window to a river swollen in flood, toward which a lone deer was fleeing from some invisible pursuer. "A wolf, perhaps," he said to Kornon, then added softly, still watching the deer, "We'll be getting out at Petrovsk."

"What's there?" Kornon asked.

"An airport."

"Are we *really* going to Moscow?" asked the general. "Or was my wife right?"

"I told you what I was told." Ustenko was sitting up, looking back now at the deer skittering for its life across marshy ground. "There might not be another animal—perhaps it was frightened by the train."

There was a long pause. The general, not interested in the fate of deer, was about to say something else, when Ustenko sat back yawning, feet apart as if now that he was mobile all his cares had been left behind. The action, Kornon thought, was almost too relaxed, too intentional, as if they were being—

Then it began to fall into place—along with the colonel's comment to him about having been "away too long." They were being watched.

"But why no vodka?" asked Kornon, adopting the other's intentionally offhand manner, watching the forests flashing by faster and faster as they increased speed. He saw a peasant and a dog, the peasant leaning on old wooden poles. Had it not been summer he would have thought the sticks were skis. Then he thought of his humiliation in the winter gone by when young Tanya found him weeping with rage.

"No vodka," said the colonel, "because when you face them they want you sober."

There was a burst of laughter from the card-playing Buryats. They had stopped playing Preference and were now dealing the sticky cards again, preparing for a game of Fool.

THE CO OF THE LORAN BASE gave Hall a message. The MV *Petrel* was sixteen hundred miles west of the Alaskan Panhandle doing a hydrographic and geological survey of fjords for the

University of Alaska and the U.S. Hydrographic Service. Captain Tate, skipper of the research vessel, had replied that he would end the bottle cast he was doing for salinity and oxygen content of the bottom layers, and the corer sample he was in the process of hauling in from five hundred fathoms, as soon as possible and be on his way to assist.

"Just as I thought," said Bremmer. "It'll take them at least forty-eight hours to get into the area."

"All right, Nostradamus," Hall joked. "But I've worked on that ship more times than I can remember, and it's one of the best-equipped oceanographic ships in the world. I know the crew and they know me."

"Fine, but we're not on an oceanographic cruise here."

"I'm not so sure, Lieutenant."

"How do you mean?"

"For starters, none of the Navy ships have state-of-the-art side scanners. Their sonars are built to detect other ships."

"I thought that's what we're looking for."

"Yes, but the Navy's sonars are more to detect ships on the attack, not wrecks on the bottom where you need good pictures of bottom topography—the shape of the sea bottom."

"Okay, the *Petrel* has got this super duper sonar stuff, but what good's it going to do us when it's hundreds of miles away?"

"Well, you know, Mike, the opera isn't over till the fat lady sings."

"What the heck's that supposed to mean?"

"That even if we find the sub, we have to get it up," said Hall. He was about to go on, then changed his mind. If no Navy ships had yet located the *New York* there was no point in his raising the myriad problems that salvage alone would present, including the possible use of the atmospheric diving suit, or AD suit. But neither did he want to lie to Bremmer, who as liaison officer would ultimately have to field the inquiries of the anguished families and friends of the one hundred and fifty officers and men. Concerns about salvage expressed now would be mere speculation, great grist for ratings on the TV wars. Such speculation would, in fact, be much worse than telling the hundreds of anxious families the truth—that you simply didn't have any answers yet. Hopefully, he told Bremmer, if the Navy was successful in "keeping a lid on the entire operation" until "something concrete" turned up, then Bremmer wouldn't have so hard a time of it.

Bremmer said he was confident that with the President's help there wouldn't be a press leak.

Yes, thought Hall, and my name's Flash Gordon! He recalled how a few years back the Navy couldn't even keep their secret codes secret.

Hall didn't like self-righteous types, believing his mother's frequent admonition that pride in one's virtue invariably came before a fall, and so it would have come as a shock to him to know it was he who, albeit unwittingly, had given the press its first whiff of what the tabloids, in characteristically screaming prose, would be calling the GREATEST U.S. NAVAL DISASTER SINCE PEARL HARBOR. But though it was Hall whose quick-thinking rescue attempt on the woman on the Oregon beach had led to a reporter sensationalizing the oceanographer's necessary, if unorthodox, method of rescue in the *Oregon Sentinel*, it was a secretive Russian, five thousand miles away, embittered by exile and arriving in Petrovsk, who, quite unexpectedly, was soon to blow the lid off completely.

# 13

"COMRADE KORNON looks cold," Admiral Litov observed, looking down from the small, dingy, off-duty room in the Petrovsk control tower.

"He looks unrepentant!" said Ilya Skolensky, not so much in his capacity as Head of the Pacific Ocean Department but as a fellow member of the Party.

"Perhaps. But after all, Comrade Director, Ulan Ude isn't Moscow. There's certainly no question of his loyalty. Borgach attests to that."

"Huh!" Skolensky responded dismissively. "Borgach would. He recommended Kornon for promotion to alternate membership to the Politburo. Borgach was lucky not to be sent to this wasteland with Kornon."

"Ah, yes," the admiral enjoined with a tone of begrudging admiration. "But Borgach was too old a fox to get too close to his protégé director. As soon as it became clear that Kornon had been outwitted by this American, Holt—"

"Hall!" said the director of the Pacific Ocean Department.

"Well, whatever his name is, he certainly causes problems for whoever's been in charge of Ocean Resources. They tell me he knows parts of the ocean like the back of his hand—every submarine canyon, every seamount and—"

"Rubbish!" Skolensky interrupted. He was becoming increasingly annoyed by the admiral's veiled goading about the unfortunate fate of anyone in the Oceans Department who had come up against this Hall, whether their ships had been searching for sea gold or trying to establish a Russian presence in the Pacific islands within what the U.S. regarded as its economic and security zone. The fact that Admiral Litov was correct, that the American oceanographer had outwitted and thwarted Soviet plans in the past, only made the admiral's needling of Skolensky's Pacific Ocean Department that much harder to take, particularly when Kornon, as onetime deputy minister of defense handling liaison with the Department of Fisheries and Ocean Resources, had in effect been Skolensky's predecessor, before he fell, or rather crashed, from Party favor after his attempt to grab a slice of the Pacific for the Soviets had been foiled by the American oceanographer. And it wasn't just the Soviets who had fallen afoul of the American. This Hall, Skolensky's file told him, had beaten out foreign multinationals—notably Swiss Rhine Petrochemicals, one of the world's largest, with whom the Soviets did clandestine business—when it, too, had tried, as the U.S. ambassador had so undiplomatically put it, "to muscle in on American" claims.

Skolensky was watching Kornon and Ustenko walk across the airport's potholed parking lot. From the Petrovsk station, Skolensky had instructed Ustenko, the two of them could take a taxi, no Party car would be provided. They had to walk through a maze of new construction around the airport all the way to the control tower. Skolensky had been adamant about this treatment for the general. After all, he was an exile and should be treated as such. Skolensky pointedly told Admiral Litov, in front of a number of their aides, that as director of

POD he wouldn't show the slightest hesitation in sending Kornon back to the "woods" around Ulan Ude if the general couldn't help him.

"He will say he can help you," replied Admiral Litov wryly, with a man-of-the-world air that Skolensky found irritatingly pompous in the Commander of the Eastern TVD—the Eastern Military Theater.

"And why are you so sure he'll say that?" challenged Skolensky.

"Who wouldn't in his position?" Litov retorted. "He's got nothing to lose but frostbite." His own remark struck the admiral as quite humorous and he grinned at his aide, who dutifully spluttered, confirming Litov's view of himself as the senior wit of the Eastern Theater. But it only made Skolensky more determined to question Kornon closely to see if the exiled general had anything to offer, or whether the long, boring flight from Moscow had been a complete waste of time.

"He'll need vodka to put him at ease," said Admiral Litov, turning to his aide.

"No vodka," cut in Skolensky. It wasn't simply that he was being churlish with the admiral, though he did enjoy the petty demonstration of who was who in the pecking order. The absence of drink would be a further signal to Kornon, now being escorted up the long flight of stairs to the control tower, that he was still in as much of a state of internal exile as he had been when he left Ulan Ude, and that he shouldn't assume that anything had changed. Everything would depend on Kornon's estimate of the situation off the Komandorsky Islands—and on whether he was contrite enough.

The moment Kornon entered the room Skolensky was struck by the marked contrast between the neat pressed look of his uniform and his distinctive odor, the sour, vinegary smell that exiles carried with them. Some said it was merely the smell of fear, that exiles were no different from anyone else facing a Party disciplinary hearing. Skolensky, however, firmly believed it was the perspiration of someone no longer able to afford the arsenal of body salts and deodorants that had become de rigueur for senior "revolutionaries" in Moscow—one of those small but telling details that differentiate those on top from those on the bottom, and that the Englishman Orwell had written about so splendidly, recounting his days as a dishwasher and tramp in *Down and Out in Paris and London*, a favorite of the younger Party members of Komosol, whenever they wanted to exemplify the evils of capitalism.

The general appeared humble enough, Skolensky thought, and between him and Colonel Ustenko, another of Borgach's protégés, who had so willingly gone to fetch Kornon from Ulan Ude, eager for his own reinstatement to Party favor, it was difficult to tell which of the two would go the farthest, do the most, do anything that was asked of them to get back from Outer Mongolia, as the Russians proper contemptuously referred to the territory east of Lake Baikal. This disdain for Ulan Ude, Skolensky knew, continued even in his own department despite the fact that the city since 1978 had been the headquarters for the Far Eastern Theater, which could now boast over fifty divisions, twenty-five hundred combat aircraft, and the Pacific Fleet, largest of all Russia's fleets, which included over a hundred and forty submarines, from diesel electrics to hunter/killers to the massive Typhoon SLBMs, which were the nearest Soviet scientists could get to the super-quiet American Trident.

It was Litov who had first brought the point home to Skolensky as head of the Pacific Ocean Department that in the vast oceanic arena stealth made the difference; it wasn't simply a matter of one sub over another but of national survival—just one of the giant subs, either the Trident or Typhoon, would decide the outcome with its ability to wipe out over a hundred and fifty enemy cities and military bases. It was the Trident's super-quiet technology that Moscow desperately needed to close the gap.

This was Skolensky's mission. Now it was his career on the line. In front of him stood a general, badly in need of a bath, but one who, if old Borgach was right, might be able to help. Or was Borgach as senile as the rest of his cronies who idled away their retirement playing chess in Gorky Park in the summer and indulging themselves watching endless reruns of old Chaplin movies down at the Illuzion? In any event, Skolensky knew that Borgach was right when he said that of all the Russians since the days of Gorbachev who had been involved in expanding Soviet influence in the Pacific, the one who had had the most experience going up against the Americans was Kornon.

Thanks to the American tabloids' sensationalist reporting of Hall's run-in with the Oregon police and his subsequent release from jail, Skolensky was convinced that Hall had been called upon by Washington to find and salvage the downed American submarine. True, there had been no absolute identification from the POD's agent on Attu, but the man's height fitted the description of Hall that the KGB *Rezident* in the San Francisco consulate had sent Moscow.

Acutely aware of time passing, and dispensing with any of the normal salutations, Skolensky held out a hand without taking his eyes off Kornon. The aide passed him a map showing the North Pacific and the funnel of the Bering Sea.

"We know there's a crippled American submarine somewhere here," said Skolensky brusquely, the stubby index finger of his right hand encircling the area from which the loud pop had emanated. "We're reasonably certain that it is a Trident, the *New York*."

"How can you be sure, Comrade? You monitored its egress?"

Skolensky didn't mean to glance around for help from either Admiral Litov, the admiral's aide or Ustenko, but not understanding the question, he instinctively motioned for help. Then he reddened. All right, if Kornon wanted to be an insolent, he could stay in Outer Mongolia, freeze his balls off and stink like a goat.

"What I mean, Comrade Director, is . . . did your department, or whoever, monitor the *New York* as it was leaving Bangor base in Washington State? Have we got a prop signature?"

Admiral Litov was intrigued. The well-dressed exile might stink, but he was obviously in what the British would call the admiral's "line of country." "Yes," said Litov, "we did. Or at least I should say we did take a sound signature, but they run a lot of surface traffic around them to confuse us, as well as the normal blocking." By *blocking* the admiral was referring to U.S. frigates keeping Soviet intelligence trawlers at bay.

"Linear chair?" Kornon asked. He meant the string of aerials along Hood Canal using electromagnetic signals to scramble the otherwise telltale electronic signature coming from the U.S. submarine as it was underway.

"Yes," answered Litov, increasingly impressed by the disgraced general's grasp of the technology involved, and trying unsuccessfully not to show it. "I'm afraid, Comrade, it means that we're only guessing it's the *New York*."

"The name of the submarine is irrelevant," cut in Skolensky. "The important thing is that our sonar and depth analysis confirm that it is nuclear. Moscow insists that we be the first to reach it and . . ."

Kornon was shaking his head. Imperiously Skolensky demanded to know why.

"The Americans have much better sonar, Comrade Director."

"Perhaps," countered Skolensky sharply. "But they haven't found it yet, General. They're crisscrossing the area I showed you on the map."

"Perhaps they're playing games with you, Comrade."

"Games? What are you talking about?"

"I am thinking," said the exiled general, "if I found it first and my surface rescue ship hadn't arrived yet, Comrade, would I stay on the spot?"

Admiral Litov sat down at the air controllers' tea table, its cheap plastic inlay chipped and speckled with stale crumbs—clear evidence to Kornon that the VIPs hadn't been expected at the out-of-the-way tower, that the unexpected arrival was an intentional part of the comrade director's secret trip. The entire meeting was to be unofficial—no special flight permits in your wallet, no bureaucratic carbon copies of a flight from Moscow or a train trip from Ulan Ude, and so no risk of telephone taps between Moscow and Outer Mongolia. But for the comrade director to come himself—that didn't fit, Kornon thought. An aide like Ustenko, crawling on his belly to get back on the promotions list, could surely have come this far to question an exile, draw out his expertise. Then again, if the decision had to be made on the spot whether to bring Alexander Androvich Kornon back on the team, that would explain the presence of the director of the Pacific Ocean Department.

Kornon fought against any optimism, but it was no good; the glimmer of expectation he'd sniffed the moment he walked in and saw a full admiral and the director himself before him had become almost a tangible thing once they began asking him questions in his area of expertise. His glimmer of expectation had become a raging hope; if he had been a believer, he would have made all the obeisances necessary to all the saints so that he might finally escape his wretched expulsion in the Transbaikal.

The admiral had taken off his cap. Kornon noticed that, unlike the official photographs he had seen of Litov, the admiral was balding, with only sideburns of white and a suggestion of soft white hair above his temples. He looked like some character out of a Chekhov play he'd seen once in Moscow, in that faraway time when Alexander Kornon was one of the Party VIPs for whom tickets to the theater or to the big international hockey games against the Americans and Canadians were simply a matter of a call to his secretary in the plush offices behind the Kremlin walls.

The memory of Moscow, of the Kremlin's stunning winter beauty, and in spring—he dared not even think of spring—all but brought tears to the general's eyes. Apart from anything else that he and Natasha might want for themselves, reinstatement would mean a proper ballet school for Tanya again. And he would be back in power. Humility could be good for the soul, the Party told him. Agreed, comrades, but too much of it, as he'd experienced in the past three years, was as corrosive as acid in your gut, eating away at your very being. And the forced idleness—he thought it must be akin to what unemployment was like in the West, doing nothing for you but eating away your sense of worth, your sense of confidence, your very sense of being, like the Arctic wolf he'd seen tearing the guts out of a crippled dog.

"Then tell us, what would *you* do, Comrade," asked the admiral, "if you had already found the sunken submarine?"

"Pretend I had not—until the surface craft arrived."

"General, how is it you know so much about submarines? I thought you were an old army man?"

"I'm not so old, Admiral." It was meant as a joke, but no one laughed. Be careful, Comrade, Kornon told himself. Be very careful. "As a junior officer," he went on, "I was attached to Spets."

Spets was the serviceman's shorthand version of SPETS-NAZ, the acronym for Special Purpose Forces, Russia's equivalent of Britain's SAS, trained by all three branches of the armed forces but under the control of the GRU—the Intelligence Directorate of the Soviet General Staff. A brigade-size unit of Spets was attached to every one of the four Soviet fleets and trained in everything from scuba and hard hat diving to meticulously planned hit-and-run sabotage attacks against high-priority targets in wartime, such as enemy—which meant primarily American—nuclear bases, especially sub bases from Kings Bay, Georgia, to Bangor, Washington, to Rota in Spain. *Wartime* was clearly understood by all Spets to mean all the time and anytime.

"I was with the Spets until I was transferred to staff college in Moscow." The handful of aides in the room had visibly straightened up, Kornon thought, after he'd mentioned Spets.

"And then you went onward and upward?" said the admiral.

There was an awkward silence.

"Until," interjected Skolensky, smiling, with all the timing and subtlety of a Molotov cocktail, "you encountered the American, Hall?"

The transformation in Kornon was so electric, so violent he almost fell, took a faltering step, stopped, collected himself as best he could. He looked tired and drawn, his skin blotched here and there where the flush of embarrassment and anger combined robbed him momentarily of all the rising confidence the admiral had unwittingly been resurrecting in him with his question concerning the general's proud past in the elite of the Russian brigades.

"If," said Kornon, "I have been brought here to be questioned again, Comrade Director, I request an official reading of the charges as is my right...."

"Sit down!" said Skolensky, but Kornon didn't move and there was a palpable tension in the air.

"Sit down, General—please. There are no charges here. I merely wished to...to remind you of your, how should I say it, your official standing."

"I have been reminded, Comrade Director, of my 'official standing' every day for the past three years. I have been re-

minded of it every time I have invited a local party function-
ary in the great metropolis of Ulan Ude and every time he has
refused. My daughter is reminded of my 'official standing'
every time she makes application for reentry to her old Moscow school. Every time another pipe freezes and my requests to
the local committee go unanswered, I am reminded. I know my
official position, Comrade Director, and I will not eat more
shit. You understand.'' It wasn't said loudly, nor was it a question. It was a statement that Alexander Androvich Kornon had
been, at least in his opinion, punished enough.

It wasn't all bravery, though, and both Litov and Skolensky
knew it. Whatever his disgrace, Kornon knew, and they knew,
that he had taken the fall for the failure of his subalterns to
outwit the American. They all knew too that with this visit to
Petrovsk not being official, the comrade admiral and director
obviously weren't sure exactly what to do about the American
sub. There had never before been a situation quite like this, no
Party manual existed on how to find a nuclear sub of the enemy, downed close to Russia. And more important, there was
no manual on how to bring it up if they found it before the
Americans, nor most critical of all, if it couldn't be brought up,
how best to get at its secrets.

Litov dropped the other shoe. "The navy wants that sub,
General. Moscow wants to destroy it—like the KAL airliner.''

Kornon remembered the incident well enough—Flight 007,
en route from Alaska to Korea, strayed over Soviet airspace and
the air force shot it down to show the world that Russian territory couldn't be violated with impunity. Kornon had agreed
with the air force. He still did. The only thing the Americans
understood, Kornon held, was a punch in the face. The Americans had made a great song and dance about women and children being aboard. Of course they did—they thought that
somehow you could exclude women and children from war.
You might as well try to exclude them from life. Hadn't Tanya
been part of his exile? Americans were too soft. He believed
that through that softness you could ultimately defeat them, as
the North Vietnamese had done, sending in children with booby
traps. Americans were insufferably sentimental; it was what
Kornon despised about them most. He was sure that if he had
been allowed more time to work on the problem, he could have

made his mark in the Pacific office by quite simply giving the Americans more of the KAL treatment. Most civilians on the Politburo were for it, too; they just didn't want to be seen doing it. Well, all right, then, he would make it all look accidental, like the French tried to do but bungled when they blew up the *Rainbow Warrior* in the Auckland harbor and got caught.

But why did Moscow want to destroy a Trident close to Soviet territory, before getting its secrets?

"What the admiral means, Comrade, is that Moscow believes that seeing, as you point out, we cannot hope to find it as quickly as the Americans, then rather than face the, ah, shall we say embarrassment . . ."

"Humiliation," the admiral cut in.

"Very well. Rather than face the humiliation of not being able to find it before the Americans, the best possible solution if we are not—and Moscow places great emphasis on this, Comrade—if we are not to lose the confidence of our allies vital to maintaining socialist solidarity in Eastern Europe, is to demonstrate the inviolability of our territory, as we did with the KAL, and destroy the submarine once the Americans have found it."

Kornon knew very well what they meant beneath all the "socialist solidarity" propaganda. Russian technology, at sea and particularly in defense of its own homeland seas, would suffer enormous political and ultimately military damage if Moscow couldn't show the world that Russia could seek out and destroy the greatest single threat in her history—a fully armed American Trident.

"I take it you don't agree, Admiral," said Kornon with increasing confidence.

"Do you?"

"No."

"Why not?" pressed the director, who was becoming noticeably uncomfortable as he tried weighing Moscow's Party line against the navy's. Though Kornon didn't know it, the argument was still unsettled in the Politburo, where the split was about fifty-fifty.

"Well," said Kornon, "I would agree with destroying the submarine *if* the Americans found it before we did. That wouldn't be too difficult, would it, Admiral?"

Litov shook his head. "Not at all. A deep homing torpedo would do it."

"Then we always have that option if worst comes to worst," said the general. "But if there's a chance of retrieving it ourselves, then we ought to try. Our biggest sub, the Typhoon, is so noisy that we have to allow for a fifteen-foot buffer zone between the pressure hull and the outside casing. . . ."

"That space is not just to buffer noise," the admiral joined in. "It's a buffer against explosions if the sub's under attack."

"The point I'm making," said Kornon, "is that one of the reasons the casing's there is that our Typhoon is so much noisier than the Trident and therefore more vulnerable, because we haven't the technology of the Americans in submarine warfare. We all know this whether we admit it publicly or not. But if we're to catch up with and move ahead of them, I say we must try to get at the Trident."

Admiral Litov beamed. He turned to Skolensky. "I think we should order in some vodka."

Skolensky ignored the request. "If Moscow goes along with the navy, it will do so only if it is sure that the submarine can be captured intact—or at least intact enough to be of use, for us to study its—whatever is inside. But how can we possibly assure the Politburo of that, Comrade General, when we don't know precisely where it is and when this American—your old foe, Hall—will be searching as avidly as we?"

Kornon sat down at the mention of Hall's name, but his movements were no longer out of control. He appeared markedly relaxed, his arms lolling over the sides of a torn imitation leather chair, like a gambler who suddenly realizes that the odds are turning in his favor. It was as if there was a God, he thought, a great odds keeper in the glorious Russian sky, who was suddenly showing the road to deliverance—and not merely an escape route from exile and disgrace but a means of wreaking vengeance on the American Kornon hated so deeply. Vengeance so sweet to contemplate, he would never get tired of going over it again and again in the years ahead. Vengeance so simple yet so grand in its conception that he couldn't bear to tell them of it at one sitting. And why should he? They had left him in the bone-cracking cold of Outer Mongolia for three long years, for the past 1,113 days, to be exact. And now he would win back all that he had lost. And more.

"I have a plan," he said simply.

"What is it?" asked Skolensky, trying to contain his impatience. He leaned forward on his pudgy hands, clasping the oily vodka glass Litov's aide had placed before him or rather seizing it, Kornon thought, as an unwilling gambler anxiously holds the cup of dice.

"Well," Kornon began, thrusting out his glass, waiting until Ustenko had served him with Stolichnaya, the very best. "No offense, Comrades, but, ah . . ." He looked around at Litov's aide, then at Ustenko—they were all riding him, he decided, riding him and his knowledge of Hall to advance their own stinking careers. It wasn't a fear of security, of hidden microphones that had made him pause, reluctant to tell them of his grand plan to seize the sub—if it hadn't fallen into the trench. Nor was his hesitation a kind of bait he was holding out for promises of what he knew would be his full restoration to power when his plan against the American worked. Rather, his reluctance to speak about the plan in any detail was born of his deep suspicion of everyone around him, a suspicion that had been nurtured by the system he grew up in, where the only law was survival, the system wherein Comrade Skolensky was now the director of the Pacific Department, a new name for what used to be, and still should be, Alexander Kornon's job. To tell Skolensky and Litov his plan—though he trusted Litov, or rather he suspected him less than Skolensky—would be to throw away all his cards. Besides, why would Skolensky want to see him restored to power, most likely to his old position?

No, Kornon concluded, his insurance lay in telling them just enough to convince them his plan was not only workable but bound to succeed, reserving for himself the myriad and vital details without which the puzzle couldn't be solved. It was the only way he could guarantee that he would be in charge of the operation. He would begin immediately, if they agreed to execute the first step of the plan. Already he was thinking of the Spets units and others he could call on quickly—*if* Skolensky and Litov would agree to get Moscow's immediate permission to proceed. The first volunteers he would ask for would be any qualified family members of those who had been with him against Hall in the old days. And then he would ask more generally for anyone qualified to be part of bringing off the greatest Soviet coup of modern times: the capture of America's most highly prized and deadliest warship, the deadliest in history, now lying crippled like a stricken killer whale on the ocean bottom, unable to move, waiting to be taken.

And while it would be a revenge that was too much for an individual to accomplish single-handedly, he nurtured the hope, born in exile when his heart had turned to stone against Hall, that he might yet get the opportunity to come face-to-face with the American, whom he had never met but whom he felt he knew well enough to kill. Slowly. He took another glass of vodka and immediately felt warm as though a fire had started in his belly. Then he told them the first part of his plan.

Even Skolensky—who plainly didn't like him and who, he knew, would see to it if the plan failed that Kornon's exile would be as permanent as the permafrost of Siberia—even Skolensky was struck by what he had to grudgingly admit was the simplicity of Kornon's plan. It was, the general admitted, suggested to him by the stupid and congenital sentimentality of the American people. They loved generosity. That was the key. Give them generosity and they'd become suckers in an instant.

"But maybe not their Navy," cautioned Litov.

"Of course not their Navy," answered Kornon, "but the people—the peace groups, the church groups, the bleeding hearts of America. They—"

"I love it!" said Litov. "Yes, it's brilliant. Congratulations!"

# 14

ON THE SOUTH COAST of the coarse, lizard-head shape of Attu Island, the bow of the hundred-and-sixty-foot MV *Amlia*, a trawler named after one of the smaller U.S. islands, was bucking sharply in the once-long Pacific swells that were now concertinaed together in the backwash as the Kuro Siwo current smashed against Attu's rocky, scarred coastline. Joe Cherco, the trawler's skipper, his face creased and worn by the sea, his body that of a middleweight boxer in good condition, paid no attention to the swarms of glaucous-winged gulls and long-necked cormorants peppering the air above his trawler. He was giving all his attention to the silver slide of pollack that were oozing out from the long, pendulous net being winched from the stern while he tried to keep the trawler's bow into the swells to prevent waves from flooding the open aft section, held down now by at least fifty tons of fish. Cherco had ordered the cook on deck to help the other eight deckhands man the short, wide shovels. All of them were working frantically, pulling and pushing the fish down through the deck grates into the freezer hold as quickly as possible so that they could move on to another school several miles away. Their next location was indicated by a black, smudgy trace on the *Amlia*'s depth sounder, which Cherco had switched onto high-resolution magnification, its stylus racing across the paper in a frantic regularity, producing a trace of squished-up sine waves.

"Cod," Cherco announced to the helmsman. "Right under us. Goddamn! C'mon, you guys, move it! Empty those nets."

When the bottom fell out of the crab market in the early eighties, Joe Cherco had mortgaged his car and his house to finance the conversion of the *Amlia* from a crabber to a mid-depth trawler. The mortgages meant he needed to catch all he could as fast as he could. The conversion alone—with stronger radios needed for the longer journeys a trawler would make, plus the structural changes to the boat—had cost him, like most of those who elected to go for the middepth trawls, more than two hundred and thirty thousand dollars.

The helmsman watched as Cherco took up his powerful binoculars and swept the horizon to spot any competition. For all he owed, his boat was known as a lucky one among deckhands; he was quick to get from one catch to the next, and they felt they could rely on him because he was a fighter. The stories of Joe Cherco's fistfights with the other crabbers in Dutch Harbor were legendary. In his crabbing days, if someone poached on his pots, each pot capable of holding over two hundred crabs, Joe didn't bother launching complaints with the Alaska Fish and Game Department—he'd board the poacher's boat if he could and settle the problem right there and then;

"putting it right," he called it. If the seas were too rough for such direct action, as they usually were off the Aleutians, or if the offending boat was too far off when Joe spotted it through the binoculars, cleaning out his pots, he'd scribble down its name or registration number, and once ashore he'd go up to the tavern with a baseball bat and settle it there. He'd been fined more than once and locked up on occasion, but with the profits in crabbing then, the fines had come out of petty cash. But that was all before the big crash, before the sudden boom-to-bust in crabbing, before old profits were wiped out in the conversion to the new trawler.

While many of the two hundred-odd crabbers had decided to wrap it up, heading back to the mainland for jobs that offered more security and safety in the long run, the thought of leaving had never occurred to Joe Cherco. He'd been born and raised on the Aleutians and now, by choice, he lived alone on Attu in one of the dugout sod-roofed houses of the native Aleuts, close to the teeming fishing grounds off the island. Cherco not only felt he belonged to the Aleutians, but he could trace his ancestry back to the very first Aleuts and Russian fur traders in the mid-eighteenth century. He was admired through the whole length of the islands by those who had befriended him, and feared by those who had run up against him. He loved his boat and the sea, and his courage was legendary. While most fishermen would turn back to port in bad weather, when the williwaws reached over a hundred miles an hour, Cherco would keep the *Amlia* heading into the wind and let her ride out the storm. He knew he'd be the first out to the lucrative fishing grounds when the storm passed by, while the competition was boozing it up or riding it out in the safe little harbors dotted throughout the volcanic chain.

"C'mon, Cookie, put your back to 'er."

"Hey, know where you can put that shovel?"

"Cut the gab," Joe called out from the wheelhouse, one hand on the wheel, the other holding the binoculars. Through them he saw the flat slab of the air base on Attu and a civilian walking toward the Hercules accompanied by several Air Force men and a naval officer. He slid his binoculars over the runway until he picked up his competition, another trawler bobbing up and down about two miles northwest of the air strip, coming in his direction in search of a new school to trawl. One hand still on the wheel, he steadied the binoculars against the open doorframe. It took him a minute or two, but soon he could make out the name on the other trawler: the MV *High Star*. He knew her—a midsize trawler out of Kiska.

"MV *Amlia* to MV *High Star*," Cherco shouted into the mike. "MV *Amlia* to MV *High Star*. Stay clear of my school. Fuck off!"

"Up yours!" came the reply.

On Attu the Coast Guard operator picked up the exchange on the open channel, shaking his head.

"Right!" answered Cherco and he was off the air.

The Coast Guard knew that "Right!" from Cherco meant a fight, and so he cut in on the channel. "Attu Coast Guard to *Amlia* and *High Star*. Attu Coast Guard to *Amlia* and *High Star*. Bad language is not permitted. Repeat. Not permitted on the public airwaves. Repeat. Bad language is not—"

"Balls!"

"Who said that? *Amlia . . . High Star . . .* Who said that?"

All the Coast Guard operator could hear was static.

Aboard the *Amlia*, the deckhand working nearest the wheelhouse continued to drag and push the fish through the grate. "Here we go," he said. "A punch-up with the *High Star*."

"Not me," said the cook, looking decidedly frightened. "I'll be down below. Making soup."

"Lucky bastard."

But there was no fight, not because the *High Star*'s captain or crew were afraid but simply because the MV *High Star*'s depth sounder hadn't picked up any school of cod or anything else on its sonar. There was none.

Replacing his mike, his catch in the cargo hold, Cherco spun the wheel, bringing the *Amlia* about. He reached over to the depth sounder and adjusted the stylus control to a slower speed so that now the bunching up of sine waves began to spread out, more like a stretched-out accordion; soon they were no more than mere undulations of the sea bottom, now and then showing the bumps of rocky outcrops. Cherco was always careful. If anyone had wanted to check later on, they would see a bunching up of the lines, looking like a school of fish, his excuse for getting on the radio and warning off another trawler.

ON THE SOUTHERNMOST of the two Komandorsky Islands, two hundred miles northwest of Attu, the signals officer of the day, a major dwarfed by the huge blue-and-white wall map of the North Pacific, picked up Cherco's warning to the other trawler not to muscle in on the *Amlia*'s school.

"He's lucky," commented the lieutenant who was monitoring the various wavelengths. "If he hadn't had another trawler near him . . ."

The major merely shrugged. "That's unlikely. Where there's fishing to be done there's bound to be more than one trawler. In any case it wouldn't matter. He could have used any one of a dozen messages, from passing on a bad weather report to the Attu Coast Guard to asking for a weather update himself. Anyway, it's the letters he uses rather than the words that make up the message. *A* means *S*, *B* means *K*, and so on—random pairs that are changed every other month. Simple but effective. I like the obscenity touch—that was Vladivostok's idea. The swearing sounds natural."

"How much do we pay him?" asked the lieutenant, idly turning the palm ball vector control that had superseded the by now ancient bakelite disks and knobs.

"A thousand a month."

"A thousand!" whistled the lieutenant. "What I could do with a thousand rubles in—"

"Dollars," said the major, enjoying the look of utter surprise on the lieutenant's face. "No," the major went on, chortling, "I have no idea how much we pay him. That's got nothing to do with us, Comrade. All I know is what the messages mean. We keep it very simple. He gets one question, something we want to know, and we give him three possible replies: no, yes or he doesn't know."

"What does his warning off the other trawler mean?" asked the lieutenant.

"It confirms for us that there is a civilian involved in the American search."

The next transmission they received was Joe Cherco joking with another midtrawler that the competition, the MV *High Star*, had "taken off," but that by the time his crew had stopped "screwin' around" and gotten all the pollack into the hold, the cod were well and gone.

"What's that all about?" the radio lieutenant on Komandorsky asked the signals major, who had been listening intently to Cherco and writing furiously on one of the gray foolscap message pads.

"It means we'd better contact Vladivostok. And quickly!" answered the major. "Damn it!"

"Trouble?"

"The bastard's mad!" said the major. "He's not going to the search area by ship, after all. We thought he'd be going out on that frigate they have at Attu. They have his submersible lashed down on her stern near the helicopter hangar."

"You mean he's—" the lieutenant began.

"They're flying him out."

The lieutenant was confused. "But, Major, he won't be able to do anything till the submersible reaches the area, will he?"

"Lieutenant," answered the major impatiently, "do you know when a submersible is used?" The major lit a cigarette. "I'll tell you. When you know where something is, or at least think you know where it is. A submersible's slower than a wet week. Three to five knots tops. First, they'll have to find where their sub went down."

While the captain encoded the message for Vladivostok's headquarters, attention ASP—Admiral of Soviet Pacific Fleet, the lieutenant sat surveying the huge wall map of the Bering Sea and the northwest corner of the Pacific. It was over a hundred and fifty miles from Attu to the area the American surface ships were searching for the submarine—about the same distance it was from the Komandorsky Islands. So what if the frigate's helicopter was going to fly the civilian expert ahead instead of him going on the frigate itself? Surely it was the natural thing for anyone to do in a hurry, and everyone was in a hurry to find the submarine. Including Vladivostok. So why was the major so nonplussed all of a sudden?

Perhaps, thought the lieutenant, it was because Vladivostok had planned on using the *Amlia* as a shadow on the frigate—though surely that would be too obvious.

"Here," said the major, thrusting a thin buff-colored sheet of telex paper at him. It was the latest weather advisory, reporting winds of a hundred to a hundred and forty kilometers per hour—williwaws, the major said—roaring out of the Sea of Japan.

"That means," said the major, tapping the weather report with his indelible pencil, "that they won't use a helicopter to take him out to the search area. The wind gusts are too powerful. One second you might be hovering above a ship's pad, the next second a wind shear hits you and you're in the chuck—a pile of rubble and everybody dead. Kaput, Comrade."

"But . . ." pressed the lieutenant. "Vladivostok must have figured they might fly him out of Attu rather than use the frigate."

"Yes, but in a chopper," said the captain. "I just finished telling you—in this weather they won't use a helicopter."

Then the lieutenant finally saw it. "You mean . . . fixed wing?"

"Yes. The Hercules. High wind, head wind, tail wind—makes no difference to those monsters, only to the airspeed. The worst they can do is drop a few hundred feet or so in a shear."

"All right," conceded the lieutenant. "You know more about it than I do. But even I know a fixed wing plane has to land somewhere. Wait a second. . . . You mean to tell me the Americans have a carrier out there? But I didn't think a Hercules—"

"No, they haven't got a carrier. That's just it. Vladivostok didn't think of this one."

"Of what?"

"That the American civilian . . ."

"Hall," said the lieutenant, "I think that's the name Vladivostok gave us—"

"Yes, yes," said the major impatiently. "Hall. Well, Vladivostok didn't realize that he's crazy."

"What do you—"

"If you ask me again what I mean, I'll cut your throat. Here, transmit this to Vladivostok. Fast as you can."

The lieutenant smiled to himself. For all the major's knowledge about aircraft, weather conditions, et cetera, it was he, the lieutenant, the younger man, who was faster on the transmit key.

# 15

IN MOSCOW not far from the Tanganka Theater at 15 Verkhnayaya Radishchevskana, in the smoky, crowded warmth of Vysotsky's Bar—named for his and millions of other's favorite folksinger—Vladimir Lebdev was staring across the bar at a tall, blond woman. In her thirties, he guessed, East German. She had big, firm breasts that he didn't have to guess about. He knew he had a better than even chance of bedding her before the night was out. The trick was to stay sober enough to do it and, more important, to enjoy it. Lebdev was editor of Red Tass. Unlike the confidential White Tass, concerned with internal affairs and issued to all government officials, or the more common Green or Blue Tass sold to the masses, Lebdev's Red Tass was the edition that gave the Party bosses the uncensored truth about both internal and external affairs. It gave Lebdev occasional ulcers and a great deal of power and influence.

He had had a long day being truthful, passing most of the time beside the fax machine in his Boulevard Ring Road office while waiting anxiously as copy came in from Japan and the United States on whatever could be found in the media there about the downed U.S. nuclear sub. There had been nothing. The American oceanographer, Hall, had been dispatched from Oregon, according to one Tass representative in the American Northwest, who was so pressed to provide any more information he could report only that the American had left his girlfriend, Gloria Bernadi, behind. From another Tass reporter, whom Lebdev had had flown to Komandorsky Island, Lebdev learned that the Americans would have to fly in pretty rotten weather to reach the search area, toward which elements of the

Soviet Pacific Fleet, including one ship with an underwater rescue vessel aboard, were steaming out from the Sea of Okhotsk, north of Japan. But so far the American press had reported nothing about the Soviet fleet. In view of the fact that the U.S. Navy's sonar underwater surveillance system, via its relay to Hawaii, must have picked up the Soviet fleet under way, the silence could only mean that the Americans didn't want to advertise the fact of a downed sub—particularly when the vessel could well be on the Russian side of the border.

After spending hours in the Ring Road office watching the fax and telexes click and clack away, he had left word that he be notified if the situation changed. If it did, he would have to go back to work immediately, so as to keep the Politburo informed of American moves reported by the U.S. press or any other.

Lebdev thus had two reasons to guard against getting too drunk: it would impair his ability both to edit copy and to penetrate the secret regions of a blond loyal socialist ally who possessed such glorious breasts that her nipples were clearly outlined despite a heavy white angora sweater that must have cost more money than Soviet workers earned in six months. She probably wasn't wearing a bra. Perhaps if he got closer... She was returning his oily-lipped smiles with polite interest. The fact that she was in Vysotsky's Bar meant that she was probably a journalist like himself. Before making his move, he fished for the black cherry at the bottom of his glass; some idiot in the factory that made the fake seaweed cherries had apparently, or so the story went, put in the wrong coloring, thinking that this month they were making olives. He wanted to see which it tasted like.

The bar was filling up rapidly now at day's end. Peering through the smoke and noise, he lost sight of the woman for a moment, then caught a glimpse of her sweater. She was moving toward the exit. He swore, but as he pushed himself away from the bar, he saw her stop. She wasn't leaving after all. Accompanied by two young Tass reporters, she was gazing up intently at the portrait of the folksinger above the doors. Then, chatting amicably to the two young "sniffers," as Lebdev was already calling them to himself, she returned to where she had been, pretending not to notice the increasing number of stares

and comments she drew but obviously, from the look in her
eyes, enjoying it to the hilt.

After ordering a refill, Lebdev called out to her across the
bar. When she glanced directly at him, he took the cherry,
sucking it clean off its stem, biting it hard and raising his glass,
spilling some of his drink. She acknowledged his toast graciously, then still smiling, turned to her two young escorts so as
to avoid Lebdev's gaze. They quickly downed their vodka and
beer chasers in an attempt to get their shapely comrade out of
the bar and away from Red Tass One, as Lebdev was known.
The musicians on banjos and a piano began a fast but melodic
tune of long ago, while the young Lotharios, one on each side
of her, hustled her toward the door.

They passed under the forlornly drooping moose's head on
the wall, called Faulty by British correspondents, and had
reached the statue of the dwarf, Dopey, from *Snow White*,
when the Ukrainian bouncer stopped them and gently but in-
sistently ushered them to one side. They began arguing with
him.

He listened to them grandfatherlike, cocking one ear as if he
was hard of hearing and then talking to them above the beery
hubbub, pointing back toward the bar. "Mr. Lebdev says
there's a fire at the Tanganka Theater. He wants reporters there
immediately."

The two reporters continued to talk animatedly, one of them
waving his hands about, showing his watch and pointing to the
blonde, then looking back at the watch again. After another
minute or so they gave up and left, and the bouncer, in the
gesture of an ancient gallant, placed one hand gently behind the
small of the Fräulein's back and, like Moses, separated the sea
of faces staring at her as he guided her without obstruction toward the bar.

Her name was Elga. Lebdev hated the name Elga—so German, so ugly.

"Nice name," he said.

"Thank you, Comrade Lebdev."

"You know who I am?"

"Of course, Tass."

"How long have you been in Moscow?"

"Two days. I'm on a socialist journalist club exchange."

"What for?"

"To learn more about the socialist homeland."

Lebdev smiled, ordering another round. "I know all about the homeland."

"That's wonderful," she said.

"Yes." He handed her a vodka and pulled her closer. "Do you know all about the fatherland?" Before she could answer he said, "A week on the Black Sea—a beautiful resort. I've been there myself. Sun and saunas and food—" his eyes closed "—you wouldn't believe." He opened his eyes again. "Would you like that?"

"But of course," she said.

Up close her breasts were so big that they seemed almost obscene. He loved it. "I want to fuck you," he said.

"Yes," she said, putting down her drink. "Are you ready?"

He downed the vodka. Realpolitik—that was what he liked about the Germans. Quid pro quo.

Going home in his ZIL limousine, leaning back and luxuriating in the real leather upholstery, Elga told him that she hoped he wasn't like most Russian men—slam, bang and roll off like pigs out of breath, like schoolboys having it the first time.

"What do you like?" he asked her.

"I'll show you. Are you in good shape?"

A typical German—all muesli for breakfast and push-ups. "I'm in terrible shape," Lebdev said. "Look." He pointed to his gut. Realpolitik. "When the hell do I get time to work out?"

"It doesn't matter." She unpinned her hair and shook her head, creating a blond cascade against the deep chocolate-colored calfskin of the rich upholstery. "Don't worry," she said. "We'll begin slowly." She turned to him, smiling, sliding her hand down, turning it to a cup then closing it slowly between his legs.

"Not now," he gasped excitedly. "Not in the car. I want to spread out."

She laughed. She liked older men; by the time they were his age—late fifties, she guessed—they'd learned the sweet torture of drawing it out until it ached.

MOMENTS BEFORE BOARDING the Hercules, Lieutenant Bremmer, in his capacity as communications officer as well as liaison between Frank Hall and the Navy, was given the latest
twenty-four hour Sigint, the signal intelligence printout from
Adak Island. There, if atmospheric conditions were favorable,
all the messages transmitted across the northwest Pacific and
beyond were monitored by U.S. intelligence-gathering ships,
AGORS, and/or satellite.

One of the hundreds of daily transmits across the Aleutian
arc was the message from the *Amlia* to the *High Star*. Like
dozens of others, it was part of the traffic relayed twice—that
is, not only between the *Amlia* and the *High Star*, but picked
up and retransmitted by another ship, in this case by several
North Korean trawlers, at least one of which was designated as
an AGI—enemy intelligence-gathering trawler. Relays were
often suspect because the relay was seen as a "kicker," a
booster to pass the message over longer distances. But unless
the message had some specificity that the decoders were suspicious of in this, the highest area of suspicion in the world because of the geographical proximity of the two superpowers, it
had to be disregarded as simply another message relayed as
general interest from one fishing boat to another. Such messages were often about bad weather or a fish sighting reported
for the benefit of other company boats, though the companies
usually had their buzz words, unknown to others. Most messages, however, had been kicked from one trawler to another
for no other reason than to pass the time during the long, boring hours between frantic bouts of fishing.

Besides, Joe Cherco was a known character among the fishermen, so disrespectful of authority, so much a "free fisher,"
as the Aleuts proudly called him, that any exchanges involving
the *Amlia* were seldom, if ever, annotated, except to bring to
the reader's attention a new or highly original obscenity.
Bremmer passed over Cherco's message, his attention not
completely on the printout anyway. He was distracted by what
Frank Hall, not yet in his seat, was saying, or rather yelling,
through the shattering roar of the Hercules's warm-up, to the
sergeant standing across from him in the huge cargo bay.

As the four turbo props thundered in unison, drowning out
normal conversation, Hall fastened his seat belt, flicked down

the helmet's lip mike, plugged the cord into the midbay panel on the left side of the aircraft and adjusted the sound level. He took up the conversation with the sergeant again, who kept nodding as Hall seemed to be numbering off some kind of shopping list on his fingers.

Bremmer, only a few feet to Hall's right, plugged into the conversation even before he belted up. He could hear the sergeant's Southern accent clearly despite the crackle of static. "Always carry 'em. This baby can carry sixty—with full packs. Ninety without."

"Without what?" Bremmer cut in, forgetting at first to release the Speak button for the Sergeant's reply.

Bremmer thought the sergeant said, "Shoots." He was feeling hungry, and for an absurd moment found himself thinking of the bamboo shoots he enjoyed so much on the sandwiches he had custom-made in the upscale Washington, D.C., restaurant he frequented on Navy expense accounts. Washington, D.C.—plush carpets, the quiet clinking of cocktail glasses, svelte waitresses in slit-sided Chinese patterned silk—a world away from the bone-shattering roar of the Hercules about to take off.

Until that moment Bremmer had thought Hall, in his haste to do a magnetometer run—that is, to look for any large metallic object beneath the sea—was planning merely to fly low over the search area. It certainly made more sense than the infinitely slower method of doing magnetometer grids by towing the "fish" or magnetometer behind the frigate—even a fast guided-missile frigate. Then, in a stomach-wrenching moment of revelation, Bremmer realized what Hall and the sergeant were talking about. They were discussing chutes, not shoots! In this weather? Hall would kill himself.

"Hey, Frank, you're not going to jump?" Bremmer said, leaping into the conversation.

"Why?" asked Hall, turning, his face framed by the white flying helmet, his rugged features and imperturbable blue eyes the incarnation of coolness, a composite of those select few, Bremmer realized, who had the right stuff.

*"Why?"* said Bremmer. "Christ, you'll kill yourself in this weather, that's why."

Hall shrugged. "It's the usual way when there's no airstrip." He said it as if it were as logical as expecting butter with bread.

"Well, yeah..." Bremmer spluttered. "But, Jesus, Frank, you aren't a paratrooper."

"So?" said Hall easily. "Neither are you."

"What's that got to do with—Christ! You don't mean—"

"You're liaison officer, Mike."

"Hey, now... Listen..."

Several seconds elapsed, devoid of conversation. The cacophony of the Hercules as it taxied now was thick vibration, filling the air, threatening to shake everything loose, including Mike Bremmer's courage.

"Well, look...yeah," said Bremmer, conceding that he *was* liaison officer and recalling Hall's well-taken point that Bremmer would be valuable as surface interpreter between the on-scene ships and Hall in the submersible—if they found the sub.

"We need you, Mike," Frank stated simply.

It was, Bremmer knew, an enormous compliment. "Yeah, right, Frank."

The sergeant's Southern twang penetrated the scream of the engines. His seat was reversed so that he could see Bremmer as he addressed him. "When you're in the air, sir, your speed is the same speed as the plane's. It's all relative. Nothing to it, sir. High winds seem much worse relative to ground speed, that's all. Imagine you're in an elevator. And, sir?"

"Yes," said Bremmer, his throat parched.

"Enjoy the ride, you hear?"

Bremmer said nothing, imagining himself in winds of over a hundred miles an hour—in addition to airspeed—plummeting toward the sea thousands of feet below. And he should imagine he was in an elevator?

"Yeah, fine," said Bremmer, "but I've never jumped before. That's the only problem, you see. I—"

"Nothing to it," Hall assured him. "Just follow me."

Bremmer nodded but he was very unhappy. He was a communications officer, not a paratrooper. "How come you've done everything before, damn it?" he asked Hall, forcing a smile.

"Don't sweat it," said the sergeant. "We'll rig you up, sir. Immersion suit, inflatable raft and—"

Hall saw Bremmer's face go ashen. He flicked the On switch and announced breezily, "I doubt we'll need the raft, Sergeant," but he was really talking to Bremmer. He knew he was asking a lot of someone who had never jumped before, but Bremmer's liaison aboard the *Boise*, Hall well knew, could be the vital link, saving a few minutes here, a few minutes there, the crucial difference that could help save anyone still living aboard the trapped sub.

Bremmer now was embarrassed, ashamed that his fear had surfaced so quickly and had been so apparent. But it had been the shock of one minute thinking he'd be simply flying over the area, literally high and dry, and the next instant suddenly realizing that he was expected to jump out into the maelstrom above one of the most violent stretches of water on the planet. Inside, the Mike Bremmer of Annapolis was scrambling to regain the dignity so essential to his self-respect, not only as a man but also as a naval officer. If it become known that he'd balked—in front of a civilian, and a brave one at that—his career curve would plummet faster than the *New York* must have. Then the ultimate humiliation came upon him as the sergeant noted through the crackle of the intercom, "Yeah, don't sweat it, Lieutenant. Frank hasn't jumped before, either."

It was now or never for Bremmer's sinking ego. "Hell, then, I'll go first."

"No, listen, Mike," began Hall. "If you really don't want to—"

"Hell!" Bremmer's excited voice was almost a shout. "Hell, *no*. Listen, you guys. Navy's the senior service, right?"

"*Was,*" said the Air Force sergeant jokingly, but Bremmer, still flushed with embarrassment, saw his reply as a possible slight, and it further egged him on.

"*Was*, bullshit. Navy *is* number one. I'll go. The civilian follows *me*. Right, Frank?" He said it with all the brio he could muster.

Hall knew better than to interfere with a man's pride, especially a man he liked. If Bremmer had the guts to face down his fear, he deserved support. "All right," Hall agreed.

Bremmer pressed the Talk button. "Alphabetical order, right, Sergeant?"

"Yes, sir," answered the sergeant, taking his cue from Hall's response. "Okay, Lieutenant. Let's get forward and I'll suit you up first."

Suit me up, thought Bremmer. Hot damn, it makes me sound like an astronaut. He was feeling better now. Besides, it was almost unknown nowadays for a chute not to open. "Lead the way, Chief," said Bremmer. "Lead the way."

As he passed Hall, the oceanographer slapped the lieutenant on the shoulder. Courage, Hall thought, was always more impressive when someone acknowledged his fear but chose to go on. He knew the fear himself. The only difference was that Bremmer had been caught off guard. In reality, Hall was willing to bet, as Tate, the captain of the *Petrel*, would have said, that Bremmer would turn out to have a "ton of guts."

Then came a surprise. The Hercules had climbed to cruising height and speed and had received the meteorological reports telling them that westward, in the area they were heading for, the weather was worsening. Now another report told them that the USS *Boise*, the fast frigate in the search area and the sister to the one just leaving Attu with the submersible, was reporting a definite sonar trace—an elongated bump registering high on the magnetometer. The report also stated that an underwater photo taken by an Edgerton phased-flash unit lowered over the object, situated just over two thousand feet below, showed in one corner of the photo what looked like a protruding metal object. It looked very much like part of a sub's sail.

# 16

GENERAL OF THE United Soviet Socialist Republics, Alexander Androvich Kornon, too excited to sleep on the flight from Vladivostok to Mednyy, the smaller of the two Komandorskys, was now in Mednyy's only VIP room. By Moscow's standards, it was modest accommodation, but it had hot water, and Kornon was enjoying shaving with a new safety razor, his stubble of the past forty-eight hours now a memory and the clean, bright sheen of his face making him look years younger. The tunic of his new tailor-fitted uniform was bedecked with the ribbons of medals won from the dry highland air of Afghanistan to the steaming jungle of Angola to the two short, fierce actions during the Sino-Soviet hostilities along the Amur in the late sixties and the seventies. Even his boots shone brightly, despite the weak beam of overcast light. Outside, a staff car, or rather *his* car, was waiting, freshly painted red stars on the stiff khaki metal flag. All were the sweet accoutrements of reestablishment to the echelons of power.

But Kornon was under no illusion, knowing the privileges would last only if he succeeded; if he didn't—he would be doubly damned—his exile permanent. Nevertheless, he was prepared for the danger of being Moscow's point man. If he miscalculated, whatever actions he would have taken would be self-righteously deplored by Moscow as the "overzealous activity of an unstable Party member" and would be followed by his return to the Siberian wastes.

He took down a bottle of cologne, made in the GDR, and splashed his face liberally with it until the freshly shaved skin tingled with a bracing chill that brought tears to Kornon's eyes, then he started down the stairs to the waiting car.

Though weary from the flight from the mainland, he was keen to start things moving, to explain to everyone his brilliant plan. But silence, he reminded himself, was still his best protection, and so in order not to become expendable he would release the details of his plan piecemeal. And then only to those who needed to know and who, like himself, would fall if his plan became coopted by the director of the Pacific Ocean Department or Admiral Litov. That way he would remain master of the puzzle.

He had chosen Ustenko as his aide. They didn't like each other at all, but each one's professionalism was respected by the other and both had an equal stake in retrieving the Trident's secrets. He had originally estimated he had at least fourteen hours' start on the Americans, fourteen hours in which to effect the arrival of U.S.S.R. surface ships, because the listening post on Komandorsky had obtained a better fix on the sub's approximate position because of the closer proximity of the sub's pop as its nose cone sonar had collapsed, an advantage that the U.S. Navy would seek to close.

Then at 8:10 a.m. unusually heavy radio traffic from the U.S. frigate *Boise* and the fact that she was now circling, strongly suggested that she had found something. Suddenly the four-teen-hour advantage Kornon had assumed was his was cut to nothing. The only edge he had now was that he was already on the Komandorskys—closer to the general search area than the Hercules. But this lead time would soon disappear unless he was airborne immediately, heading for the search site. Before he left his quarters he had ordered the major at Mednyy station to leak the information to ham radio operators immediately. Kornon knew that Hall, his nemesis, the civilian on Attu, was in the air. The course of the Hercules had been plotted from the moment of its takeoff on Attu.

Kornon's staff car took six minutes to drive along the narrow two-lane road from the officers' quarters to the new airport next to the major ship anchorage on the west coast of the narrow, thirty-seven-mile-long island. Without preliminaries he joined the crew of one of the latest MiL-24 helicopters, deliberately not parked in groups on the air base but scattered widely for defense purposes. An AN-12 Cub, with a shape almost identical to the U.S. Hercules, had just arrived, bringing sixty fully kitted special Russian Spets to Komandorsky, bolstering its already strong garrison of two thousand regular troops.

The helicopter Kornon approached was somewhat different from the rest, for while it was an MiL-24, modifications on the fuselage made it look remarkably like its American counterpart. As both he and Ustenko climbed in, Kornon smelled fresh paint. Immediately his sinuses seized up, as if they had been plugged with cotton wool, and he felt a dull ache starting behind his eyes and down through his cheekbones. He'd told the doctors in Moscow about this, but they had found it difficult to believe that just one whiff of paint, thinning lacquer or turpentine, for that matter, could plug him up, and had failed to prescribe a remedy. Roundly cursing the new paint, he buckled up.

"The paint was your idea," Ustenko reminded him, smiling for the first time since he'd been sent to fetch the general from disgrace in Ulan Ude.

"I know it was my idea," Kornon retorted irritably, "but it's still wet."

Ustenko shrugged. "They've been working on it all night."

Kornon was introduced to the helicopter pilot and shook hands, noticing the man looked Oriental—a Soviet from one of the Far Eastern republics. He had been specially chosen and trained for the hazardous job of flying in rough conditions.

"It has to be low," said Kornon. "I want to see them, but I don't want them to see me."

"He's been around quite a bit," Ustenko assured Kornon.

"We'll get our feet wet, General," said the pilot, half jokingly.

"Never mind about that. Just keep low."

"Fifty meters low enough?" asked the pilot. "We won't be able to stop and hover anywhere. The wind shear is too unpredictable in these strong winds. We'd be airborne one minute, six feet under water the next."

Kornon said nothing but glanced around at the electronics warfare officer, cloistered in his cubbyhole jammed with electronic equipment. All Kornon was concerned about was that the helicopter's maximum speed was three hundred and fifty kilometers per hour—making it the fastest chopper in the U.S.S.R.—though in the present weather conditions the ride promised to be an extremely bumpy one.

Ustenko soon felt queasy but said nothing and tried not to look down at the racing blur of angry, flecked sea, at times only a few meters below. Spray spattered the lower windshield and plastic bubble where the observer sat directly below and in front of them, his swivel mounting capable of rotating a high-resolution camera or machine gun through an arc of a hundred and eighty degrees. Only a few minutes out from Mednyy Island, the pilot began chattering away in fluent Japanese, telling his observer/gunner below to be sure to get good zoom shots of any American surface ships.

"Where is he?" asked Kornon impatiently, referring to Hall on the Hercules.

"You mean, do we have a fix on him now?" The EWO answered his own question. "Yes, sir, we do."

Kornon caught a flash of the boiling sea beneath them, then heard the EWO telling him they had the Hercules on a vector of one nine six, heading west-southwest.

"When will we see him?" pressed Kornon.

The EWO punched the two vectors into the computer, first his own helicopter's and then that of the Hercules, which was flying much higher. "Intercept point," he announced, "is . . . twenty-one minutes."

"Double-check it," Kornon instructed. "And no tracer. Understand?"

"No tracer" came the confirmation from the observer/gunner below, the snout of the .50 protruding like the proboscis of some malevolent mosquito skimming the rough sea.

"Good," said Kornon, satisfied that all his detailed instructions were being followed. To his left he caught a glimpse of Ustenko throwing up his breakfast into an air bag, filling the cockpit with an overwhelmingly sour stench. Ustenko crimped the top of the bag, opened the side window a foot or so and threw the bag out quickly. It exploded like a bomb on the tarmac-gray smear only meters below.

"Twenty minutes," announced the pilot of the Hercules.

Mike Bremmer was excited about the USS *Boise*'s report that they had possibly found the sub. Hall, though, was noncommittal, unintentionally dampening Bremmer's enthusiasm. "What's wrong?" pressed the lieutenant. "Don't you believe them?"

"Do you ever watch clouds?" Hall asked him.

"Not particularly." Bremmer shrugged. "Occasionally. Why?"

"Ever see faces, or shapes of things in them?"

"Sometimes. So?"

"They're not really there, are they?" said Hall. "The faces or the shapes of things, I mean. We project our images into them. Like looking for lost coins on a beach—pretty soon anything that shines looks like what you want to find."

"You think the guys on that frigate are daydreaming?"

"Not dreaming. Hoping."

"They want it to be the sub, you mean? But you've forgotten something, Frank. The camera doesn't lie."

Hall unzipped the bright watermelon-pink immersion suit to his waist. The heat inside the Hercules had risen uncomfortably. "The camera's the biggest liar of all," said Hall. "Ask any newspaperman. Still, you could be right, if they've detected metal."

"How about its long shape?"

Hall reached over for the frigate's report. "How long did they say this magnetic anomaly was?"

"At least a hundred feet," answered Bremmer, handing Hall the report.

"Doesn't give the scale they were using, how many feet to the inch. We'd need to see that first."

"Well, I think it's the sub," said Bremmer. "Come on, place your bet."

"No, you're probably right," Hall conceded. "Hope I'm wrong."

Bremmer smiled. He admired Hall. Unlike so many other experts he'd met, Hall didn't let pride blind him to the fact that he could be mistaken. The other thing Bremmer liked about Frank Hall was his caution, balanced by a refusal to be bamboozled or pushed to any decision until he'd seen hard evidence. All the stories Bremmer had heard about the consummate oceanographer seemed to be borne out. He had a cool head, but also a heart. He could have humbled Bremmer or at least laughed at his fear, but instead he had agreed to let Bremmer make the first jump so that the Navy men aboard the on-scene ship, the *Boise*, would know it was one of their own who had volunteered to be the first out into the maelstrom.

Bremmer knew that when he splashed down he'd be the first one to be picked up, for even with the immersion suit that would keep him afloat as well as protect him from hypothermia, there was no protection if you were lost sight of in a curtain of rain or heavy seas. For a moment he felt his heart beating faster. He remembered that off the coast of Maine a Navy flier had actually had his skull split open by the bow of an overeager rescue launch.

# 17

IN THE SUBDUED pinkish glow of a lamp, Lebdev was lying naked between cream-colored silk sheets in his apartment overlooking the Moscow River. He was chewing mints to cover his tobacco breath while waiting for Elga. She'd left the bathroom door slightly ajar, her shadow cast on the bedroom wall. She undressed very slowly, combing her long blond hair and tossing it back. The movement thrust her breasts into high relief so that by the time she emerged, Lebdev was so aroused, tired though he was, that his erection made a tent of the sheet. His arms were extended on either side of him, his hands clutched the down-stuffed pillows, and he groaned in anticipation at the sight of her. Her nipples were the size and color of dark cherries in the rosy light. He grew bigger the longer he gazed at her.

He asked her to tease him further, and obediently she sat on the end of the bed in a coy pretense of innocence. Then she lay voluptuously on her back, her body at right angles to his, stretching her arms and legs like a playful cat, her movements lithe, unhurried and surprisingly supple for a woman of her height. The weight of her body pulled the sheet tighter on him. Her right hand moved slowly across her body toward him.

Lebdev released his grip on the pillows, relaxing as much as he could, waiting for what seemed an eternity for her fingers to touch him and stroke him. She turned her head away toward the door of the apartment, brought her hand back across her body, trailing it over her breasts to the edge of the bed where she let it fall loosely to the carpet. At the same time she arched her back and raised her pubis, gyrating slowly in the soft light and sighing longingly. For a moment she seemed a fleeting, unobtainable promise, and it nearly drove him mad.

"*Nyet,*" he begged her, "no. No, I didn't mean it. Don't tease anymore. Let's do it. Elga, Elga, let's . . ."

Suddenly she rolled back toward him, then on all fours, moved her head rapidly from side to side. Her hair whipped across his heated body. He could stand it no longer. He sat up and lunged at her. She drew away quickly, and he cursed.

"Lie down," she said. "Lie down."

He hesitated, breathing fast, then collapsed on his back, staring at the ceiling, its cheap pyrite glistening in the pink plaster sky.

"Only *one* week?" she said playfully, the forefinger and thumb of her right hand forming a ring that slipped over, down, squeezing, the pulsating silk now a tight sheath over him. She was referring to the promise of a Black Sea vacation.

"Two..." he began, but could barely speak. "Two weeks," he promised weakly. "But you'd better do—" He didn't finish. The next instant her breasts enfolded the silk sheath, her lips closed about it, her tongue darted frantically. He wanted to yell, shout, scream with the sheer pleasure. Then cool air rushed over him as she tore the sheet aside, mounting him, bending low. Her breasts touched his face, their soft, warm fullness burying him.

There was an insistent knocking at the door. She slowed.

"Comrade Lebdev?" inquired a voice.

"Go away, damn you!" he gasped, out of breath.

"Official business, Comrade."

Elga rolled off him. "It's official," she whispered. Before Lebdev could say anything to stop her, she had quickly tiptoed to the bathroom. This time she shut the door.

He'd get rid of them. He'd kill the bastards. "What is it?" he shouted, the violence of his tone enough to terrify any mere official. But the two men outside were unmoved. They *were* on official business—from Tass, which he discovered after grabbing his robe and opening the door just wide enough to see them.

They told him the newspaper's correspondent, whom Lebdev himself had sent to the Komandorsky Islands, had reported that heavy radio traffic among the USS *Boise*, Attu, Fairbanks, Alaska, and Washington suggested that the Americans had found something—most probably the Trident. The ham radio operators, said the reporters, had also picked up the increased traffic, and their speculation that something was amiss in the area had been passed on by several of the operators to the Western media. Finally Washington, under increasing pressure, had been forced to admit that a "naval vessel does, in fact, appear to be missing."

Lebdev, still breathing heavily, still descending from the near peak of ecstasy, found it hard to reply, to think clearly.

"Sorry to disturb you, Comrade, but we thought you should know."

He mumbled his thanks and shut the door. Damn them! he thought. Damn everything!

But they were right. The Politburo would need to know how Tass was going to handle the news that must now break everywhere, especially in the American media. The six-ship contingent dispatched in haste from the Soviet Pacific fleet were still—he turned and glanced at his watch on the side table—at least six hours away from the area. Right now the Politburo would have no choice but to implement the second part of General Kornon's plan, which involved Tass. But the Politburo, inherently secretive, not liking Kornon's revolutionary plan in principle, yet at the same time seeing no alternative, wanted Lebdev to arrange a full-blown press conference. This was something Kornon had insisted upon as being essential to his plan once the story, with the assistance of certain ham radio operators, broke in the world's press. The Politburo were very uncomfortable with press conferences for Western journalists. Nothing like this had happened since Gorbachev had first come to power.

Elga touched his shoulder. "Some other time," she said sweetly, the sharp profile of her white sweater arousing Lebdev all over again.

"Yes," he grumbled as desperately as a disappointed schoolboy. Then his face brightened. "You're a journalist," he said. "By God!" Snatching his briefs, he began to get dressed, turning away from her with a modesty that at once amused and charmed her.

"The German Democratic Republic will need to know about this," he intoned.

"About *us*?" she asked. "I hope not."

Now he turned back to her. "The biggest story you'll ever report, Elga." He paused. "What's your last name?" They both laughed.

"Kirche," she said. It was the German word for *church*.

"Christ." He laughed, then stopping he stared at her. "I can't wait."

"For what?" she asked ingenuously.

"To screw you. I'm going to push it right up to your chin."
He began to button his shirt. "Are you married?"

"No."

"Even better," said Lebdev. "How would you like a *month*
on the Black Sea?"

"It keeps getting better and better, Comrade. What do I have
to do?"

"What you did for me."

"*Did?* I was just getting started."

"Damn," he said, grabbing her violently, pulling her toward him and kissing her passionately. "I want you to tear it
off," he said. "After the press conference." He laughed. "But
first file your copy to Berlin."

She pushed her thigh hard into his groin. "You said a
month?" she reminded him.

"Oh, that's for someone else."

"Who?"

"Not yet," he said. "Come on."

In the limousine he told the chauffeur to take him to the Tass
office on the Garden Ring Road, then he pulled down the
blinds and slid the middle panel closed. He made the two reporters who had come to get him sit in front with the driver so
that he could have his privacy with her, so that she could fon-
dle him. Sitting back, he went to guide her hand, but she already knew what he wanted. He looked at her, drinking her in,
at the same time realizing he'd have to do a security run on her.
She could very easily be a British or American plant. Or West
German, for that matter.

By the time they got through the heavy traffic and arrived at
the office, Lebdev lay back, limp and exhausted, feeling completely drained and calm. "There's not an ounce left in me,"
he murmured sleepily, "not an ounce. I couldn't give you another ounce." He was impressed by her unselfishness, she had
given him everything she could and had taken nothing. Of
course, her reward would be the Black Sea resort—but still . . .
"How about you?" he asked dreamily, his eyes still glassy from
the ecstasy.

"I can wait," she said matter-of-factly. "I have strong willpower." She was making herself presentable, applying lipstick, blotting it.

If she wasn't a plant, he thought, she'd be perfect for it, for the second part of Kornon's plan. He was sure that no man could resist her. He pulled out a Tass card from his wallet. "Give this to the doorman when we arrive. It'll get you a front seat in the conference."

In the wallet she glimpsed a photograph of a woman, probably in her early fifties, and two children in their late teens or early twenties.

"Your wife?" she asked.

"What? Oh, yes. After the conference, wait for me in the foyer."

"I will."

He leaned over and kissed her so hard that he smeared her lipstick. He loved it—it made her look like a slut.


THE MESSAGE FROM the Komandorsky Islands to Moscow was encoded and short. "They can't contact him now," the Politburo's Moscow signal and cipher chief informed Lebdev.

"Why not?" asked Lebdev, cradling the safe line scrambler phone between his right shoulder and cheek as he arranged papers in front of him on his desk to prepare for the press conference. Even while he was talking to the cipher chief, a full colonel, in his mind he was going over and over Elga's body. He imagined she could swallow him whole. Involuntarily he moved forward in his seat as if he was still with her. It had been wonderful in the back of the car—the best in years, totally unexpected in its intensity.

"Because he's on radio silence," said the colonel.

"What?" asked Lebdev distractedly.

"Radio silence. He's on board an MiL-24, approaching the U.S./Soviet line. We can't send or receive without alerting the American ships."

Lebdev didn't know much about military equipment beyond knowing that an MiL-24 was the assault gunship that they'd used most in Afghanistan and that it was renowned as an antitank helicopter as well, with short, sturdy rings supporting antitank rockets in pods. But even if the Americans heard no radio traffic to and from the helicopter, surely they'd pick it up on radar.

"No," the cipher chief explained, exasperated by the civilian's ignorance. He wished that Lebdev would stick to being an editor for Tass, where he knew what he was doing. "The helicopter is skimming just above the waves. Even the best American radar won't pick them up. They'll be below the Americans' radar horizon, especially in the heavy weather conditions out there. Backscatter will just give the Americans fuzz on the screen."

"Well, will the press conference go on without his approval?"

"Comrade Lebdev, General Kornon is still, shall we say, on probation. The Kremlin gives the orders. It approves or disapproves his plan."

"But at the moment you're approving the press conference, as well as his flight?"

"We're approving both, Comrade."

Yes, thought Lebdev, until the poor bastard does something wrong. Then it will be back to Outer Mongolia. And there was no way Lebdev was going to join him if anything got screwed up. "I'll want written approval for the press conference, Colonel."

"I'll send it over by courier immediately. But you may start the conference now if you wish."

"Very well," said Lebdev. Cupping his hand tightly over the mouthpiece, he instructed his subeditor on the intercom to postpone the conference for another half hour. Lebdev hadn't become editor-in-chief by going ahead without written authorizations in hand.

"Comrade Lebdev?" said the cipher chief.

"Yes?"

"One more thing. If you must carry on with German tarts, please be more discreet."

"Why? Is there some doubt about her security clearance, Comrade?" Lebdev asked cheekily. The cipher chief was very powerful, but so was the editor of Red Tass.

"Oh, not at all," said the colonel. "She's one of ours. But she says you're very loud, groaning and thumping things. Quite out of control."

"Really?" The bitch, thought Lebdev. She has it both ways—enjoys and reports. The remarks betrayed obvious jealousy on the cipher chief's part. He was married, too, but afraid to dip his wick out of mortal fear of his wife. He was one of the most powerful men in the Kremlin officer corps, yet his wife, Tina the Terrible they called her, ruled the roost. In the Great Patriotic War she'd killed a German sergeant major, snapping his neck in an arm lock. She had a thing about Germans—East or West, it didn't matter. But if the cipher chief thought he'd enrage Lebdev by revealing Elga's duplicity, causing him to give her up—"one of ours" meant KGB—then the colonel was in for a big surprise. Lebdev knew that almost everyone in an official position had had to "help out" the KGB at some time or other. In fact, the first copies of Red Tass went straight to Dzerzhinsky Square, and when three or more were gathered often someone would ask, "Who's KGB tonight?" and they'd concoct a harmless report for the one to hand in—and then get down to what they really thought. No, Lebdev knew he'd have her again if he could, but he'd have an answer of his own for her blabbing; he didn't like the "You're very loud" bit. He'd talk to Dzerzhinsky Square himself, point out how valuable she could be in the present "acute situation"—meaning the Kremlin's determination to get the secrets out of the American Trident at any cost.

Lebdev smiled to himself as he lit one of his favorite Turkish cigarettes and inhaled deeply. He put his feet up on his desk, relaxing yet thinking. He saw clearly how, as the Americans used to say when he was based in Washington, he could have his cake and eat it, too. For a moment he thought of firing his chauffeur, thinking that he might have reported the back seat escapade and that Elga was just being used to cover the true source. But he decided not to bother—all chauffeurs were conduits to the KGB. *Everyone* was a conduit to the KGB—except the Baptists who were in the camps or the exiles like Kornon. No, he'd keep the same chauffeur and he'd keep Elga. It would be an offense against socialist realism to let Elga's tits go to waste.

## 18

THE MiL-24 PILOT'S FACE was streaming with perspiration, not
so much from fear as from the sheer concentration required to
keep the helicopter as steady as possible in the high winds. The
twin Isotov-117 turboshafts were screaming above him with
their combined thrust of forty-four-hundred horsepower, and
the cabin was too hot because of a faulty thermostat. The
windshields, one in front of him, the other in front of the electronic warfare officer below and forward, were constantly
misting up as the wipers worked overtime. The sea spray
steamed at them in a constant salty rain that splattered against
the bulletproof blister windows and against the short, stubby
wings, which gave the helicopter twenty-five percent of its lift
at cruising speed; the spray also encrusted the weapons pylons
with salt, causing them to grow heavier. The salt buildup, together with occasional icing, added dangerously to the weight
of the hundred and thirty-two 57 mm rockets and conventional and chemical bombs of the kind used in Afghanistan
against the hill tribes.

The pilot switched on the electrothermal de-icing equipment
both for the five-bladed main rotors and for the offset port side
tail rotor as the helicopter, with the help of a tail wind, ex-
ceeded its maximum two-hundred-mile-per-hour cruising speed
to almost two hundred and twenty, flying only yards above the
storm-tossed sea. The hillsmen the pilot had warred against in
Afghanistan were far from his mind, his target now being in
one sense much easier—only one man; but on another level this
was one of his most difficult assignments, for this time he'd
have to continue flying close to the sea below the enemy's radar screens. Visibility was no more than ten yards in the torrential rain and spray, but they couldn't use active radar to warn
them of any especially high seas for fear of the radar's signal
alerting the thicket of American receptors, which as a matter
of routine would be revolving constantly, monitoring the mist-
and rain-shrouded sea. Despite the roaring of the turboshafts
above and the whine of the wind through the various ducts,
deflectors and the tricycle-type landing gear, the pilot could
hear the short, sharp retching of Ustenko, General Kornon's

aide. Soon the suffocating stench of vomit and hot oil fumes filled the craft.

"Open the port window," he called back to the cabin where Kornon was sitting trying not to feel claustrophobic in the gloomy cabin designed for eight men. From where he was sitting Kornon could see only the pilot and the top of the EWO's flying helmet.

The EWO kept his eyes averted from the churning sea racing past just below him and instead concentrated on the metal hinge that allowed his canopy to swing open starboard if they were forced to ditch. He had checked all weapons systems at least three times since they left Cape Yuzhnyy, the southern end of Ostrov Mednyy in the Komandorskys, but now he went over the procedures again—especially defensive measures. No one believed that even American radar was good enough to pick them up when they were flying so low, but the weapons officer had never underestimated American technology, and neither, he reminded the pilot, had the Kremlin; otherwise the four of them, counting Kornon and Colonel Ustenko, wouldn't now be racing just above the waves on a mission to stop the one American most likely to prevent the Soviet capture of the Trident's secrets, which the Kremlin wanted at any cost. The EWO checked the firing procedures again because, like the pilot, he knew they would have time to make only one pass before, their cover blown during the attack, they'd have to turn sharply and head back full tilt to Mednyy Island base, a hundred and thirty-four miles northwest at the limit of their operational-fuel-combat radius.

THE HERCULES BEGAN to hum, its fuselage reverberating with the lowering of its rear ramp door—the drawbridge, as the pilots call it—revealing to Hall and Bremmer an enormous rectangle of thick gray before them, the sea hidden far below by swirling clouds whose currents resembled nothing so much as whirlpools going crazily in every direction. Only after staring downward for five minutes could they detect the occasional wink of a whitecap two thousand feet below before it was swallowed again in the grayness.

"Red light on," said the Hercules pilot.

"Red light on," the copilot confirmed.

The second the sergeant saw the flashing light he tapped Bremmer and then Hall on the back of their vivid Day-Glo immersion suits. "Hook up!" he instructed them. He snapped the two canvas slit-eye clips onto the thin guide wire and moved them up, checking the chute straps for the proper tension as the men approached the huge, gaping opening. The interior of the aircraft seemed so big that Bremmer thought of Jonah inside the whale. He said a prayer for safe deliverance—for both him and Hall. As they moved forward, feeling the temperature drop, their faces suddenly chilled, the sergeant instructed each to press the slide-start switch on the miniature radio transmitters sewn into the immersion suit where a left breast pocket would normally be. The small radios were surprisingly heavy, their nickel-cadmium battery good for giving off a locator signal bleep at one-minute intervals for almost a week.

The Hercules pilot confirmed latitude and longitude with the USS *Boise* and one of two deep-sea trawlers in the area, neither of which was visible but should, if the Hercules's navigation had been correct, be about fifteen miles dead ahead, which at three hundred miles per hour meant three minutes away.

"Drop recognition flares," instructed the pilot. The copilot pressed the button and the first of six flares dropped, the others following at thirty second intervals; five of the flares were vivid red, the last a bright, incandescent green.

"THERE IT IS," said the MiL pilot. "Let's go!"

THE SECOND THE GREEN "drop" light came on in the cavernous interior of the Hercules, the sergeant shouted, "Go!" Hands outstretched like a high-wire walker, Mike Bremmer began the longest walk of his life, off the ramp into the ice-cold world that sucked his body away from the aircraft's slipstream and whisked him into the grayness. Then the chute, a vivid orange, blossomed in the turbulent dark clouds and, remembering what the sergeant had told him, he pulled the right shoulder strap and the identification flare, a vibrant canary-yellow, streamed above him as he descended.

Aboard the Hercules the sergeant unhurriedly began the safety margin count: "One, two, three, four, five—go!" Hall stepped out of the plane.

THE FAST FRIGATE, the USS *Boise,* was steaming with all stops out at flank speed through heavy rain toward the estimated intercept point for picking up the two jumpers. The ship's normal bridge complement of lookouts had been doubled, and most of the off-duty crew lined the rails for the first glimpse of the telltale yellow stream of smoke that should spiral upward from the jumper's shoulder canister.

"Yellow flare!" shouted the starboard lookout. "Five points starboard."

"Steer zero three two," ordered Captain Peters.

"Zero three two," the helmsman confirmed.

"Pickup party to the starboard side," announced the executive officer over the PA. "Pickup party, starboard side." The exec would have liked to launch the frigate's chopper, but hovering in these gusts was inviting tragedy. It was much colder but safer for everyone to pluck the men out of the chop.

Steadying himself against the steering console, Peters brought up his binoculars, focusing on the trail of smoke a mile or so dead ahead. He still couldn't see the parachutist through the rain.

"Sir," came the voice from the CIC—combat information center—seeing an unidentified aircraft appearing on the screen. "Bogey approaching—zero three two."

"Range?" snapped the officer, grasping the roll bar.

"Four miles and closing."

"Are we inside the U.S./Soviet line?"

"Barely!"

The captain pressed "General Quarters", and the klaxon immediately started its strangled cry throughout the ship.

The captain noted the complementary bearing, 212 degrees, the vector on which the unidentified aircraft would be approaching, and switched onto the all-frequency band. "Unknown aircraft. This is a U.S. Navy warship on your 212 four miles. Identify yourself and state your intentions. Over."

There was a crackle of static, as if the bogey was trying to respond but was experiencing technical difficulties. In the dim red light of the combat information center amidships and directly below the bridge, the executive officer ignored the banks of red, green and orange electronic eyes blinking frantically about him, instead fixing his gaze on the blue-green radar screen where the faint blip of the bogey came and went, its luminescence appearing for a second then disappearing for several in the backscatter of the heavy seas.

Once more the warning went out. "Unknown aircraft. This is a U.S. Navy warship on your—"

"He's changed course, sir," interjected the radar operator, one hand adjusting his headset, the other on the static damper control. "He's off the screen."

"What the—"

"On screen again," the operator reported, his tone rising in its urgency. They had been trained for this a thousand times, but now it was real. The blip was pulsating on a heading of 025, approaching the ship on its starboard "blind" side or quarter where the frigate's array of aerials, revolving radar meshes and other defensive paraphernalia blocked the field of fire of the radar-controlled Phalanx Mk-15 Close-in Weapons System.

"Off screen again, sir. He's skimming."

"Magnification? Silhouette identification?" asked the exec.

"Can't be fixed wing unless he's ditching. Possible Cobra. Possible Hind-A."

The Cobra was a U.S. attack gunship, Hind-A, the NATO designation for a Soviet MiL-24. But now there was nothing on the screen but wave scatter bouncing back the frigate's radar, the blue screen covered in a swarm of dancing dots, none of them distinguishable from one another.

"Missile indicators?" snapped the exec.

"Negative."

Nevertheless the exec switched the Phalanx antimissile system from manual to automatic mode, fully activating its search-and-track radar-guided 20 mm Gatling gun. Once the system had a clear sight of the target, it could spray a hail of depleted uranium bullets, any one of which could deflect or destroy an incoming missile.

Then came a crackling voice. "This is a Japanese search helicopter. Experiencing engine trouble...request assistance..."

The executive officer, glancing up at the computerized situation screen, saw three other blips, much larger, three ships just entering the search area. Where had the chopper come from—another search ship? A Japanese mother ship farther away, backscatter drowning the *Boise*'s bounce-back radar? Or had it come from any of a half-dozen islands clustered in the western tip of the Aleutian chain?

On the bridge Captain Peters was swiveling the big infrared binoculars, but all he could see was a white-scratched gray circle, huge waves passing in and out of view like rain-shrouded hills. He ordered the ship ten degrees port, denying the potential attacker the ship's blind quarter, the *Boise* now in condition 5—maximum readiness for defensive measures. The descending flare was less than five hundred feet above the water a half mile ahead, its earlier bright yellow "fizz" now an amorphous, dirty lemon-colored smoke, whisked away by the wind, the parachutist still invisible in the low gray stratus.

"NICE OF THEM," said the MiL-24's electronics warfare officer, looking down from the helicopter's forward blister cockpit, intently watching the pin-sized but brightly pulsating dot on his passive radar receiver while keeping one eye alert to the infrared suppressor indicator.

"What do you mean?" cut in Kornon.

"Your friend is wearing a locator beeper," explained the pilot without taking his eyes off the altimeter and low light level TV gun camera. "We didn't expect that much help."

Kornon began to say something, but the pilot ignored him, asking the EWO for the range.

"Three thousand meters...two five zero zero...two thousand..."

The EWO was now adjusting the cross hairs on the four-inch circular screen until, leaving their phosphorescent ghosts fading off to the screen's perimeter, they neatly intercepted the blip that was the descending parachutist. He was now at three hundred feet. The gun camera whirred.

The pilot put the MiL-24 into a gut-wrenching turn, ordering, "Release chaff!" Kornon felt the helicopter rise, the pilot compensating for the downward push of the forward firing foil canisters as they arced upward ahead of the MiL, exploding, the sound like two short cracks of a whip.

THE EXECUTIVE OFFICER on the *Boise* saw the distinct blip that he knew was the parachutist descending a few degrees off the starboard bow just before the radar screen went crazy with the confetti of interference caused by the rain of millions of tiny pieces of foil. He had two seconds to stop the Phalanx from firing and possibly killing the parachutist along with destroying the bogey. Either that or risk the lives of the *Boise*'s two hundred and twenty men.

"Sir! Bogey has released chaff."

"I know..." The next instant they saw a cluster of four or five especially bright dots flying apart on the screen like an exploding meteor.

"Possible missiles," reported the operator.

The Phalanx was already firing its deadly curtain of uranium bullets even as the executive officer released five of the *Boise*'s Mk-13B heat-seeking antimissile missiles, the ship's SLQ-32 radar warning and electronic countermeasures system quickly interpreting, incorrectly, the five decoy flares fired by the MiL-24 as the exhausts of incoming missiles. He heard one missile, then another detonate, then two more, the fifth either a dud warhead or having missed its target altogether.

"Jesus Christ!" It was the radar operator, looking up at the situation board to his right.

The executive officer saw that he had made an error that might cost him his career; two of the other three ships in the area were in the line of fire, the bogey nowhere in sight in the crazy pattern of the radar screen.

MIKE BREMMER hit the water, the shock of cold snatching his breath away. He submerged, then quickly bobbed to the surface again in the immersion suit, trying to get his breath without taking in more saltwater. Then everything closed in on him, the chute collapsing in a huge, sodden sheet, its stretch-weight threatening to pull him under. He heard four enormous explosions. The scarlet flashes rending the sky were grotesquely visible to him through the heavy transparency of the nylon canopy clinging to his face like thick sandwich wrap; having brought him down safely, it was now threatening to suffocate him. He had the presence of mind to force himself under, diving, kicking hard to counter the natural buoyancy of the immersion suit, attempting to swim beyond the undulating parachute's extent.

Panic began to well up within him, then he suddenly realized he'd forgotten to hit the release buckle. As soon as he did so he felt an enormous weight shifting rapidly away from him. The next moment he saw gray sky and the monstrous driving sea all around him, and he thanked God he had remembered in time. Then, not more than three hundred yards off, he saw deliverance coming toward him—a chopper with the bright red ball on the white background that told him it was Japanese. He would love the Japanese forever after.

THE MIL'S WARFARE OFFICER saw the parachute now, a crinkled orange patch sliding up and down the swells. "There he is," he said, pointing it out to the pilot.

"Yes, I see him. Stand by to release V-7 pods."

"Ready to release," acknowledged the warfare officer.

"We'll be over him in ten seconds. Release on eleven."

"Understood. Will release on eleven."

ALL BREMMER SAW, apart from the flicker of debris still burning after the *Boise*'s missiles had struck the flares and exploded, was the helicopter approaching in a world of gray sky and sea. He turned around, looking for Frank, but all he could see was sea and sky merging into one. His panic was subsiding now and in its place was a rising excitement that he was about to be rescued, for even if the chopper couldn't hover in such weather, it would surely be guiding the Navy ships toward him—which explained to him the explosion of the flares. The ships were no doubt using these as visual indicators, as well as their radar, to pick him up.

The chopper swung away to his left and he saw the pilot wave. The chopper circled him, dropping three or four canisters, each tumbling freely then bursting open on the sea, giving off thick white smoke that rolled across the water like clouds of dry ice vapor, quickly dissipating into the grayness.

He was dead in two minutes. The V-7 nerve gas sent his central nervous system into agonizing spasm, causing him to defecate and vomit blood simultaneously.

THE LAST THING Kornon saw, peering through the rain-streaked port window, was the bright orange immersion suit floating facedown. Then the MiL went into a tight turn, still just a few meters above the waves, racing at maximum speed with a tail wind assist back to Mednyy Island. The beauty of it, Kornon explained to Ustenko, who was so airsick he couldn't have cared less, was that the American would appear to have drowned, lungs full of water, no sign of physical battering.

"What if they do an autopsy?" asked the warfare officer.

Kornon shook his head, smiling knowingly. "I've thought this out to the last detail, Comrades. Oh, there'll be a great row between the U.S. Navy and the Japanese chopper defense force. I'll warrant the *Boise* didn't even see us. And even if they did, what have they got? A Japanese helicopter off course, trying to identify itself with flares."

"But what if they do an autopsy?" pressed the pilot. "They're sure to find him. That damned beeper's still going."

"I tell you it doesn't matter," Kornon explained. "This is V-7. To detect that in the body you'd need the Mayo Clinic and the Moscow Institute combined. And you'd have to do it within twenty-four hours."

"No," continued the general, leaning back against the vibrating fuselage in a mood of deep satisfaction, "no, they'll bury Mr. Hall at sea. A hero's death." He paused, smiling. "America will weep and our flotilla will have reached the search area where they have found the sub. With Hall gone *we* will be the first to the Trident."

"I don't know about a burial," said the warfare officer.

"What do you mean?" Kornon asked, suddenly sitting up and forward in his seat. The warfare officer was jerking his thumb downward toward the sea, but Kornon, situated right behind the pilot, couldn't see straight down.

"It's infested," said the WO.

"What is?" Kornon asked irritably.

"Sharks," said the WO. "They can smell shit a mile off. Your friend Mr. Hall will be dinner."

Kornon sat back again, smiling, closing his eyes contentedly, chuckling. "Even better, eh, Ustenko?"

Ustenko nodded, looking white as a ghost, interested only in getting back to the Komandorsky base. The motion of the helicopter was neither smooth nor steady as he had imagined, but rather it seemed to be skidding and bucking through the air like some crazy Afghan horseman. Trying desperately to regain his sense of equilibrium, he tried the pilot's suggested remedy once more, fixing his eyes on a point as far out to sea as the poor visibility would allow. He glimpsed a spume of mustard-colored smoke, dimly impressed by the fact that the dead man's identification flare must still be bubbling away beneath the sea's surface like a live thing attached to the floating corpse.

Kornon switched on the lip mike, addressing the pilot. "And now, Comrade, radio ahead to Mednyy base. I must be in Moscow and back in twelve hours."

"Don't worry, General. The Tu-22 bomber is supersonic. You'll be there and back before you know it. Mind you, you'll be pretty tired, General."

"Yes," said Kornon. He would be exhausted, most probably, but he would never feel better. It was a long way from Ulan Ude.

# 19

LOOMING OUT of the mist-shrouded area, the *Boise*'s sharp bow came punching rather than slicing through the huge swells. The frigate proceeded slowly, at no more than three knots, the foam sloshing briefly along the warship's port side, the acute angularity of the Jacob's ladder running down to the heaving water line breaking the curve of her flank. Then Hall saw the long bosun's hook coming out at him like a harpoon in slow motion. Taking the yellow canvas harness line dangling from it, he slipped it over his shoulders, raised his right hand for the pickup party to see and in a few seconds felt the steady tug as the bosun's party began hauling him in.

Shivering on the metal serrated platform at the bottom of the ladder, chilled by the wind, he was ready for the usual light-hearted banter of sailors, but instead was surprised by the serious demeanor of the officer of the deck and the rest of the crew who now started making their way up the ladder. Two of them were standing immediately behind Frank, making sure he didn't slip on the sea-slicked metal slats, his balance a little off after having bobbed up and down, waiting for the ship to close in on his signal flare. As he stepped onto the main deck just forward of the bridge and behind the forward Mk-13 missile launcher, he still felt unsteady on his legs, the wallowing roll of the ship more prolonged than the shorter, staccato buffeting experienced aboard the Hercules, requiring different timing, making him feel unusually awkward for the first few minutes aboard.

He also realized the moment he stepped onto the deck that something was seriously wrong, suspecting that his initial skepticism about the ship's having found the sub was justified, after all, and that, not surprisingly, no one wanted to tell him. Yet the sailors' tone, especially that of the officer of the day, was more one of sadness than embarrassment.

"Follow me, sir," said the OOD. "Your quarters are this way." The officer, a lieutenant, led off, stepping over the sill of the starboard hatchway, then turning right up the stairwell toward the captain's sea cabin, situated immediately aft of the wheelhouse.

"Was Lieutenant Bremmer picked up by one of the other ships?" Hall asked as the OOD opened the door to the starboard side cabin, usually the first officer's.

"No, sir."

"So you had to fish out both of us?" asked Hall, heading for the lower bunk, where he began taking off the immersion suit.

"Ah . . . yes, sir." It was in the OOD's hesitation, his eyes looking down for a moment at the hard gray metal decking instead of straight at Hall. "Captain Peters has requested you see him as soon as you're dried out, sir."

Hall didn't have to be told. He felt it, a chill passing through him as frigid as the Bering Sea itself. "He's dead?" he said softly.

"Yes, sir, afraid so."

"What happened?"

"You'll have to talk to Captain Peters about that, sir." With that the OOD opened the metal closet to reveal two sets of blue denim work clothes, heavy-weather gear on wire hangers, swaying silently back and forth, like ethereal bodies, with each rise and fall of the ship. "Toothpaste and shaving gear in here, sir." The OOD nodded toward the phone on the bulkhead cradle. "You need anything else you punch 011 for the duty officer. He'll get you what you need."

Hall heard him as one would a public announcement at an airport, lost in the shock of Bremmer being dead, and in speculation about what could have gone wrong. "Was it a Roman candle?" he asked the OOD. "Didn't the chute open?"

"You'll have to speak to the captain, sir."

More and more it sounded like a Navy screwup. Why the hell couldn't the OOD give it to him straight out?

"Sorry, sir. Chain of command," continued the OOD.

"All right," said Hall. He understood—bureaucratic bullshit was the same the world over, only this time dressed up in Navy uniform. That was what it was—everybody already protecting their ass. "Son of a bitch! You didn't fire at the Hercules, did you?"

"No, sir."

"At Bremmer then . . . ? All right, all right," Hall snapped irritably. "I'll see the captain. Peters?"

"Yes, sir. Commander J. R. Peters, Jr., sir."

Why was it, thought Hall, that it always had to be "junior"? Right now he needed a senior. Steadying himself against the rolling of the ship, he finished unzipping the immersion suit, wincing as the zipper caught in his chest hair. He tossed the suit aside and stepped into the cell-like shower cubicle, wanting a hot shower before the frigate picked up speed and changed course again, when it would roll and pitch heavily with him trying to do a Houdini while washing the salt out of his hair.

The lieutenant moved toward the cabin door, about to excuse himself, when Frank called from the shower, "The sub? Have you located it or not?"

"Believe so, sir," said the OOD, his eyes brightening, relieved the question wasn't about Bremmer. "CIC—Combat Information Center—made the fix, and radar has a printout."

"How far are we from it?"

"Not far, sir. Ten to fifteen miles."

"Well, can you find it again?" Hall couldn't remember the number of times—especially if no one aboard was trained in oceanographic research—that a ship had reported finding a wreck or whatever and had given its "exact latitude and longitude," only to have to spend days trying to relocate a magnetic anomaly; despite the loran and satellite navigation systems, a search at sea was still an imprecise art. This was especially true in the far north, where the magnetics were notoriously changeable, often playing havoc with instruments, and where a small miscalibration, a millimeter here or there on a chart, could result, when extrapolated in the vast areas of the ocean, in a massive error of hundreds of square miles.

"I think we've pretty well got it nailed, sir," said the OOD confidently.

"I hope so," said Hall. "I'd like to see the coordinates after I talk to the old man."

"Very good, sir. I'll arrange to have you brought down to the CIC. We should be over the sub site—" he glanced at his watch "—in about an hour. Around 1000 hours. Unfortunately your submersible won't reach us for some hours yet, sir. It should be here well before dark, but if the frigate from Attu is held up for some reason, we've got deck lights positioned for night work."

"Great," said Hall, turning on the shower. "Why didn't you just send them all engraved invitations?"

"Beg pardon, sir?"

"The Russians," said Hall, reaching for the soap. He ripped off its wrapper, scrunched the paper into a tight little ball and threw it across the cabin at the wastepaper basket. He missed.

"We might need lights, sir—unless we're only going to try the rescue during daylight hours."

"No, we can't afford a delay," said Hall. "There's over a hundred and fifty men somewhere down there, beyond crush depth if our bottom charts are anything to go by—and they aren't much to go by, because some of those hydrographic maps of this area are more guesswork than anything else. Haven't been plumbed since Job was a boy.''

The OOD looked perplexed. He knew about the famous *Challenger* expedition with Darwin aboard, and Cook had also made many of the charts, but Job he couldn't place.

"They could be in the trench, for all we know,'' Hall continued. "No, we're not putting off anything. We start working as soon as we get to the site—if it is the site.''

The OOD had to be polite, but he wasn't going to let the oceanographer have it all his own way. "If it's dark by then, we'll need to see what we're doing, won't we, sir? We'll need the lights.''

"If it is the site," said Hall, pressing the point unnecessarily, but he was tired, and the OOD's obvious lack of experience irritated him.

"Yes," said the OOD, "but if you're going down in the submersible during darkness, you'll need to see everything on deck before we start winching—''

"I know that, Lieutenant," Hall cut in. "The point is, I don't want this ship lit up like a Hollywood pool party at any time—at least not all by itself. Let's get whatever on-scene ships we have into the act as well, and three or four whaleboats launched for good measure, all spread out at least ten to fifteen miles apart. Confuse the hell out of the Russians. They can't cover all of us at the same time.''

The OOD was impressed with Hall's foresight; the oceanographer was already measuring up to his reputation. But he told Hall he'd have to clear this idea.

Hall agreed. At least there weren't any Russians on the scene. "Well," he said to the OOD, "maybe they don't know about it yet.''

"No, sir.''

The OOD was trying to be civil, and Hall called out to him as he stepped over the doorsill.

"Yes, sir?''

"Sorry for sounding off. It's been a long day. For you, too, I imagine.''

"I understand, sir.''

"Thanks," said Hall. But he knew the lieutenant didn't understand at all. There was no way, he thought, for the Russians not to know about the sub going down. The real worry was what they were going to do about it. The last thing he needed was a lot of damn Russians trying to run interference.

And there was another thing the OOD didn't understand—that it was he, Frank Hall, who had let young Mike Bremmer jump first. And so he bore at least part of the responsibility for whatever had happened to Bremmer—Roman candle, strangled in the chute, pulled under, the buckle not releasing. Or maybe, Hall thought, the Navy chopper he'd heard somewhere overhead had botched the haul-up and dropped him—that had been known to happen. Or while being winched up, maybe he had been hit by a gust and, swinging like a pendulum, had smashed into the side of the ship. If so, the *Boise*'s Captain Peters didn't know what the hell he was doing, putting out a chopper to hover in such dangerously gusty weather. And if that was the level of competence on the bridge of the USS *Boise*, it didn't augur well for any rescue—even with *Serena I*'s formidable depth capabilities, known only to Hall and his mechanic, Bill Reid, in Astoria.

On the port wing of the *Boise*'s bridge, ten minutes later, the wind was howling about the flap of Hall's wet gear collar, the rolling sea now brooding, heaving all about him in the sullen overcast. While dressing after his shower, he had remembered that Mike Bremmer had two young children, a boy and a girl. Bremmer had shown him snapshots of them as he and Hall had sat chatting inside the belly of the roaring Hercules, as Mike Bremmer, unknown to any of them, was flying to his death. The oceanographer recalled another man, a young seaman on one of Hall's trips aboard the *Petrel* who had died his first time out, and for a moment it struck him that he, Frank Hall, might be a jinx. He rejected the thought immediately as idle superstition. Worse than that, it seemed a kind of creeping, residual self-pity that he found contemptible in himself—a kind of self-indulgence that would do no good whatsoever for the men trapped in the sub beneath the vast weight of the Pacific.

A gust hit him full on, stinging his ears as he swore, not at the elements raging about him but at himself. There was a job to be done, and to do it, he had to be positive, like it or not. He didn't like it. Tough. It had to be done, anyway. He couldn't eliminate Mike Bremmer from his thoughts, but he could compartmentalize his mind, deal with first things first. If the sub had been found, he would bring it up.

Well, he then confessed to himself as he heaved open the port side bridge door, it wouldn't be quite as simple as that, but with a little initiative here and there they could bring the sub up, if it wasn't already lost in the trench, within three days at the most. By then the *Petrel* should be there to assist should *Serena I* need any super-high-resolution radar readouts.

The frigate was rolling heavily and had begun to toss and pitch with jarring regularity. Entering the warm, almost cozy bridge, he heard the weather advisory predicting decreasing winds. It made him feel more optimistic, against his better judgment. But then he had no way of knowing what was going to happen in the next two days, especially in those hours before the dawn that sailors from time immemorial have called the dog watch, those predawn hours when the ability to see, or, more accurately, to distinguish one object from another at a distance or even up close, is at its worst; the time when apprehension turns innocent shapes into ominous forms and harmless-looking objects into ominous portents; the time when men were most certain they would sail to the edge of the world and fall off.

# 20

WITHOUT HER ACTIVE sonar the *New York* was like a once able blind man deprived of his cane. Still, as often happens with the blind, her other senses became more finely honed—her heat and current sensors and the like. If the sub could no longer propagate active radar signals that could then be bounced back from any other object in the sea, she could at least receive, through her passive receptors in the long array of hydrophones that trailed several hundred yards aft like a long, thin tail, the sounds of other ships—if any were coming her way. There was already a lot of incoming noise, for as the sonar operator knew and as Dyer was discovering, the sea wasn't, as popularly believed, a silent place. It was one of the noisiest places on earth.

On the oscilloscope dancing patterns told of massive schools of fish constantly moving and changing direction so swiftly and at such acute angles—one hundred and eighty degrees in a split second—that they could be nothing man-made. Even the HUKs—hunter/killer submarines—couldn't move with such grace. Adding to the cacophony was the distant, and at times almost constant, rumble of volcanic activity throughout the long arc of islands. At times Dyer could hear the roar of an avalanche begun by what he could only guess were localized turbidity currents, and through it could be heard the squeaks, clicks and yawning sounds of whales, twenty to forty miles off but still audible because sound traveled so much more quickly in water than in air and in salt water than in fresh water, sound waves being transmitted faster from salt particle to salt particle than through the less dense particles of air.

"Where the hell are our guys?" complained Marty Knead for the umpteenth time.

For Chief Ryman, Knead was becoming a first-class pain in the butt—always whining and second-guessing every command. To get him out of the way, the chief had assigned Knead to cleanup duty in Sherwood Forest. It wasn't normally one of Knead's jobs, but it was one where the chief figured he could avoid arguing with the rest of the crew—except for the occasional passerby on shift change when some of those on duty in the auxiliary turbine room and engine rooms aft would have to negotiate the narrow, raised walkway through the thicket of missiles. Ironically, around the missiles, so deadly in themselves, Knead could do the least harm; the hydrogen bombs atop each were encased in the steel tubes towering four stories above him. But the chief knew that even so, he would have to keep a close watch on Knead, who was plainly having problems that he either couldn't or wouldn't talk about.

The chief had requested that the *New York*'s medical officer have a chat with Knead, but under the MO's gentle probing, Knead denied there was anything bothering him. "I'm just pissed off," he had said, "that Captain Wain is just sitting on his ass waiting. Waiting for what? How the hell can they find us if we don't help them, by firing up a flare or sending up the haul line attached to the messenger-buoy? That's what the frigging thing's there for!''

When the doctor offered him a cigarette, Knead said, "You're trying to stop cancer, and what do you do? You feed us weed! Jesus!'' Then suddenly Knead's face changed. It had occurred to him that the doc wasn't trying to comfort him, but to make him feel at ease so he'd spill his guts. Maybe they'd even put something in the cigarettes to zonk him out.

"I don't have to talk to you," Knead told him, and he got up and walked away.

His response alarmed the doctor more than the obvious fact that Knead was disturbed, under some abnormal psychic strain. Here was a sailor selected and trained by the Navy, where hierarchy and chain of command were more strictly observed than in any other service, than anywhere else in the world, and yet Knead was being as disrespectful as any teenage delinquent.

It was this crack in the man's discipline alone, in his otherwise exemplary record, that moved the doctor to talk the matter over with the captain, something he wouldn't normally have done, especially given the strain that Wain himself was under. But the doctor's wider concern was that there were younger men who looked up to Knead with all his experience on the pig boats; for them to see a veteran buckling under the strain would be a threat to discipline and morale throughout the whole boat.

"We may see others start to crack," warned the MO.

What bothered the MO even more, something he didn't tell Captain Wain, the executive officer, Sloane or the chief was that Knead—stressed out and wild-eyed as he was, whether from something that had happened on the boat or from some domestic crisis he wouldn't admit—did have a point. If the captain would only send up flares or a sonobuoy, there was a good chance that someone sooner or later would get to them.

On the other hand, the MO knew that the captain's reasoning was sound enough in itself. They were much closer to Soviet territory than to American, and the risk of alerting the Russians first was too high, at least until the *New York* had given their own Navy more time to find her. Against this, however, there was the radiation leak that had forced them to close down the generating capacity of the sub—if the leak, or the level of radiation, increased to unacceptable levels, they'd all die, anyway. The problem there—and in this the MO realized the captain was Navy through and through—was that if it meant sacrificing the sub's crew rather than giving the Russians first crack at the Trident's secrets, or of sacrificing the sub's crew rather than polluting the food chain as a result of a bigger crack in the reactor wall during a dicey haul-up and possible drop, then Wain would let the deep claim the *New York* and all aboard her.

The MO was Navy, too, but he wasn't *that* Navy. Knead was a little crazy, but he had a point. Why weren't *they*, by which he meant the captain, doing something?

Then something struck the MO with the force of a blow, and he slumped down in his chair. Maybe Wain had already decided it was no use releasing a flare or sonobuoy with haul cable attached? Maybe the radiation leak was already too high. And where *was* the rest of the U.S. Navy, anyhow? Sunning themselves in Oahu? Surely to God they should be showing up on the passive sonar by now?

Walking forward, his body inclined like that of a cross-country skier leaning into a gentle hill, the MO decided to put the question directly to the captain. Not man-to-man—he wasn't that stupid or careless about his career—but in his official capacity as ship's medical officer, responsible for the men's well-being. That way his suspicion would remain under the protection of Navy rules and regulations. It also bothered him that the question wouldn't have been necessary at all had all the men worn dosimeters; instead there had been a switch over to the automatic radiation sensors located throughout the sub.

The doctor paused on the gangway going through Sherwood Forest, feeling slightly out of breath. He knew he was in better shape than that. The shortness of breath told him there was a further falling off in air quality.

Knead was nowhere to be seen. As the MO passed the missile containers, the twenty-four steel tree trunks of Sherwood Forest, he noticed they were beaded here and there with condensation. The temperature was still rising.

A minute later he entered the cherry-red glow of the command and control center below the boat's sail. The red light, he knew, only protected one's sight should a sub have to suddenly surface, particularly during nighttime patrol, but it also had the additional and unintended effect of causing voices to be more subdued. Even so it was abnormally silent in the CCC as he entered. He felt a tenseness among the men, a waiting for something to happen, the possibility of slow death heavy on them. The light whir of the automatic controls powered by the battery reserve had the eerie effect of reminding him that many of the controls would keep working for days, even months perhaps, after everyone on board was dead.

He glanced at the clock set into the sonar on the forward port side of the control room. It was almost 1000 hours, halfway through another watch, but already the men looked tired, shuffling in their soft-soled slippers rather than walking. It wasn't simply the reduced oxygen due to the damaged carbon dioxide scrubbers and the shutdown of power that kept the oxygen generator going; it was the heat, too. The temperature had now reached eighty-five degrees Fahrenheit and was still climbing.

The temperature rise didn't make sense, not with the reactor shut down. Admittedly heat was still being emitted from the electrically run machinery in the control room, and there would be some residual heat from the reactor as it cooled. Even so, at such a depth, the sub's temperature should have been dropping.

The captain was moving around the control room from one position to another like an expectant father. The bow planesman was mopping his forehead, sweat pouring from him despite the fact that most of his watch was spent sitting.

Seeing the MO enter, Wain nodded. "Problems, Doc?"

"I was wondering what the radiation level is?"

"In the reactor room?"

"Throughout the sub."

"Can't tell you on either count."

"How's that?"

"Automatic dosimeters are on the blink. The humidity, I guess. We're working on it. How's young Knead?"

"I talked to him, but..."

Wain nodded. "Good. Good."

"Can the radiation leak be found, Captain?"

"Negative. The electronic leak scanner seems shot to hell. One thing I'll say about the old diesels, Doc. A hell of a lot less could go wrong with 'em. At least electronically."

"I guess," replied the MO. "Why is it so damn hot in here?"

"Air conditioner's run off reactor power. We had to shut her down."

"But it shouldn't be as high as this, should it?"

"We're on auxiliary power, Doc. Batteries. We can only use 'em for absolute essentials. Without enough ventilation, no breeze. Ever been in Hawaii when the trade wind falls off?"

"Was there once," replied the MO, reaching around uncomfortably to peel his sodden khaki shirt from his back. "Can we get some fans going?"

"Sorry, Doc. We need all the power we have left for this stuff," said Wain, indicating the banks of electronics.

"Well, I'd feel a lot better if we knew what the level of radiation was in here."

"If it's high, it's high, Doc. If it's low, it's low. We can't do anything about that. Dials won't correct it."

Wain had a point, thought the doctor, who had been working up to asking Wain about their not having fired the buoy or the flares. Wain hadn't denied that the radiation level might be high, might be too high. He was so straightforward in his answers to the MO, or so it seemed, that the doctor felt a twinge of guilt, as if he had been acting as paranoid as Knead.

Suddenly the sonar operator clasped the earphones of his headset, pressing them in hard to shut out the MO's conversation with Wain. Then they saw a slight but definite green hiccup on the oscilloscope.

"Sonar contact! Bearing one niner two." Someone cheered, but it was a hushed, strained cheer. The shuffle of slippers crowding around the sonar set reminded the MO uncomfortably of a covey of psychiatric patients gathering about a nurse's station for drugs—for any kind of hope to sustain them. The question was, however, whether the hiccup made by the luminescent sine wave was friend or foe.

"Can't identify, sir," announced the sonar operator. "Not until the signal gets stronger."

"*If* it does," said the doctor.

"Distance?" asked Wain.

"Sixty, possibly seventy miles."

Wain looked again at the bearing, now appearing automatically as a vector on the screen. Almost south-southwest. "Size?" he asked.

"Signal's not sharp enough, sir. I'd only be guessing right now."

"Then guess."

"I'd say...about three to five thousand tons."

"A frigate?" suggested the executive officer.

"Or a trawler?" added Wain.

"It's alone," said the sonar operator. "Almost due south now, sir."

Wain was biting his lip. "Alone? Then it could be a trawler?"

"Sir..."

"What is it?"

"Another contact."

"Same area?"

"Affirmative."

"A trawler fleet," put in the executive officer. "Or rescue ships."

"Second contact's bigger, sir. I'd say around ten thousand tons. Twice as big."

"Factory ship," added the executive, quickly retracting the sudden mood of optimism his suggestion of rescue ships had raised. "A mother ship to the trawlers?"

"Possibly," said Wain. "Or...maybe you're right. A cruiser maybe."

"Run the signatures," ordered Wain, even though he knew that at sixty to seventy miles the signatures would probably be too faint to identify the actual vessel. The signatures, or engine patterns, sped down the computer screen adjacent to the sonar like a speeded-up menu, searching for a matchup with the two signatures of the incoming signals, using all the known signatures stored on the disk.

"Doubt if we'll get a matchup for the second blip, sir. Too faint. We might get lucky with the—" But the signatures had all run through. "No matchups, sir."

The message on the computer screen was flashing, "Incoming Sig Too Weak."

"How long do you figure till we get a strong enough incoming?" asked Wain.

"Speed seems to be around thirteen knots. Should have a matchup—" he glanced up at the clock, which said it was 15:31. "I'd say about 1700 hours, sir—possibly earlier, 1630."

"Very well," said Wain. "I'll be in my cabin. Call me when you have anything."

"What if it fades off, sir?"

"Then don't wake me," said Wain simply, taking off his goggles, and he left the redded-out command and control center.

One of the seamen on the port side monitors, without taking his eyes off the dials for a second, mumbled to the man next to him, "Son of a bitch's gonna take a nap. Isn't that fucking dandy? Why doesn't he fire a goddamn flare? Who gives a shit if the Russkies see it first?"

"He does," replied the other sailor, an electronics technician, third class.

"And," the MO butted in, overhearing, "so does everyone else on the Tridents. The Russians get a good look at all this wizardry—" he gestured at the banks of winking green and red monitors "—no Trident will be safe."

"Yes, sir," said the sailor, looking straight ahead at the air pressure gauges. There was a very slow leak in one of the forward starboard tanks—or was it the pipe leading to it? Sometimes it was hard to tell just what was going on.

The doctor patted the sailor on the back. "Don't worry, son. We're still kicking and bitching. That's a good sign."

"Yes, sir."

As the MO left the control room, the sailor was still monitoring the air leak, his voice more subdued but just as tart. "'Don't worry, son,'" he echoed the doctor. "'We're still kicking and bitching.' Well, we've still got a fucking radiation leak and the fucking carbon dioxide scrubbers are all fucked up. We won't be kicking for long."

"Don't panic, Popcorn," countered his shipmate. "I heard the old man's going to start bleeding the spare oxygen cylinders from the torpedo room and the sick bay if necessary."

"It'll be fucking all right."

"Ah, c'mon. If we don't move around too much—save our energy—we'll be all right."

"Save our energy? You mean like take a fucking nap, like the old man?"

"Captain's got to keep fresh. He's got to think."

"Yeah, well, he'd better start thinking about firing a fucking flare or two or that sonobuoy, or by the time he gets around to it, it might be too fucking late. If any fucker does see it—" He nodded over toward the sonar. "Even those guys sixty or seventy miles away. By the time they get here we could have snuffed it."

"Then why fire a flare?" cut in the other crewman. "If no one's around to spot it?"

"Aircraft'll be around. They'll have sent out AWACS, won't they? Even the Navy's not that fucking stupid. AWACS sure as shit'll pick up a sonobuoy bleeping away."

"Johnston!" It was the executive officer. Letting them blow off a little steam was all right, probably beneficial, but too much would only start stirring everyone up. "Keep quiet and do your job, sailor!"

"Yes, *sir*!"

"And keep that tone civil, sonny, or you'll be on report."

"Yes, sir. Ah, sir?"

"What?"

"Request relief, sir. Have to go to the head."

The executive officer gave his okay, motioning one of the standby crew forward from the periscope island. "Very well—five minutes."

Johnston got up quickly from the perspiration-soaked seat, too quickly, for he felt light-headed and, stumbling forward a few paces, had to steady himself on the roll bar girding the attack center.

In the toilet Johnston splashed his face and neck, trying to get some relief from the heat. He expected bracing cold water, but instead the tap ran lukewarm. He let it run for a while, but the water only became hotter.

Swearing and making his way back along the corridor, he heard a sound like a shower being turned full on, then a babble of voices and a soft rush of slippered feet. A tiny pipe running through the pressure hull had finally given way to the enormous pressure above, creating a spray of water jets that were blinding the men in the data processing room. Crewmen there were tightening the valve and setting emergency clamps by feel, and soon the rush of water ceased.

Another ten seconds, and a major rupture in the valve would have made it necessary to shut off the room from the rest of the sub. They hadn't been able to close off the leak completely, and it kept dripping like a bathroom tap, the sound audible in the control room, like the clock of a time bomb ticking away. For a moment Johnston thought of the millions of tons of water pressing in on them, how the leak signified the flexing and stretching of the sub's hull caused by such enormous pressures on the thin metal skin separating him and his shipmates from instant death.

By the time he reentered the CCC the temperature in the sub had mysteriously risen another degree.

"Signature match!" It was the sonar operator. The executive officer and everyone else glanced toward the sonar. With a quiet ratchet sound the computer's printer disgorged the size, type and—if they were lucky, thought Johnston—the actual names of the two ships whose signals were now strong enough to have triggered the computer's automatic matchup mode. They were still coming from the south, heading more or less due north—fifty-four miles away.

The printout read: "Alfa—SSN—Disp: 3500 Sur 4200 Div—Max D 3000—TT 21in—WG. Prop 1 NR SP—42 Div. Cr 60. SON LF."

Dyer, the civilian sonar expert who had been quietly and unobtrusively sitting nearby on the orders of Wain, more or less sitting in as instant mechanic or "nurse," as the crew called him, to the passive sonar—now the sub's major sensor—didn't understand any of the printout, only how the computer and sonar worked. He asked the sonar operator for a translation but the latter, telling him to hold on, punched the bar for the captain's cabin.

"Yes, what is it?" asked Wain, his voice coming over the intercom not sleepily as the operator had expected but as if he hadn't been resting at all.

"Signature matchup, sir. I haven't got the ship's name yet, but—"

"All right, what have we got?"

"HUK. Alfa nuclear attack sub. Displacement, thirty-five hundred tons surfaced, forty-two hundred tons dived. Maximum depth three thousand feet. Torpedo tubes twenty-one inch—wire-guided. Propulsion—one nuclear reactor. Speed forty-two knots submerged." Someone whistled. "Crew sixty. Sonar low frequency."

"Second signal?" asked Wain.

"Negative, sir. Only have a printout on this one."

"They picking us up yet?"

"Don't think so, sir."

"Damn!" said Dyer in an uncharacteristic outburst.

The sonar operator looked up at him puzzled.

"Well," explained Dyer, seeing the executive officer, too, looking at him strangely, "I mean, if he can't hear us he can't help us, can he?"

"I don't think you understand, Doctor," said the executive officer, tearing off the printout. "Alfa class is a *Russian* attack submarine. Fastest they have."

"Damn!" said Dyer.

# 21

THE FRIGATE USS *Boise* was slicing her way through the heavy seas, getting closer and closer to the magnetic anomaly and sonar bump found earlier and marked on the chart. Aboard the frigate, Frank Hall listened closely as Captain Peters, a fifty-two-year-old veteran of "peacekeeping" duties in the Persian Gulf, explained as clearly as he could the confusion during the time the frigate was to pick up Bremmer: the approach of an unidentified aircraft later reporting itself as a Japanese helicopter in trouble, its firing of what seemed to be missiles, then its sudden withdrawal, and the near miss in almost hitting one of the other two surface vessels when the *Boise* had fired on the chopper.

"So it was the chopper that killed Bremmer?" asked Hall.

"I'll bet my pension on it," said Peters, who was turning out to be far more friendly than the OOD's tone had led Hall to expect. "But there's not a mark on him. Maybe I'm wrong, and maybe it was just coincidence—a chopper in trouble turning up like that at the same time. But I doubt it. Anyway, what the hell were all those flares from the chopper for? And the foil? Unless it was a diversion for something else."

"What else?" asked Hall.

"I don't know. I've got no ideas on that one."

Neither had Hall as he steadied himself against a heavy roll. The clouds had started to lift but the wind was as strong as ever, whipping the sea into a vast grayness streaked here and there with a metallic sheen from sunlight that was piercing the stratus. "Where is he?" asked Hall quietly.

"Sick bay. You want to see him?"

"I should."

"All right, I'll have the sick bay petty officer come up and take you down. There is one thing, Mr. Hall—"

"Frank."

"All right, Frank. I do have a problem here. If we can't clearly ascertain cause of death from injury, external marks, whatever—I'm authorized to dispose of the body as soon as I deem it prudent. We have a chief petty officer as medic, but no ship's doctor. So it's up to me." What he was trying to say, as delicately as possible, was that he couldn't afford to keep a corpse that might be harboring some kind of communicable disease.

"A sea burial?" asked Hall.

"Correct. Don't know how long we'll be out here, anyway. It's the best solution really. Also, he is—was—a Navy man."

"Yes," agreed Hall. "I think Mike would have..." What Mike Bremmer would have preferred, Hall knew, was not to have jumped. And who had told him that he had to?

"Hard on his wife," Peters was saying.

"Yes."

"He have any children, do you know?" asked Peters.

"Two," replied Hall.

"You knew him well?"

"No." It was a conventional response. Hall could hardly say he'd known Bremmer well. All of two days, but sometimes under unusual pressure and danger in a high-tension situation, like the one facing Bremmer before he jumped from the Hercules, you got to know a man better in twenty-four hours than others you had known for years. Bremmer had been willing to help, fearful yet in the end courageous, trying to do his part to help find and rescue a hundred and fifty men trapped somewhere in the primeval darkness of ancient seas. And now all he would be to his two small children was a memory, a smile here, a hug there, a photograph in fading color of a father who had one day gone far from home and never come back. And Hall knew that Bremmer's wife wouldn't blame him. Like Navy wives all over, she would understand only too well, and suffer, which made Hall feel angrier than he had in a long time.

When Hall arrived at the sick bay, the chief petty officer told him it had been unusually busy, several men complaining of chest pains and nausea.

"Not unusual after combat," said the medic, his twenty years' experience evident from the four "hash marks," black cotton slashes angled in parallel, on his left sleeve. "It often happens after an engagement. In the middle of it they're so busy doing their job they don't notice anything else, then a few hours after, it starts. The building tension hits 'em—headaches, gut aches, sinus, throwing up. The whole fucking lot. Most of the chest pains are stomach acid. They bend down, think they're going to upchuck and have pain all over. Think they're having the big one."

"Where's Lieutenant Bremmer's body?" asked Hall.

The CPO pulled back a curtain enclosing the starboard corner of the sick bay. Hall felt his gut tightening, though he'd seen death at sea often enough before—accidents aboard ships, sometimes to men who were drunk, some simply dropped dead of strokes or heart attacks. Maybe Mike Bremmer had had a stroke or heart attack—but he was too young for that.

He pulled back the sheet. It was horrible. The face he saw was distorted, as if one side had been pushed up like putty into the other. They'd taped the eyes shut but it didn't help.

The petty officer pulled the sheet right off. "Not a mark on him."

The orange immersion suit was hanging nearby on a bulkhead hook, swinging back and forth with the motion of the ship, its soft neoprene not making a sound. He went over to look at it, turning it around, looking for what the petty officer had called any sign of "external trauma." What Hall was looking for was any sign of blood, or a tear in the fabric. Suddenly his head shot back from the suit, and he turned away from it, his hip hitting the end of the bed, knocking a curved surgical needle and the tray it was in clean off the bed to crash on the hard metal floor. "Son of a—" His expression was one of disgust.

"Yes, I know," said the CPO, with what Hall thought was a strangely perverse matter-of-fact tone. "We got the shit out of the suit, but vomit—I tell you, you have to soak that stuff for hours. You can wash out blood, shit—anything you like—but on that material . . ."

"Neoprene," said Hall, moving still farther back.

"Yeah, neo—well, whatever. Vomit goes into it like ink into blotting paper. It still stinks after the goddamn thing's hosed. A goddamn fire hose, at that."

Most of the time Hall paid no attention to the constant obscenity and vulgarity aboard ships, but the petty officer was rubbing him the wrong way. It was a kind of toughness, a hardness that Hall didn't admire. Or maybe it was simply that he was feeling guilty about Bremmer.

"Is that common?" asked Hall, needing to know but wanting to get away from the CPO and his macabre, offhand vocabulary as soon as possible.

"What?" asked the CPO. "Throwing up like that? Oh, yeah, in drowning victims especially."

"You think that's what it was?"

"Sure. Maybe he blacked out coming down, I don't know. Water probably brought him around but, whatever, he upchucked, and when you're not fully conscious... Lots of drunks buy it that way. Automatic reaction. Of course, he mightn't have blacked out, could have been wide-awake all the way, know what I mean? Just panicked. Under the chute maybe, gobfuls of water. Ever swallowed saltwater?"

"What . . . pardon?"

"Ever swallowed saltwater? Makes you barf right away."

Hall nodded solemnly. "Thanks," he told the CPO. Parting the curtains, he stepped through, then stopped, turned around and looked through the curtains again, wanting to assure himself that Bremmer's locator beeper had been working. He froze. "What the hell—"

The petty officer was pushing the big curved sewing needle through the lower part of Bremmer's nose where it joined the lip, and pulling it out the other side.

"What?" asked the petty officer. "Oh, this," he went on nonchalantly. "It's a Navy tradition when there's no doctor aboard. You don't have to do it, but I figure I might as well."

"Might as well what?"

"Well, see, I mean, some guys in the water a long time go into hypothermia, right? Everybody thinks they're dead, but they're not really. We don't want to slip somebody overboard when they're just in a heavy coma." He tugged on the needle as if testing the stitch. "One of the most sensitive parts of the body, this. No reaction to this, then you're dead, buddy. D-E-A-D. We stitch you to the canvas bag."

"Christ!" Hall walked out, feeling sick.

It took him a while to get the experience in sick bay out of his mind long enough to try to figure out what had happened to Mike Bremmer. No one could be sure of exactly how the Navy lieutenant had died, not here anyway, and he didn't have the luxury of time to worry about one man, not when there were more than a hundred others depending on them, depending on *him*. But when he looked at the charts and saw that the nearest landing area for a chopper, which couldn't have a radius of much more than two hundred miles, was the Komandorsky Islands, he was willing to bet sea gold to doughnuts that somewhere along the line, and not far away at that, a peace-loving comrade from the workers' paradise had murdered Mike Bremmer because he was thought to be Frank Hall, the American sent to rescue the downed Trident.

"All right," he said to the hostile elements all around him, "so they want to play hardball."

By late afternoon the frigate from Attu had arrived and effected the tricky but successful transfer of the submersible to the *Boise*.

Now Hall felt he was ready to do battle.

# 22

TAXIS WERE ARRIVING by the score and there was a traffic jam outside the Novosti Building. Inside it seemed as chaotic as sale time in the GUM, but this was the auditorium on the second floor of the freshly painted, cream-colored Foreign Ministry, and not Moscow's biggest department store. With the babble of voices in more than a dozen languages, the harsh glare of klieg lights and cables snaking across the floor, Western correspondents—well over a hundred of them—given preferential treatment, were seated at the front while reporters from *Pravda*, *Izvestia* and the Eastern Bloc countries had to be content with the back rows.

The old commissionaire in the second-floor auditorium hadn't seen anything like it, "not since the crush of '83," he told the young, less bemedaled comrade after giving up trying to control the sudden surge of foreign reporters.

"What happened in '83?" asked his young assistant.

"The Korean airliner. Surely you remember that."

The young man was trying. "A crash, was it?"

"Shot down," said the old man. "The Koreans said it was off course. CIA lies, of course."

"Ah," replied the boy. "I think I remember. Over Kamchatka . . . right?"

"Yes. Trying to take pictures of our submarine bases. That's right. We had to . . . It was General Oligov then—he was chief of staff. But," said the old man, clearly disapproving of, yet impressed by the sheer size of the crowd now pushing and shoving into the auditorium, "this is much bigger. Look, there's not enough room. They're spilling right down to the mezzanine." The old man, one hand behind his back, brought the finer points to his assistant's attention in the manner of a professor of biology pointing out strange species to a young student.

"There, you see?" the old man said, the medals he'd earned in the Great Patriotic War glinting sharply in the glaring white light. "That's CBS—American network, Central Broadcasting System—and ABC over there." The young man didn't correct him about CBS. "Ah," commented the old man. "No show without Britannia, eh? You see, the British have come, too."

The young man thought the elderly commissionaire was getting the three Russian TV cameras, which would feed all the foreign networks, mixed up with the foreign networks themselves. It was confusing, he had to admit, with so many officials gesticulating crossly to the mass of reporters to sit down, the reporters ignoring the officials' pleas and gesticulating just as fervently to the cameras and crews that might block some of the reporters' view of the dais and whatever was behind the red-curtained screen that formed the backdrop to the table with five chairs and two water decanters. Others were already speaking into shoulder-held tape recorders, testing them on playback, adding to the din.

"It's a madhouse," said the old man, shaking his head. "An absolute asylum."

His assistant spotted a beautiful, tall, blond woman in the front row, the seats on either side of her already occupied by admiring American reporters. "Where's she from?" he asked the old man. "The one with the big melons?"

"Ah, American probably. They let their women do anything. Imagine walking around like that. I don't know . . . it's a wonder they wear anything anymore."

"It's all right by me."

"Don't be filthy, boy."

Suddenly they were in darkness.

There was a collective groan from the assembled reporters, especially those still trying to push their way up the stairway from the mezzanine. Now all the commissionaire could see was the glow of dozens of cigarette ends frenetically jumping about in the auditorium and down the long staircase. The smoky air somehow seemed thicker in the darkness, which was filled with much cursing and shoving.

"No manners, these foreigners," the old man said. "The lights will come back on in a minute. They're like a bunch of hooligans."

"Well," suggested the assistant, "they didn't get much notice. We only heard about it an hour ago ourselves, didn't we? Anyway, they all probably thought it would be held in the little hall, not an open-invitation press conference. Must be something big, eh, Uncle?"

"Still no cause for bad behavior and all this cussing and—hello! That's better, you see." The lights were on.

Cheers and clapping.

"The big man, over there, pushing his way through at the top of the stairway—see him?" asked the commissionaire. "Like a gorilla. He's from *Stern*. German magazine. I'd know him anywhere. And those, see them jostling and carrying on? British press! You ever heard of the *Daily Mirror*?"

"No," replied the assistant, brushing down his gray uniform, still gazing at the blonde.

"Breasts and things. Yes, on the front page! I'm not lying. All on the front page. No respect."

"No, Uncle."

"Well, that's it," said the old man resignedly. "It means they've invited everyone and anyone."

"How do you know all this...about this pornographic *Mirror*?"

"Well, ah, when the ministry's finished with, ah, you know, going over them for, ah, all the rotten lies they tell about us, well, then we have to burn the trash, don't we? Can't let that filth loose, can we? Course we have to know about it, so that we can stop it, you see. It's very important that we stop it."

"Yes, of course, Uncle."

The old man was shaking his head, looking distressed. "You should see them. I tell you, it's disgusting."

"When do you do all this—burning all the capitalist papers?"

"Night shift does it."

"Oh," responded the lad. "Night shift."

"It's no good, you see," said the old man. "Ruins your social life, night shift. You end up sleeping all day—can't go out at night with your friends, playing cards. No good for young people like you."

"No—no, I can see that, Uncle. Uh, who assigns the night shift? Must be a sadist."

"Chomsky. You stay away from him. Otherwise he'll have you on it. I never wanted it, but you know the missus, always for the extra ruble, eh? Extra time. If I won the lottery, I'd tell Chomsky to shove it.''

"Yes, yes. If it's extra work, Uncle, maybe...perhaps I should help you.''

"No, no, son. I'll do it, don't worry. Somebody has to do it. I'm used to it. It's awful stuff, mind.'' Now the old man was pointing excitedly down at the stairway. "Look, what did I tell you? There's a fight on the stairs. See?'' There was a lot of shouting and somebody looked as if they were falling against the marble railing.

"Koreans!'' said the old man.

"How do you know, Uncle? It's too far to see.''

Now a hush fell over the room.

"Always Koreans,'' said the old man in a whisper. "North and South, you see. Quiet now. He's here.''

*He* was Leonid Muravyev, first deputy chief of foreign policy, stepping onto the dais. On his left were two naval officers, admirals, and on his right, one army general and a civilian. As they sat down there was a great shuffling of the plastic metal-legged chairs, coughing, clearing of throats in general, and everyone who could sit did so, those on the stairs, unable to get any farther, straining to get a look at the dais. Some too short to get any kind of view simply gave up and began taking notes; others, unable to see, lowered their heads, ears cocked as if better to hear the first deputy through the crowd. The red velvet curtains parted to reveal a movie screen.

The cameras had already started and there was a quiet whir as they provided the satellite feed, monitored and relayed by control booths to other rooms off the auditorium and throughout the building.

Muravyev was a tall, gangling man, well-dressed and almost shy-looking with hard-cut rimless glasses that kept catching the light. He had long white hands like those of a pianist or a magician, which he raised to ask for silence. Then he clasped them behind his back, looking like the friendly headmaster of a school.

"Ladies and gentlemen of the press,'' he stated, "we welcome you to this open-invitation news conference. In the spirit of international peace and brotherhood and in compliance with the Supreme Soviets' principle of furthering goodwill between all peoples of the world..."

Some of the Western correspondents, especially the old hands, looked bored, not writing but leaning back staring at the ceiling, or glancing around to check whom else they recognized, their earlier expectant postures slumping into world-weary attitudes of glazed impatience. On the stairs someone had fainted; there was a lot of "hushing" and "shushing," and a small opening appeared in the crowd as two burly plain-clothesmen moved in to carry someone out. "A Frenchman!" said the old commissionaire to his assistant, though it was plainly impossible to tell, for they were standing near the top of the opposite staircase.

Muravyev kept droning on in what one correspondent, who indeed *was* a Frenchman, standing near the old commissionaire, denounced as "the usual shit." The commissionaire glared at him, and the Frenchman smiled back. Only the correspondents from *Pravda, Izvestia, Komosol* and other Party newspapers were taking notes as if this was hot news; Lebdev had instructed them that they must appear not to know what was coming.

Then Muravyev signaled to an aide and the red draperies parted dramatically. Suddenly a transformation came over the assembled press corps, the mood now one of intense interest. People leaned forward in their chairs, craning their necks; some of those on the stairs took little hops, trying to catch a glimpse of what was going on. Everyone's gaze focused on a ten-by-twenty-foot map projected on a screen by a small projector that Lebdev wheeled in closer before he turned and left the stage.

At the top of the map in the middle was the white funnel formed by the southern end of the Chukchi Sea tapering down to the narrow waist of the Bering Strait, Siberia on the left and Alaska on the right, both land masses colored pale blue, and then below the funnel, spreading out wider and wider again, the deep blue apron of the Bering Sea, spreading fanlike beyond the Aleutian arc into the vastness of the North Pacific. In the area to the middle left of the map, about a hundred and fifty miles west of Attu and a hundred and forty miles southeast of the two Komandorsky Islands, a large red circle had been drawn between longitude 170 degrees and 168 degrees and latitude 50 degrees 30 minutes and 52 degrees. It covered approximately eight thousand square miles, bisected diagonally from top right to bottom left by the U.S./U.S.S.R. boundary agreed upon in 1867.

"Our radar and other tracking stations tell us," Muravyev went on, "that an American Trident submarine illegally probing Soviet defenses has suffered a malfunction...." He paused. There was absolute silence, not even a cough. Muravyev repeated the word, "...a malfunction, and has apparently sunk. Even though this is an unprovoked and unacceptable intrusion on the integrity of the Soviet Union, in keeping with the Soviet Union's traditional spirit of friendship for all peoples of the world..." Even the Frenchman was sitting forward, tense, scribbling as fast as he could.

"...the Soviet government expresses sincere condolences to the families of those already lost in this tragic accident, and to those of the few survivors, who will also be lost unless immediate steps are taken to find the exact location of the sunken submarine and to retrieve it if possible. The Soviet Union wishes to give all possible assistance in this effort and has already dispatched elements of the Soviet Pacific Far Eastern Fleet, including our latest decompression chamber, to help in any way we can. Whatever is in the power of the Soviet people to do to prevent further tragedy, we do as a gesture of goodwill in the interest of peaceful relations between the American and Soviet peoples and in compliance with American wishes. Any other countries wishing to join us in assisting the United States Navy in locating the disabled submarine and in returning the trapped U.S. sailors to their loved ones as soon as possible, in the spirit of world peace, are most welcome to do so. Thank you."

The four men, two on either side of Muravyev, rose. There was a barrage of questions, but Muravyev declined to answer any and the five men walked off the dais and out of the auditorium, despite the urgent chorus of reporters' questions following them. Pandemonium broke out. Now those on the stairs and the mezzanine had the advantage, for they were first out of the building, disgorged into the street through the revolving doors of the ministry. There was a stampede—for taxis, limousines, embassy cars, anything on wheels—as the world's press raced to file the unprecedented story. In less than five minutes the footsteps of the commissionaires and janitors who had already started to clean up in the auditorium were echoing like voices in a vast and empty cave.

"Why weren't there any questions?" asked the young assistant.

"There were," said the old man. "There weren't to be any answers, that's all."

"Then why did those four bigwigs come on the stage with Muravyev?"

"Did you see Lebdev?"

"Who?"

"Lebdev. Chief editor of Tass. He was running the show—off to the side of the dais by the curtains, looking at his watch all the time. If there had been questions most of the American networks would have missed the evening news. He's no fool, that Lebdev, let me tell you."


"CUNNING BASTARD!" intoned the aide to Admiral Gill, Chief of Naval Operations. "Now what do we do?"

Admiral Gill was shading his eyes with his right hand, the gold braid at his wrist a rich amber in the television's fading light. He could see his career ending as quickly as the television images from Moscow were fading from the TV screen. He watched the green dot until it was no more. "Play back the video," he told his aide. Before the aide pressed the Playback button on the remote, the phones had already begun ringing.

"I'll speak to the President only. No one else."

"Yes, sir," answered the aide. He entered the adjoining office and closed the door after himself.

"Goddamn it!" said Gill, turning brusquely to another aide. "Got a cigarette?"

"No, sir."

"I want one."

"Ah, begging your pardon, Admiral, but you told me not to—"

"Never mind what I told you. Go get a cigarette. Give me the remote."

"Yes, sir." The second aide exited the room.

Now there were only two of them left in the Pentagon room—the CNO and his director of undersea warfare. Gill let the news conference run for a while until the first deputy had almost finished his speech, and then he took a zoom shot and paused the video. "Who's *that* ugly bastard?"

"They're all ugly bastards, John," said the director of undersea warfare.

The aide returned with a packet of cigarettes and lit one for the admiral."

"Yes," said Gill, "but I know the two ugly bastards on the foreign ministry guy's left—Litov, Pacific Far Eastern Fleet, and his sidekick, the commander of the submarine fleet out of Petropavlovsk on the Kamchatka Peninsula. And the civilian on his right—"

"Skolensky," said the director of undersea warfare. "New minister responsible for the Pacific Ocean Department. Overlaps with the old fisheries portfolio."

"Right. I make him," said the CNO. "But who's the general—looking so happy with himself? Can you zoom in any closer?"

The aide tried but the picture only got fuzzier.

The CNO shook his head. "Goddamn Soviet TV. What can you expect?"

"Well, sir," ventured the aide, "if I didn't know better, I'd say it was Kornon—former Politburo alternate. Hitched his wagon to Borgach before the old man retired."

"Yes," cut in the DUW, "Kornon—fisheries, right? That is, fisheries and dirty tricks?"

"Yes, sir," said the aide. "I think that's who it is. He was mixed up with that Eagle Island business with the, uh, Frank Hall ship, the *Petrel*, when it was looking for sea gold—metalliferous muds."

"Yes, yes," said the DUW. "But I thought the son of a bitch had been canned."

"Yes, sir, so did I."

"Then what's he doing back?" interjected Admiral Gill.

"Well," suggested the DUW, "he's the one who's been up against Frank Hall before. By all accounts, he hates his guts. Hall's not in love with him, either. He got internal exile as I remember. That right, Lieutenant?"

"Yes, sir. Siberia somewhere."

"Well," said Gill, "don't tell me it was the salt mines, because they don't have any goddamn salt mines in Siberia. You know that?" He looked all around.

"No, sir."

"Well, they don't. Gold mines, silver mines, you name it, but they haven't got salt mines. Who the hell made that up?" It was as if he was accusing someone in the room. He was trying to compensate for not knowing as much about Kornon as he figured he should have. "I don't care where the hell they sent him," Gill continued. "What's he doing back in Moscow? Think *he's* the head honcho?"

The DUW shook his head. "Hard to say, Admiral. You never know what the hell those Russians are up to."

As the DUW and Gill were mulling it over, Gill's aide was watching the stilled zoom shot. In front of the first deputy he recognized several correspondents from the American TV networks and a reporter from the *Washington Post*—one of them was obviously ogling a luscious blonde sitting in the front row. He wanted to run the film back and have a good look at her; all he could see now was her profile—not that that wasn't good enough.

"So what happens now?" said Admiral Gill. "They move in their 'elements of the Far Eastern Soviet Fleet.' Wasn't that what that foreign ministry joker was saying? Well, if they think I'm going to let any Russian ship within ten miles of where the *Boise* says that sub went down, they're crazy. I'll order every goddamn thing we've got in that area to form a protective ring around the salvage operation. That way those bastards won't get anywhere near Hall or the sub. Everyone understand?"

"Yes, sir," said the aide.

"But we don't want to escalate it unnecessarily," advised the director of undersea warfare.

"Hell, George, it's one of your subs up there. If push comes to shove—"

"I'm not disagreeing, Admiral, but we have to know *what* area. We don't know if the *Boise's* correct."

"George, I know Peters. He's a good man. If he's fairly sure that what he's got on that sonar blip of his is the *New York*—then I'll bet my pension it's the *New York*."

"Admiral?" It was the aide from the adjoining office.

"Yes. What is it?"

"The President, sir, on line one."

THE PRESIDENT OF THE United States rose and shook hands with his chief of naval operations and ushered him toward the sitting area in the middle of the Oval Office. "I thought we'd have some coffee."

"Thank you, Mr. President," Gill said. "I could use some. I have a feeling this is going to be a long night."

After both men had sipped their steaming coffee, the President wasted no time getting to the point. "I know you've seen the telecast from Moscow, Admiral. Do you agree that the Russians want to get their hands on the *New York* and go over it with a fine-tooth comb? To steal every technological advance we've made?"

"I'm sure of it," the admiral stated, relieved that the President had on his own seen through the Soviet "gesture of goodwill," recognizing it for what it was—a play for the intelligence coup of the century. Gill's audible sigh of relief seemed to fill the Oval Office. "I've told the DUW to get a couple of his subs up there fast—in addition to the on-scene ships—and to keep those charitable gentlemen well clear of the search area."

"Oh, we can't do that, Admiral. The 'charitable gentlemen,' as you so aptly put it, have us behind the eight ball. One thing about the Soviets I learned long ago—never underestimate their deviousness. Behind the simplest-sounding phrase a bog of intrigue is waiting to trap you—to suck you under."

An aide brought in a silver tray with an insulated coffeepot, fine china and a plate of assorted cookies and left immediately while the chief executive poured.

Gill prided himself on his quick intelligence, his ability to rapidly assess any militarily strategic problem and to react speedily with a cool, clearly thought-out solution—after all, he told himself, it was what they paid him for. But the President's reluctance to seal off the search area perplexed Gill. On the other hand, he was only too willing to concede that if his forte lay in military affairs, the President's resided in matters political. "I must confess, Mr. President, I don't see any problem in stopping the Soviets...."

"From a military standpoint, of course not—if you don't care about risking a war. But you explain to me, Admiral, how in God's name I can tell the Soviets to get lost, to back off, when they've so *generously*, in front of the entire world, offered to help our sailors in a—what did they say—oh, yes, 'in the spirit of international peace.'"

The President got up and walked toward the high mantel. "I know it's their prime chance to get at the prize, the one thing that in any eyeball-to-eyeball confrontation will make the Soviets blink—the Trident. But even if you know it, I know it, the CIA knows it and Moscow knows it, how can we tell them to keep their distance when they have a flotilla on the way, ready with a deep-sea rescue vehicle, so ABC News informs us? My God, it's a ready-made gift for them. Not just the sub, I mean, but a propaganda victory like they've never had. Every peace group, save-the-whales, save-the-maggots outfit in the country'll be screaming on the White House lawn by morning."

"I agree, sir, but if we can find the sub first and get down there, we can beat them to the punch."

"But can we, Admiral? Can we beat them to the punch? That's what I've been asking all morning, and no one can tell me."

The admiral was smiling in the soft peach-colored cone of light that reflected his career in the rows of miniature dress uniform medals. "Yes, sir, I believe that we have. The USS *Boise* has signaled that they've found what they think—"

"Never mind what they *think*, Admiral. Have they found it or not?"

"I believe so, sir. At any rate, Hall, the oceanographer in charge of the retrieval, has been taken aboard. We should know in an hour at the most."

# 23

FRANK HALL BRACED himself on the bridge as the *Boise*'s prop shuddered violently; the section that had been repaired in Attu had cleared water briefly. He made his way to the chart table, situated directly behind the steering console, and examined the sonar trace. It indicated a definite hump, an *elongated* hump, on the sea floor at two thousand plus feet, the magnetometer reading high for the area around the Aleutian Trench.

But these weren't the things that interested him. The magnetic anomaly was simply that, an anomaly—a higher reading then normal—no more significant in his experience than an apparent abnormality in a person's heartbeat or blood pressure. Its significance depended on a host of other factors, among them the depth of water that at two thousand feet would be approaching the sub's crush depth, the shape of the hump, which could resemble a sub seen from one angle but not from another, and the six best photographs from over a hundred and fifty, ten-by-fourteen-inch black-and-white blowups taken by the stainless-steel-encased Edgerton strobe flash/camera unit. The camera was affixed to a four-legged metal frame or scaffolding lowered into the pitch-dark, the long, three-foot strobe unit preset to start popping away every thirty seconds. A small pinger bounced its signals off the sea bottom to start the synchronized camera and flash unit automatically, allowing a safety margin of twenty feet above possible rocky outcrops that would otherwise smash the unit to pieces. A compass, its needle encased in a transparent, oil-filled housing, was suspended below the metal frame scaffolding by a three-foot lanyard, and its needle was visible in most of the shots unless washed away to the side by currents. Now and then the camera frame would twirl or tilt in the deep localized currents swirling about the trench, and fail to photograph the compass, so that observers couldn't tell, after the film had been developed, in what direction the camera had been facing.

"There," said the *Boise*'s executive officer, holding up one such photograph. "The water's very cloudy, light reflecting off sand and mud and some broken shell, probably stirred up by the unit as much as by local currents, I guess—but you can see the definite rectangular outline.''

"Yes," said Hall, studying the photo carefully, sliding the magnifying stand up and down, then across the print. The executive officer was correct—the outline was blurred, possibly lying well beyond the focal length, but it *was* a long, definite hump—the same as that recorded on the sonar trace but more squashed. The scale had been understandably magnified on the *Boise*'s bridge to pick up the smallest anomaly its depth recorder was capable of. It was impossible to estimate the distance from the camera lens; the executive officer had assumed it was about two hundred feet, though he conceded this was only guesswork, an extrapolation from the shape and scale on the sonar trace.

It was then that Hall noticed that the bottom left-hand corner of one photo was blank, as if someone in the darkroom had accidentally put his thumb on the edge of the paper as it was being exposed. "What's this?" he asked the executive officer.

The officer reached for the photo, sending a yellow pencil rolling across the 1:1 million operational chart. "Hmm," he mused. "Don't know. Somebody's thumb got in the way, I guess. To tell you the truth, I've been too busy looking at the sub—I mean the shape—to be worrying about anything else."

That's just it, isn't it? thought Hall. He isn't worried about anything else. In Hall, however, the careless thumb mark aroused the nagging suspicion of an amateurishness in the photo development and interpretation—in fact, in the whole operation. As the signal that the sub had been found was being sent through the rain-slashed skies over wild ocean to Mike Bremmer, full of life and optimism, boarding the Hercules on Attu but now stone-cold and dead and about to be committed to the deep chill, an equally hopeful executive officer might have committed a simple but fundamental error—understandable among those who hadn't handled the underwater camera assemblies more than a half-dozen times. Through such an error the executive officer might have brought the *Boise* and its crew and the on-scene U.S. flotilla *off-scene*—by how many miles, God only knew.

"Is the strobe/camera unit still assembled?" Hall asked, his tone even, simply inquiring. There was no point in raising the alarm here on the bridge; it would cost the executive officer, a man about the same age as Bremmer, his career. "May I see it?"

"Sure," said the executive officer. "Yeoman, will you take—"

"No," Hall cut in as easily as he could. "I'd rather you show it to me."

The yeoman looked from Frank to the executive officer. Captain Peters was coming onto the bridge, stopping for a second as the *Boise* plunged headlong through a high wave, a burst of spray sweeping across the twin sliver of the forward harpoon missile launcher.

"Mr. Hall." Peters nodded formally but good-naturedly.

"Frank'll do fine."

"Very well. Ah, we've scheduled sea burial for Lieutenant Bremmer at first light—pending search priorities."

"Very well," replied Hall, momentarily unaware he was echoing the time-honored naval response to the captain. His mind was on other things. They could be in big trouble. And the Russians *were* coming.

"Have you any update on the position of the *Petrel*?" he asked the executive officer.

"No, sir. Last we heard was six hours ago. No position since then."

"Well, she should be approaching our area. Could your radioman try to raise her while we're having a look at the unit?"

"Certainly."

"Thanks."

Although the executive officer was the OOD, Captain Peters was quite happy to relieve him, for like all captains in rough weather, he preferred to be pacing the bridge where he had the pulse of the ship.

Down in the helicopter hangar near the stern pad of the frigate, Hall dogged the watertight entrance hatch, making sure he would be alone with the executive officer. The strobe/camera unit was still assembled, standing lashed to the workbench. Both camera and flash were pointing down within the frame at forty-five-degree angles that would have met about twelve inches below to form the apex of a triangle.

Looking around to make sure that the stern entrance through the helicopter hangar's slide door was also closed so that no one could come in on them unexpectedly, Hall walked over to the frame. Six feet long, two feet wide and four feet high, it resembled a giant galvanized-steel Meccano set. The Edgerton flash and camera units were still in their glistening stainless-steel watertight cylinders bolted inside the diagonally cross-beamed frame.

"Has it been altered in any way?" pressed Hall. "I mean has anything been taken off or added?"

"No," answered the executive officer. "Not that I know of. Of course—" he gestured toward the strobe/camera unit "—the Nike batteries have been removed, as well as the film from the camera."

Hall was kneeling down by the frame, running his finger around the rubber O-ring seal of the camera tube. It was sparkling, now that the saltwater had been hosed off by fresh water.

"You think saltwater got into it? Blurred the film?" asked the executive officer.

"No," Hall responded slowly. It was the very slowness, the deliberation in his tone, that worried the executive officer.

"How many ASA?" Hall asked casually.

"A thousand ASA, I think. Very fast, anyway," answered the executive officer.

Hall nodded. "The shots might have been clearer with the two thousand film." But it was really beside the point. He pulled up the navy blue lanyard that was attached to the compass until he came to the end of it, where it was attached to an eyelet atop the oil-filled bulb of the compass. Then he let the unattached end of the lanyard fall onto the hangar's grease-spotted deck like a loosely coiled grass snake. Getting up, steadying himself on the frame as the *Boise* rolled hard to starboard, he asked the executive officer to bring the small overhead beam crane over the unit, lowering its hook until he could attach it to the U-bolt, which was in turn attached to four chains that suspended the unit as it was lowered to and raised from the sea bottom.

"All right," Hall instructed, waving his right index finger around in short, tight circles after the hook had been attached. "Take the frame up slowly, about two feet above the deck."

The crane's winch whined in low gear; then there was a heavy thump as its brake resounded throughout the hangar. Hall was standing like someone stuck with an awkward dance partner, his weight shifting jerkily from left to right as he grabbed a low crossbar on the frame, which, though suspended from the beam crane, rocked wildly as the swivel joint above the U-bolt responded to the heavy roll of the ship. Beneath the frame the compass began to twirl and untwirl like a yo-yo. At the same time the lanyard's string was swinging pendulously, its rust-speckled metal fin rotating quickly this way and that with each turn of the lanyard, causing the compass to swing wildly beneath camera and flash unit. Hall turned his head to see if the executive officer was watching. He was.

"Oh, Christ!" said the executive officer. His pronounced Adam's apple, which Hall hadn't noticed on the bridge, was sliding up and down in surprise, in the realization of the mistake someone had made—one of the crewman assembling the unit, probably, but a mistake for which the captain and he, as officer of the deck, would take the rap.

"You see it?" asked Hall, not scoldingly or in any way sounding superior or condescending, but knowing that the officer must realize the mistake, error, call it what you like, that might cost them the race to the *New York*.

"Oh, Christ!" repeated the exec, his face pale even in the pale light of the hangar, as he watched Hall dangle the compass bulb at the end of its cord. "The rectangle we saw in the photo—"

"*Thought* you saw," said Hall.

"It was the compass—its . . ."

"Stabilizer fin," said Hall quietly. He lowered the cup-sized compass to the deck, letting the nylon cord collapse as the exec, staring straight ahead like an automaton, lowered the strobe/camera unit to the deck.

"It's not the first time it's been done," said Hall, by way of consolation. "It depends on the angle. The current twists the compass around, its stabilizer fin flashes into view. Pop—and you've got an image. And you don't know how big it really is. Could be a hundred, two hundred feet. No real sense of scale."

"But..." began the exec lamely, "there's a pinger on the unit to tell you..."

"Sure," said Hall. "But that only tells you how far you are from the bottom. A current moves the whole frame on an angle, so you've no idea how far the rectangle is in front of you."

"But I thought . . . I mean the trace on the sonar paper..."

"Well, it was impressive, I know . . . even allowing for the magnification, it looked like something well over two hundred feet long. And it was an anomaly . . . but that's *all* it was. The sea bottom's strewed with anomalies, especially around the trench. All that volcanic activity going on beneath spews out all kinds of stuff. It can look like anything from a sub . . . to a goddamn Toyota."

Hall felt sorry for the lieutenant. He had no answer, only excuses, and now he was seeing his naval career dead in the water, as dead as the magnetic anomaly that had sent back the sonar's signal all right, up through the thick sandy soup of the bottom, a long, rectangular shape that in the gloom of the flash's penumbra, and with everyone hoping, had appeared to resemble a sub, but wasn't.

"Look," said Hall, his voice echoing, "I know that—"

They heard footsteps coming down somewhere from the deck above. The sounds changed in volume when whoever it was was momentarily slowed by the shuddering corkscrew motion of the frigate as it leaped high astarboard, dropped in free-fall, then wrenched hard left. The frame jerked along the steel deck, screeching in protest and threatening to take Hall with it.

"Listen," Hall began again, talking faster now that someone was approaching. "What's done is done. You're not used to this underwater stuff. Hell, they made the same kind of mistake in '63 when they were searching for the *Thresher*."

"Yeah?" Hall was throwing the exec a lifeline, and he was grabbing it with both hands.

"Yes. Not part of the compass but the crossbeam of the frame itself. People don't understand how rough it can be beneath the surface—they think everything is dark and slow. It isn't. Some of those bottom currents..."

"Jesus!" said the executive. This time the profanity was his uninhibited expression of relief; Hall was telling him anyone could make a mistake. "You mean, you're not going to report—"

The forward hatch levers thudded up and down as if moved by some invisible force, as someone knocked them off the locked position from the other side. It was a yeoman, tattoos on both hands, holding two message sheets. "Lieutenant, sir."

"Yes?"

The yeoman handed him a message.

"We've had a reply from the MV *Petrel*," the exec told Hall. "She's a hundred miles due east of us...."

"Right," said Hall. "We're going to mow lawn, fellas."

But the next moment his buoyant mood at hearing news from his old ship receded as the exec handed him the second message and he read it. It was the text of a news conference held in Moscow. The Russians had apparently announced to the entire world how they were magnanimously going to the "assistance" of Uncle Sam. Hall immediately thought of Mike Bremmer. Someone in Moscow obviously had a plan to *thwart* any American rescue attempt, not assist it. And Mike Bremmer had been the first to pay for it.

"Any reply, sir?" asked the yeoman.

"Yes," Hall replied. "Message to Captain Tate of the MV *Petrel* from Lieutenant Michael Bremmer, U.S. Navy."

"But, sir..." The yeoman looked at the lieutenant for an explanation. He had none.

"From Lieutenant Bremmer, U.S. Navy," Hall repeated. His voice was even, but he was in no mood to brook any opposition. "Message reads, in plain language, 'Front yard overgrown stop pineapples about to fall stop at least seven inches stop hurry before all gone stop Bremmer.'"

When the yeoman was gone, looking as perplexed as the exec, Hall explained to the lieutenant why the message had to be in plain language. "The *Petrel* isn't Navy, Lieutenant. They don't use codes."

"Yes, I understand that. But what does the message mean?"

"It means," responded Hall, looking at his watch, "that if we don't move our ass and find that sub soon, the Russians will. You'd better send a message yourself, Lieutenant, to Washington. *In code.* Tell them I examined the prints—that the camera misfired and what I thought was the sub, isn't."

"But that'll make you look . . . I mean you don't have to—"

"Look," said Hall, "one mistake like this and you're canned. On a frigate for the rest of your life. What've *I* got to lose?"

"Your reputation."

Hall paused. "Thanks, but it's not all charity, either, Lieut—Hell, I'm tired of calling you 'Lieutenant' and 'Exec.' What's your first name?"

"William—William Bryce."

"It's not charity, Bill," said Hall easily. "I've been up against Russians before. Believe me, you have to think ahead."

The lieutenant wasn't following the oceanographer at all. "But I don't see how having Washington think you've fouled up instead of me will—"

"Good," said Hall. "It's good you don't see. That's the whole point."

"Look, sir—I appreciate you not reporting me—"

"Don't thank me yet."

Bryce started to walk away, then stopped and turned, still bugged by the message Hall had just sent. "But why sign it 'Bremmer'?"

"Somebody thought Bremmer was me, Lieutenant. Don't you see? They only expected one parachutist—an oceanographer, name of Hall. I don't want them to find out otherwise. So no messages go out signed 'Frank Hall.'" The oceanographer hesitated. "Anyway, Mike wouldn't have minded."

Bryce left the hangar more confused than when he'd come down. The scuttlebutt had it that Frank Hall was one weird fish. Someone—an oiler, Bryce seemed to recall—had said he heard Hall had just beaten an "indecent assault and attempted rape" charge back in the States. The trouble with scuttlebutt, Bryce knew, was you never knew how much was for real and how much was bullshit.

Back on the bridge Captain Peters asked Bryce what Hall's message to the *Petrel* meant, reading it out loud. "'Front lawn overgrown'? 'Pineapples'?"

"He didn't explain, sir," said Bryce. "I assume the *Petrel* will understand. The *Petrel* and Hall go back quite a way, apparently—a lot of oceanographic cruises."

Peters was annoyed. Hall had seemed reasonable, sound enough, but here he was ordering messages to be sent from the *Boise* without even having the decency to explain them to the *Boise*'s commanding officer. "That really frosts me," Peters informed everyone on the bridge. "Goddamn insolence! Is it true," he went on to Bryce, "that he's some kind of pervert? That he either succeeds here or he goes into the slammer?"

"No, sir," Bryce answered quickly. "I—I don't believe that."

"Well, he seems goddamn odd to me. Not the full fathom. And if he thinks—" Suddenly Peters stopped. "Pineapples don't grow on goddamn trees! What's he mean by pineapples falling?"

Frank Hall entered the bridge as the radio operator was tapping out his message to the *Petrel*. Everyone fell silent. Peters had the option either to be silent, too, or to be silenced by Hall's presence. He thought about Hall's other message about misinterpreting the all-important film. Making the *Boise* look stupid.

"Pineapples don't grow on goddamn trees!" he said to Hall.

"You're right," answered Hall easily. "Comes from an old song, 'Pineapple Picker'—picked them from the trees." Hall smiled. "Mario Lanza."

Peters's face reddened. "Mario Lanza? What's this got to do with Mario Lanza?"

"The song he used to sing," explained Hall. "'Pineapple Picker.'"

The starboard lookout could hardly keep from bursting into laughter. It was the strangest conversation he'd ever heard on the *Boise*, and on top of that, he knew that the one thing Peters couldn't tolerate was a joke that he thought he wasn't in on.

It wasn't a joke, Hall explained. As he had told Bryce, he couldn't send code to the *Petrel*; so he had to use plain language but language that only the *Petrel* would understand. As the oceanographer explained it, Peters realized it was no joke.

In fact, he told his assembled officers later in the mess that as he saw it the hundred and fifty men trapped in the *New York* had not yet been located because Hall, the "hotshot oceanographer extraordinaire," had apparently made a hash of it, giving screwed-up instructions on how to rig the camera and strobe unit. As far as Peters was concerned, Washington had made an even bigger screwup sending Hall to the *Boise*.

"What we have," he informed his officers, as the *Boise* began a new search line southwest of Attu, "is a goddamn fruitcake oceanographer, with *authority*, gentlemen—" he looked around the mess, his gaze taking in each officer as he spoke "—with *extraordinary authority* over all of us."

"What did he mean by pineapples, anyway?" asked the chief engineer.

"Who knows?"

A little later, as he drank coffee in the chart room, Captain Peters was thinking of the hundred and fifty men who wouldn't be drinking coffee, or who if they were, were maybe drinking their last. He called in Chief Hospital Corpsman First Class Cooper. "Cooper, I think we could have a situation here with this Hall. I want to see how you read it."

"Can't say, sir. I haven't met the man," replied the thin, gangling corpsman. "The boys said he came down to see Bremmer's body, but I was off-duty at the time."

"Well, that's what I'm wondering about—him seeing Bremmer like that. He's a civilian. That sort of thing can shake a civilian up, unbalance him for a while. I've seen it happen before."

"He must be the best, though. Washington did send him posthaste."

"*Was* the best, Cooper. That's the operative word here. I've seen that before, too. Top guns suddenly losing their touch. Going along fine, then one day, bang! They can't handle the stress anymore." Peters ran his fingers through thick, graying hair. "The thing is, I can't afford second-raters. We've got a hundred and fifty boys down there, and by God . . ."

The corpsman was sipping his coffee. The captain had a point, he acknowledged. No one could take a chance with anyone who wasn't up to it—not with a hundred and fifty men trapped. The corpsman was also shrewd enough to understand that Captain Peters didn't want a second-rater, and a civilian to boot, torpedoing his career.

"Well, sir, I expect we'll soon be rid of him, anyhow."

Peters, his hand locking onto the coffeepot as the frigate went into another roll, turned about. "I don't get your drift."

"Well, the scuttlebutt has it that this civilian research ship—"

"The *Petrel*," said Peters.

"Yeah. Someone said it'll be in our area in the next few hours. Is that right?"

"So?"

"If we find the sub, won't he want to work from the *Petrel*, seeing he's so familiar with it? I mean, instead of the *Boise*."

"By God, Chief, I think you're right!" Nevertheless, a frown crossed Peters's face. "That might get him out of our hair, but does the son of a bitch know what he's doing?"

"Lord, I hope so," said the corpsman. "I sure as hell hope so."

"Look," said Peters, "strictly on the QT. If this guy seems to be—I mean, if he is a bit weird..."

"No problem," said the chief. "I wouldn't do anything, of course, unless I had hard evidence of abnormal behavior, but if it is a case of someone losing their grip—and we've both been at sea long enough to know it can happen..."

"A shot of some kind?" Peters suggested quietly.

"Easier than that," answered the chief. "In his coffee, tea, whatever. He'd never notice it."

"What could we put it down to?"

"Extreme motion sickness. You know yourself how some men get so ill from seasickness they can't get out of the bunk—"

"Damn it, Chief. He's been to sea for years."

"Yeah, yeah. Sorry, I forgot. Oh, hell, Captain, don't worry. There's any of a dozen ailments. After all, his friend..."

"Bremmer."

"We don't know what put him out of action."

"The goddamn Russians put him out of action."

"Nope," replied Cooper. "We might suspect them, but there's not a mark on him. I think he blacked out and drowned."

"Well, I don't."

"Neither does Hall, from what the exec says."

"Well, that's one thing we agree on."

There was a knock on the door. "Sir?" It was the bosun's mate.

"Yes, Johnston?" asked Peters.

"It's about Hall, sir. He wants us to start dropping grenades."

The chief looked perplexed, but Peters reassured him. "No, this one's okay, Chief. It's standard search procedure. We didn't do it earlier because of the danger of alerting the Soviets to the fact that we'd lost a sub."

"Well, why are you going to do it now?" pressed the corpsman.

"That's what I'd like to know."

"Well," Hall said, following the bosun's mate in, "it's obvious the Russians know we haven't found the *New York*—otherwise there'd be all sorts of underwater activity. Now we know for sure they know we've lost a sub, there's no point in being extra cautious. We might as well start dropping the grenades. If the *New York*'s still alive, she'll pick up the explosions and hopefully respond. It's the usual drill, right, Captain?"

"Yes," Peters conceded, "but—"

"Yes, Captain?"

"It's still my ship, Mr. Hall."

"Ah...that's debatable, Captain." With that, Hall left the bridge.

Peters was so enraged he couldn't speak. "Insolent bastard!" he finally boomed in the chart room. "By God, I'll have his guts for garters!"

Hall was already between decks but still he could hear the captain's outrage. It was too bad. He hadn't enjoyed saying it; he liked Peters. But there was no other way.

That evening, as he entered the crew's mess where some men were watching the evening television satellite relay broadcast, he saw, as part of the CBS news, the shots of the Moscow press conference. He thought he recognized a face on the panel. He started toward the TV to press the zoom button, but by then the news clip had ended and the Moscow segment was gone.

As Hall looked intently at the last few seconds of the conference fading away behind the reporter, one of the sailors joked, "You must be hard up."

"Maybe he's just hard," said someone else.

"Hell," said a third, looking back from inside the galley refrigerator, "I didn't think any of 'em looked good."

"Picky picky!" came a chorus, followed by general guffawing.

Hall took the ribbing in good humor but was more interested in the TV. "Is this being taped?" he asked, thinking they might do it for the eight-to-midnight watch.

"No," said one of the sailors, flicking down the cover of the control panel. "No, the red light isn't blinking."

"You get the eleven o'clock news?"

"You want it taped, sir?" It was the young yeoman with the tattoos.

"That'd be great. Thanks," said Hall. "I'll be at the sonar watch." There was another dull thump outside, and for a moment the TV commercial for Japanese McDonald's shivered, was speckled with black and white, then came clear again with an image of french fries.

"How many of those you gonna dump over, sir?" asked one of the crew.

"Until they hear us," said Hall, and suddenly the mood changed, the crewman's question bringing everyone, whether they liked it or not, back to the immediate task at hand.

"What can they do, sir, if they do hear us?"

"Break radio silence—the most serious thing a Trident can do. But they'll count the explosions first. It's the regularity that'll tip 'em off. Then they can release their sonobuoy with the haul cable attached to it, and once the buoy pops through the surface and starts giving off that bleep, we've got their location. Then we hook up with the haul cable and we're in business."

"How would we get them out, sir? That deep-sea rescue vehicle the Russians have got?"

"Depends what kind of shape the sub's in. That's what I'll have to find out first."

"How you going to do that, sir?"

"I go down in the *Serena I* with strobe light and camera and—"

"Then you're the seeing-eye dog for the *Petrel* before she tries to salvage. That it?"

"Yes," said Hall, struck by the aptness of the man's metaphor. "Yeah, that's exactly it. I guide the *Petrel*, the *Boise* or whatever other on-scene ship is involved into position for the best pull-up."

"How about the Russian DSRV? How does that work?"

"Three eight-foot-diameter pressure spheres—pressure hulls if you like—are welded together. It has about a fifty-foot outer hull or casing over it. They copied it from ours. It looks like a long, fat cigar tapered at both ends, but one end has a variable pitch prop in a control shroud and both ends have two-foot-diameter bow thrusters. The linkup with the sub is made by bringing the DSRV at right angles to the sub. Close-circuit television cameras and sonar guide the DSRV over the sub's escape trunk, aligning the escape trunk with a skirted flange that fits over the trunk. Then the DSRV lowers itself until the metal skirt encases the escape trunk—sort of like hovering over the sub's escape hatch and lowering an upside-down funnel over a pipe."

"Male to female!" someone said.

"If you like," said Hall.

"Yeah. I like."

Hall smiled. "Okay, then the connection is made and the skirt or funnel part is pumped dry from the DSRV, the hatch is opened from inside the sub. In the new Trident K class—the *New York*'s—as well as the escape hatch in the sail, there's one just forward of the sail with an interlock chamber. Anyway, the first few sailors get a good cold shower, and then they start coming up through the escape hatch into the DSRV one by one."

"How many does it hold, sir?" asked the yeoman.

"Forward sphere holds two—pilot, copilot and all the electronic gear, second and third pressure hulls carry two crewmen—both medics—and twenty-four passengers maximum."

"Piece of cake, eh, Frank?" asked one of the stewards.

"No," answered Hall. "There are no portholes in the DSRV. That makes it more resistant to water pressure, but it also means that everything depends on the electronics inside. TV monitors, et cetera. I've got nothing against electronics, but personally, I like to see what I'm doing as well. Anyway, there's another problem with the DSRV. With a maximum of twenty-four passengers it means you'd have to make at least six perfect trips down and up to get everybody out of a Trident.

"Then the DSRV's only got fourteen hours' endurance at a maximum of eight knots before you have to recharge the batteries. More realistically you run them at around three—maximum four—knots, which gives you about sixteen, seventeen hours maximum." Said quickly, seventeen hours sounded just fine, but Hall knew if you did a little arithmetic—six trips up and back, time down, transfer time, time up, transfer of personnel to the mother ship in dangerously heavy seas—it was very much a matter of coming in on a wing and a prayer. As one of the world's most experienced oceanographers, Hall knew that Murphy's Law was always operative; he'd seen so many sophisticated pieces of equipment tested and tested and retested ashore and in tanks and offshore, only to foul up once they were tried in deep seas.

"I prefer bringing up the sub in one go," said Hall.

"But even if we find it," asked a skeptical seaman, "how do you bring it up in one go?"

Hall nodded. He sat down at one of the Formica tables and accepted a cup of coffee that one of the stewards had brought. The crewman's question was exactly the kind that would be asked by the news hounds who would be sure to show up following the world headlines of the Moscow conference. If he could help someone get it right the first time, then all the better. "You go down with spreader bars," he explained. "Like taking down two giant pairs of blunt scissors opened fully up with the finger holes on the top. One pair of scissors or spreader bars forward of the sub, one pair aft. Then you attach a separate cable to each of the four finger holes and slide one pair of the scissors or spreader bars under the sub so that when you start to haul up on the four cables, which are attached to one big swivel joint, the scissors start to close, cradling the sub in two steel Vs four hundred feet apart—seeing a Trident's about six hundred feet long. You can attach cross cables, et cetera, to make everything more secure. There are other ways, too, of helping her up once you start to haul. If the—"

"But, hell," cut in the steward, "can we lift anything that heavy? I mean, the Trident's around eighteen thousand tons, right?"

"That's right," answered Hall. "And if she isn't already crushed and the crew are alive, still she must be pretty near crush depth if she's anywhere in this area."

"That's what I mean. Eighteen thousand tons and we're only—"

"Hold on," said Hall. "Remember it's not a dead lift of eighteen thousand." Someone refilled his coffee mug and, cradling it in his hands for its warmth, he thought for a moment, searching for another analogy. "Look, remember playing with toys in the bathtub when you were a kid. Some things went straight to the bottom. Others with more buoyancy, like a sub, would sort of half sink—like a heavy log. A little push and they'd keep going down, a little pull and they'd pop up."

"Yeah, but the *New York*'s no toy."

"Same principle, though," explained Hall. "If her pressure hull's not ruptured, she'll have air in her, and if we can slide some cable netting and those two steel slings under her, we might stand a chance. We could take down some syntactic foam."

"What's that?"

"You know that lightweight packing stuff you see all around electronic gear these days when they ship it?"

"Styrofoam," someone said.

"Well, yes, sort of," said Hall. "You take a great bunch of it down using heavy weights, attach it to the sub, then release the weights. You get a lot of lift from that. Point is, remember, that all the sub needs to go down is a bit too much negative buoyancy. Even then she has to *drive* herself under. So, as I said—if we can get her started up, she'll just keep coming up. And each foot she rises there will be less and less pressure on her. The problem could be to slow her down when she gets enough of an up angle—positive buoyancy."

"Think these grenades are going to help us find her, Frank?"

"Sure. If her active sonar's working. Trouble is, it's housed smack up in the nose, between the pressure hull and the outer casing. It was probably the first to implode—"

"Implode!" said an oiler, sitting with his back against a stanchion, both legs up on the bench and rolling his own cigarette—something Hall hadn't seen for years. "Better me than them," the oiler went on. "Fucking coffin with a propeller on it, my old man used to say. Give me a surface ship any day. Bet you're glad you're not down there, eh, Frank?''

"Well," said Hall, getting up from the mess bench, "thanks for the coffee."

"No problem," said the steward. "Here, take a piece of pizza with you."

Hall took a slice and immediately had to start tossing it from one hand to the other.

"Sorry, Frank. Should have told you it's pretty hot."

"Now he tells me!" Hall quipped as he left the galley to make his way up to the combat information center to check on the sonar.

"You spongehead," said the steward to the oiler.

"What'd I say?" asked the oiler glancing up, licking the cigarette and damping it.

"He *is* going down there," said the steward.

"So?" replied the oiler. "If he goes down, he must know what it's like."

"Yeah, but you don't have to rub it in."

"Right," one of the cooks joined in, looking across at the oiler disapprovingly. "You should be on a carrier, Lawson. You could tell all the pilots how they might crash."

"Well," said Lawson, reaching for his lighter, "Boo fucking hoo! He gets paid for it, don't he? I mean he doesn't *have* to go down there, does he, Mommy?"

"Point is, Lawson," added the cook, "he'll have the Russians to deal with as well."

"Aw, horseshit," said Lawson, smoke seeming to come from every part of him as the ship went into a particularly violent roll, continuing the search pattern.

"What do you mean, *horseshit*?" protested the yeoman. "Didn't you see the news? The Russkies are on their way, supposedly to help us—that means they're going to try to get it."

"They won't get near it," said Lawson confidently. "For Christ's sake, you guys. Wise up!"

The yeoman wasn't saying much; he didn't like Lawson, but he knew he was no slouch, that there was a cool brain somewhere behind all the smoke and obscenity.

"Look," continued Lawson. "Turn that fucking TV off, will you? Can't stand that frigging ad. I wouldn't drive one of those foreign imports if you—"

"Come on, Lawson," pressed the yeoman. "What about the sub?"

"What?"

"The sub."

"Well, look, you're the man, right? I mean you're the President of the United States of America. The Russians are coming to get your sub. Now—you gonna let 'em?"

"Course not."

"Hell, we know *that*, Lawson. If that's all you're—"

"Hey, Coonshit Brains!" snapped Lawson. "Stop jerking yourself off and listen. You think the Russians are going to keep away from us 'cause we ask 'em? Real nice like?"

"No."

"Or keep away from the sub?"

"No. So what—"

"So," Lawson began, taking another long drag at the cigarette. "We've got a Mexican standoff."

"Shit!" drawled a Southerner, one of the *Boise*'s missile launch crew. "Don't take squat to figure that out."

"No, well, maybe not squat," said Lawson. "But what would you do?"

"Give 'em a Harpoon missile—right up the ass."

"And they'd do squat, I suppose?" gibed Lawson.

"We can outshoot those bastards anytime."

"Might be easier not to start a rumble. You think the President wants a war? You think anyone wants a war?"

"Course not," answered the Southerner.

"Then there'd be one way to stop it, wouldn't there? I mean, just get everybody back on track."

"You mean everyone . . ."

"Yeah." Lawson nodded. "Everybody just goes home."

"Then what happens to the sub, genius?" said a sailor, finishing off the pizza.

"Oh," Lawson replied nonchalantly, "I guess she'd never be found. One hell of a big ocean."

There was a silence in the galley that made all other sounds of the ship suddenly become louder, unbearably loud. The yeoman shot up from his bench, flaring at Lawson. "You're nuts! No way we'd stop looking for her."

"I didn't say that, Yeo."

"Then what the hell did you mean?"

"I mean who's going to risk a war over a lost sub?"

"Yeah, but look," said the Southerner. "The Russkies aren't gonna pass up an opportunity to get it. Eh?"

"No," said Lawson. "I don't think they would."

"Then why the hell would they go home?"

"If the sub had imploded," said Lawson, and he sat back.

"Imploded?"

"Yeah. You heard what Hall said, *imploded*. Flatter'n a skillet—with all that pressure. It'd be no use to anyone then."

"Holy..." began the Southerner, but it was the yeoman who got to the full import of Lawson's thinking aloud. "The President would never do it."

They heard another dull thump. "I don't know about that," went on Lawson unhurriedly, "if it looked like we were going to lose it to them. I mean, if they locked in on her first, beating out Hall. What would you do, Colonel," he said to the Southerner, "if *you* were the President? Let the Russians get it? Intact?"

"Goddamn it, Lawson, you've got a mean streak in you wider'n the Mississippi."

"Uh-uh," Lawson denied without much conviction. "Not mean at all, Colonel. I'm just a realist. And—" now he was poking, or rather jabbing, his cigarette at his Southern shipmate "—when you're the President that's one thing you've got to be, Colonel. A realist."

"Well, if you're right," said the Southerner, "I'm glad I'm not that Hall fella. What was that word you used? Im—?"

"Imploded," said Lawson.

"That really happen?"

"Hell, yes," answered Lawson. "Pressure on those subs is somethin' fierce—thousands of pounds per square inch. Once that tin can around you goes, it's like squashing a bug. All you'd have to do to finish her off is drop a deep depth charge."

"The *New York*'s not a tin can, Lawson. It's top steel. Top of the line," the yeoman protested.

"Don't matter a shit with that pressure. When it starts to go, it starts to go."

"One thing, it'd sure be quick," said the Southerner.

Another grenade exploded.

"Very quick." Unconsciously everyone was waiting for the next grenade.

"You think the President would really *do* that?" asked someone. "I mean order the sub destroyed rather than let the Russians get it?"

"Yeah, I do," said the oiler.

"Don't forget to tape the eleven o'clock news," someone called out to the yeoman, deliberately changing the subject.

As Lawson watched a man put a cassette in the VCR, the Southerner fired one last broadside. "Hell!" he said. "They got enough food and water on those subs to last 'em for months."

"If all systems are working," said Lawson, "and if any of them are still alive. Come on, Colonel, you're a realist, aren't you? Or are you one of those guys who believes everything comes out all right in the end? Eh?"

# 24

THE AIR WAS CLAMMY and fetid, and the temperature in every part of the sub was still rising, from the closed-down engine room and reactor compartment through Sherwood Forest—which took up a full third of the vessel—to the control room, living quarters, radio and radar compartments forward and the torpedo rooms immediately below on the second and third decks. The Mark 48 torpedoes, beaded with perspiration, lay on their smooth-tracked trolleys, looking as if they were somehow alive, waiting and suffering along with the crew. With the reactor and the engine room shut down now, the sense of congestion amid the foul hot air was beginning to oppress everyone—some, like Knead, more than others.

Knead was desperate to get out, to get back to Bangor, to hold Jo again, to say he was sorry, admit he was insanely jeal-

ous, tell her he knew how difficult it was for her with him away
for months at a stretch, but that this time he'd really try—
they'd really try—to keep it together. The thought of her lying
against him, of him awash in her perfume, of her breathing
against him, with him, put him in such an agony of anticipated ecstasy that he felt strong enough just to break out of the
damned sub. And then he'd see her in his mind, a mere glimpse
for no longer than a second or two, all tarted up, waiting for her
lover. The seediness of it all, the condom wrapper in the kitchen
garbage, the cigarette butts. It was the smells that drove him
mad—the sweet fragrance of her hair, the ripe odor of garbage, the acrid stench of the cigarette butts, goddamn frog
cigarettes, Gitanes. The very thought of its being a Frenchman
who was making a cuckold out of him sent a white-hot flash
through his brain. He wanted to mash in the son of a bitch's
face until he was dead.

But in a growing mood of burning rage and hysterical con-
gratulation, he had figured out that it had to be a Navy guy, not
a Frenchie after all—just somebody who'd picked up French
cigarettes on leave, from one of the long Pacific patrols. Tahiti, or New Caledonia, where the natives were trying to kick
out all the frogs. Yeah, a three-month cruise—that would be
where he got the frog cigarettes. Goddamn it, there weren't any
Frenchmen in Bremerton, or near Bangor anyway.

If he ever found out who it was, it would be all slow and nice
like: "Hi! I'm Marty Knead. How ya' doin'? Fine? Terrific!
Hear that, Jo? Your hot cock's fine. Well, I think we'd better
sit down and have a beer." And if it was a frog, "How about
it, frog cock? How about a little all-American beer?" Then
sipping the beer, no rush, just everything cool, and she and her
torpedo shitting themselves. Oh, he'd love the frog to have a
try. He'd blow the frog's whole face off—point-blank. But he
didn't want it that way. No, he'd wait and see, see her get all
pasty-faced and the frog—hell, maybe it wasn't any Pacific
cruise at all, maybe it wasn't a real frog but a Canadian frog
from Quebec. That'd be like Jo. She liked foreign stuff. American wasn't good enough. Menu à la carte. He could feel it now,
beating the frog to a pulp. No Marquis of Queensberry
bullshit—just Marty Knead's rules. Hammer the bastard to the
floor, kick his friggin' face in till it was gooey like raspberry

jam, all the bones sticking out, then one tremendous kick in the balls. Then he'd take Jo and slap the living—

"You okay, buddy?"

Knead was aware of someone looking at him, and he felt tears streaming down his face. "No, I ain't all right."

"Listen—" Chief Ryman had to look at the man's name tag; his failure to remember the name, he knew, was a sign of stress. "Knead, don't you worry. We're gonna get out of this. You hear?"

"Yeah?" Knead answered defiantly, staring at some point beyond the chief. "How do you know?"

"Listen, man. Haven't you heard it?"

"Heard what?" Knead blew his nose, red-faced but recovering his composure.

The chief was looking down at the second hand of his watch. "Listen—one, two, three, four, five, six—" There was a faint pop. He glanced at Knead.

All Knead saw was a figure in a clinging uniform and a face covered in sweat, wearing a smile.

"Grenades, sailor! Every seven seconds. Lord, it's just about tearing Sparks's ears off on the headset. We can't tell distance very well, 'cause we lost the active pinger from the bow. But we can still hear it. Coming closer, man. Go up to control. You can see the audio waves coming in on the passive. Come on, I'll show you."

They were heading forward through Sherwood Forest when Knead asked, "So what's El Supremo going to do about it?"

"What?"

"What I said. Is he going to do anything about it, or just sit on his ass?"

"Keep your voice down," said the chief.

As they approached the control room they heard Wain's voice. "Flares laid out?"

"Flares laid, sir."

"Very well. Prepare to eject."

Everyone was waiting. There was another pop, amplified over the PA. Somewhere high off to starboard they could hear the faint hum of surface props, the sine waves on the oscilloscope barely visible. Knead's head jerked around as his gaze darted from Wain to Sloane, the executive officer, to the sonar operator and back again. The control room was crowded, expectant, men whispering with growing excitement, waiting for the order for the flare to be fired.

What the hell were they waiting for? Knead wondered. The captain was looking across at the civilian, Dyer. The scientist looked frightened, anxious and doubtful all at once, but when Wain caught his eye the civilian averted his gaze guiltily. It was Dyer's doubt that gave Wain pause.

"Everyone shut up!" hissed Wain. "All of you. Sonar?"

"Sir?" The operator looked back at him, eyes bleary from overconcentration.

"Signature?" asked Wain.

"Aye, aye, sir."

Sonar tapped out the computer code for the ASR—acoustic sign recognition—surface vessels. The screen display jerked downward again and again in its rapid search. After five seconds it flashed No Matchup.

"New ship?" the sonar operator suggested. "Not yet fingerprinted."

"Or commercial vessel," the executive officer put in.

"We should have all commercial vessels above five thousand tons," answered Wain. "What do you think, Sonar?"

"My guess is . . . maybe it's a smaller factory ship or one of its trawlers, sir. Signature isn't recognizable if we don't have commercial vessel data under five thousand tons."

Wain looked over at Dyer, who had remained silent. Another pop came through on the oscilloscope, less audible than before. Wherever the unidentified ship was, off to starboard, it had begun moving away from them. It was now or never.

"Doctor?" Wain asked Dyer. "You're one of the outfit that built this gadget." He gestured toward the sonar console. "Any suggestions?"

"Could be a warship after repair in dry dock. That would alter the sound signature—especially if . . . well, if some work had been done on the shaft."

"Sir, if we don't—" began Sloane with urgency.

"Yes, yes, I know," Wain snapped. He grabbed the sound phone, which worked by diaphragm vibration and needed no electricity. Every amp of electrical power was being saved now that the reactor and auxiliary diesel had been shut down. "Eject flares! Release buoy!" Wain ordered.

There was a sigh of relief in the control room that suddenly gave way to applause and loud whoops of joy. Then Lieutenant Forbes, Jr., torpedo and gunnery officer, replied as his finger pushed the buttons, "Fire flare—flare away. Release buoy—buoy released."

Another cheer went up from the *New York* as Wain's imposed reign of silence, having strained everyone aboard, was suddenly ended, drowned by the thud of the flare being ejected, the clank of the buoy being released and the applause. Even Dyer joined in the laughter and joy of general relief.

In the torpedo room the lieutenant pushed the venting button that would blow the water out from the flare tube and close the outside seal, so that there would be no water in the tube should it be needed again. He heard an unfamiliar rattling noise and made a mental note to enter it in the log for the yard birds to check out back in Bangor, then realized that his doubt about getting back to Bangor had begun to disappear the moment he'd pressed the buttons to release the flare and sonobuoy.

ABOVE THE SUBMARINE, through the pitch-black of the bottom ocean layers, then the semidarkness and finally the deep blue of the upper layers, the USS *Boise* proceeded westward. Her new signature was quite different from the old because the work done on her prop in Attu dry dock had significantly changed her sound emission patterns.

The bosun's mate continued to toss grenades every seven seconds. All lookout stations—port, starboard and mast—were double-manned, other men stationed on the stern and three extra lookouts along each side in heavy wet gear as the *Boise*'s bow smashed into, then rose through yet another wave in the sea's endless onslaught, rolling into the valley of an oncoming swell. Her helipad was rocking so badly that there was no hope of getting a chopper off to help in the search until the weather calmed down. But every other instrument from the frigate's sonar to the big Zeiss binoculars mounted on the starboard rotary and the keen eyes of duty and off-duty sailors scoured the white-combed swells for any sign of the lost sub.

On the *Boise*'s bridge Hall and the senior officer of the four-to-eight watch saw nothing on the fathometer but a slightly undulating bottom, the reflections of the active sonar signals causing a marked lack of definition after the surface and sub-surface turbulence did their share of scrambling the signals.

"What is the *Petrel*'s ETA in the search area?" Hall asked Bryce, the officer of the deck.

Bryce busied himself over the chart table and in a few minutes gave his latest estimate. "Six hours—give or take."

"'Give or take'? Can't you figure it out more accurately than that?" It was uncharacteristic of Hall to criticize his host ship's equipment.

"Wish to God we could, but in this weather we're lucky to—"

"What the hell is wrong with this paper?" Hall cut in sharply, pointing to the fathometer. "It's Hardinger, I hope."

"Hardinger?" Bryce frowned. "I'm not sure..."

"For Christ's sake, man. *Hardinger* paper, or have you got some other inferior crap on here? Look at the trace—all gray and fuzzy like a kid with a crayon. How the hell are we going to tell whether anything's down there or not? How wide a track can you get with this?"

"About a quarter mile, give or take—"

"See what I mean? It's always 'give or take' with you jokers. Don't you *know*?"

"Yes, sir," replied Bryce coldly. "A quarter mile, *sir*."

"No damn good. What we need is the side scanner on the *Petrel*. It covers six acres in one swath. At this rate it'll take us months, and if she's gone down into the trench, then it's goodbye."

"This isn't an oceanographic rescue ship, Mr. Hall!" Captain Peters stepped onto the bridge, throwing back the hood of his wet gear and scowling at the oceanographer. "It's a warship."

"Yes, well, your sonar needs upgrading, Captain. Looks like it came out on the *Mayflower*."

Peters reddened again. "It's not meant to scan the bottom of the ocean in detail, Mr. Hall." Hall realized that he must have heard him on an intercom. "Its job is to give us depth and some profile."

"Depth?" Hall shook his head disgustedly. "Might as well put a ball and string down. It'd probably be a damn sight more accurate. But the problem isn't the electronics, it's that you people don't maintain it properly."

Peters was about to retort but held himself in check. Hall had been given overall command of the search, even though Peters had responsibility for the ship. What the arrangement meant in reality—and what had put Peters on slow burn ever since Hall had started being so rude—was that while Hall could order Peters to carry out any maneuver to accommodate the oceanographer's search pattern, if anything went wrong, if anything happened to the USS *Boise*, it wouldn't be Hall standing before a naval court of inquiry. And it wouldn't be Hall's file on which the appropriate notations would be put that could confine Peters to the command of a tender, or less, for the rest of his life. The captain, his rough step defying the sharp pitching of the ship, strode out to the starboard wing of the bridge, glaring furiously down at the enormous ocean. He personally believed the *New York* would never be found, and yet if he didn't control his temper, a submarine that he had never seen could, ironically, be instrumental in damaging his rise to flag rank.

Hall, equally worried about the sub's chances of being found, faced the biting wind on the port wing of the bridge as he took a break, leaning against one of the hard white plastic Beaufort drums containing a roofed and provisioned life raft that would break free of the plastic shell and automatically inflate once it hit the sea. He, too, scanned the ocean, thinking of Mike Bremmer's death, of how long he'd been out here and of how he'd been so busy with the search that he'd barely had time to think of Gloria back in Portland. For a moment he was lost in a daydream of her, seeing her run down the track on the cliff, remembering how whenever he caught her she'd be laughing, her eyes as soft and trusting as a doe's and her skin firm and soft where he wanted it soft, and yielding to him and he to her, the ecstasy...

"Mr. Hall!"

Hall swung around.

"The *Petrel* reports she's picked up our search pattern. On her new vector she could be joining us in about four hours."

Hall nodded. Chopping two hours off his ETA meant that Captain Tate on the *Petrel* had hauled all oceanographic gear aboard, anything that might create drag on the ship or might be damaged as the *Petrel*'s four GM engines wound up to their full speed to help an old friend. With the *Petrel*'s side scanner Hall knew they would stand a better chance, in effect covering the area it would normally take three other ships, working full-time, to profile. In sonar terms the *Petrel* would be the only real equalizer they could mount against the Russians coming in from the west, where the Soviet hydrophone arrays, stretched from Mednyy Island, the southernmost of the two Komandor-skys, might give the Russians a better idea of where the sub went down—unless the volcanic activity that was always going on somewhere in the chain had scattered the sound waves so much that the Russians weren't any better off than the Americans. But Hall didn't believe that. The Russians wouldn't have started all the ballyhoo if they didn't think they stood a good chance.

"How's the magnetometer reading?" Hall asked on returning to the bridge.

"Anomalies to port and starboard," reported Bryce. Hall had a look at the anomalies, gruffly agreeing that the OOD had been right in not calling his attention to them earlier. Neither anomaly was high enough to be a sub—only slightly higher than the average magnetic reading in the area.

Just then the starboard lookout shouted. Bryce quickly joined Peters on the starboard side, while Hall returned to the port wing with binoculars. The lookout was pointing about two to three degrees off the starboard bow, several hundred yards out. Hall swung his binoculars in that general direction.

"I see it!" said the excited port lookout.

Through his binoculars Hall could see nothing but the black hair gradations running down the center and across the circle like a serrated, inverted T. Then he saw it, too. Huge air bubbles erupting over hundreds of yards of wildly undulating ocean.

## 25

FIFTY-ONE MILES NORTHEAST, off the southern extremity of Mednyy Island, the Russian battle group—including several frigates, the cruiser *Leningrad* and the *Karpaty II*, a Nepa class submarine rescue ship of five thousand tons, four hundred feet by fifty feet wide—was running at full speed.

It was exactly one hour and twenty-three minutes after they left port when Russian AGIs—intelligence gathering trawlers—as a result of their intensive analysis of the radio traffic between the U.S. naval warship *Boise* and the U.S. oceanographic ship *Petrel*, reported to the naval commander of the battle group, Admiral Litov, and the overall commander of the operation, General Kornon, that the American oceanographer, Hall, was apparently still alive and operating from the *Boise*—that, in fact, the parachutist shot down off the *Boise* earlier had been someone else.

Kornon took his raging disappointment at not having killed Hall after all onto the *Karpaty*'s starboard bridge wing to let the ice-cold wind at once calm him and brace him with new resolution. For a moment he closed his eyes. Would he never be rid of this American? Yes, he would, he decided, and not from mere wish fulfillment—he was much too realistic a man for that, especially after Ulan Ude. He knew that Hall was finished because the odds of the battle group—especially the deep-sea rescue vehicle aboard its mother ship, *Karpaty II*—gave the Soviets the overwhelming advantage.

With the assist of the eastbound Japanese Current and the howling wind fresh out of Asia, the submarine rescue ship's speed had increased from twenty to twenty-three knots, her high, acute-angle stern in fact a heavy lift platform capable of a six-hundred-ton pull, three of her lifting points situated amidships and one on the bow. On her stern was lashed the Russian DSRV. She also carried an emergency ward with doctors and nurses. Normally only ten or so of her two-hundred-and-seventy complement were women, but this trip everything was different. There were at least thirty members of the press aboard, including Elga, whom Lebdev had very easily managed to gain a place for.

Soon after General Kornon left the bridge and went to the VIP suite, Lebdev had joined him there. He pointed out to the general that the Americans' certain failure to rescue their submarine—that is, Hall's failure—would be guaranteed to appear on every major network, in the East and in the West. He would arrange for Elga to interview the defeated oceanographer.

"That would be wonderful, Comrade," Kornon answered. "But what makes you think the American will agree to be interviewed?"

"Elga," replied Lebdev. He ushered in the East German blonde as if she were foreign royalty. "Hall likes women, Comrade General. Is that correct?"

Kornon nodded his head. His old sense of authority had returned in full flood now that he'd been given another chance—not merely to be reinstated but to clinch one of the greatest Soviet naval triumphs of all time. And when he succeeded, Elga could interview *him*. He saw no good reason why she should not be his official press aide during the ecstatic welcome he would no doubt receive at the forthcoming annual meeting at supreme headquarters of the Warsaw Pact.

In addition to Elga, the submarine rescue ship media contingent included members of the French, Italian and British press, all brought along to witness the magnanimity of the Soviet people who, "like peace-loving peoples everywhere, sought a continued lessening of tensions among the superpowers."

Lebdev, though Tass representative, had been forced to give up what would have been his normal stateroom to a BBC television crew. But he didn't mind not sharing the top-deck cabins with Elga and the members of the foreign press, even though the pounding of the Nepa's engines made it difficult for him to sleep. He was tickled by the irony of the situation. While the foreign journalists were enjoying their vodka and plum brandy above, waiting hopefully to see if the sub could first be found and then be rescued, unknown to them above in the cluster of the *Karpaty II*'s aerials and masts and deep below her keel where they could not see, the submarine rescue vessel was also serving as a *sudno svyazy*—a quaint phrase for electronic spy ship.

According to Kornon's carefully laid-out plan, the *Karpaty II* was a mile ahead of the two Krvak class SS-N-14 missile frigates and a six-thousand-ton Kresta class cruiser, twice as large as the submarine salvage ship and three times as large as the two guided-missile frigates.

The Russians' open "commitment," with their rescue ship going to aid the Americans, was being beamed on television the world over, from Azerbaijan to West Berlin, from London to Sydney to Los Angeles and New York. The ships the Russians were sending to aid in the rescue numbered no less than the American contingent, and—what was more important—their lead ship, the sub rescue vessel *Karpaty II*, was noticeably *not* a warship, unlike the Americans' *Boise*.

The submarine rescue attempt was already a Russian propaganda triumph.

"It's a plume," said Hall, lowering the binoculars, not even trying to hide his disappointment.

"What's that, sir?" asked the lookout.

Hall looked across the bridge at the starboard wing and saw that Bryce had changed the course of the ship to bring it closer to the bubbling surface.

"It's what oceanographers call an upwelling," Hall explained. "A lot of water travels through thousands of miles of aquifers or channels in the rock below the seabed. There's a lot of volcanic and thermal activity down in those regions. On the way the water often gets superheated and, when it comes out, it shoots up like a jet from the bottom, a plume that bubbles on the surface. Hundreds of years ago sailors used to think it was sea monsters."

Hall crossed to the starboard wing and explained the phenomenon to Peters, who said he had figured that's what it was as soon as he saw it. After all, upwelling occurred in all the oceans; one had to expect it especially in and around the Aleutians.

"Just thought you might not realize what it was," said Hall coldly, almost condescendingly, before he started back to the port side.

ABOARD THE DISABLED SUBMARINE, Captain Wain suspected something else was wrong. "Torpedo room," he said.

"Yes, sir."

"When did you last check that sonobuoy?"

"The day we left Bangor, sir. Signal was fine."

"Well, the ship that was approaching us is now moving away. Better fire another flare."

"Yes, sir."

In the torpedo room Lieutenant Forbes took another of the new RAND-2 smoke flares and began to spin open the flare tube. He stopped the instant a jet of water shot out from the seal and, dropping the flare quickly, he spun the wheel clockwise to close it. By then, three other men in the room were racing to help him—one slipping on the water-slicked decking, sending the flare skittering across the floor. The two other men had managed to help the lieutenant tighten the wheel, but damage to the O-ring seal had already occurred.

The tube was still leaking saltwater as the seaman apprentice who had fallen was scrambling up from the floor. Again he slipped, his heel ramming the flare hard against the bulkhead, scoring part of the flare's exposed phosphorus strip. Instantly the phosphorus burst into flame, the flare spinning madly on the deck. In seconds the whole torpedo room was filled with brilliant vermilion-colored smoke. The seaman apprentice took only an instant to recover, then went straight to the nearest water extinguisher, only to have it snatched from his hands by the lieutenant. Another torpedo man, coughing violently, pulled out the carbon dioxide extinguisher and aimed its funnel. The next moment a cone of white foam shot forth, smothering the flare.

"Clamps!" yelled the lieutenant, and in two seconds the flare tube's seal was finally secured, its fast dribble now reduced to a mere drip.

The torpedo lieutenant turned on the hapless seaman apprentice. "You goddamn idiot! You put carbon dioxide on a flare, not water. The goddamn flare is designed to keep burning in the sea. That's why it's made of goddamn phosphorus. Got it?"

"Yes, sir, Lieutenant."

By then Sloane, the executive officer, had reached the torpedo room. His eyes watering from the smoke, he couldn't see the clamps on the flare tube, but could hear the slow leak that meant that the tube's outside seal must have failed to reseal properly after the firing.

"Sorry, sir. Damn tube sprang a leak. Pressure's too great, I guess, for the outer seal."

"It shouldn't be."

"I know, sir, but the mother's leaking all right." He pointed to the dripping, the drops giving off a sound disproportionate to their volume as they plopped loudly into a bucket. "The clamps should hold, though, sir. On our test dives we once had—"

"Yes, all right," Sloane responded impatiently. "It's this damn smoke I'm concerned about. We'll try to suck it out with the portables and vent it through one of the tanks. Trouble is, the damage is done. It's already used up more of our oxygen."

The torpedo officer refrained from mentioning how the young seaman had panicked, almost using the water extinguisher, which would have kept the flare burning, consuming more of the vital oxygen.

"God, it stinks in here. Like rotten eggs," commented the executive.

"Wasn't me, sir," said the torpedo man's mate, trying to infuse a little humor into the situation, but the few laughs he got were forced. Everyone knew that with less oxygen in the boat, now that the scrubbers were gone, their chances of survival were worse.

"All right," ordered Sloane. "Get cleaned up in here." As he left he noticed that everyone in the torpedo room seemed to be suffering more from the heat. He didn't understand it. With the reactor and diesel auxiliary completely shut down the temperature should be dropping. It wasn't.

"Enter this in the log," Sloane told the torpedo officer.

"Yes, I will, sir."

"Very well."

As he obeyed the order, entering in the log the flare mishap and the fact that the temperature had now climbed to eighty-nine degrees Fahrenheit, the torpedo officer wondered what use the entry would be after they were dead.

Back in the CCC, Wain and Sloane tried to figure out what had happened with the flare tube.

"You sure the tube opened?" pressed Wain.

"Yes, sir. I trust Forbes. If he says it fired, it fired."

"Could have been a leak in the compressed air."

"No, sir. Forbes had maximum pressure in the tube."

"Captain?" It was the sonar operator.

"Yes?"

"Sir, I'm getting a ping. Real close, sir."

"How close?"

"Seems to be right nearby, sir."

"A surface vessel or—"

"I'd say a sub, sir. The pitch is very bad. When we hit the bottom, it shook the hell out of this gear, sir. The hydrophone line must be damaged. Whatever—the signals are scrambled."

"If it's a sub, it's a Russian," said Wain. "Our own boys would be transmitting contact noise by now. Damn it! We should never have fired that flare and buoy. That was a Russian ship above us. That's why they didn't turn around. Once they saw the flare—or the buoy—they let their sub know and now he's onto us." He turned to Sloane. "Battle stations!"

There was no sound. Aboard the most sophisticated vessel the world had ever made, the order to man battle stations was communicated by the most ancient method of all—man to man, whisper to whisper, guarding against any sound that might possibly be picked up by the passive, that is, the "listening" sonar of the enemy.

"If the bastards are going to take us out, we might as well make 'em pay," said Wain. He knew the *New York* was a sitting duck, but at least a Mark 48 torpedo might get the Russian. Of course, he couldn't fire at such close quarters; the concussion would cave in the *New York* as well as the enemy. Nevertheless he knew he must be ready. "We'll use tubes one and four."

"One and four, sir."

A minute later came the quiet confirmation over the sound telephone. "One and four armed and ready, sir."

"Sir?" said the sonar operator.

"Yes."

"Sir, there's no turbulence coming in on our passive. Just soft noise. It's weird but . . ."

"But what?" Wain asked sharply.

"Sir, I don't think the incoming on our passive is noise from the Russian sub. Not without turbulence."

"What the hell is it, then?"

"Sir . . . I think it's our pinger coming from our buoy."

"Are you sure?"

"No, sir, but it's the right frequency."

Wain was gripping the back of the sonar man's seat so hard that its cushioning was flattened. Before he could say anything, there was an angry shout.

"You idiot! You let that ship go right by us!" It was Knead—racing into the redded-out control room, his face contorted in rage and despair. "You heard the goddamn grenades and you let them go right past us. You never released the flare, you bastard!"

"Get yourself under control!" Wain snapped.

"You bastard," Knead repeated. "You conned us." He turned to the others in the control room, even as Sloane was moving quickly toward him. "Don't you realize what's happened? There was *nothing* in that tube. Forbes didn't release a damn thing."

Sloane grabbed him, but Knead was still shouting, struggling, yelling at the operators on watch in the control room's semicircle of consoles. "Don't you see, you stupid bastards! He won't call for help until he hears 'The Star-Spangled Banner' coming through the hull." Knead threw himself at the green button of the diving alarm.

Sloane pinned Knead against the rail of the attack island, but in his rage the seaman had the strength of two. Bursting free of Sloane's grip, he sent him reeling back. Striking his head hard on the rail, Sloane was stunned for a moment. Knead was only inches from the button when Wain and the bow planesman charged into him. They managed to haul him away, but he lashed out, kicking Wain in the groin. The captain crumpled. The other seaman tried desperately to overpower Knead, but the madman outreached him. Quickly he flicked up the protective cover and hit the button, sending the strangled cry of the Klaxon reverberating throughout the *New York*, sending exhausted men running everywhere on the sub to a state of what they believed was final alert. As if in a daze, some stumbled into the torpedo room, in the event that the *New York*'s attack would be launched from there.

# 26

TWO MILES TO STARBOARD, the USS *Boise* kept steaming on. The sound waves emitted by the *New York*'s Klaxon were so mixed by the subsurface and surface turbulence of the heavy seas that they weren't picked up as anything more than a non-specific fuzzy trace at the outer limits of the fathometer's narrow cone.

Six miles ahead, however, where the sound shot through the deep layers where salinity remained the same and surface turbulence didn't reach, the *Amur*, a hunter/killer sub, picked up the trace of the Klaxon on its low-frequency array. The signal was too faint to be identifiable, but its frequency and oscilloscope trace were such that it couldn't be a school of fish and at such depth was certainly not a whale. Knowing they were in the general search area defined by the Mednyy station and that not far away was the *Boise*—which they had already matched up on the computer—they assumed that the sound might well have come from the downed American sub.

"Their surface ships can't hear her," said the *Amur*'s captain.

"Not surprising in this weather," said the first officer, a short, stout man from Soviet Georgia. "There's a storm above us. It will be difficult for any surface ship to—"

"Yes, yes, I know," answered the Russian captain impatiently. He knew very well what to do; as captain of the *real* lead ship of the Russian battle group, which was ostensibly being led by the *Karpaty II*, the Russian submarine captain already had his orders from Kornon on what action to take if he suspected they might have found the American submarine. There was no time to lose.

"Vent auxiliary fuel tank," he ordered. "Slowly, remember."

"Auxiliary fuel tank venting, sir" came the steady reply.

"Altering course. Silent running. Steer three oh two."

"Three oh two, sir" came the confirmation from rudder control.

TWO MILES DEAD AHEAD of the *Boise*, the heaving surface of the sea bubbled as if some monster were ascending from the depths. But the only thing that appeared was a wide, ugly brown pool of oil several hundred yards in diameter and still spreading like a filthy windblown sheet over the gray-green swells, turning virgin-white foam to a dirty-dish brown.

Off-duty seamen crowded the *Boise*'s rails. "Nuclear subs don't carry oil, do they?" asked a steward, shivering as he stepped on deck without wet-weather gear, afraid he'd miss something. "They run on nuclear power, right?"

"You donkey!" retorted a machinist's mate. "What the hell do you think they run their auxiliaries on? Something goes wrong with their reactor, they have to run a lot of stuff off a diesel engine. That means diesel oil."

The steward shivered more violently from the cold. "So it means they've had it, right?"

"Nah," answered the machinist's mate. "Probably a signal to let us know where they are."

"Oh, yeah?"

"Yeah. They blow fifty gallons or so. More maybe. Easy to spot."

"Or maybe it means they've bought it," said another voice from the cluster of figures on the port side. "Fell below crush depth and whammo!"

"You're a cheerful bastard!" said the machinist's mate.

"Just facing facts, man. Just facing facts."

"Well it ain't over till it's over."

"Yeah, well, I think she's down. For good."

The men started making bets on whether or not the oil came from the *New York*—and if it did, whether anyone was left alive.

The *Boise* slowed, ready to turn, as Hall leaned over the forward port side, attaching the eighteen-inch Neilsen stainless-steel water-sampling bottle to the port winch's one-quarter-inch cable; both spring-loaded ends or lids of the long four-inch-diameter bottle were open, its thermometer encased in a protective sheath down its side. When Hall released the grenade-size brass messenger he was holding, it would slide down the wire, hitting the top easy-release clamp and springing the lids shut. The bottle would fall away from the wire in a back somersault, its top becoming its bottom, attached by one clamp instead of two. The thermometer, having reversed itself in the somersault, would break the mercury column, so registering the water temperature at the precise moment the messenger struck the wire.

"What are you using that for?" inquired a sailor nearby.

"To have a look at that oil," Hall said.

"What for—to see what kind it is? I can tell you that—it's diesel. Tell by the smell."

"You sure?" said Hall, though he knew the man was right. The *Boise* came to a stop in the slick, all its intakes shut down so as not to gum up the pumps. The diesel oil's stench was overpowering, swept over the *Boise* by the steady west wind.

Hall clipped on a ten-pound anchor link weight and waved his hand clockwise for the winchman to take up the slack, then using a boat hook, he pushed the cable away from the ship. Aboard the *Petrel* Captain Tate would have had the ship maneuvered so that the wire's incline to the ship was a near-perfect fifteen to twenty degrees, wide enough to clear the side yet close enough for the oceanographer to work easily forward without having to lean out dangerously in the heavy seas, straining the safety harness. But the Navy's job was warfare, and though they were required to take oceanographic measurements now and then, they were unused to accommodating an oceanographer on deck.

Hall complained to the OOD through the intercom about the angle between the ship and the wire. Captain Peters answered. Hall could see him up on the bridge, a blur behind the *Boise*'s water-smeared bluish-gray bridge glass, all but pushing the OOD to one side as he responded to the oceanographer.

"You wanted to get a water sample quickly, Mr. Hall."

"That's correct," answered Hall in a formal tone he hardly ever used on deck. His right hand pointed down at the sea; the winchman eased off the brake, letting the bottle go down in low gear. "But this angle is too acute, too close to the ship," he went on, his voice through the open deck intercom rising and falling with the wind. "She should swing her ass sternway, so I don't have to use this boat hook to push the wire off."

He heard Peters start to answer but simply kept on. "I sure as hell don't want the wire scraping the side when you bring it in. That could break the thermometer, and we'd lose the reading." Then, turning his back on the bridge and watching the wire slide down toward the stern, like a fishing line, Hall could hear the muffled outrage of Peters scattered by the wind.

Hall held up his hand and the winch stopped with a thump. "Christ, sonny," Hall shouted into the intercom at the winchman. "Don't you come to a stop like that on the stern line if I go down in the *Serena*. The shock would jolt the hell out of the electronics, let alone me. Got it?"

"Yes, sir."

"I'd like to jolt him," came an anonymous voice on the intercom.

"Keep quiet, sailor!" The reprimand was Bryce's, the officer of the deck this watch. Captain Peters didn't know whether Bryce sympathized with the man who'd made the remark, but as OOD Bryce had acted properly. It was one thing for the captain to vent his spleen—that was his privilege. It wasn't in regulations, but it came with carrying the whole responsibility for the ship's discipline and safety on his shoulders.

Nevertheless, while he agreed with the sailor in being piqued by Hall's rudeness, Peters resolved himself to be more restrained. Yet as soon as he had made the resolution not to challenge Hall so much, Peters experienced a moment of self-disgust, for he knew that he had determined to control his intense dislike for Hall not so much to set an example of restraint for his crew but rather because he was afraid of what Hall's report to the Chief of Naval Operations could do to his career. It was enough to make him angry all over again. What use was a man if he merely reacted in fear? He'd seen it become a habit with ambitious men, who overnight had become so career-oriented that they had become what the Australians in Nam called "gutless wonders," and "don't-rock-the-boaters."

Well, hell, Peters told himself, everyone occasionally had to temper their conduct for the sake of their careers. He just didn't want it to become a habit, to run permanently scared of who might say what to who—or, as they'd taught him in Annapolis, to whom. Dammit, who did Hall think he was, anyway? Hadn't the man flashed cock or something on a beach? The only reason he was here was that he was supposed to be a hotshot oceanographic salvager. At least so Bryce claimed—something about being able to read underwater photos like X-rays. Well, a man could take only so much from hotshots or anyone else.

HALL CLIPPED the eight-ounce brass messenger to the wire and, lifting it high, threw it down the one-quarter-inch wire. A white puff of dried salt rose from the wire as the messenger sped down its length and splashed into the sea. Two seconds later the slight vibration on his forefingers, as they felt the wire with a deft touch born of years of experience, told Hall that the bottle had tripped.

It was a useful skill, especially for the times when he sent the water bottles down thousands of feet where sea slugs and other jellylike creatures sometimes wrapped themselves around the wire like gelatinous scarves, stopping a messenger as effectively as a wet sponge. So after waiting hours for the cable to reach the bottom of a twenty-thousand-foot trench, and allowing time for proper flushing of the bottles and the first bottle to trip and the temperature to set, he would start the long haul up, stopping the wire to take off a bottle every five hundred feet—forty-one bottles in all, including the one at the surface—only to find that only the first half dozen had tripped because of the blockage caused by a lone sea slug or jellyfish that by then had disintegrated, having exploded as it passed from the enormous pressures in the deep chill of the ocean to the higher surface layers of decreasing pressure.

Hall held up his hand again, and the winch came slowly to a stop, so slowly that the lone clamp by which the bottle was attached to the wire almost passed through the block on the davit.

"Hold it!" Hall yelled, muttering ancient Indian obscenities he'd picked up from Gloria in her redder-faced moments.
"Not that slow!"

The sailor lowered the bottle to what he thought was rail
level, but the next swell put it two feet below Hall's farthest
reach. It was easily done—Hall had done it himself—an almost impossible calculation to get perfectly right in a heavy sea,
but every delay could mean lives lost. Somewhere below,
hopefully below the rapidly spreading oil slick, a hundred and
fifty men were waiting—or were they dead? Ever since the days
of the first submarine, the ugly telltale blotch of an oil slick had
signaled disaster below.

Bending down to reach the clamp as the bottle jerked nervously upward, streaming frigid water, Hall overbalanced in a
particularly heavy roll. The clang of the thermometer casing
striking his forehead could be heard through the intercom, and
the port lookout informed the bridge with a straight face what
had happened.

"Oh, Jesus, that's awful!" said Peters in a tone that conveyed the exact opposite.

The eight-to-twelve watch erupted in laughter as the old man
exited the port wing for a better view. They stifled their
amusement when he returned a moment later and, with forced
solemnity, told the exec, who didn't seem amused, to ask Mr.
Hall if he required medical assistance.

"No," Hall replied, his voice surprisingly loud given his angle to the intercom by the base of the davit. "Tell you what I
could do with, though."

"What's that?" asked Peters.

"A bit of seamanship, from the bridge on down. The more
screwups there are, the more time lost. Unless you don't give a
shit about your buddies down there."

"We do give a shit, Mr. Hall, as you so eloquently put it"
came Peters's sharp reply, made with as much control as he
could muster.

"Wouldn't know it, Captain. I'm glad we're not doing a long
cast."

Peters was caught off balance, not sure what the oceanographer meant. The delay cost him a chance to retort. Peters
could see the insolent civilian, legs apart "like some goddamn

pirate," he said to Bryce, defying the pitch and roll of the ship now that they were under way and out of the slick. Hall was heading toward the closed copter hangar, holding the water bottle aloft out of harm's way, "as if it's gold," commented Peters sarcastically.

Peters didn't know how right he was.

Once in the hangar Hall called for the bridge to send down the electronics warfare officer, then, clipping the bottle to its wooden cradle, which was lashed firmly to the bulkhead, he opened its tiny faucet. A dirty brownish-green stream, in the words of the EWO, "like a cow peeing on a flat rock," arced out of the bottle. Now that any microscopic traces of stainless steel that might have collected at the bottom of the Neilsen sampling bottle were flushed out by the initial jet, Hall quickly held a fifty-milliliter-necked flask in the stream. After noting the temperature of the fluid, he drew off another sample for the chemical spectrometer. Then he reached for the microspectrometer, the size of a transistor radio, fitting snugly on the bottom left of the eight-foot-diameter Perspex sphere or bubble that was the front of the eight-hundred-pound *Serena I*.

A crowd of interested off-duty crewmen gathered to watch. It was the same no matter what ship you were on, Hall thought. Was it boredom with routine, like city office workers on their lunch hour watching bulldozers, or was it a genuine fascination with the sea from which we all came, where, as he had told Gloria, the rain peppering the sea this instant was the same water that had fallen a million years ago, formed ice fields, melted and run back to the saline seas wherein the salinity was remarkably similar to the mother's saline sea in which we were carried to birth? Probably, he thought, the men were bored.

Some of the crew members were more interested in looking at the submersible. Its supporting L-shaped chair frame was made of lightweight carbon-resin-wafered supports, and its two elbowed arms, which extended from either side of the frame, were now at rest in a high-lock position, giving the whole vehicle the appearance of a giant, round, transparent crab in a frame, back against the bulkhead, ready not only to defend itself but to fight to the death.

"Hey," said one of the twenty or so men gathered around. "I know what he's looking for in that oil."

"So tell us, Einstein."

"Garbage . . . He's trying to see if there's any of our garbage floating about in it."

"There's nothing floating in it," said another. "Not that I saw, anyway."

"I don't mean stuff you can see with the naked eye," said the first man. "Coke cans, food, can labels, that kind of stuff. I mean, you know, pieces of food, tiny bits our eye can't pick up. Right?" the sailor asked Hall.

"No," said Hall, causing the other sailors to laugh at their self-appointed expert as Hall dropped a magnetic stirrer, the size and shape of a drug capsule, encased in a gray rubber noncontamination sheath, the magnet spinning and stirring the dirty brownish oil-seawater mixture uniformly for a good representative sample ready to pass through the spectrometer.

"What the hell *are* you looking for then?" asked a sailor.

Hall took a second to answer, checking the settings on the spectrometer. "A fingerprint," he said, adjusting the speed of the stirrer.

"He's jerkin' you off," said another sailor, but no one answered. They had moved off to the rear of the copter hangar, where through the scud of low, dark clouds several miles westward they saw the horizon segmented by the gray slivers that were the Soviet battle group.

Silence continued for a few moments until a bosun's mate announced confidently, "Well, our boys'll be here pretty soon. Heard the OOD say there's a hospital ship on the way from Pearl."

"Need more than a nurse to keep those mothers away."

"Don't sweat it," added the bosun's mate. "In twenty-four hours we can have our mother ships here and match 'em ship for ship."

"Yeah? What about *that* lot, mate?" It was the same sailor who'd been asking Hall what he was looking for. The fierce wind billowing his sleeve, the sailor's arm was moving through a wide arc from southwest to east, pointing to another group of ships far in the distance. He stopped counting at twenty-five. "Russian trawlers," he said.

"Not all of 'em," put in another crewman. "Lot of other foreign boats in that lot."

"Yeah, but how come they're all up here all of a sudden?"

"This is one of the richest fishing areas in the world, that's why. They probably picked up some big schools on their sonar."

"Maybe," responded another sailor. "But don't you think it's funny how they just happen to be here at the same time as the Russkies are showin' up?"

"Ah," said the bosun's mate, increasingly feeling the responsibility of his rank to calm the crew. "Most of 'em are Japanese, Korean..."

"Yeah, *North* Korean," someone piped up.

"Hell," said another. "They're no problem. You can recognize them straight off. It's the others—South Korean and Japanese—that bother me."

"Why?"

"Well, beanhead, they mightn't *be* South Korean or Japanese, right? They might be AGIs sticking it to us, listening in on every goddamn signal we put out. Look at 'em." The Russian ships formed the western horizon, while the trawler fleets, a big mother ship here and there, curved south in a semicircle, in all spreading over fifty miles from west to east.

"Goddamn shape is like the Commie sickle. We're surrounded."

"Don't sweat it," said the bosun's mate. "We've got the Mark 13 hammer, comrades. Couple of those babies'll sort things out real quick."

"Is that a fact?" chimed in another sailor, staring at the long gray line of the Russian battle group. "What the hell you think *they*'ve got aboard, slingshots?"

As the bosun's mate caught himself from being thrown hard into the port rail of the copter landing pad, he saw Frank Hall also fighting the roll. The oceanographer took hold of the *Serena*'s starboard arm, his gaze still fixed to the readout of the gas chromatography/mass spectrometer unit, its digital readout changing by the millisecond. He had a look of surprised relief on his face.

"So, what's the story?" the bosun's mate asked him.

Hall was so preoccupied that he heard the voice but not the question. He couldn't believe what he was seeing as the sample from the flask vaporized and, excited by an injection of helium, separated into its constituent molecules. In particular, he was watching the count-out of the alkanes, the long hydrocarbons and also the pristane molecule count.

"It's *not* Russian," he said. "I thought it might be a Russian trap."

"A Russian sub?" asked the bosun's mate. Some of the crew who heard him crowded back into the hangar now, jockeying for position to get a look at the digital readout's flickering green stream of luminescent lights.

"Yes," answered Hall, checking the sample again. "Of course, if a Russian sub was down there and wanted to make us believe the oil was coming from the *New York*, they wouldn't have simply blown oil—that's the oldest trick in the book. If they were going to do that they would've chucked in a lot of garbage as well, to make it look more like a wreck. That's what I would have done."

"Yeah, funny thing there's no garbage," said the steward. "You should see the garbage we have to—"

"So what's the story?" pressed the bosun, ignoring the other sailors. "You...Christ, you mean you think it's the *New York*?"

Hall wasn't sure. "All I know is that this isn't Soviet fuel oil. Composition's not right."

"Your machine okay?"

"It's fine," answered Hall. "First thing I checked. No, that oil out there is American. Alaskan North Slope, to be exact."

"You can be that accurate?" asked the bosun.

"Sure. You can't see it with the naked eye, but each bead of oil has its own molecular structure. Put it under a big enough microscope, which is what the spectrometer is in a way, and you'll see the difference. Right here—" he motioned to the sample passing through the chromophotographic-gas analyzer "—we're not looking at Russian crude from the Baku or any other Russian field. This is Alaskan North Slope." He tapped the analyzer. "It's how we trace oil pollution spills, or when some bozo decides to pump out his bilges in coastal water. It's like an oil X-ray. Every field's different."

"Shoot!" said a missile technician. "You keep all that stuff in your head?"

Hall reached over from the analyzer and picked up a white plastic-covered eight-and-a-half-by-eleven-inch book more than two inches thick. "Hell, no," he said. "I have trouble remembering my zip code. It's all in here—an international what's where of the oil industry. Still—" Hall paused as an unusually strong swell shoved the *Boise* hard aport. He grabbed the *Serena*'s mechanical arm to steady himself.

As he did so, Bryce entered the hangar, the crew making way. "Hear you've found something," the executive officer said.

Hall was deep in thought, his body moving with the roll and pitch of the ship as if under automatic pilot. "Of course a Russian sub wouldn't have American waste—different labels . . ."

"Yeah," said the bosun's mate, caught up in the dilemma facing Frank. "But then why would they have American oil?"

"To fool us," said Hall.

"A lot of trouble to go to."

"The *New York*'s worth some trouble," said Hall with measured understatement. "It'd be a gold mine for the Soviets."

"If they get it."

Hall shut off the counter. "Anything on your sonar?" he asked Bryce.

"Negative. Humps here and there—fuzzy with all this surface churn."

"No response to the grenades?"

Bryce shook his head. "Not a thing."

"Well, there's something down there."

"Then why ain't they answerin'?" asked one of the sailors.

There was silence among the men then. All they could hear was the creaking of the nylon rope holding the *Serena* captive as if she were a live thing straining out of her element, longing to be free. For a moment Hall felt as one with the faithful machine he'd piloted so many times in various deeps all over the world—but never in such a wild place as this.

By then the sailor who had asked why there was no answer from the *New York* if she was somewhere below them had found the terrible answer in the silence of the men around him, the realization of what it could mean now that Hall had discovered it was an American oil spill. Flustered, the sailor went on with brio. "Ah, well, uh, how do we know the oil's from a sub? I mean—"

"Because," said Hall quietly, "if it had been from another vessel it would have dispersed by now. Which means it must have come to the surface less than an hour ago, and we know there hasn't been any surface ship near here in the past several hours except us."

But the sailor wouldn't let go. "Yeah, but I heard that sometimes oil leaks up from the sea bottom—like those freshwater springs." The *Serena* was straining against the ropes even more loudly now above the low moaning of the wind as the *Boise* began turning to commence a new zigzag in the search pattern.

"What's he talkin' about?" interjected another sailor, impatient with his fellow crewman's persistence. "Springs?"

"He's right," said Hall. "Oil does bubble up like that sometimes, especially in a volcanic area like the Aleutians. Fissures—cracks—appear all the time. All kinds of stuff bubbles up but ..." He turned to the sailor. "The trouble here is that there's no more coming up. Besides, the analyzer's told us it's Alaskan North Slope, not western Pacific. The North Slope's a hell of a long way from here."

A sailor handed Hall back the big plastic-covered book, and he put it back where it belonged, then continued. "Anyway, this is *refined* oil, not crude. I've never seen a hot spring of refined oil." He tried to smile to lessen the shock of the implication, but the smile was overcome by his own apprehension that the *New York* lay dead, the life squeezed out of her below crush depth somewhere near the Trench, or worse, deep in it. In which case they might never find her.

But he knew, and they all knew, that he had to try, and that he couldn't afford even the four-hour wait for the *Petrel* to arrive with her state-of-the-art side scan deep sonar that, unlike the *Boise*'s, could be hydraulically lowered well beneath surface turbulence.

He began unlashing the *Serena*, informing Bryce, "Tell Peters to bring her into the wind and keep her there." He thought of the line of Russian warships approaching and added, "If he can. And I want your best man on the after winch. And for Christ's sake, whoever's on that winch, when I say stop I don't want him jerking the fuck out of the wire. Ease her off in low gear. If I want a dead stop, I'll say so. Then I'll release the submersible and go down solo."

The sailors began to break up, a sudden sour mood in the air.

"Why do you *do* that?" asked Bryce, still grateful for Hall's covering for him about the botched-up photos but angered by the contemptuous tone the oceanographer had used to the sailors and the captain. Bryce knew, and he thought the oceanographer should know, that everyone on the *Boise* would do everything in their power to help him find their fellow sailors—dead or alive—on the stricken submarine.

"Why do I do what?" snapped Hall.

"Insult people like that. I heard you were an all-right guy. Lieutenant Bremmer told—"

"Bremmer's dead."

"So?" asked Bryce, perplexed.

"So doesn't that tell you something?" Hall shot back, checking the oxygen bottle directly behind the *Serena*'s lone pilot seat and making sure that the carbon dioxide scrubber was topped with lithium hydroxide crystals.

"Tell me what?" Bryce returned. His tone had an edge to it now.

"That he wasn't smart enough to stay alive."

"Jesus, that's a mean thing to say."

"It's a mean sea out there, Lieutenant. Look, buddy, I've got a good-looking girl waiting for me back in Oregon. I intend getting back, that's all. So I want your boys on their toes. All right?"

"Yes, *sir*," Bryce replied, saluting to rub it in. As he clanged shut the hatch to the inside of the ship's main corridor, Bryce saw the bosun's mate light up and take in a deep drag.

"You know what, sir?" the sailor said.

"What?" snapped Bryce.

"Some of the crew would like to throw that moody son of a bitch overboard."

Bryce told the bosun's mate to put out his cigarette and to haul ass, or he'd be on captain's report and lose his pension.

Then, passing the crew's mess, he heard someone say loudly, "Reckon he's got a screw loose."

Bryce stopped as if to go in, then moved on, his back bent. He had to walk up a steep incline as the *Boise* pitched steeply, yawning hard astarboard. An avalanche of crockery and obscenities reverberated throughout the ship.

In the hangar Hall patted the *Serena* as a cowhand might his favorite workhorse. "Hate to be rude, old girl. But you have to think well ahead. Right? Right."

ON THE BRIDGE Peters was receiving more bad news. Four competing television crews—three from the U.S. networks and one from the Canadian Broadcasting Corporation—and other "media representatives" were en route, with the approval of the Chief of Naval Operations, aboard four deep-sea trawlers out of Attu. Their ETA in the area was ten to twelve hours, only five hours after the *Petrel* was due. On top of that, Washington was advising that the Russians were also bringing a large European media contingent.

"That's all we need," Peters told Bryce. "The damn press crawling all over the ship. Get bosun to rig Classified Area—No Entry signs. We don't want any snooping around, especially near Missile Fire Control."

Peters picked up the PA mike. Walking toward the port wing, the spiral cord uncoiling until it was almost taut, he watched a deck party of six men hauling on the pulley guys, trying to work in unison while fighting to keep their footing, moving Hall's submersible on its multiwheeled rubber trolley toward the *Boise*'s stern. Peters waited to make his announcement until the trolley was fully braked and beneath the *Boise*'s big A-frame and until the five-eighths-inch cable from the winch drum on the port side of the copter hangar had been passed up and threaded through the A-frame's block down, six feet below, where its U-bolt swivel connected it to the *Serena*'s swivel ring bolt. The submersible, its eight-foot-diameter high-pressure acrylic bubble resting on its two ski-like legs, its crablike arms still in the defensive "up" position, was being splattered unceremoniously by wild sea spray, salt particles encrusting it like coarse sugar.

The captain's voice was whisked away by the roaring westerlies, only snippets of his order audible.

"What'd he say?" bellowed one of the deck crew, turning his back on a breaking wave that lifted the stern then dropped it with belly-wrenching suddenness, sending foam rushing among the legs of the crewmen, and streaming off the scuppers. Frank Hall, standing alone in the hangar's huge, gaping mouth, zipped up an orange-glow immersion suit, preparing for the dive.

"Captain said the media's on the way," replied one of the deck crew. "He's given us a gag order. Just smile."

"They sending Dianne Sawyer?"

"You'll be lucky. Probably all guys."

"I'm not fussy."

"Degenerate! Mount that winch."

"What for? We'll never get 'er off the deck in this weather. Swing like a bitch."

They saw Bryce coming down from the bridge in wet gear. "Don't worry about the weather," the bosun told the others unconvincingly. "It'll settle down once we're headed into the wind."

The winchman saw Hall putting on a navy blue skullcap that looked the worse for wear. "Scruffy-looking bastard."

"It's his good-luck charm," answered the bosun.

"Says who?"

"He does. I offered him one of ours. He says he got it after Eagle Island."

"What the hell's that?"

"An island, dummy."

"I know that. Where?"

"Somewhere off Oregon. Apparently he got caught up in some rumble."

"I'm not surprised. He's got a chip on his shoulder as big as a goddamn log."

"I dunno," replied the bosun. "He seemed nice enough when he came aboard."

"Sure, when we fished him out of the drink. Now he's dry and fucking high."

"Well, he won't be for long," put in another of the deck crew, watching a huge swell looming monstrously above the stern. "Lot of chop down there."

"You'd better pray he keeps dry," said the bosun. "Son of a bitch or not, he's our only chance of finding the *New York*."

"Yeah, well I think that machine of his is full of it. How the hell can it tell Russian oil from American oil?"

"Well, what would *you* do, smartass?" pressed the bosun. "We've dropped grenades—no response. He double-checked it—the machine says American oil."

"Ah, it's probably on the fritz."

"So tell us?" continued the bosun as the ship now came full into the wind.

Suddenly it was a different world. The pitch was still dangerous, but the wild rolls of the swells were gone. It would still be hazardous, though, getting the *Serena I* off deck in the heavy seas, an operation that in normal circumstances—such as fixing a submarine cable off Washington State, mending a punctured pipeline in the Atlantic or spot-welding an oil platform's ruptured flotation legs—would have been suspended until the weather abated. But with over a hundred and fifty men missing and the world press closing in on both sides, nothing could wait.

"So I'm asking you, Einstein," the bosun repeated, "what would you do if you were Hall?"

"Mend my fucking manners."

"Yeah, yeah, all right. Then what?"

"Your gizmo tells you it's American oil, and it's in the area that the sub went down in."

"That they *think* she went down in," cracked the bosun.

"All right. They *think* she went down in."

"What would you do?"

"Check it out," said the sailor grudgingly.

"So," ordered the bosun, "go man the friggin' winch. And when he says stop, pump the brake, don't stab it. Get it?"

"Got it!"

"Good!"

Bryce, meanwhile, had been taking out the headset and earphones from the A-frame's intercom box. "Testing . . . Bridge. You read me?"

"Loud and clear, Lieutenant."

"Okay, plug me into the *Serena*'s radio-phone circuit."

"Roger. You're plugged in, sir."

Bryce waited, watching the oceanographer pull back the plastic bubble's curved door on its left side, dogging the door inside, strapping himself into the pilot's seat. The orange immersion suit was in stark contrast to the black half-moon shape of the submersible's controls, spread in a waist-level semicircle, red and green lights visible, here and there a blinking amber warning light coming on as Hall went through the cockpit check. Bryce heard a rush of static, then Hall's voice. "You hear me, Bridge?"

"Yes, sir."

"Bryce?"

"Yes, sir."

"Call me Frank."

"Yes, sir—Frank."

Bryce couldn't make him out. One minute informal and friendly, as Bremmer had said, and then the next minute rude and abrasively insulting. Bryce recalled that Hall's first noticeable mood swing had occurred when he'd found out about the Russian battle group. Personally Bryce was convinced that Bremmer's death had thoroughly shaken the oceanographer.

"How do you feel?" he asked Hall before he'd had time to consider the appropriateness of the question.

"Rotten," Hall replied. "Sick as a dog. I always am, first day or two out."

Bryce was surprised. It was something a sailor would rather die than admit to, and Hall seemed the last type to admit to any weakness.

"You need a Gravol?" It was the captain's voice on the line.

"Christ, no! It'd make me too sleepy. Just get me off this rust bucket. Once I'm under surface it should calm out."

Bryce felt his face warming with anger, despite the biting wind. Hall couldn't even accept Peters's offer of a pill without insulting him. If it hadn't been for the men in the *New York*, Bryce wouldn't have cared if the oceanographer was sick all the way down and up again.

"Ready to lift?" he asked Hall matter-of-factly.

"Yes," said Hall. "Let's go before I barf."

"Take her up slowly," Bryce instructed the winchman evenly. "Deck crew take strain on the guys."

"C'mon," said Hall impatiently. "Get me off this damn thing."

Suddenly Bryce was sure he knew what was bothering Hall. It wasn't Bremmer's death at all, he thought, it wasn't seasickness: it was sheer, unadulterated *fear*.

But he couldn't have been more wrong. Frank Hall was the calmest he'd ever been. He was convinced that within the hour he would find the missing nuclear submarine, and within two weeks, possibly one, he'd be back with Gloria.

# 27

SINCE THE WORLD PRESS had been alerted by Moscow, scores of reporters and paparazzi had descended on the families and friends of the *New York*'s crew members, running the whole gamut of approaches from polite persistence on the telephone to brazen invasions of privacy, most of the latter coming from "national" U.S. papers, British tabloids and European "pix" magazines.

At first Gloria Bernardi had naively thought she would be left alone, that press attention would focus entirely on the loved ones of the submariners, and she was correct—until the London *Evening Standard* got a tip on Frank Hall, blaring, SUB SEARCHER ON SEX CHARGE, the headline devoid of any mention that the charge had been the result of a monumental misunderstanding and had been immediately dropped by the Astoria sheriff's department or, most important of all, that Frank Hall had, in fact, been attempting to save a woman's life. The story, taken off the wire feed by scores of others throughout the world, soon became even more lurid because of several sensationalist and sloppy translations including, in one South American paper, pictures of the "attack" area, purportedly showing a stretch of cold, lonely beach in Oregon; to its credit, ABC's *Nightline* pointed out that the photo had palm trees in the background. A "correction" was run by the paper, but as Gloria quickly learned, people never see the corrections. Within forty-eight hours after the first Peeping Tom photographer had popped up outside her bedroom window as she began undressing, not only was her privacy being invaded, but she found herself in a state of siege. The other women in the dorm, excited at first by all the fuss, quickly became downright resentful about having to waste their time getting through a ring of university security personnel just to leave the building.

Then Gloria's usual cool deserted her in a crush of reporters, whirring cameras and popping flashbulbs. One reporter, timing his move just as an Italian free-lance photographer was angling for the most sensual profile of what they were, truthfully for once, calling her "cover-girl figure," asked her, "Is your boyfriend a pervert?" She turned on him indignantly, the sheen of her silky blond hair caught in the flashbulbs, her biology texts clasped tightly against her breasts. "No, he is not," she replied angrily. The photo ran in all the tabloids, with an accompanying four-inch headline: GIRLFRIEND DENIES HALL IS PERVERT.

At first Gloria tried to get the sheriff's office, then the Chief of Naval Operations, on the *MacNeil/Lehrer News Hour* to confirm her story of how the whole incident had been a case of mistaken intent that had become "completely distorted." But she was out of her league, soon discovering the wisdom of what the CNO's public relations office had told her: that any such high-level government denial as the one she sought and got only confirmed the story in the minds of many in the media; that more denials would only increase the already gossip-infected stories that a cover-up was under way; that the President was so concerned about the political damage as well as the strategic damage involved in losing America's most powerful weapon that he and his advisors had decided to use the best man for the job, regardless of the man's personal morality, and had decided to concoct a cover story for the Astoria affair.

Watching a late-night talk show, trying to unwind, Gloria heard a host joking about "a news item . . . that public health officials in Oregon were thinking of hiring oceanographer Frank Hall as a shark alarm—just put him on a beach and you'd clear it in thirty seconds!" As the audience rocked with laughter, she broke down and cried. Didn't they know he was just the opposite of what they were saying? Didn't they understand he was even now risking his life to save others, that he might never come back?

Despairing, alone, she phoned her two closest friends but couldn't get through to them; their lines were busy. Either that or they'd pulled out the jacks, tired of the pestering journalists who were pursuing anyone who knew, however remotely, either Frank or her. She wanted Frank with her to hold her, to protect her, to tell her he loved her, that it would all go away—that everything would be all right. For a moment she was angry with him, leaving her to face all this alone, then she felt guilty for her anger, so unreasonable, and she began to cry, choking with sobs as she futilely tried to stem the tears. On the one hand, crying helped relax her; "Better than a Valium," she often told her friends. On the other hand, it made her eyes red and puffy; in the morning she had lectures to attend, and not only because she wanted to; she'd learned enough now about the press to know that not to attend would be to stir up further wild speculation. Yet to appear in sunglasses would be equally suspicious, making her look as if she was trying to hide something. At a time when she most needed someone, no one was there.

ONE THOUSAND FEET below the circular glimmer of sea the blue-black walls of the deep slid by, giving Hall the impression that he was stationary, cliffs of dark velvet sea rising all about him. At eleven hundred feet the faint, coin-size surface glimmer became a mere pinpoint of light, then all was pitch-dark, the slightly rocking motion of the *Serena I* from unseen currents giving him the only sense of movement. The submersible's interior was a softly lit orb descending, the adagio of the active sonar's pinging comforting to Hall's ears yet eerie in that the sounds inside the plastic bubble also served to reinforce the powerful sense of aloneness. His only contact with the world, with the *Boise*, was the mouthpiece-activated sound phone transmitting on 9.5 kilohertz. He hadn't switched on the sonar until he was well below the surface, to avoid any false echoes from the *Boise*'s hull in the immediate subsurface turbulence.

He constantly monitored the indicator lights clustered before and above him, recording depth, rate of descent, salinity, factors that would affect the transmission of sound through the varying thickness of the ocean's layers, and the *Serena*'s degree of variation from the horizontal—which had to be accounted for automatically so as to keep the active sonar's narrow cone of outgoing sound at a predetermined angle. He had been down in the *Serena* and a dozen other underwater reconnaissance vehicles and submersibles hundreds of times, yet the sense of awe in descending into the deep never left him, returning full force each time he entered the vast blackness of the earth's most unforgiving realm. It was a mother sea that covered two-thirds of the globe, from which all things came and to which all would return, as the incessant volcanic upheavals kept shifting the great ocean plates, inundating and altering continents in the unending reshaping of the earth.

He turned on a time-phased 35 mm camera which, though mounted in front of the instrument panel inside the bubble, was waterproof. He then pressed the time marker on his sonar trace. In a trade-off, the active sonar's narrow cone—which sacrificed area of bottom covered in return for high accuracy in giving the precise depth of water to the bottom—showed very little of the bottom itself. He kept radio silence, apart from speaking into the throat mike connected to the submersible's Walkman-size tape recorder. There was no need for chatter between the *Serena* and the *Boise*, especially when he didn't want anything to interfere with his concentration on the sonar.

Aboard the *Boise* the *Serena*'s globular shape wasn't discernible on the fathometer, but her position was, as residual echoes from her radar bounced off the bottom fifteen hundred feet below the heavily pitching warship, dissipating themselves in the turbulent upper layers.

Hall pressed the automatic buoyancy adjustment button, proceeding to level out in the inky blackness, reducing his rate of descent to avoid the danger some other submersible pilots had succumbed to when, like space-walking astronauts, they became so engrossed by the task at hand that they had forgotten to watch the fathometer, crashing into the bottom, drifting laterally into unseen turbulence, or in a gentle bottom convection current, smashing into the precipitous outcrops of sea canyon walls. In one such accident, which he witnessed from the *Petrel*, the plastic bubble had fractured and imploded with such violence under the thousands of tons of pressure that it had disappeared off the *Petrel*'s sonar screen in milliseconds, leaving no record but the straight "dead" line on the oscilloscope, replacing the once-dancing waves of life.

Now he was deep enough for the spotlights to be of some use. A haze of blizzard-white burst forth from the *Serena*, the beams of the halogen lamps reflected off millions of microscopic organisms that filled the water like a fog, reducing visibility to little more than ten to twenty feet. The *Serena*'s fathometer showed the bottom was only a hundred feet below, as her descent slowed until the tiny craft in the vast world of ocean was barely moving, sinking into the soupy white haze.

Whether the profusion of tiny sea creatures was scrambling the sonar's signals, in the way some electrical signals were scrambled by the rise and fall of plankton-filled scattering layers at sunset and sunrise, Hall didn't know. But something seemed to be upsetting the *Serena*'s readings. All he was sure of was that the sonar screen was blurring beyond recognition and that sediment stirred up by the *Serena*'s down draft was obscuring his vision. Then off to his starboard side, in the whiteout that, like a snowstorm, was robbing him of any sense of depth, he glimpsed a fleeting form of what appeared to be a huge, gaping mouth, like that of a giant white shark coming toward him.

ON THE BRIDGE of the *Boise* Bryce held the sonar earpiece to his ear. Captain Peters was hunched over the chart table, calipers and double parallel rule in hand as he marked off the positions where more American naval vessels still en route to the search area from Pearl Harbor should be most strategically placed to act as "picket" ships. These would form a protective moat between the *Boise* at the center and the Russian flotilla that would doubtless press in as soon as the *New York*'s position was confirmed. Peters waited for a deep trough to pass before completing the T that would mark another picket position in a two-mile-diameter circle that he would, in effect, declare a salvage "keep clear" zone.

"Sir, we've lost radar contact!" It was Bryce.

Peters swung about, the bakelite rule slapping the edge of the chart table. "Nothing at all?"

"No, he's flat," said the mate, indicating the sonar screen's lifeless amber line.

"Can you get him on the radiophone?"

"Negative."

"Last reported depth?"

"Twelve hundred feet."

"Bottom?"

"Fifteen hundred, dropping off in places to two thousand plus."

"Keep trying," Peters instructed.

But his order was unnecessary. Bryce was already squeezing the down bar on the underwater phone. All he could hear was a sound like french fries sizzling in oil. "*Boise* to *Serena*. Do you read me? *Boise* to *Serena*."

There was no answer.

"Maybe he's caught in bottom currents," said Peters. "A small submersible like that could be blown right off course, though he might have turned off his active."

"Why would he do that?" asked Bryce, puzzled.

"To save power. No point draining his batteries if he's being rolled about down there. The first thing is to regain equilibrium."

"He could be on his way up," suggested Bryce hopefully. "If he found nothing, that would explain him switching off the active sonar. If he *is* coming up, we should pick him up on the fathometer at five hundred feet."

"He would have let us know, surely," retorted Peters. "We'd have to ready the hook, move the ship into maximum recovery positions."

"Maybe he's too tired to let us know," continued Bryce, "or the radiophone's on the blink."

Peters's frown conceded the possibility. "You tried the full range on the phone?"

"Yes, sir. Eighteen to twenty-seven kilohertz."

"And back to nine point five?"

"Yes, sir—no reply. Only static."

"How far away is the oceanographic ship?"

"The *Petrel*? Twenty miles, sir. You think she might be able to help?"

Peters shook his head. "Don't expect so. But she might be able to figure out what might have happened to the poor son of a bitch. Washington doesn't like inconclusive reports."

"I know, sir."

"LOOKS LIKE HE'S HAD IT!" remarked Kornon's aide, Colonel Ustenko, wedged comfortably into the starboard corner of the *Karpaty II*, sipping the best coffee, real coffee, he'd had since he went to collect Kornon from Ulan Ude.

Kornon didn't answer Ustenko. Ustenko, he thought, could afford to be optimistic; it wouldn't be his head, his reputation, on the line if Hall succeeded in getting to the *New York* first and raising her.

"Don't worry, General. I think your plan is working. I have already written a release for the press people aboard, informing them of the unfortunate 'demise' of our American colleague due to an apparently serious malfunction in his underwater reconnaissance craft."

Kornon continued leafing through a sheaf of translations from the English chitchat aboard the *Boise* that had been intercepted by one of his signal intelligence gathering "trawlers" between the battle group of the *Karpaty II* and the cruiser *Leningrad*, and the *Boise*'s search area. Kornon was heartened by the news that there was confusion aboard the U.S. missile frigate, that they didn't know what had happened to Hall. Still, he told Ustenko to hold the precooked press statement. It would be better, he told Ustenko, not to be impatient, to wait a little longer until he had visible evidence of the wreckage of the *Serena I* on the surface.

"It's a pity," said Ustenko, "that 'our Victor—'" he referred to the Russian sub *Amur* "—cannot report whether its mission has been successful."

"And alert the Americans to her position near them? No, she must remain absolutely on silent station—on the bottom. Not a sound from her."

The *Karpaty*'s radio officer handed Kornon the latest transmit intercepts as Skolensky continued explaining, "When the *Sabrina*'s—"

"The *Serena*," Kornon corrected him.

"Yes, well, some wreckage will pop to the surface, depending on buoyancy of its debris—some, of course, will fall back to the bottom eventually. But pieces of torn clothing, some flesh, limbs, should be visible on the surface to confirm the accident for our media colleagues."

Kornon held up the latest intercept of the communication between the *Boise* and the approaching *Petrel*. The *Boise*'s captain had sought the *Petrel*'s expert advice on how best to recover the presumably crippled submersible should it suddenly surface. The main concern of the *Boise*'s captain seemed to be that perhaps Hall, tossed about by the violent turbulence that the *Petrel* confirmed wasn't at all uncommon off the Aleutians, might have been knocked unconscious, unable to assist in a recovery, if indeed recovery was at all feasible.

"It's possible he was knocked out," Tate, the *Petrel*'s captain, had answered. "He should have been strapped in, though."

Here the transcript between the *Boise* and the *Petrel* became difficult to follow, not only because of some surface scatter but because it seemed some strange dialect was being spoken. The "trawler" suggested to Kornon that whoever had spoken, whatever the dialect, sounded very depressed at hearing the news of the lost contact between the *Boise* and the submersible. Possibly a close friend of Hall? Kornon tried again to read the garbled portion of the translation. It began with an English word that sounded like *ock* and another, *canna*, and then *soons*.

Kornon called for the *Karpaty*'s translator. "Can you tell me what this is, Comrade?"

The translator's lips moved, while everyone in the *Karpaty*'s second "security-sealed" control room waited. The seas outside, Kornon noticed, hadn't abated since Hall left the *Boise* for what Kornon fervently hoped had been the last descent ever for the American. He had thought of letting Hall find the *New York*, as Admiral Litov, now commanding the *Leningrad*, had first suggested, and then exploiting that fact. But the imminent arrival of the *Petrel* had necessitated a quick and, for Kornon, welcome change in strategy, for the *Petrel*'s state-of-the-art side scan was bound to find the *New York* eventually, with or without Hall. Whether it did so in time to save the American sailors, he didn't know and didn't care. But with Hall out of the way it would be that much easier to move in on the Trident and wrench out her secrets, once the *Petrel* had pinpointed her exact position.

IT WAS THE LIGHTS that had saved Hall, for even in the pea soup his eye had caught the turning, racing shadow coming in for the kill....

He had less than half a second to react. With one swift movement of his arm he switched off the active sonar and hit the jettison ballast button, sending the *Serena* shooting upward, the lead shot ballast streaming from her underbelly like a shower of sheep pellets. The malevolent predator flashed past the acrylic bubble in a rush of greenish-white turbulence. The next instant, as he killed the lights, there was a violent crash against the *Serena*'s arm. He was upside down, the sound of the lead shot like marbles cascading over the plastic bubble as it continued rising. Then more sounds of marbles, but not above him—instead, all around him *in* the bubble.

But that would mean there was a hole in the bubble, and if that were so, surely there would be flooding—water roaring in under enormous pressure. And there wasn't. But the bubble was rocking from side to side and yawing violently. Still strapped in, spinning upside down, Hall heard instruments rattling and something thumping like a clothes washer with an unbalanced load, its sound waves punching hard into his entire body. Nauseated, like a fighter pilot in a spin, he fought to regain trim. At the same time he tried to stop the jettisoning of any more shot lest his rate of ascent be too fast, like a balloon suddenly released from the bottom of a deep pool. But the shot door was jammed, no doubt by the impact. He switched off the prop surge he'd used to increase the *Serena*'s initial jump, but still she was rising fast, the fathometer needle spinning counterclockwise, the shot emptied from the ballast tank. Pulling hard, fighting the control stick, he felt her roll again and worked the trim to steady her. He switched on the emergency lamp fixed to the left side of the pilot's seat and saw immediately what was making the sound of running marbles *inside* the bubble; it was the lithium hydroxide crystals spilling out of the backup carbon dioxide scrubber, low down behind his seat.

As he wrestled with the controls to get the *Serena* right side up, she was still rising, but though all the lead shot from the ballast had been jettisoned, her rate of ascent, according to the fathometer needle, was slowing, to about thirty feet instead of sixty per minute. But then, just as the fathometer told him he was seven hundred feet from the surface, the *Serena*'s decreasing rate of ascent was suddenly explained—the skin of his immersion suit felt cold. He looked down. The bottom of the acrylic sphere was bubbling with water, and he was staring cold death in the face.

He pressed the light switches, but only one of the *Serena*'s eyes glowed weakly, a halogen lamp on the port side. It was enough to reveal that the L-shaped legs of the submersible had been completely sheared off by the impact, not only flipping the vehicle upside down but fracturing the bubble at a bolt join. The crack had not been enough to cause the *Serena* to implode, but enough to create a fast leak in the bubble. The water level was rising quickly. Hall knew that when the water reached a high enough point, near the base of the pilot's seat, the bubble's rate of ascent would stop altogether. And then, as the water kept seeping in, the submersible would begin to sink, slowly at first but then gathering speed as the volume of water inside her increased, making the bubble heavier and heavier; at the same time the weight of the water column above her would be increasing. The bubble would be driven down faster and faster, to crash into the ocean bottom at over a hundred and seventy miles per hour.

The fathometer showed Hall he was ascending too slowly with five hundred feet still to go. For a moment he tried to trace the source of the leak, but the constant slopping of the rising pool of water in the sphere made that impossible. He sat strapped in the pilot's seat, knowing that his life depended on the ratio of depth to rate of ascent. The immediate danger was that the submersible would come to a stop too soon and begin to sink back into the deep, the mounting water pressure above pushing it to a speed he couldn't control, so that he would drown, trapped in the plummeting bubble. Or he might perish in the ultimate frustration of the submersible pilot, of being within a hundred feet or so of the mirrored surface, able to exit the door hatch but unable to slow his free ascent to prevent nitrogen-forming bubbles in his blood, so that he died in the agony of the bends.

If only the leak would slow, he thought. But it wouldn't. The *Serena*'s rate of ascent had slowed further, from seven feet per minute to four, the water rising so high that soon he would have no air left. In the dying amber light of the *Serena*'s interior he could see the lithium hydroxide crystals floating about like dead insects. And now he felt a chill grip him through the survival suit, which, though it protected him against sudden hypothermia, would do nothing to stave off the bone-twisting pain and death from the bends.

# 28

ABOARD THE BEAR BOMBER out of the Kuril Islands west of the Aleutians, the European press contingent was living it up, with the best sturgeon caviar and any drink they wanted except vodka. The base commander at Ostrov Paramushir, not wanting any drinking on the plane, had been interpreted as saying there was to be absolutely "no vodka aboard," and so the military press relations officer from Moscow had obeyed him, allowing no vodka but permitting the Scotch and rye that were the favorites of the foreign media contingent. When, however, the PR officer saw the huge patch of oil floating like a scab on the white-flecked blue of the sea far below—a different spill from the one the *Boise* had come across—he knew that no amount of Johnnie Walker or Southern Comfort would be sufficient to hide it from the eagle eyes of the journalist from *Paris-Match*.

*"Qu'est-ce que c'est?"* asked the Frenchman, pointing with his glass through the rain-spattered cockpit, every word he spoke sending the smell of Scotch over the copilot's face. Then, thinking the PR man didn't understand him, he reluctantly shifted to English. "Down there—oil?"

"Ah...I don't know, *monsieur*. It could be seaweed. There's a lot of kelp that floats to the—"

"Kelp, my ass," cut in the British reporter from the *Daily Mirror*.

The PR man had seldom seen the likes of this lot before, though he had to admit to himself that the Russian reporters were the worst. Of course most journalists had livers like sharks; booze was as necessary to them as gasoline to a car, a kind of constant liquid meal, something they could trust not to kill them with typhoid or dysentery or any of the thousands of other diseases that waited for them in diverse parts of the world. What astonished the Moscow man, however, was how they could actually do their job yet drink so heavily, alcohol apparently driving them on rather than slowing them down.

"Well," conceded the PR man sheepishly, "perhaps it is oil."

"Let's go down," said the *Paris-Match* man. "I want close-ups." He turned to the pilot. "Where are we, *mon ami*?"

Before the PR man could do anything about it, the pilot indicated a spot about one hundred and thirty miles southwest of Attu, but as the Bear banked into a slow turn, losing height and heading toward the oil slick, the PR man bent down by the pilot and said something. As the Frenchman's camera started whirring and clicking and whirring again, the pilot nodded.

"Hey!" called out the *Daily Mirror* reporter. "Aren't you going to call it through on the open channel? Everyone in the area should have this. This could be it, mate. The *New York*!"

"Ah...perhaps," agreed the PR man, smiling. "But we cannot be sure yet...."

"Well, have your blokes check it out, Comrade."

The media relations officer informed them, beaming, that that was precisely what he intended to do, the moment they cleared the cockpit for "safety reasons" during the dive.

"Ah, bugger safety reasons, mate. Can't see a flippin' thing back there. Don't worry. We won't say anything rude on the airwaves."

The PR man had no choice, unless he wanted to look as if he was covering up. "All right," he told the pilot. "Call it in."

"Quiet, you bastards!" called out the *Daily Mirror* man jokingly. "Let the comrade have his say."

The reporter from the *Times* ignored the vulgar levity of his countryman. The *Paris-Match* man shifted to his Leica backup camera, while some less dedicated journalist called for more ice.

Halfway through the pilot's report to the *Karpaty II*, which was given, as per international rules, in English on the open channel, it wasn't the English reporter but the French who turned around sharply, looking nonplussed. "Those aren't the right coordinates, *mon ami*," he said, pointing to the automatic readout in the banks of dials.

The PR man's face reddened as he sharply corrected the pilot who, without conceding he had made an "error," proceeded to read out the correct coordinates. The incorrect coordinates he'd given the *Karpaty II* were only a minute or so different from the automatic readout, but the difference would have sent any search ship many miles off. Then, the more cynical reporters suspected, the real coordinates would no doubt have been given later in code. Even among the hard-bitten boozers of the press corps there was an awkward silence as the Bear, its engines thundering, dived toward the suspected oil spill.

"Ah, yes," said the PR man, producing a small ice bucket with all the verve of the professional. "Now, ladies and gentlemen, there is more ice."

"Ladies?" scoffed the *Daily Mirror*'s reporter. "There are no bloody ladies here. Unless you mean the bloke from the *Times*."

The PR man flashed a phony smile, while the reporter from the *Times* ignored the innuendo with editorial disdain. But above and beyond all the banter and insincere pleasantness, everyone knew that the PR man from Moscow had flubbed it. In trying to divert their attention from the spill, he had achieved precisely the opposite.

The *Daily Mirror* man said his *Paris-Match* counterpart was full of it and bet him twenty pounds the oil wasn't from the *New York*. The *Times* reporter said gambling was a fool's game. No one mentioned the men on the lost sub. The assumption seemed to be they, if not the sub, were goners, because nothing, absolutely nothing, had been heard from her.

KORNON WAS ON THE BRIDGE with Ustenko and Skolensky as the *Karpaty* bullied its way through a run of swells. "Hall is finished," said Ustenko.

"Yes," agreed Skolensky, handing back the sheaf of intercepts from the *Boise*, where it was obvious that consternation was growing by the minute. "Even if he jettisons the hull weight, there's only a fifty-fifty—"

"Hull weight?" interjected Kornon, alarm infusing his earlier mood of satisfaction. "What's that?"

"The base square weight to which the submersible is attached. Otherwise it would never sink. The square weight has lead shot ballast pods inside. Normally you release the shot bit by bit, but in an emergency you can jettison the whole bottom weight."

"Then why hasn't he?" Kornon asked.

"He might have, General. These latest intercepts don't mention any surface debris. The submersible might well be damaged, but he could still be on his way up."

"Surely he would have jettisoned the base weight holding him down?"

Skolensky shook his head. Officially the director of the Pacific Ocean Department didn't bear the direct responsibility for the operation as did Kornon, but he knew that insofar as he had supported Kornon's plan, he was, in fact, as committed to ensuring its success as anyone else involved. Accordingly he had done his homework, and took no small pleasure in informing Kornon, "No, General, he wouldn't necessarily have released his base weight, for if there was a leak and he went up too fast, the pressure change could narc him." Though aware the general was unfamiliar with the lexicon of the diver, Skolensky continued. "When a body rises from the deep too quickly, Comrade, the nitrogen in the blood expands under decreasing pressure. What were liquid particles of nitrogen become gas bubbles in the bloodstream, and this produces the bends, because the decompression is too fast.''

"Does it cause death?" asked Kornon. "If Hall comes up too fast will he die?" He could think of no more fitting end for his American enemy.

"Yes."

The answer quickened Kornon's hope. He had just received the Bear's report of a new oil slick fifteen miles north of the *Karpaty II* and closer to the ragged lip of the Aleutian Trench. The *Boise* and the *Petrel* were about the same distance due east of the new slick. This would mean that while the *Petrel* would see a picture of the bottom before any other ship because of its side scan, it and the *Boise* would have to travel almost twenty-two miles to the new slick. It would be a close race against the Russian battle group. If Hall was finished . . .

"What's our maximum speed?" asked Kornon, his disposition improving by the second.

Ustenko could tell by looking at him that the general was forming yet another contingency plan. Ustenko was no close friend of Kornon and never would be—their rank and background were too far apart—but the colonel had learned to admire the general's catlike ability to change direction in midair and still land on his feet, his prey dead beneath him. "Maximum speed," Ustenko answered, "is thirty knots."

"And the *Boise*'s?"

Ustenko's lips pursed as he mentally ran through the ship recognition and specs he'd been studiously memorizing, while the *Leningrad*'s OOD merely called it up on the bridge computer console. "*Boise*—maximum thirty-five knots."

"We could still beat her to it," said Skolensky. "Once the *Petrel* finds it. We're much closer."

"The *Petrel*'s speed?" asked Kornon.

"Thirty knots," replied the OOD. "With a tail wind and everyone pushing."

Everyone on the bridge laughed, except Kornon. "So we are going to beat them to this newly reported oil slick. You forget something, Comrades." There was a silence broken only by the surging of the sea as the Russian battle group changed course, slicing across the swells toward what Kornon insisted on calling the "reported" oil slick. The general, bracing himself against the steering console, looked from Skolensky to Ustenko and back to the OOD. "You forget that the *Petrel* has the best side scan and forward-looking sonar the Americans can make. They can be five to ten miles behind us and know more than we do about what's on the bottom."

"They still need their expert to go down, General," answered Skolensky. "And that was Hall. And he's dead."

"You can afford to be so sure, Comrade Director Skolensky?"

"In Gorky there's an old saying—"

Skolensky was interrupted by an officer entering and handing a new sheaf of pink intercepts to Kornon.

"*Bozhe moy!* My God!" said Kornon, turning on Skolensky. "They've picked up an echo from his submersible! Five hundred feet below the *Boise*."

"Don't worry, General," said Ustenko easily. "Five hundred feet is too deep for a diver to come up fast. Without a full breathing suit and helmet, he'll be narced even if he's still alive."

"No question," said Skolensky.

"What other option has he got?" asked Kornon.

Skolensky looked at Ustenko. "None. And if he stays in the bubble, he's dead, anyway."

Kornon was thinking hard, not about all the technical information he'd heard in the past half hour or so, but about Ulan Ude, where the winds could blow so bitterly and so long that you became locked in by a sea of ice. He was determined—had promised Natasha, Tanya and, above all, himself—that he would never go back. He could leave nothing to chance. "Would he still be *alive* if he managed to get out from that depth and come up?"

Skolensky shrugged. "If he could jettison weight from inside the bubble itself, I suppose. That would squeeze a little longer life out of it, that is, get it to rise another hundred feet or so. He could do it, but he'd probably be in bad shape when he came up. If he'd been at the same depth for any time, he'd have the bends on surfacing, for sure. He'd be in terrible pain."

"Well, that's something," said Kornon. "But could the bastard talk? Would he be able to tell them it was an acoustic torpedo that hit him?"

"If he knew that's what it was," answered Skolensky. "The *Amur* took all possible precautions." Then Skolensky laughed, an unusual occurrence for the director of the POD. "Actually, I'm told that the *Amur* crew took the idea from the American fliers in China in World War II. Apparently the Americans used to paint the front of their planes with a great gaping mouth like a tiger—The Flying Tigers, you see. It worked even better on the *Amur*'s torpedo—after they'd deactivated its warhead so we wouldn't have any giveaway explosion. Quite frankly, down so deep and with the acoustic torpedo being able to move around like a fish as it twists and turns, zeroing in on its sound source, I doubt whether the American had any idea what hit him. The Spets divers tell me that underwater it looks *exactly* like a shark roaring out at you."

"Yes," Ustenko cut in, "but if he's still conscious at the surface... There are different reactions to the bends. Some victims are fully conscious and screaming in pain. With others, the pain alone keeps them blacking out."

Kornon was biting his lower lip. "These transcripts say the American media are on their way to the *Boise*."

Ustenko confirmed it. "In fact, they should arrive in about an hour." Then Ustenko, too, saw the threat; if Hall wasn't dead, as they all hoped he would be, then the press might hear something to arouse suspicion—or, at least, speculation. That would be dangerous, for in a matter of minutes, via satellite relay, the world might know, or at the very least suspect, that the Russians had tried to kill the American oceanographer. The lid would be blown off the Russians' "humane concern," revealing it in all its naked cynicism—a bold, callous ploy to get to the American Trident's secrets, with no real concern at all about the men aboard the stricken sub.

Kornon could almost see Ulan Ude station right before his eyes, its bone-chilling desolation standing for everything he hated in exile from his beloved Moscow. "We must get to him," said Kornon.

"I agree, General," said Ustenko. "But how?"

"They have no doctor aboard the *Boise*?"

"No," said Ustenko. "They carry a medical corpsman instead."

"And special equipment for this—this bends?" asked Kornon urgently.

Ustenko looked for the answer to Skolensky, but he had to turn to the OOD, who had to consult the computers. "No HOT-C, sir," he said, using the universal English designation.

"What's that?" snapped Kornon.

"Hyperbaric oxygen therapy chamber," explained the OOD. "Latest recompression/decompression chamber to get rid of the nitrogen bubbles—slowly. It takes hours."

"Do *we* have one?"

"On our sub *rescue* ship?" interjected the ship's captain. "Of course. It's standard equipment aboard the *Karpaty II*. The Americans have one, too, but it's still en route from Pearl Harbor."

"Quickly!" said Kornon, almost jumping from his chair. "Offer our chamber to them!"

"But, sir," interjected Ustenko. "Even if they used their helicopter, by the time they got him to us, he'd be—"

"No, no," said Kornon. "We take it to them by helicopter." He turned to the *Karpaty*'s captain. "Or is it too big?"

"No, no. Our helicopter can airlift it easily. It wouldn't take long. It's made to be mobile, quickly transportable within the fleet. But, General, I'm willing to bet this American is dead."

"Have you ever been up against *this American* before, Admiral?"

"No."

"I have." He swung around to Ustenko. "So has the colonel. What would you do, Colonel?"

"Send the chamber," Ustenko agreed. "With our doctor. Someone has to stay with the patient, watch him at all times. Yes." Ustenko nodded. It would go over well in Moscow—keeping up the cover of "Soviet Savior of the Americans." It would go over well everywhere. What was even better, the *Karpaty*'s OOD had just written up on the situation board that American TV crews on the four trawlers out of Attu had now reached the *Boise* and were boarding her. Ustenko could see the headlines now: SOVIETS RESCUE WOULD-BE RESCUER. The benefits as propaganda would be enormous all over the world....

Kornon called in Lebdev to help arrange the press coverage, and it was Lebdev's idea, indeed inspiration, to recommend that a nurse go along for added effect.

"Yes, but the most crucial business of all," said Kornon, "will be to get him into the chamber before he can say—"

"Or scream—" Skolensky said, smiling.

"Yes, or scream anything. Once he's inside the chamber our doctor can look after him."

Kornon lifted the phone, and as he punched out a three-digit number for the head of the Moscow and East European press corps, he ordered the *Karpaty*'s captain to dispatch the life-saving chamber to the *Boise* at once. Suddenly his hand froze as he held the phone to his ear. "The *Petrel*. She will have a chamber?"

"Yes," said Ustenko. "But she's over an hour away, General. If Hall is still alive, he must surface in the next half hour or he will drown."

"What about our sub?"

"It will move only when the *Boise* has passed on, heading for the new oil slick reported by the Bear."

"You are all certain it's an oil slick?" said Kornon. "That it's the *New York*?"

"Yes, General. Aren't you?"

"I don't understand why there is only oil. If they could have released oil, as we did from the *Amur*, then why not flares, a sonobuoy?"

Ustenko didn't answer. He was wondering, too, if it really was the *New York* under the oil slick? Or was it a trick, this time by the Americans to divert the Russian salvage ship in the same way Kornon had tried to divert and eliminate Hall? Was it even oil? After all, the Bear had only seen the patch from the air.

Tired as he was, Ustenko went below to help undo the ring bolts that held the recompression chamber to the deck and tighten the U-bolts on the slings that would allow the Hind helicopter to lift the chamber off the *Karpaty II*, bound for the *Boise*.

The members of the big Eastern European press contingent were swarming about the deck despite the cold, blustery

weather, taking photos and videotapes of the preparations that
would testify to the peaceful intent of the Soviet Union and her
determination to replace the old, outdated cold war images with
scenes of true international fraternity and brotherhood.

# 29

JETTISONING THE *Serena*'s heavy square base at first increased
the bubble's acceleration, but this was soon negated by the increasing weight of water caused by the leak. Now, still almost
three hundred feet from the blurring shimmer of the surface,
Hall felt the water encasing his chest. Despite the survival suit,
the cold seemed to burn into his bones like dry ice. If he opened
the hatch here for his free ascent to the surface, the pressure of
the water itself, at 62.5 pounds on every square inch of his
body, no longer posed the danger of crushing him—but he'd
have to hold his breath for three hundred feet. Being in fairly
good condition, he felt he could do that, all right. But the
danger lay in the speed of the ascent. In the rapid decompression that he'd experience while passing from one hundred and
twenty pounds per square inch to the surface pressure of 14.7
pounds per square inch he would be narced. Narcosis, or
change of liquid nitrogen in his blood to gas bubbles that could
block blood vessels, particularly those leading to the heart,
would occur during the rapid decompression. If that happened, he would die, and he would certainly suffer that agonizing cold knife-in-your-bones pain that divers called the bends.

Now he jettisoned the extra battery pod and clump weight.
It made no difference. While the *Serena* initially rose slug-
gishly another ten feet, neutral buoyancy was soon reached, and
then slowly his companion of one hundred dives began to sink
toward the stygian darkness. Quickly he ejected the waterproof 35 mm film cartridge, slipped it into his zippered left leg
pocket and then, in an act of sentiment that only other divers
and those attuned to the sea would have understood, Hall
turned on the still-functioning starboard lamp. Activating the
beeper in the left upper pocket of the bright tangerine-colored

suit, he held his breath, exiting through the hatch. Arms extended in the form of a cross, then in the fetal position as he backpaddled and trickled out his air so as not to rupture his lungs, he rose, while beneath him the one-eyed engineering marvel of his youth sank faster and faster in a blaze of ethereal light.

ABOARD THE *Boise* everyone was uptight, its light chopper dispatched the moment the bubble had registered on the fathometer paper as a smudge emerging from the fuzzy trace of the scattering layer. The *Boise*'s light chopper was hovering low over the sea, directed by its own sonar. But then the bubble, which had slowly emerged from the dancing static of the scattering layer, began sinking again, back down into the layer that would effectively seal it off from sonar contact. Perhaps, as the Russians had suggested while listening in on the open rescue channel, the *Serena I* had somehow malfunctioned. After jettisoning everything he could, Hall might be exiting from the submersible over two hundred feet from the surface.

Two American cameramen, weighed down by their gear, staggered onto the bridge like drunken hunters bearing their kills. Peters muttered an oath under his breath. But the cameramen, apparently oblivious to him or anyone else on the bridge, decided there was nothing worth shooting there, and went away again.

"I know there's no alternative," said Peters sharply to the executive officer, conceding that with the *Petrel* still over half an hour away, he had no choice but to let the Russian rescue party with the decompression chamber aboard his warship. "But I don't want any of those Russian jokers wandering about inside my ship. Understood?"

"Yes, sir," Bryce answered.

"Wraps on all classified equipment. I don't want any of them going beyond the helideck."

"They'll have to put the recompression chamber in the hangar, sir."

"What—yes, all right. But wraps on everything else in sight, and none of them gets beyond the inside hangar hatchway.

They're to be strictly confined to the stern helipad and hangar. Nowhere else.''

As Peters reiterated his orders over the PA, he could see the big, bulbous-eyed insect a quarter mile off, a white oblong shape suspended from it: the decompression chamber. He heard one of the watchmen murmur something to the *Boise*'s helmsman.

"What was that, sailor?" The Russian chopper was quickly looking larger as it approached the *Boise*.

"Ah ... I just want to know, sir, what we'll do if one of 'em wants to, er ... relieve himself, sir."

Peters was watching his helideck crew go into action. "Tell 'em to piss over the side," he answered the seaman. "To leeward."

"Yes, sir."

"Ah, sir ..." said Bryce, "how can we stop them taking pictures? They're bound to bring some press with them. After all, we've got U.S. and Canadian networks aboard."

"Goddamn it. *All* press are under the same restriction—no internal photos and no interviews with anyone. Got it? Refer all questions to me. Be pleasant and tell them squat." There was a murmur of assent on the bridge.

"Can we smile?" someone said as Peters left the bridge with the bosun's mate to watch the Russian landing. If Peters heard the remark, he ignored it.

The Russian helicopter was less than two hundred feet away, its rotor wash whipping up canvas on the lifeboats and ballooning the deck crew's wet gear to twice its size. Holding on to the port rail of the upper deck, shouting to make himself heard above the chopper's steady roar, Peters said, "Bosun?"

"Yes, sir," the bosun replied.

"Go get the Nikon and take a shot of that ugly mother."

"Yes, sir."

"If they see you, I'll chew your ass out."

Just then a cry went up.

"Man in the water! Starboard midships. A hundred yards."

Peters looked, and there it was—a man's head, bobbing in the water like a mandarin orange, the immersion suit's flap wrapped around it. But the captain, like everyone else, knew that while there was a fair chance Hall might have survived a fast ascent, there was bound to have been internal bleeding in the inner ear, the lungs or both. Time was of the essence in retrieving his body from the ice-cold sea and getting him into the recompression chamber as fast as possible, where they would increase the pressure again, to change the deadly nitrogen bubbles back to liquid, and then decompress, this time slowly, over a matter of hours.

Peters watched the *Boise*'s chopper swing over and steady itself. The "drop" man hit the water and disappeared in the heavy seas, reappearing moments later in the wind-riven patch caused by the chopper's down draft. He was slipping the shoulder harness around the oceanographer. Both disappeared from view briefly, then Peters saw the pencil-thin wire retracting, Hall's body turning slowly in the wind, another crewman waiting at the hatch. Instead of pulling him in, the man clipped a canvas strap onto the harness, which held Hall firmly against the fuselage, while the chopper turned tightly and headed toward the *Boise*'s forward deck.

At the same time the Russian Hind was descending slowly, taking up most of the space over the open stern deck. The recompression chamber being lowered beneath it wasn't white, as Peters had at first thought, but a six-foot-diameter, rust-spotted, cream-colored cylinder. The moment it reached the deck, it was rolled, on hard rubber-ball runners that made it look like some massive, short caterpillar, into the hangar, where it was anchored to the hangar deck's recessed flip-up ring bolts.

A huddle of news types who had ignored Peters's orders were sticking big black, soft foam mikes at anyone who looked like he would talk. Ustenko, two recompression chamber technicians and a stunning nurse in virginal white refused to answer any questions. The network camera crews were fighting a losing battle in the heavy swells, trying to get some half-decent shots of the big Russian chopper and its crew for satellite relay from Attu back to the States. An NBC cameraman almost went over the stern in a particularly savage pitch. The crews of the other two American networks and the Canadian Broadcasting Corporation had seen that Hall would be lowered to a sick bay stretcher up forward, away from the tricky unloading of the recompression chamber astern; they were retreating into the hangar, arguing, cajoling, threatening and trying to bribe their way forward. But the OOD's team stood firm—no cameras in the interior passages. The press would either have to surrender their cameras to the *Boise*'s crew for transport through the ship, or wait for the sick bay party to bring the famed oceanographer to the hangar, where the Soviet colonel, Ustenko, and the American OOD jointly insisted that the oceanographer wouldn't be delayed or bothered in any way by questions or photos but put immediately into the recompression chamber. The Soviet decompression expert, Dr. Latik, and the nurse would have to stay with him right through the hours of careful decompression.

The Russian newsmen, including two cameramen from the *Karpaty II*, waited patiently in the hangar, while the Western reporters, yelling instructions at one another, positioned themselves at strategic places about the hangar, whose door started to come down, drowning the sound of the sick bay party and the news reporters' commentary.

While the jockeying for position continued, Frank Hall, on the wire basket stretcher, water dripping from the immersion suit, was carried carefully but as quickly as possible through the ship from the forward deck to the inside entrance of the hangar. His eyes were closed, he was breathing heavily, and his face was waxen in color and tripelike in texture. His horrible, lifeless look, as if his body had been drained of blood, was emphasized by the portable klieg lights that were clattering against the constantly pitching bulkhead, filling the cavernous hangar with a harsh white glare.

Peters, entering the hangar, was immediately aware of its change of smell. Whereas it normally had a faint oily odor, there was now a heavier smell of sweat and deodorant, as well as hot paint from the recently painted hangar itself. The gaggle of press, giving up on the uncommunicative Soviet doctor and his nurse, turned instead to Peters for comment: Precisely what had happened to the oceanographer? What had he found out? Would his rapid ascent prevent him from going down again?

Peters grimaced in the bright light. "I don't know exactly what went wrong, except that after we lost sonar contact with Mr. Hall's submersible—"

"How come you lost contact, Captain? Your sonar malfunctioning?"

"Our sonar was not malfunctioning," answered Peters in an unnaturally measured tone, feeling that he was being watched by millions, including the Chief of Naval Operations. "There is a sound-scrambling layer called the scattering layer, which is made up of small life-forms and rises and falls in response to light intensity."

"The sun?" suggested the CBC man.

"Yes," said Peters. "The layer rises at sunset and falls before sunrise. If it's above the object you're trying to track, then the scattering layer simply bounces back the sound you put out, scrambling the echo."

"You know how far he came up from, Captain?"

"We estimate between one hundred and two hundred and fifty feet. Possibly more." The truth, Peters knew, as Hall had so rudely pointed out to him less than twelve hours before, was that like most surface ships the *Boise*'s sonar wasn't anywhere as accurate as the *Petrel*'s. But Peters's pride wasn't going to allow his ship to be bad-mouthed by the media, most of whom didn't know a ship's head from the canteen.

"What now, Captain?"

"Well...uh, we've had another oil slick sighting to the north of us, and as Mr. Hall will be indisposed for some time in the decompression chamber and is unconscious at the moment, we'll investigate this new sighting...uh, then return here to investigate further if necessary. That is, after we talk to Mr. Hall if—I should say, when—he's recovered. Of course, as we leave this area we'll be dropping marker buoys."

"Then no doubt, Captain," began the CBS reporter, "you're happy to have a top-rated Soviet team willing to lend assistance." The reporter probably meant assistance in decompressing Hall, but his statement could have been taken a number of ways.

Peters forced a smile, the most unnatural his men had ever seen. One of the sick bay attendants noted wryly that the captain looked as if someone were holding a gun to his back—smile or die. "Yes," said Peters. He knew what they'd do—edit the goddamn videotape so that the question about him being happy with the Soviets' "assistance" would run immediately after the question about his sonar, making the U.S. Navy look either unprepared or inept.

"Are the Soviets happy to be aboard the *Boise*?" asked the NBC man.

"Yes, yes," bubbled a Mr. Lebdev, Moscow head of Tass. "Here at sea," said Lebdev, arms sweeping outward, "there are no superpowers doing battle, yes...there are only men and women who do battle with the sea. This aid to the *Boise* demonstrates how the Soviet peoples have responded in the true spirit of international peace and brotherhood."

Peters kept his grin frozen, noticing how during a roll Lebdev had adeptly moved closer to the first of the two thick double-glazed observation ports situated either side of the recompression chamber. Through the ports the cameras following him also got a good shot of Hall, obviously unconscious, being unstrapped from the basket stretcher and moved, as gently as the ship's motion would allow, to one of the four chain-suspended bunks that could be lowered as needed, two on either side of the chamber.

In the front of the chamber there was what looked like a small, box-shaped, eight-cubic-foot refrigerator that, Lebdev explained, contained drugs and food for Hall and the medical team of two who would spend the period of decompression in the chamber. The hangar then echoed with the hollow sound of the doctor inside the recompression chamber speaking Russian through a mike connected to an outside PA horn affixed above the thick, stern-facing entrance. Soft red light filled the interior of the chamber, and blinds were pulled down inside over the four observation ports. Lebdev explained that this was "for modesty's sake," following Dr. Latik's announcement that he and his nurse were about to remove the survival suit from Hall and wrap him in blankets.

While they were waiting for the first of the medical reports that would be issued periodically during the decompression period, Lebdev asked the networks if they would like to take any shots of the Hind helicopter.

"Exterior shots only, right?" said one of the world-weary CBS cameramen.

Lebdev overheard him and smiled with all the charm that had helped him survive a half century of power struggles in the

Kremlin. "Interior shots if you wish, of course," he informed the surprised CBS cameraman. His offer made Peters's stringent "off-limits" directives to the press seem petty in comparison.

Another propaganda victory for the Russians, Peters thought, wondering how his handling of the situation would go down in Washington. The peace groups would be sure to point out the contrast between Soviet *glasnost*, openness, and American intransigence. He wondered if any of the journalists would mention that the missile frigate *Boise* was much newer than the older Hind chopper, which contained no features Western intelligence would be interested in anyway.

EXCEPT FOR THE TWO Russian mechanics manning the noisy compressor hooked up to the decompression chamber, the hangar was deserted, the newsmen having moved with Lebdev toward the hangar's sliding door. Their heads bowed in unison as the door's panels retracted noisily. They were struck full force by the wind howling in from the gray ocean, the gusts snatching away their breath as they bent into the blow, heading eagerly yet cautiously on the water-slicked deck toward the big, ugly Russian chopper. The bulging eyes of the Hind's turbos atop its cockpit blisters increased the impression of some huge inflated blowfly as the press group drew near; the ugly khaki-green wavy camouflage pattern on its sides ended at the belly line, where overlapping blues and whites could easily pass for shifting sky and clouds to an observer a thousand feet below.

Inside the now almost deserted hangar the two Soviet technicians outside the chamber watched the gauges, carefully increasing the pressure slowly to a hundred and fifty pounds per square inch, more than the hundred pounds that the American captain had estimated Hall had experienced when his free ascent began. If any of the Americans asked why a hundred and fifty instead of a hundred pounds per square inch, the technicians would simply explain that it was a "safety margin."

The higher figure also meant the decompression would take longer, giving Kornon more time.

Inside the redded-out chamber the nurse slipped off her crisply starched white jacket, then her blouse and skirt, revealing matching bra and panties made of body-hugging white lace. Next she undid the severe-looking bun at the back of her head so that silken blond tresses fell loosely over her shoulders.

"Is this enough?" she asked.

"To begin with," replied the doctor. "Yes, that's sufficient."

"There isn't much room."

"Well, Helga . . ."

*"Elga,"* she corrected him.

"Well, Elga, we don't need much room, do we? Besides, we might have to do it in the cabin. Anyway, you know I used to do it in a Beetle."

She looked puzzled—puzzled and astonishingly beautiful. Her breasts, he saw, were large but firm. She was magnificent. "The Beetle," he repeated, "it's what everyone used to call the Volkswagen. Even in the West. You're German," continued the doctor in surprise, "and you've never heard of the Beetle? Of course..." he mused, looking beyond her to gaze back in time, then glancing over at her again, "they finally stopped making them—a very serious mistake. The Beetle was a beautiful car— no overheating, a gearshift that was like stroking velvet. And the mileage! Well, nothing could beat it."

"I think I remember my father talking about them," she said.

The doctor nodded; hers was another generation. "Here," he said, "take two of these."

"What are they?"

"Don't worry. They're just amphetamines. Wake-up pills. Look." He took two himself, washing them down with some mineral water. "When the pressure rises in here, it will make you tired. Like being at the seaside. It's all right for our friend here, but you and I have to stay awake."

She took the pills.

"It's commendable, Comrade," he said, a touch of sarcasm in his voice.

"What do you mean?"

"That you are willing to do this for the Party."

"I'd do anything for the Party," she responded without a smile. He didn't believe her but that didn't matter. She noticed the slight bulging at his crotch, and it pleased her. Not that it would do him any good, but it gave her the sense of power over men that she so much enjoyed. She got dressed again.

"It wasn't necessary to show me," he charged.

"I wanted to make sure it was enough."

"You know it's enough. You enjoy it."

"Don't *you*?"

# 30

ANOTHER FIVE DEGREES had been added to the *New York*'s angle of inclination to the bottom, presaged by a creaking and straining throughout the hull that filled every man with fear, though every one of the one hundred and fifty sailors showed it, or rather hid it, in different ways.

At first when the pressure in the outer tank had fallen so drastically, Captain Wain had suspected that Knead, in the grip of his seesawing madness, had purposely bled the fuel tank, sending up over two hundred gallons of dieseline. But Chief Ryman said he'd been watching Knead closely, even following him to the head by the torpedo room, where the stench of the backed-up toilets was so strong it made him want to be sick, and where under the weak battle lantern lights crewmen could be seen strewed about like corpses in some dank and dark medieval dungeon. The lights were turned down to a minimum to conserve power in the sub's batteries, but the gloom did nothing to alleviate the oppressive atmosphere in all sections of the boat. The temperature, except in the prop's crawl space, had now climbed to over ninety degrees, the humidity a dripping ninety-two percent due to evaporation of the water from the earlier rupture in the sea valve. Every metal surface seemed to be perspiring, glistening with moisture from condensation, parts of the bulkhead actually dripping. Salt tablets had been distributed, and the men off duty were told not to move around, to conserve energy and so reduce their intake of the emergency oxygen now being bled off from the reserve bottles stored in the torpedo room.

In the redded-out control room the crew on watch, stripped to the waist, moved with the heavy lethargy of humidity-induced fatigue, their steps little more than shuffles. Wearing the regulation silent-running slippers, the sailors of the most deadly machine man had invented looked like doomed souls in a noiseless but fiery red hell.

"Well, sir," said Sloane, referring to the fuel leak, "it could be a blessing in disguise. If our boys spot the oil, they'll be sure to check it out. Maybe zero right in on us."

"And what if the Russians get to us first?"

"Sir, we're getting to the end of our tether down here. Reactor shutdown, carbon dioxide scrubbers gone, auxiliary engine shot and—"

"So?" said Wain sharply. "We've fired off a flare and the sonobuoy. What else do you propose?"

Sloane stood as embarrassed as a schoolboy caught repeatedly making the same error in class. He'd momentarily forgotten the firing of the flare and sonobuoy, and this lapse of memory told him that he was, in fact, much more affected by the fatigue and unfiltered air in the sub than the captain. And if he, so conscious of the need to set an example to the men, was so affected, he could only guess at the state of mind among the crew, especially Knead. "Sorry, sir," he apologized to the captain.

Wain didn't reply. He was holding up his hand listening, sensing that something terrible was about to happen. "You hear it?" he whispered to Sloane. The faint creaking sounded again, but this time it was accompanied by an agonizing noise like that of overloaded timbers groaning at the deepest part of a mine. It stopped for a few seconds, then began anew, pressing in closer now, as if it were a live thing, advancing, stopping, then advancing again.

"Another sub?" Sloane asked sonar.

"No, sir—no incoming. There's nothing out there."

"Everything's out there!" It was Knead speaking, eyes bright, alert—the most lively man on the entire sub. "Cuckolded!" he said, his watery gaze shifting from Wain to Sloane and back again. "Cuckolded!" he shouted. "By...by..." He looked frantically around the redded-out control room. Some of the men turned to stare at him, then back to watch the myriad dials. "That's what they call it," he yelled. "Cuckolded by a Navy mother!" Glaring at the captain with wild intensity, he asked, "Guess how I know?"

The chief made to grab him, but Wain signaled no. "How do you know, sailor?" he asked Knead in a calm, understanding tone.

"The safe," said Knead. "Navy issue—in the garbage, but I saw it. Jesus!" He sat down abruptly on the captain's swivel chair. "I saw it but never thought about it till later."

"You think he's on the *New York*?" Wain asked him.

"No," Knead answered, staring into the red light as if his sight were penetrating the solid steel of the sub. "Must be someone from the other crew. While we're out they're in. Get it—they're *in*!" Knead laughed hysterically.

Wain ignored the vulgarity. Instead he told Knead gently, "When we dock you'll have time to work it out with your wife."

Knead slumped back in the captain's chair as if he owned it. "I killed her."

Wain glanced across at the chief, who was as nonplussed as he.

"You want to make a statement?" Wain asked softly.

"I killed her, Captain. I smashed her head..." He couldn't go on.

"C'mon, sailor," Sloane said, placing his hand on Knead's shoulder. Knead got up as obediently as a dog, looked around at the captain, the sonar man and the chief, then followed Sloane to the wardroom.

According to regulations, the first officer informed Knead of his rights, noted date and time and dutifully began writing with a ballpoint that smudged badly.

"The humidity," said Knead easily.

"What?"

"Plays hell with refills," said Knead. Then, "Can we do this later?"

"We should do it now."

"Later." Knead got up from his chair and walked out of the wardroom. "Too tired."

Sloane was afraid Knead would commit suicide. "You okay, Knead?"

"No."

"Then hit the sack for a while. We'll do it when you're ready."

Knead suddenly turned. "Don't worry, Mom. I'm not gonna flush myself down the toilet. I'm hungry."

Sloane managed a smile. "Okay." He was starting to like Knead; whatever else he'd done or might do, the sailor was uncowed, unafraid.

There was a call on the PA. An incoming signal. "Still quite weak and a long way off," the sonar man said, "but not changing course."

"A friggin' whale," said one of the torpedo men, wiping the sweat from his forehead.

After making certain that Knead was going to the galley, Sloane headed back to the control room, where the incoming signal made his presence, if not absolutely necessary, at least desirable.

In the galley Knead saw a crewman peeling back the gauze cloth from the pile of sandwiches the cooks had prepared and left atop the immaculately clean stainless-steel counter.

"Corned beef," the sailor informed Knead, pointing to the nearest pile. "Salmon over there." The crewman chose the corned beef and started back to crew's quarters.

Knead pulled open the cook's drawer, took the shortest of the butcher knives and, holding it so that its handle was concealed in his right hand, its blade flat against his forearm, left the galley, heading back in the direction of the control room.

The PA system crackled again, announcing the showing of a movie in the crew's mess. Shadowy figures were coming toward Knead, passing him like red ghosts.

"What's it called?" someone asked.

"Who gives a shit?"

"*The Last Picture Show*," said another.

"Very funny!"

"It's true."

No one thought it was funny.

Knead kept walking down the corridor, glancing quickly into the captain's stateroom without breaking his stride.

IN PORTLAND it was clear to Gloria Bernadi that she could no longer stay in her dormitory. The other students had not only grown weary of her unwanted celebrity, but by now were becoming increasingly vocal about the difficulty of getting in and out of the residence, which had been made worse by new security guards, who didn't know the students but had been hired by the university in a vain attempt to keep out the growing army of reporters.

Despite the security a couple of journalists had managed to lie and wheedle their way in, harassing Gloria. So this evening when she heard the knocking on her door and saw, through the peephole, two men—albeit well-dressed, so unlikely to be reporters—she nevertheless played it safe and answered warily with the burglar chain still on. "Yes?"

"Miss Bernadi?"

"Yes."

"My name is William Burroughs." As he held up his FBI badge so she could see it through the crack, he turned to his colleague. "And this is agent John Morley, Portland Bureau. Can we have a word with you?"

Weary, yet relieved, she opened the door.

"You shouldn't have done that, miss."

"What?"

"Open the door like that just to anyone."

"But you're FBI."

"We *said* we were FBI." He gave her his card. "You should have asked for this number, Portland FBI, and checked it out."

"But your badges..."

"We could have obtained these from any one of a dozen mail-order houses."

"I'll remember next time." She smiled. "Okay?"

"All right. May we come in?"

"Yes." Suddenly she felt cold inside. "Frank! Something's happened to Frank?"

Yes, they said, it had, but it looked as if he'd be all right. But they were there about the matter of her harassment by the media. Some of the work Frank Hall had done for the U.S. Navy had been highly sensitive, and Washington was afraid that if the media didn't back off, there was going to be more and more danger of classified information being leaked.

"How?" she asked.

"Well... I don't want to hit this one too hard, Miss Bernadi," said Burroughs. "But you and Mr. Hall have been close friends."

She blushed. "Yes." He somehow made it sound improper. There was silence.

"Oh," she began. "Oh, you mean they think Frank might have told me state secrets or something...."

"Not exactly state secrets, miss, but where he worked, the different naval firing ranges and such where he did recovery work. Not state secrets but—"

His colleague Morley interrupted. "Information we'd prefer not to be public, miss. You did mention to the—" he consulted a small brown notebook "—London *Sunday Times* that Mr. Hall had worked on the Nanoose Bay range, between the U.S. and Canada on the West Coast."

She grinned uneasily. "I did?"

"Yes, ma'am, you did." He showed her the clipping.

"I'm sorry. I didn't realize—"

"Washington thinks it's best," continued Burroughs, "if you move out of the dorm for a week or two. Until the *New York* situation is over. We have a place for you on the coast."

"But my lectures and—"

"We've arranged for all your lectures to be taped and brought down to you the same day."

She felt a flood of relief washing over her. She'd be free of all the media pressure.

"*And* the assignments," said Morley, smiling. "Just in case you thought it was going to be a holiday at the beach."

"Thanks a lot," she said, feigning disappointment.

Burroughs laughed. "When would you like us to pick you up? Later this afternoon?"

She shrugged. "Give me an hour or two and I'll be ready."

"Fine. In an hour then."

When they left she picked up the card she had been given, was about to throw it out, but on an impulse picked up the phone and rang the number.

"Federal Bureau of Investigation. Portland Division."

"Could I speak to Agent Burroughs please—or Mr. Morley?"

"May I say who's calling?"

"Yes. Gloria Bernadi."

"Please hold."

She heard strains of Lawrence Welk music.

The music stopped. "Hello?" It was the woman's voice again.

"Yes," said Gloria.

"I'm sorry, but agents Burroughs and Morley are out of the office. May I take a message?"

"No thanks."

Finally she felt safe. She was glad in a way that she had let the info about the Navy firing range slip out; otherwise the FBI would never have been interested in getting her away from the media and the terrible loneliness she'd felt ever since Frank went away. Then, in the silence of her room, she wondered if he'd ever come back.

# 31

CAPTAIN TATE BELIEVED he had undeniable confirmation. The *Petrel*'s state-of-the-art side scan, with its transponder or signal source so low in the water that it was free of surface turbulence and so effective that it could replace fifty thousand pictures per square mile, had picked up faint echoes of "something big, something metallic." Captain Tate reported this fact to the *Boise* on the open search channel.

Less than an hour after the *Petrel* received the signals and turned away from its intended rendezvous with the frigate, it was racing, like all the other Russian and American search ships and aircraft, toward the location of the newly sighted oil slick, now ten miles northwest of the *Boise* and a hundred and fifty miles southwest of Attu Island. The pinging of an echo following seconds after each of the outgoing pulses from the *Petrel*'s transponder held constant, and the trace, appearing more detailed by the second as the stylus delicately, swiftly, passed across the moist, gray Hardinger paper, was revealing a huge, blurred zeppelinlike shape. Its sail—or what Captain Tate and his Scottish mate, having earned their masters' tickets in a different age, insisted on calling a conning tower—was surprisingly stubby.

"It's a wee bit short, isn't it?" proclaimed the red-bearded Scot.

"It's in our angle of approach, Scotty."

"Oh, aye, I'll grant you that, Captain, but look, we've shifted five degrees here and there's still no change. We're still getting a wee conning tower on the trace but seeing the same great bloody whale of a shape for the rest of it. If the conning tower still looks shrunken from a different angle, why doesn't the hull?"

The *Petrel*'s port lookout, finishing his coffee and replacing the mug in the antiroll rack, suggested the stubby shape might be due to the downed sub lying at a severe tilt. "Maybe its sail is leaning away from us."

"Maybe," Tate said. "But if it's tilting that much, you'd think it'd roll way over on its side and we wouldn't be seeing any of the conning tower."

"Ach," said Scotty, "it's a mystery to me. How far off are we?"

Tate, surprisingly agile for his age, slid the roll rule smartly over the chart, which was peppered with depth soundings. "A tad over two miles."

"There's irony for you," said Scotty. "The *Petrel* will be the first ship there, but there's bugger all we can do until Frank's operational—if he ever is."

"We can get as sharp a picture as we can. Every bit of information we can get will help—especially now that the *Serena*'s gone. If he's up to going down again, he'll have to use the atmosphere diving suit."

"If he ever goes down again," said the lookout with an informality that was as normal between crew and officers aboard the *Petrel* as the more formal relationships were normal for the *Boise*.

"He'll go down again," said the first mate.

"I don't know, Scotty," replied Tate. "The *Boise*'s captain said Frank came up mighty fast—free ascent from well over two hundred feet—say three hundred to be on the safe side. What's that on the decompression table? It must be at least two hours."

Scotty called down to the *Petrel*'s after starboard wet lab, where the bosun was busy checking out the AD or atmosphere diving suit, the super-strong aluminum suit that permitted a diver to go to fifteen hundred feet—its crush depth two thousand feet plus—yet maintain working mobility. The internal pressure of the bulbous-limbed suit was maintained at one atmosphere, that is, at normal air pressure of 14.7 pounds per square inch, making decompression unnecessary.

"Wet lab here. Go ahead."

"Lab, have a look at the decompression tables, will you? What's the time for free ascent from three hundred feet?"

"Hang on..." Scotty could hear the lab crew in the background moving some of the fluid-supported low-friction rotary joints on the AD suit, joints that, turned by modern computer-controlled lathes, guaranteed moving yet watertight seals. This engineering feat, modified and improved by men like Hall's mechanic, Bill Reid, allowed a diver to move up to eighty-two percent of his normal capacity, while protected from the enormous pressures of the deep and able to breathe oxygen from two independently closed circuits from a spaceman-like backpack filled with four oxygen bottles. This overcame the old problem of divers having to breathe mixed gasses, which could sometimes have dangerous side effects. With the help of a carbon dioxide scrubber inside, the AD suit gave the diver almost fifty hours of submerged time.

The bosun came back on the intercom. "Mate?"

"Yes?"

"How long was Frank at three hundred feet?"

Scotty turned to Tate. "How long did the *Boise* say..." but he had to wait several moments as Tate, his brow knit in concentration, moved forward, away from the chart table, and

punched new coordinates into the steering console to counteract the effect of gale-force winds that had increased ever since
they'd turned north, knocking their speed down to seven knots.
"How long did the *Boise* say Frank was at three hundred feet?"

"They're not sure," replied Tate, "but they estimated
around an hour and a half."

In the after lab the bosun heard Tate through the intercom.
"That means six hours decompression unless they got him in
the chamber within three minutes, then they could do a surface decompression on oxygen and cut the six hours to one and
a half."

"They got him in pretty quick," said Tate. "That's what
they'll be doing then."

"Ach," said Scotty, "I'll bet the bloody comrades liked
that." Tate looked nonplussed at him. "An hour and a half,"
explained Scotty, "instead of six hours."

"I still don't get you," said Tate.

"I don't trust those buggers," said Scotty. "I've a mind
they'd like to see our Frank out of it altogether. Get at the sub
all by themselves."

"You're a cynical man," said Tate good-naturedly, but
meaning it nevertheless.

"That's true, Captain."

"Well, Scotty, all I can say is it's a damn funny way of putting our top gun oceanographer out of the game—helping him
through decompression. If they wanted him out of play, all they
had to do was not offer the chamber."

"They couldn't do that."

"And why not?"

"Because we knew they had one—ever since Moscow announced the Soviet Navy was going to help 'in the interests of
peaceful relations.' You'll notice they sent their own doctor and
nurse—at least that's what I picked up on the open channel."

"What else would you expect them to do? Hell, nobody on
the *Boise* could run the damn thing. It's a warship, not a sub
rescue vessel."

"I suppose you're right," said Scotty reluctantly. "Ach, I
still don't trust them. Remember Cuba...."

"Cuba! How do you remember Cuba? You must have been only a 'wee bairn' at the time," said Tate, adopting one of Scotty's phrases.

"My father told me. Ach, they're a scungy lot. All smarmy when they've a mind to."

"You're the life of the party, you are," said Tate, winking at the helmsman and two lookouts, all of them enjoying Scotty's unrelenting gloom. He was always the same, habitually seeing the dirty side of the handkerchief.

Scotty began to answer but was interrupted by a ping several tones above that of the constant returning ping of their transponder's pulse.

"What the—" Tate began, holding up his hand for silence on the bridge. Scotty and the other three men were watching the recorder. The shape was still the same, a blurred zeppelin with almost no sail, but the second ping, like a clarion call above the sound and fury of the violent sea all about them, told them that this sound, possibly man-made, had come from the sub.

"They're alive!" said the helmsman, his voice dry, taut with excitement.

"Ach," said the Scotsman, "it could have been something loose swingin' back an' forth—like a bloody pendulum on the bulkhead. I canna hear it now."

The helmsman glowered at the mate. Sometimes the Scotsman's accent really teed him off. Or was it that for all his annoying cynicism Scotty was usually right?

The secondary pinging started up again.

"Could be a false echo," cautioned Scotty.

"Then," said Tate, "it's a damn funny one, Scotty."

"How d'you mean?"

"Listen, man," said Tate. "It's as plain as kipper on your face."

Scotty grunted. The pinging was repetitive and spaced; it spelled SOS.

"SIR!" ANNOUNCED the *New York*'s first officer excitedly. "Passive sonar's picked up several ships coming our way."

Wain's restrained tone was an effort of will over emotion. He, as much as any man on the boat, was anxious for rescue, but he knew a ship approaching them wasn't the same as a ship finding them, and a ship finding them, Soviet or American, wasn't a ship rescuing them. And he, like everyone aboard, including the civilian, Dyer, knew the *New York* was already below its test depth, tempting the instant implosion of crush depth.

"Captain." It was the sonar man, unusually excited. Now the contacts were coming fast, one ping entering another's emission cone so that only a trained ear could differentiate one from another.

"What is it?" asked Wain.

"Three surface—and a sub."

"You sure?"

"Yes, sir, but I'm feeding them into the computer for sound print matchup."

"Very well."

"Sir, we should stop tapping out the SOS. It's scrambling my incoming."

Wain nodded and switched on the PA. "Forward torpedo room. Cease SOS till further notice."

In the gloomy red glow of the torpedo room a seaman happily let a monkey wrench clatter into a tool kit and, exhausted, his torso covered with a sheen of sweat, his blue denims soaking, he lay back without a word onto the fetid-smelling bunk.

"Initial matchup," began the sonar man, priding himself on being able to tell what type a ship would be from only the first few lines of the computer's graphics, "is…" But he had to wait. It wasn't a U.S. Navy ship at all. *"Civilian,"* he said with the surprise of a nudist spotting a clothed trespasser. Before he could say any more, the printout spewed out: "MV *Petrel*— Oceanog Ves—550 ts Sub la and rec cap. F6."

The sonar man interpreted. "Oceanographic vessel. The MV *Petrel*. Five hundred and fifty tons. Submersible launch and recovery capability to force six."

"What are we in? Can you guess?"

"No, sir. But in the Aleutians—"

"I know," Wain cut in tiredly, his clenched fist kneading his forehead hard above the right eye. "Force six is like the Fourth of July up here. Comes once a year. Normal is force eight, right?"

"Or more," Sloane said, "but I don't think it'll worry the *Petrel*. They'll try getting something down to us no matter what the weather. I've heard about that outfit."

By now a dozen or so of the off-watch crew had gathered in the control room. Had he not known better, Wain, struck by the silence and the exhausted appearance of the men, would have considered them threatening. Wain turned back to sonar. "But what if the *Petrel*—"

"But what?" someone interrupted in a tone that struck Wain as intentionally disrespectful.

"I was wondering," he said, "whether they can do anything if it's above force six. I'm not doubting intent, but *can* they do it?"

"They're very professional." This came from Dyer, who was trying to be the objective expert after his earlier panicky display.

"*We're* professional," said someone pointedly. "And look where we are."

"We hit a freshwater down draft, Novak," said Sloane. "That stuff can drive you down so fast it'd—"

"We should've been ready for that, right?"

"We were," snapped Sloane. "The vanes didn't respond quickly enough to—"

"Yeah, well they should have, if those goddamn yard birds in Bangor knew what the hell they were doing."

"Knock it off!" ordered Wain. "Let's get ourselves organized in case they do get something down."

"Second ship is the *Boise*," said the sonar man. "Navy frigate—guided missile—" There was a weak cheer.

"Terrific," said the disgruntled Novak. "So what are they gonna send down, a chopper?"

"Look, whatever's going on topside, we don't know," Wain said. "But they'll try to work out something between them."

"Third echo, Captain. It's a sub!"

"Hey, hey, hey!" said a crewman with all the reserve energy he had. "That's more like it."

"Victor class," said the sonar man. "HUK—Hunter/killer—the *Amur*." He didn't read off its specs from the computer screen. They all knew what hunter/killer meant.

"Maybe they're going to help us," said Dyer.

"Right," said Novak. "And I'm Dolly Parton!"

"I dunno," said Yeoman Smythe. "Maybe the doc's right. I mean our frigate and this *Petra*—"

"*The Petrel*," the sonar man corrected him.

"Yeah, well, they must know the Russian sub's there, right?"

Captain Wain glanced down at the sonar man in the blood-red light. "He has a point."

The sonar man nodded. "Yes, sir, reckon they all know about one another up there. Could be a joint rescue effort."

"What do you think *now*, Dolly?" another seaman asked Novak.

"I'll believe it when I see it," said Novak. "When I hear someone locking onto that escape hatch above us here, then I'll believe it."

"You'll faint if it's a Russkie," said someone else.

"Yeah," Smythe said. "Hey, Novak, you're looking more like Dolly every time I look at you."

"Watch him," said a yeoman. "He's been at sea too long."

There was tired laughter, but it *was* laughter, and Wain was glad of it. Laughter came from hope, and right now that was what they needed most. Still Wain couldn't bring himself to join in, because if they were rescued by a Russian sub's deep-sea rescue vehicle, and a Russian face was the first face he saw, then Wain knew his duty was to deny the enemy access to any classified information about the most powerful weapon in the American arsenal. Yet to do this before a possible rescue would, among other things, mean crippling the vital passive sonar, or ears, of the sub. The thing that worried Wain most, that started a steady thumping at the base of his skull, spreading all around his head like a vise, was that even if you took a sledgehammer to the electronics, there was no way, short of blowing them up—which would mean blowing up the sub—that you could prevent the Russians from painstakingly putting the pieces of the puzzle back together. What would he do—what *could* he do, if it was a combined rescue effort and it was a Russian who first reached—

"Captain!"

It was Chief Ryman at the door of the control room, and even in the red light Wain could see his face was drained of color.

KNEAD WAS HALF IN and half out of the head near the control room, slumped forward, the blood dripping from his wrists onto the scored decking in a crimson pool beneath the battle lanterns. His head leaned against the door. Eyes full of mad intent stared at them. The vinegary stench of urine was so powerful that the medic gasped involuntarily as he felt for a carotid pulse and watched for any signs of breathing.

"He's still alive, Captain."

"All right, all right, clear the area," ordered Wain. "Smythe, lend a hand here."

"Silly bastard," someone said. "All over a bit of pussy, eh, Doc?"

Dyer was shaking. He started to say something, then made a dash for the twin head and retched until he was on his knees.

"I dunno," said a torpedo man, shuffling forward. "They say there's no pain."

"Beats suffocating," said someone else.

"Hey! Everyone back to his station."

It was Sloane. The fourteen or so crewmen who had come from the forward torpedo room to see what was going on stopped and looked at the officer. He was still in full khaki officer's uniform, which was soaked through with sweat, the gold dolphin he proudly wore glinting in the ruby light. Sweat trickled down his face.

He said no more; he didn't have to. They saw it in his eyes—his resilience, his determination shaming the defeatist talk. It wasn't that they thought he was better than they or tougher, but ever since he'd been billeted to the *New York* they'd recognized him as a "mustang," a man who had earned his lieutenant's bars for working his way up through the ranks; it was this they respected. It told them he knew what every one of them was most worried about—that if there was to be a rescue it would have to be within the next twelve hours.

The unexpected rise in temperature had sapped more strength and consumed more oxygen and cooling air than anticipated.

Without oxygen the men were done for. Without cooling air, whatever vital automatic systems that had remained functioning so far would soon begin serious overheating. Even now the machines were siphoning off reserve battery power that was meant to drive the two emergency "get home" shafts concealed in two stern tanks, and that would give them three, possibly five, knots, if they had enough power left, and if they had an "up" angle—positive buoyancy—which they didn't.

# 32

INSIDE THE RUSSIAN DSRV, deep sea rescue vehicle, which was riding piggyback on the *Karpaty*'s stern deck, the vehicle's pilot was making his final checks. The DSRV was no reconnaissance vehicle; it quite simply didn't possess the agility and quick response to control maneuverability of the American's submersible, *Serena I*. But the American was out of operation, at least for the present, according to the sonar operators from the *Amur* who had locked onto the *Petrel*'s sonar.

LIKE THE AMERICAN SHIPS heading for the new spill, Commander Malik, captain of the *Amur*, believed that the object bouncing back the *Petrel*'s sonar was the lost Trident.

Malik was unstinting in his praise of Kornon, admiring the general's ability to change strategy to meet changing situations instead of being locked in, automatonlike, by the Kremlin's infamous bureaucratic inflexibility. Now that the Americans had found the *New York*, Malik reported to his officers, Kornon saw no immediate necessity to have Hall killed. That could wait until the American had served one more useful purpose. The *Boise*'s captain, no doubt with Washington's concerns pressing him, had told the press that as soon as Hall finished decompression Hall would go down again, this time in the AD suit from the *Petrel*. The information didn't surprise Malik's executive officer, who pointed out that Hall was known for being unusually determined and unorthodox.

"You mean *rude*." Malik smiled. "If we are to believe our trawlers' intercepts of the *Boise*'s radio traffic."

"By unorthodox," said the *Amur*'s executive, "I meant highly individualistic, Comrade."

"Yes, like our General Kornon," Malik said. "Well, individualistic or not, Comrade, at the moment he is our prisoner."

The first officer was nonplussed. There was no doubt it had been a clever move on Kornon's part to offer the decompression chamber in order to cover any suspicions the Americans might have originally had but, as the first officer pointed out to Commander Malik, as long as the American was alive he was surely a threat. As soon as he was through decompression, probably in less than an hour from now, he would be talking and back in action.

"But perhaps he doesn't know it was a torpedo that struck his craft. We went to great trouble, Comrade, yourself included, so that he would *not* think it was a torpedo."

"That is not what I mean, Commander. I don't think anyone, given the conditions, could have been sure what struck them. I mean that in less than an hour he could be in action again."

"An hour?" Malik asked, bushy Georgian eyebrows raised. "An hour, you say?"

"Yes. The helicopter from the *Boise* retrieved the oceanographer within three minutes of his bobbing to the surface."

"Not so remarkable, Lieutenant, given the fact they had lost contact with him and sent the helicopter out. They wouldn't have retrieved Hall in three minutes if their helicopter hadn't been airborne."

The lieutenant, however, knew this wasn't true. The Americans off Korea and Vietnam had often picked up a carrier pilot in that time, including lift-off time. They were very fast. But there was no point in irritating the big Georgian. All he had wanted to make clear, he told Malik, was that Hall would be out of the chamber in an hour. By that time the *Amur* crew would have had to untether the slow-moving DSRV, lock onto the *New York*'s escape hatch and, while rescuing a few Americans, gain access to the secret Trident. And there would be at least a hundred and fifty men aboard the American submarine, while the *Amur*'s DSRV was capable of removing only twenty-four at a time and transferring them to the surface. This would all take much longer than an hour.

Commander Malik gave the first lieutenant his broadest of bearded smiles, crow's-feet crinkling at the corners of his deeply set dark brown eyes. Sometimes the lieutenant's naiveté just plain annoyed him, as when he thought Hall would actually be able to tell a torpedo had come at him instead of what would, in fact, have been only a dark, indistinct blur, like some huge fish. But at other times the lieutenant's youthful innocence evoked in Malik the warm, fatherly feeling of someone who feels obliged to teach an innocent the way of the world for his own benefit. Career men like Kornon devoured such innocence.

Reaching out for a grease-veined mug of tea, Malik shook his head, still smiling. "What makes you think, Lieutenant, that we are going to rescue any more than twenty-four—once we've gained entry?"

The lieutenant looked stunned but recovered, Malik thought, brilliantly. "Because, sir, if you rescue twenty-four, when they are interviewed by the press, they will say there are still over a hundred more left."

"How do you know that—that there are over a hundred men left?" Malik's smile was jaundiced.

"The tapping—the SOS. By now every ship close by will have heard that."

"It takes only one man to tap out a message, Lieutenant. Perhaps the last man—just before he died."

"But, sir, the twenty-four will—"

Malik's smile had vanished. "You think we will let twenty-four Americans tell the U.S. Navy we saw what was inside the Trident?"

"Then . . ." The lieutenant stopped. "Then what will we tell . . ."

"Tell the press? The world?" Malik shrugged, took a sugar cube and, in the style of his ancestors, placed it between his teeth before drinking the hot tea. "We will tell them the truth—there was an explosion as our DSRV approached the *New York*—only debris was left, strewed about the seabed, a catastrophic accident. Possibly started by fire. Who knows?" Malik unclipped his jacket pocket and extracted a message sheet. "This is the news release General Kornon will regretfully present to the press aboard the *Karpaty II*. I think it will be very moving."

"How?" asked the lieutenant, swallowing hard.

Malik was finishing his tea. "What's that?"

"How are you—"

"*We*, Lieutenant."

"Yes, sir. How are we going to . . ."

"Explode the *New York* without firing a torpedo that the *Boise* or anyone else could pick up?"

"Yes, sir."

"An antitank mine. The latest model—very powerful. Kornon's idea. It's an army mine, no larger than a dinner plate. Pressure- or time-set. Magnetically attached, in this case. It has a very concentrated blast cone. I saw one demonstrated in Vladivostok. It blew a substantial hole through a German Leopard. Do you know how thick the armor plate on a Leopard tank is?"

The lieutenant shook his head.

"Neither do I." Malik laughed, turning to check the situation board monitoring the DSRV's imminent departure from the *Amur*. "But however thick it is," Malik continued, "it's many times thicker than a sub's pressure hull. The *New York* will implode just like that." He snapped his finger and thumb. "Everything flatter than unleavened bread."

"And the twenty-four men in the DSRV?" inquired the lieutenant.

"Ah . . ." said Malik, the lines on his face harder and deeper than the younger man had ever noticed before; his was the face of a commander who didn't flinch, a man who knew how to win. "The Americans in the DSRV will be 'released.'"

"From the DSRV?"

"Yes."

"They will fight," said the lieutenant. "I would. And there is only room to push one out at a time through the belly hatch."

Malik had finished his tea. He burped, excusing himself. "No, no, no. Of course they won't volunteer. *Bozhe moy!* My God!" The lieutenant was starting to annoy him again, even though it was true that as torpedo officer he couldn't be expected to know the finer points of DSRV operational procedure. "You don't *ask* them, Lieutenant, to open the watertight hatch. The DSRV crew close their watertight hatch, then open the sea valve to the passenger compartment. The men drown like rats. *Then* you release them."

The lieutenant could see their bodies streaming toward the surface a thousand feet above at over a hundred feet a minute, swelling and exploding like puffer fish, innards and limbs floating evidence of the tragic "catastrophic accident" aboard the *New York*.

"Then we'd better hurry," said the lieutenant, an edge to his voice, looking at his watch. "Before Hall makes another attempt."

"Don't be an idiot!"

The lieutenant's face shot up. Malik charged on. "Hall won't know how long it took them to get him aboard. Three minutes, five, ten minutes. The difference in decompression time is exponential. In this case three minutes means an hour and a half in the chamber. Any more and it's—"

"Six and a half hours," answered the lieutenant.

"Correct. So he'll stay in there as long as our doctor tells him. We won't even have to use the Spets team we brought along. He *is* our prisoner now, Lieutenant. On the American warship."

"Unless he feels well enough to insist he be released."

Malik nodded impatiently. "Yes, yes, that's possible. But do you think General Kornon hasn't thought of that? Kornon is fighting for his life, Lieutenant. *He's* thought of everything, what the Americans call 'every angle.' It's Hall or him. You'd better toughen that soft heart of yours, Comrade, or you'll end up the oldest lieutenant in the Soviet navy. We're not here for a tea party. In the end it's the Americans or us. Which would you rather be?"

"Us," the lieutenant answered unequivocally.

"Good," said Malik, grinning again and putting his hand on the other's shoulder. "I want you to go along as an observer in the DSRV." He looked at his watch. "You'd better go now, up through the escape hatch before they unhitch the skirt."

The lieutenant said, "Yes, sir," and did as he was told. Someday he wanted a command of his own, and if he impressed the skipper and Kornon his career would take a quantum leap. It was no good being sentimental about the Americans. Commander Malik was right—they weren't out here for a tea party.

"MR. HALL IS STILL unconscious, Captain. I assure you that you may speak to him as soon as he is able. In the meantime, I ask you to reduce speed." The Soviet doctor was on the intercom talking to Peters from the decompression chamber.

The doctor's accent was thick, but Peters understood the request clearly enough. "What's the problem?" he asked the Russian.

"The rising and swinging," replied the doctor.

"He means pitch and roll," Bryce explained.

"What about it?" asked Peters. "I'm not in charge of the weather."

"But more slowly would reduce motion—yes?"

"Not necessarily," replied Peters, at the same time gesturing to Bryce, off to his side by the steering console, that he maintain flank speed en route to the *New York*'s position as given by the *Petrel*. Then Peters turned his attention back to the doctor. "What's the problem? Is it too rough for you?"

"For us, no, but for the patient, Mr. Hall, it is not good. When he wakes he will have no horizon in here to fix upon. I think he may suffer auditory vertigo, also—you know this word?"

"Yes," said Peters. "Well, I'm sorry, but my orders are to proceed with all due haste to the *New York*."

"What is the point of hurry, Captain, if your leading oceanographer is too ill to work? He will require much more straightness to help recover his equilibrium. You understand? His balance."

Peters and Bryce exchanged glances. They figured that by "straightness," the doctor meant running with the sea, due east—away from the *New York*.

"Can't help you," said Peters firmly. "Hall will have to recover as best he can. We don't know what the situation is aboard the *New York*, but we may be able to assist your people as soon as we arrive. The *Karpaty II* informs us they've dispatched their DSRV. They'll want your recompression chamber pronto."

There was a pause and a crackle of static. Peters and Bryce could hear the Russian doctor consulting the nurse. Finally he came back on. "What is this pronto?"

"Right now. It means your people will want the chamber right over the *New York*. I have to say I agree with them."

"I am a doctor, Captain. My concern is for my patient."

"Well, I'm sorry," said Peters firmly, his voice mixed with static. "We stay at flank speed."

THE DOCTOR LOOKED down at the American. He still looked pale, his pallor made worse by the reflection of the redded light. Except for the steady pulse he could easily have been taken for dead.

"Well, what now?" Elga asked.

"The general should not have requested the chamber so quickly. It gives us less than forty-five minutes."

"But we simply tell him—" she motioned to Hall "—that he needs another four to five hours decompression. There is no problem."

"Yes, yes," said the doctor. "I know this, of course. But a slow arrival would have given us more time away from the *New York*. When we get there he will want to leave the chamber. Don't you see? Kornon's orders were to appear considerate of the American but, insofar as no harm could come to him while he was on board the American ship, at least to delay him until Kornon's DSRV had done its work."

Elga smiled sweetly. "You worry too much, Herr Doktor. I'm here to help, remember?"

The doctor gave a fleeting, if anxious, grin. "That is a great comfort." He meant it sincerely—the whole situation placed too much responsibility on his shoulders, and soon Hall would be awake, which would cause even more difficulty—but he could see the East German took his remark as Russian arrogance. They were both speaking English—perhaps he had used the wrong word. "No, I meant it, Fräulein. I am glad you are here, Comrade. Truly."

Elga sat down on the seat beside the American. "We'll manage. After all, he is our patient. With the world press all about us nothing must happen to him." She tightened one of the three antiroll restraining straps on Hall's bed. The *Boise*'s rolling was becoming much more severe as the frigate reached flank speed of thirty-five knots less ten for the head winds coming out of Asia. She pulled down the calico sheet. "I thought so. He has an erection."

The doctor looked down over his bifocals. "Water retention and a full bladder—volume expansion during free ascent."

"Interesting," she replied. The doctor was about to reply when a violent pitch made the ship rise precipitously, their stomachs rising with it. For a moment the *Boise* was suspended, motionless, before she crashed down in an explosion of white spray. Elga felt her stomach drop as if through an endless vacuum of space. It was one of the most disagreeable sensations she could remember.

# 33

LIKE A RUNNER from whom all others take their pace, the *Petrel*, now more than a thousand feet above the downed sub, swung into action with all the panache of the no-nonsense professional she was. Her sharp white bow was jockeyed into position by Tate's use of the bow thrusters, their switch-on, switch-off circuits hooked up to the ASK-C—automatic station keeping computer—which was capable of keeping the *Petrel*, unlike any other American or Russian ships, including the *Boise*, within a hundred and fifty feet of a fixed point on the ocean bottom in forty-knot winds, eighteen-foot swells and twelve-foot waves. The waves were now as high as twenty feet and the winds higher, so the best the *Petrel* could hope for, even from ASK, was a plus or minus four hundred feet—a remarkable achievement of late-twentieth-century technology, yet one that could do little alone to rescue the other modern engineering marvel trapped by its negative buoyancy in the deep below. For this a man was needed.

HALL WAS JUST WAKING UP. A thick, cloying perfume plugged his sinuses. He tried to focus his eyes on the small, dark circles of the curtained portholes, certain he was in a ship's cabin. Gradually he became aware of the gut-wrenching roll and fall, of a man bending over him in the red light, of a woman, her long hair a lurid pink. The cabin seemed tiny. The doctor, with a heavy accent, was saying something about nitrogen...narcosis...recompression and decompression, while the woman sat on a chain-suspended bunk opposite and to the left. She was smiling. She looked like a nurse, her hands thrust into the pockets of a white jacket, the fullness exposed by its V-neck holding his gaze captive. Then she spoke, at once sensual and motherly, her lips soft, perfectly formed, as she inquired in mellifluous tones how he was feeling.

"Fine..." He looked about, finding it difficult to raise his head. Behind the doctor he saw a printed graph, meters plotted against time, with Russian letters in the margins. He lay back, remembering the *Serena* going down. "Recompression chamber?" he asked.

"Yes."

"Aboard the *Boise*?" asked Hall.

The doctor stood, startled. Elga smiled. Both wondered how the American knew which ship he was on, especially when the decompression graph was in Russian. Perhaps he'd had a moment of consciousness after he'd been picked up. Elga had no idea, but she could see that Hall's words had jolted the doctor's confidence in any delaying action.

"How do you know," asked the doctor, unable to mask his surprise, "that you are on board the *Boise*?"

Hall, his voice raspy from dehydration, answered, "You mustn't have been on many ships, Doc."

"No," said the doctor, his tone making the word sound more like an admission of guilt than a simple fact. The American's quick deduction didn't allow him time to recover his usual professional, confident air. "But how did you know?"

"Every ship," said Hall, "has its own peculiar motion. The *Boise* rises high, swings hard to port, then slides to starboard."

The doctor didn't know whether to believe the American or not—perhaps he had heard them talking before. But then he would have gone along with them. Or would he? Whatever, the American wasn't stupid. But if he had been conscious longer than they thought and had heard them talking, then in order not to give away his pretense of unconsciousness, the American would have to say he didn't know how long he'd been in the chamber. Baiting his trap with a smile the doctor asked, "Do you know how long you've been here, Mr. Hall?" It was a perfectly innocuous-sounding question, just the kind any doctor would ask a recovering patient, testing for possible concussion.

"About an hour," answered Hall.

"Oh . . ." said the doctor. "Then you must have been wakeful?"

"Awake." Elga corrected.

Hall noticed she was fidgeting—or was it playing?—with the top button on the white silk blouse under her jacket. A nervous nurse or a sexual come-on? He wasn't sure. Maybe both. "No," he answered, his voice even raspier than before, "I wasn't awake." He turned his left wrist toward her, showing the faint greenish-yellow phosphorus dots on the Omega's face. "I wear a watch."

Elga smiled demurely, the sensual parting of her lips and fixed stare communicating more than mere good humor to Hall. The doctor wasn't amused, however, by his and Elga's overlooking the small but potentially crucial detail of the watch.

Dr. Latik tried to excuse his bungling to himself. After all, he was a medical man, not KGB. But he knew that it wouldn't mollify Kornon, wouldn't make it easier for the DSRV to do what it had to do in less than an hour. In fact, he was becoming so worked up about the prospect of having to face Kornon that when he moved away from the bunk to check the decompression gauges and heard Hall's question, he was quite disconcerted for a minute, until Elga repeated the question in a casual, apparently unconcerned tone.

"Mr. Hall would like to know if he can leave the chamber soon, Doctor. He wishes to go aboard the *Petrel* as soon as it rendezvouses with the *Boise*. I was telling him he needs more rest, and in any case it seems that the *New York* has been found and we are heading there. So until we get there, there is no need for Mr. Hall to—''

"Exactly," the doctor agreed quickly. "The nurse is correct, Mr. Hall," continued the doctor, adopting his best no nonsense stance with his patient. He indicated the array of pressure gauges fixed to the bulkhead behind him at the end of the bunk, arranged in a parallel but offset series. "You are not yet well enough."

"Why not?" Hall insisted, half rising from the bed, then suddenly lying down again, realizing he wasn't even wearing his briefs. "The gauges are at one atmosphere, right?"

The doctor was perspiring. "Yes, er, yes, of course. The gauges are at one atmosphere. Yes, certainly they are, but you still need more rest—much more rest, as the nurse says. You realize—'' and now his voice rang in the small chamber, growing in power with his reassertion of authority "—what happens to your lungs in the free ascent, I assume?"

"I know," replied Hall. As a diver he remembered vividly the first demonstration he'd seen of a small fist-size balloon released from the bottom of a deep tank; the balloon rose, rapidly expanded and then exploded at the surface.

But the doctor didn't hear him, and continued with a description of all the possible horrors following free ascent from great depth. "The membrane expands... bleeding... unless you—'' He stopped, unable for a moment to think of the English word he wanted. He turned to Elga and used Russian.

"Trickle," Elga suggested.

"Yes. Without trickling your breath instead of holding it."

"I did that," replied Hall. The jittery Russian was starting to get on his nerves. "I backpaddled as well to reduce the rate of ascent."

"All the same," Elga interjected, her voice smooth, her tone unflappable, "I do think the doctor is correct, Mr. Hall. Here." She touched the side of his neck, her fingers feeling for the carotid artery. "Your pulse is still quite fast. You are very tense, *ja*?"

The touch of her hand tingled through him, the most exciting thing his body had experienced since he last made love to Gloria. He could feel his pulse throbbing against her skin, feeling her feeling the pulse throbbing, her fingers trailing eas-

ily down onto his shoulder where her delicate yet powerful grip
squeezed his trapezius. She was correct, he thought. I am tense.
It's not every day I almost die. Her fingers began kneading the
rope-taut muscle, and he felt himself relaxing, but he didn't
want to admit to anyone he had been so wound up. He knew he
needed to go down again quickly—not only because there were
a hundred and fifty men trapped but, because like any driver
or pilot following an accident, he needed to return to the scene
as soon as possible before unbridled fear had a chance to move
in as permanent tenant and take over as a phobia that might be
difficult or impossible to shake. "Fast pulse or not," said Hall,
"I'll have to go see Peters and tell him what I saw, or rather
didn't see...."

"Of course," agreed Elga. "But first you need to relax. How
will you go down from the *Petrel* when she arrives—in a submarine boat?"

Hall smiled. He liked the Fräulein, not just because she was
a stunner but her turn of phrase, "submarine boat," evoked an
innocent little-girl quality that was attractive, cute. "No," he
answered, feeling more relaxed by the second. She was right, his
trapezius had been like steel, but it was feeling better now the
more she massaged it. "I go down in a suit, a metal suit," he
explained.

"Ah," she said happily. "Like a robot, *ja*?"

"*Ja!*" he answered. His eyes had fully adjusted to the red
light. As they met hers, for a moment he imagined she was
squeezing something else.

"You should go soon, then," she said encouragingly, dis-
armingly, refusing to look at the doctor. She was certain he was
staring at her. "But first you need to be rid of all this tension,
*ja*?"

Before he could answer, Hall felt her hands moving firmly,
confidently beneath his shoulder blade. "Turn over please!"
He obeyed, protesting, "As soon as the *Petrel* comes alongside, I—"

"*Ja, ja,* of course," said Elga. "But enough of work for the
moment. You should worry about yourself. The doctor will go
up and tell the captain. Also our ship should make ready for
our helicopter. We must be leaving, too." All the time she was

working Hall's shoulder, she was glancing at the doctor and at the door. Finally he got her cue.

"I will leave you now," Dr. Latik said. "I will be coming back for a blood sample. Sometimes a bubble or two of nitrogen remains. If this happens, and they become lodged later in one of your blood vessels, you could die. You must know this, yes?"

There was a mumbled confirmation from the pillow that told the doctor and Elga not only that the American understood but that his tired body was yielding to her deep but supple kneading of his tight muscles. The doctor left the chamber to report on the open radio channel that the American oceanographer, or "aquanaut," as the doctor more accurately described him, had now been decompressed to one atmosphere. He was, in effect, warning Kornon that although they were doing their best to delay him, the American would sooner or later be going down a second time to find the *New York* and to supervise its salvage from the deep—if that was possible.

In the curtained chamber, as if she had only been waiting for the doctor to leave, to do so, Elga told Hall to call her by her first name. He said she could call him Frank.

"I am going to apply some rubbing alcohol, Frank. It may be a shock at first. Are you ready?" she inquired jovially.

He moved his head to the right, away from the bulkhead, to glance up at her, thinking a little guiltily of Gloria as he watched Elga unscrewing the lid of the plastic bottle. Her sweet perfume washed over him, and he saw that the top button of her blouse was undone. As she leaned forward over his bare back, her breasts, hardly restrained by her white lace bra, began moving voluptuously back and forth as she pushed and pulled against his upper back. Then, in one long, slow downward movement, she pulled her hands over his thighs. He buried his face in the soft foam pillow and could feel her breasts— or was it her thigh?—pressing against him, her hands sliding over his buttocks then under, her fingers trailing in a long caress beneath his hips down the full length of his leg. He stiffened with the sudden excitement.

Her voice was a whisper. "You must relax. Do not be embarrassed. Have you never been massaged before?"

"Not like this."

"You do not like it?" She sounded professionally offended.

The last thing he wanted to do was offend her. He might as well enjoy it. He heard a faint rustling noise.

"It's so hot in here," she said softly. He felt her again, his arms limp by his sides. His breathing deepened, until the heat, her touch and the motion of the *Boise*—much less violent now, coming about and running with the sea instead of against it, readying to rendezvous with the *Petrel* within the hour—all combined to lull him into somnolence. Images of him and Gloria in bed together vied with ones of him and Elga. Her massage became more and more tantalizing, until he knew if he let it, the conflicting images, fighting for precedence, would fuse in an explosion of release.

The phosphorescent dots on his watch slid into his view like so many beady eyes in the soft red light, reminding him of the last thing he had seen as he abandoned the *Serena I*—the dying red eyes of the instrument panel, which had blinked like a living thing when the submersible was hit by the rushing shadow of the shark.

Or was it a shark? He told himself he mustn't think of the attack, only of the present, of the deep satisfaction the masseuse was giving him. But the more he tried to put it out of his mind the more he was drawn back to it, not so much to the creature itself as its speed. The more he thought about it the more it struck him just how fast the attacker had been—a blur of gray—almost as if it was a torpedo. But that was nonsense, of course; if it had been a torpedo, he wouldn't be here now with the beautiful Elga. But . . .

He turned his head to see her. "Where did you put my survival suit?" Her breasts, he saw, were glistening in the heat that had made him perspire, too, making him feel drowsier and drowsier.

"Don't worry," she said schoolmarmishly. She was disappointed, for she had thought him so aroused that nothing would distract him. "You worry too much, you Americans," she said. "The suit is all right. It's hanging in the cupboard. Now for goodness' sake, relax."

He lowered himself again to the bed, but there was residual tension in his back. He was in such good condition that Elga could see the outline of the muscles plainly as they flexed. She went to work on him again.

Why, he wondered, would anyone use a dummy torpedo? The noise!

He sat bolt upright, wrapping the blanket about his waist. Elga stepped back, alarmed. Her blouse was soaked with perspiration, the lacy white bra pushing tightly against it. She'd been working hard on him, all right.

"Where's the intercom?" he asked as he got to his feet. Then he saw it across the chamber, and in a second he was speaking to the bridge. "Peters? Frank Hall here. You read me?"

"Yes. How are you feeling? That was quite a—"

"Fine. Can you send a crewman down to the chamber? On the double."

"Yes, but what—"

"Send him down. Now!"

On the bridge, Peters shook his head at Bryce. "Well, I see his good manners are back."

Elga, in the decompression chamber, was scrambling to keep up with events. "He cannot come in here!" she complained.

"Don't worry." Hall sat on the edge of the bunk. He added gallantly, "You think I'd want to share you?"

She beamed. Perhaps she'd win, after all.

As Hall waited for the crewman to arrive, he found his survival suit in the closet where Elga had told him it was. He dug into the pocket on the side of the leg and removed the 35 mm film. He could have done the job himself, but it would take time, and as yet he had no dry clothes. He pulled back a blind on one of the ports to see if the crewman was coming but could see nothing but the hangar's bulkhead. Then he heard an argument going on between a crewman and the two Russian technicians outside, who apparently didn't want to let him into the chamber. Hall opened the door leading into the safety interlock room between the chamber proper and the outside, then looked back at Elga. God, he thought, she's beautiful. "Be right back," he assured her.

"I hope so," she replied cheekily.

The technicians outside the chamber could hardly refuse to let the two Americans speak to each other, on an American Navy ship where the technicians were, strictly speaking, guests.

Hall gave the film to the crewman. "How far are we from the *Petrel*?" he asked.

"Still about half an hour, sir."

"All right, listen, take this to Lieutenant Bryce and ask him to develop it. Fast. Bring it back the moment he's finished. Never mind printing it straightaway—just bring me the negatives. It'll be the last few frames I'm interested in. They should only take fifteen, twenty minutes to develop. Remember, tell him I want to see it right away."

"Yes, sir." The sailor's voice was louder than necessary, probably, Hall thought, to rub it into the Soviet technicians that this was *his* ship, not theirs.

"And, sailor?"

"Yes, sir?"

"Bring me down some dry clothes if you can."

"Yes, sir."

"One more thing!"

The crewman turned around. Hall told him as forcefully as he could, "If anybody fouls up *this* film, I'll personally drown him!"

When the sailor had gone, Hall looked at his watch, calculating what time it would be when the *Petrel* drew alongside. There wasn't a thing he could do until then. He looked at the technicians. "How you boys doin'?"

The Russians nodded politely and smiled.

"Everyone's happy today. That's nice," said Hall. "Well, any one wants me—" he nodded in the direction of the chamber "—I'll be with Comrade Elga." The technicians were still smiling.

When he reentered the chamber, he understood one reason why the technicians were smiling, and why the doctor hadn't returned. Elga was patting the bed, her invitation as unmistakable as it was blatant. He closed the hatch, dogging it firmly behind him.

"What was all that about outside?" she asked playfully.

"I wanted some dry clothes sent down."

"There'll be time for clothes later," she said sweetly. She paused. "There's plenty of time for *everything*, Frank." The difficulty, she knew, was that this world-famous aquanaut had a girlfriend back in America. That was why he was holding back; it was all a matter of war between natural desire and petty bourgeois conscience. He wanted it all right and couldn't quite bring himself to say no. She switched off the intercom and dimmed the red light further, until they were barely visible to each other.

The sailor's knocking on the hatch was the most unwelcome sound Hall had heard in a long time. Elga was furious. "Who is that?" she called out sharply.

"Clothes for Mr. Hall, ma'am."

"Leave them."

"I have to get them," Hall said rather reluctantly, walking to the door, again using the blanket as a wrap. It suddenly struck the worldly Elga that Hall had been playing a game with *her*.

"Sir."

"Yes?" Hall asked.

"We developed that film."

"So what did you find?"

"Ah . . . sir—" the sailor began hesitantly. "The technician developed 'em real careful like but . . . well, sir . . ." The sailor seemed frightened. "There ain't anything on them. They're all black—overexposed."

Hall nodded. "Or deliberately exposed," he murmured to himself, looking in Elga's direction, "before the film was developed." He thanked the sailor. "Well, we'll never know then."

"Don't get your drift, sir."

Hall took the bundle of freshly pressed clothes and turned back toward the chamber. "Come into my parlor," he said.

"Pardon, sir?"

"Tell the captain that I want a chopper to take me over to the *Petrel*. Now."

"Yes, sir—but, sir, we're only a half hour away from her."

"It takes fifteen, twenty minutes at least to get suited up. The sooner I get there the sooner I can go down. Free descent's about a meter a second. That means I can be on the bottom— right smack on top of the *New York*—if it is the *New York*—ten minutes from the moment the *Petrel* stops. And right now, sailor, I figure I need any edge I can get."

The sailor was shocked. Hall was the first he had heard to even hint that the sub the *Petrel* was getting on its sonar screen might not be the *New York*. But then Hall was a funny guy—one minute being polite, the next minute being rude as hell to the old man.

"YOU ARE FOOLISH TO GO," said Elga, her face flushed. She was properly dressed now, her jacket making her look bustier than ever. A clutch of *Boise* sailors stared, their mouths agape. "You're a fool," she repeated to Hall. "It can be very dangerous to go down there when you're so tired." Never before had a man walked away from her favors. Never. She was angry, contemptuous and humiliated all at the same time. "Why?" she asked him out of earshot of the crewmen, and the doctor, who had reappeared, looking more worried than he was before. "We could have had a wonderful time."

Hall's eyes met hers, and he said slowly but truthfully, "Elga, I don't know where you've been."

She turned abruptly and walked away, angrily grabbing the rail that girded the chamber, to keep from falling as the *Boise* rolled. The doctor came quickly after her. "What happened?"

"We failed," she snapped, without looking back at him, switching quickly from German to Russian. "Tell Kornon we failed. He'll have to know. Hall is moving earlier than expected. We can't delay him any longer."

"*We* can't? You mean *you* can't," said the doctor churlishly.

She wheeled on him. "You sniveling coward," she said. "I suppose you would have sat up like a puppy as soon as I'd touched you?" The doctor's head shot back, withdrawing from the ferocity of her retort, but she hadn't finished with him. "He's the enemy, but he's twice the man you are. You can't even share responsibility for our failing."

"No," Dr. Latik answered simply. "And neither would you if you knew Kornon."

"I know Kornon."

"No, you don't. You've only just met him. Who was it—Lebdev?—introduced you two? You don't know Kornon. Kornon kills people."

"A lot of Russians kill people," she said viciously.

"You needn't be so upset, Comrade. Is he the first man you've failed to seduce—for the *Party*?"

"He's a fool," she said, transparently unconvincing.

"*Ja,*" said the Russian, slipping into German much more easily than he did English. "And he'll die for it."

"Good riddance!" she said. "It's nothing to me. But if I were you, *Comrade*," she spit sarcastically, "I'd draw up a contingency plan. Mr. Hall is much more unpredictable than you think."

"Oh, we already have," Dr. Latik said proudly.

"What?" she shot back.

"A contingency plan. Now I suggest we get back to the *Karpaty II* with the recompression chamber as soon as possible—before your lover descends the deep." He paused. "Have you ever seen them, Fräulein? When they pop up?"

"What are you talking about?"

"Men. Divers, I mean. Popping up to the surface from a thousand feet."

"No."

"It's very unpleasant—all the orifices being distended, then they disintegrate. The eyes are extruded."

"You're disgusting."

"Yes," answered the doctor. "That's why I work for Kornon. But he pays well, *ja*?"

"I work for Lebdev."

"Ah, a fine distinction." He laughed. "But I must say I've never taken so much pleasure in any such mission before."

"You hate him, don't you? You're jealous?"

"What? Oh, yes, I hate all Americans. They're too soft."

"Hall isn't soft," Elga returned.

"Well, you know about that."

"You are disgusting."

"And I will enjoy seeing him die and all the others he's so heroically trying to rescue. The Americans are always trying to help somebody. It's a national obsession."

"And you? You call yourself a doctor?"

They said no more as they boarded the Hind, which was ready for lift-off and the delicate operation of hooking and raising the chamber. During most of the time, they waved graciously to the news media whose cameras, still in place from when the Hind had landed, recorded every second of the helpful Russians' takeoff. The doctor knew that if Kornon had his way they would soon be shooting scenes that would make them vomit but that would gain enormously high ratings. The coverage of the greatest American naval tragedy since Pearl Harbor, "probably caused by leaking propellant from the missile bay," would be flashed in vivid color on the networks' evening news around the world. Moscow would send an official delegation, for the first time ever, to Arlington National Cemetery, "the graveyard," he explained to Elga with unconcealed delight, "of dead American heroes." If, he added, they found enough to bury.

# 34

INSIDE HIS GLEAMING WHITE AD suit, with Old Glory painted on the backpack of its built-in oxygen cylinders, and tethered to the ship by a thin but strong hydrographic wire, a black communication cord snaking around the wire like morning glory vine, Hall had descended countless times from the *Petrel*. Today he was taking down the wrist light, with its temperature dial, and the cane. The six-inch-long, three-inch-diameter light was powered by a nickel/cadmium battery. Because of the hostile environment it would be working under, the whole unit was made with clockwork precision and to Frank's specifications by his highly talented mechanic, Bill Reid, in Astoria. The flashlight could slide from elbow to wrist on a tubular track that was slightly raised above, and so did not interfere with, the aluminum-Teflon joints, while the cane was a thin, telescopic steel probe built in the same way above the right wrist.

As always the sheer beauty and wonder of descent enthralled him. Once the effusion of bubbles subsided to a single silvery stream rising in the cerulean-blue column above, he felt

again the calming rapture of déjà vu, the recurring wonderful
feeling that although each diving site was different he was
somehow returning to the same ancient family home. And all
the while he was descending in the state of negative buoyancy,
the sense that he was at once alone yet part of everything persisted, with only the hollow sound of his breathing inside the
spacemanlike suit reminding him that he was also a stranger to
the watery domain. A moment of miscalculation, either at
thirty-three feet or in the ice-cold darkness of a thousand feet—
where the pressure on each of the thirty-two Teflon-ringed
aluminum joints had to withstand over thirty times the pressure, or more than four hundred and fifty pounds per square
inch—would be fatal. A single mistake, puncturing the suit,
would crush a man to a pulp of flesh and splintered bone,
squeezing him to less than half his normal volume. Years ago,
working near the Marianas Trench off the Philippines, he had
seen a hard-hat diver whose air line fouled and twisted in the
ship's tether. The man had strained the watertight fittings in a
final frantic struggle to free himself. With contact broken off,
no one knew if he was alive or not, and it took several hours to
bring him up, because of the necessity to decompress at stages.
When the surface was reached, his rubber suit appeared collapsed, as empty as a depleted wineskin. The diver wasn't in the
suit. Instead, when the big brass helmet was unscrewed, the
man, or rather what had been a man, was found compressed
into a bloody, amorphous jelly inside the helmet.

Glancing up now through the AD suit's hemispherical helmet, Hall could see the *Petrel*'s tether cable—a fine, one-
quarter-inch hydrographic wire snaking through the silvery
water column, its curvature like that of a longbow, its con-
tours dictated by surface and subsurface currents and the layer-
cake differentials in salinity. Then one of the sea's apparent
miracles appeared, a halo of quicksilver—fish against the
translucent blue above. The effervescence of the bubbles from
his breathing obscured the halo for a moment and, as quickly
as they had appeared, the fish became a solid mass, blocking
the twilight's rays. The next instant they were gone. Shifting his
gaze to the water immediately about him, Hall saw the light
rapidly fading. A shark or two, gray nurses, passed him, un-

interested, fifty yards away, the graceful, lazy movement of their tails a thing of beauty.

The light was fading now at a much faster rate, and soon he switched on the wrist light; powerful though it was, its beam was of no real practical use beyond thirty feet. After that all detail was lost in the increasingly murky water, which was made up of a profusion of microscopic marine forms and of sediment stirred up by bottom currents as these moved about the mud and on occasion the rocky outcrops that marked the upper margins of the ten-thousand-foot-deep Aleutian Trench.

In keeping with standard procedure when working off the *Petrel*, Hall began giving his three-minute DS or dive status reports. Unlike the hard-hat diving suits of old, the AD suit had bulbous rotary joints at the elbows and above and below the knees, which were cut on the bias rather than the horizontal, permitting him much greater movement in the neutral buoyancy of the suit; in fact, NASA was now training new astronauts in the AD suits, getting them used to eighty percent of normal movement and to working in neutral buoyancy in general. But the astronauts trained in carefully monitored tanks. At a thousand feet near the Aleutian Trench, Hall knew there could be no quick recovery, and while his backpack of four thermos-sized oxygen cylinders freed him from the encumbrance of an enormously long oxygen feed line from the ship, the four cylinders, making up two independent closed-circuit systems, were his only life-support system. He had to constantly think ahead, anticipating possible problems at the same time as carrying out his work during the dive.

He shifted the wrist light ninety degrees to his left, then to his right. There was nothing but a sweep of brownish water, and beyond, the stygian darkness that emphasized the solitude of the tiny descending island of light, like a man alone on the darkest winter night. The temperature was barely above freezing, his only line of sight a short beam of foggy flashlight, through which passed a dirty snow of microorganisms and sediment in the constant symbiotic relationship of earth and sea. He inclined the light more steeply, at an angle of about forty-five degrees to his body.

"Laddie . . ." It was the *Petrel*'s first mate.

"Loud and clear, Scotty."

"Side scan says you should be nearing the bottom. See anything yet?"

"Negative."

"Ach, are you blind, mon? The scan says it's right at your feet. Maybe a hundred, a hundred and twenty feet."

"There's a lot of stuff stirred up down here. Like Scotch broth."

Hall had descended fifteen feet or so while they were talking. "Still can't see a damn thing." Moving the wrist light until it was directly in front of him, he then tilted it until it was perpendicular to where he thought the bottom would be. For a second or two his legs went from under him, so that in his negative buoyancy he went into a slow-motion somersault, though still descending. "Damn!"

"What's up?" asked Scotty.

"Hit my gun belt." It was slang for one of the arms of the suit hitting the belt of umbilical weights around the waist of the suit. In the event of anything untoward happening topside, preventing the *Petrel* from reeling him up, he could drop the weights and go up at a hundred feet a minute in free ascent in the one atmosphere suit, without having to undergo time-consuming surface decompression.

"Anything yet, Frank?"

"No. Visibility's fallen to fifteen feet."

"Then be careful you don't bump into the bloody thing."

"If I do, Scotty," Hall answered jovially, "you'll be the first to know, mon." His voice was clear on the open rescue channel, undistorted by the speeded-up Mickey Mouse effect once produced by the helium mix gases before the invention of the AD suit with oxygen feed.

Listening on the open channel aboard the *Boise*, Captain Peters grunted, "He's sounding civil for a change. Must be ill."

The comment made Bryce feel awkward. Hall had been decent enough over the blunder Bryce had made in misinterpreting the photo of part of the compass as part of a sub's sail. At the same time, the first officer had to admit Peters had a point—Hall hadn't exactly been cordial to Peters. Perhaps it was the kind of personality clash that remains a mystery even to people who know and admire both parties. The irony, as Bryce saw it, was that in many ways the two men seemed so much alike: confident, highly professional, possessing an ability to delegate as well as command—although it was true that Hall had a lively sense of humor, while there was little that moved Peters to laughter. But the more he thought about it, the more Bryce decided that it wasn't so much a case of like repelling like at all. The similarities between the two might only be superficial, the face of the human psyche, as with an iceberg, only one-quarter visible, the greater part of a person's nature hidden beneath the surface, often in deep turbulence.

"You think he's friendly?" asked Peters, sensing the first officer's ambivalence.

"Ah . . . I think he can be, sir. If he wants. He's worked a lot with the people on the *Petrel*. Anyway," said Bryce, grinning, "I guess it pays to be on good terms with whoever's got your tether line."

"Maybe," Peters shot back. "But we're the bigger ship around here. If it is the *New York* down there, and we manage to get her to negative buoyancy, we'll be the one hauling her up. I would've thought Hall, being he's so damn smart, would've taken the time to be on good terms with—" Immediately he shifted the emphasis away from himself. "I mean he's alienated half the *Boise*'s crew already, with his boss arse tone."

Bryce had to agree with the old man's assessment. "Could be," he replied awkwardly, "he blames us for calling him and Bremmer out from Attu on a wild-goose chase."

"So we made a mistake," said Peters. "It wasn't the sub. So all right. But with the sonar equipment and underwater photo gear we have it was the best call we could have made. Goddamn it, we're a warship, not a research vessel."

Bryce wanted to get away from any more talk about who goofed, misinterpreting a part of the metal compass for a sub in the photo, and was grateful for a crackle of static on the open channel. "Down there yet, Frank?" It was Tate's voice from the *Petrel*.

There was another burp or two of static, then a faint, inaudible voice from the deep.

"Christ," said Peters sarcastically, "don't tell me their equipment isn't perfect, either."

But he rang the *Petrel* immediately, her sleek white lines plainly visible despite the swells a quarter mile away, asking if the *Boise* could offer any assistance.

"No-o," replied the Scotsman. "No panic. I think we've got a wee kink in the communication cord. Sometimes it gets in a tangle. It'll probably straighten itself out soon enough. But thanks for the offer, Captain."

"Not at all," said Peters. "They're our boys down there."

"Aye. And if anyone can help 'em, it'll be Frank. He's a good lad."

No one on the *Boise* said a word as Peters replaced the mike in the cradle and walked, hands clasped behind his back, out to the starboard wing. He turned his cap, peak to the back, braced himself against the big binocular turntable and swung the glasses about in the direction of the *Petrel*. The crisscross pylons of the *Boise*'s air-search radar antennae immediately behind the bridge and the disk of the target illumination radar obscured Peters's view until the frigate slid and rose high on the next swell. In the magnificent circle of darkening blue ocean, slashed white by the wind, the big articulated hydraulic arm on the *Petrel*'s stern was clearly visible. Peters could see a glint of gold as the silvery tether wire was reflected in the last of the sun's fading rays, the tether wire bisected here and there by the darker communications cable.

That the fate of one hundred and fifty men, men like him and his crew, either joy or tragedy, hung upon such a slender thread spoke to him again of man's vulnerability whenever he ventured into the vast watery main that was most of his planet. Whatever else Hall might be, Peters knew he was brave.

Just then another message came over the open rescue channel. Kornon told the *Petrel* and the *Boise* and the cluster of other American and Russian picket ships and news boats that the *Karpaty*'s DSRV, the *Lenin I*, had also been lowered to assist in locating the *New York* and to help in whatever way possible.

PASSING FROM BLUE to dark blue into the zone of pitch-black, the *Lenin I* was now showing up as a definite echo, an oblong shape of orange light the size of a small, fat cigar blipping in the middle of the *Petrel*'s big nine-square-foot tinted video screen, its image relayed by a sled camera and lights lowered independently from the *Petrel*'s bow winch to the nine-hundred-foot level.

Slightly above the cigar shape but five inches to its left on the screen at eleven o'clock there was a much smaller white image, in the shape of a figure eight, an inch high on the highest plusten magnification scale—Hall. And only yards below the cigar-shaped DSRV a long, fuzzy outline was gradually emerging, more than ten times the size of the DSRV.

A submarine.

The long shape stretched at an oblique angle for two and a half feet on the *Petrel*'s video screen, extending across most of the screen. Fuzzy as the image was, unlike the sharper, smaller images of the DSRV and the AD suit above it and slowly descending toward it, the outline confirmed that the sail, or "conning tower," as Scotty called it, was on a definite lean, as first thought. It meant, Scotty informed Tate, with the help of the sonar trace, that the sub seemed to have rolled "at least twenty degrees starboard."

"But why is it so blurry," countered Tate, "compared to the DSRV and Frank?"

"Ach, probably pollution and wee organisms near the bottom."

"Better put it in the log for attention when we get back. That's pretty poor for the money the government paid. Over a million dollars for this lot."

"The main thing is we have 'em all on screen."

"Can't see the damn hatches on the sub," commented Tate.

"No-o. 'Cause of the roll, Captain. We should've come at her from the other side." But then Scotty pointed to more fuzziness behind the stationary bulk of the submarine. "No, that wouldn't have done any good. I think that's a ridge there." He ran his hand against the screen. "You see, the sub's come to rest alongside this ridge or whatever. That could be why we're getting so much fuzziness from the sub—our signals are bouncing off the ridge as well as the sub—a kind of double echo."

Tate nodded. "All right. Can we cut down the magnification and see whether that ridge runs out?"

Scotty did so. The ridge didn't run out, though; it seemed endless.

"Christ! It's a bloody great cliff."

"That's what I suspected," said Tate. "Means she can only come out one of three ways—forward, astern or port. No starboard access."

"Aye," said Scotty. "So?" It was a mild insolence that only Tate and Scotty's long partnership could have tolerated.

"So," explained Tate, "the Soviet ships are on the far side. Behind the cliff. If their DSRV isn't enough and they want to help haul up, they'll have to move their ships in closer—in over the spine of the cliff."

"The *Boise* won't like that," said Scotty.

"Neither will Frank. Neither of them likes the Russians."

"Neither do I," commented Tate. "But we might need all the help we can get if we try to salvage."

"I'm on the bottom." The voice was Hall's—the communication line had been cleared of its tangle.

"And about bloody time!" said Scotty.

Hall returned an equally cheeky but infinitely more vulgar Oregonian expression.

At that moment General Kornon was aboard the *Karpaty*'s helicopter en route to the *Leningrad*. Minutes later, pacing excitedly in the *Leningrad*'s combat center, he had its captain, Admiral Litov, break in on the open channel to tell everyone that for ease of operation on the DSRV they would be using Russian not English.

It made perfect sense and no one objected.

# 35

ON THE OPEN CHANNEL Tate and Scotty could hear Admiral Litov speaking to the group of five trawlers milling around the Russian control ship.

"What's up with him?" asked Scotty.

He was answered almost immediately as Litov, rushes of static creating the illusion that he was short of breath, addressed the *Petrel* in labored English. "Have you please been bothered by the shar—fish?"

"Starfish?" inquired Tate.

"*Shark* fish," repeated Litov. "They have been attacking the transponders. We are getting very bad images from sea bottom."

"Sharks," said Scotty. "I'll check on it and get back to you."

Scotty was looking at the *Petrel's* big screen. He could see two black images in the dim photographs provided by the sled camera lighting—one was the Russian rescue vessel and the other was Frank Hall. The images were about three hundred yards apart. The sluggish DSRV was moving toward the stern of the sub at no more than a knot or two, while Hall, at about the same speed, was making for the big, bullet-shaped nose. But even though Scotty knew the *Petrel's* state-of-the-art side scan and sled light photography were miles ahead of the Russians', what he and others in the field called SWTR—shallow water type resolution—wasn't yet possible in such depths as these. It probably never would be, due to myriad sea life and currents in the deep that affected both the sharpness of optical resolution and the vectors of the sound waves traveling from transponders. These transponders, or sound sources, usually buckling electrical plates, were often placed in mountings on the hull, or sometimes, as in the *Petrel's* case, lowered from the hull by retractable cable, which meant the transponder could be positioned far enough below surface to minimize noise interference from ship and wave action above.

Scotty got back to the Russian, and informed him that while the *Petrel's* images weren't so good, either, the transponder seemed to be working fine, not bothered by sharks.

"I thanked the bugger anyway," Scotty told Tate after he finished talking to the Russian on the open channel.

"That was nice of you," said Tate.

"Ach, I don't trust the buggers as far as I could kick 'em."

"You miss your porridge this morning?"

Scotty was about to deliver a friendly equalizer when the *Petrel's* bosun, who'd been listening to the open line chatter, asked him, "Why're we putting down both the DSRV *and* Frank?"

"International waters, sonny," Scotty explained to the bo-sun. "Anyone who likes can go down. Besides," and he moved well away from the mike as he said it, "we're not sure if Frank can help anyone doon there, sub or its crew. If he can't figure a way to salvage her, we might be grateful for a wee bit of help from Ivan. At least to get the men out. On the other hand, if that escape hatch forward of the sail is buckled, even by a few hundredths of an inch, the Russian DSRV won't be able to lock on for an airtight seal. In that case the DSRV's bloody useless, and it'll be back into our boy's court."

"Glad I'm not him."

"So am I, laddie. So am I."

"I can't see any hatch," said the bosun.

"No," said Scotty. "We canna get that kind of resolution there—the water's too soupy with microorganisms. But Frank knows what the sub looks like inside and out."

"How can you be sure of that?" asked the bosun.

"Laddie, Frank never goes on a job without knowing all the ins and outs. Why do you think the Navy hires him? There're only two things he reads—The Brothers Karamazov and man-uals."

"Brothers what?"

"Karamazov. Aboot a lot of Russians."

"You kidding me? I thought Frank doesn't like Russians."

"No. It's the Kremlin he doesn't like, and all those who do their bidding."

In the background, the open channel was still squawking and spitting, the Russian captain trying to find out whether the *Boise* had been harassed by sharks. Once it had been thought that sharks, especially the great white, were so aggressive they would attack anything, but now most skippers knew what oceanographers had discovered, that it wasn't naked aggres-sion that moved sharks to attack. Rather, like so much marine life, sharks would approach a foreign object out of sheer curi-osity. The shark's sonar, while working well at a distance, went haywire the closer it got to a metal surface, sending the fish into a blind panic, and creating the myth of its viciousness.

"I think," said the Soviet captain, addressing the *Petrel* again, "you should be telling Mr. Hall to keep sharp eyes open.

Our other boats are reporting them, too. Hammerheads mostly."

"Thanks for the warning," Tate acknowledged. "We'll keep open sharp eyes."

Scotty laughed and Tate joined in. It relieved the tension, but the bosun ruined it by asking what the hell good it would do to warn Hall. "He's got enough to worry about thinking about that sub. Anyway, what's he got to ward off a goddamn shark with? A shark'd puncture that aluminum skin like going through a tin can!"

"Don't be so gloomy, Bosun," said Tate. "Anyway, he's got two claw hands. They've got quite a grip."

"That'll be nice. Maybe he can ask it to dance."

Scotty frowned at the bosun. "I'm as worried aboot him as you, mon, but let's try to be positive."

Just then there was a thump on the hull, then more in quick succession. The video screen went blank, shrinking to a small green dot that quickly died. Either the camera and light sled's electrical lead from the *Petrel*'s bow had become disconnected, said Tate, or the lights on the sled had fused.

"No," said Scotty, "they're independent fuses. All four wouldn't go at once unless the lead's been ripped out." He exhaled deeply, his face dark with concern, but as usual he was cool under pressure. "So we've lost the telly from our bow cable—tough titty for the networks. But we can survive without pictures."

"Then it's sonar image alone," said Tate.

"Aye, that's the ticket. Still, I don't expect the boys at the networks'll be too pleased. Sonar images on trace paper aren't going to make the evening news."

"Don't you worry about that," said Tate. "They'll use whatever they can get. Anyway, we've got Frank and the DSRV closing in on the sub. That'll be something to give the families some hope."

"Why are you so sure?" asked the *Petrel*'s bosun. "Why's everyone so damn sure the sub is the *New York*? Maybe it's like last time—that joker on the *Boise*. He brought out Frank from Attu, remember? A big rush, and it was nothing. They just *thought* it was a sub."

"Ach," said Scotty, "then look at the sonar trace. You don't get that kind of image from nothing, laddie. That's a great bunch of metal reflecting the sound waves we're beaming down from the transponder. Bet my bottom dollar it's the *New York* this—"

"What is?" asked the bosun, leaning over the sonar trace recorder, watching the two stylus heads skimming over the twelve-inch-wide Hardinger paper, the styluses spaced so as to give the illusion of one stylus racing over and under the paper every second.

"Look at the image," answered Scotty. "Where the stylus burns the paper you can see how far apart Frank and the—"

"I can't see anything. There's no mark."

Scotty walked over. The bosun was right. Scotty listened carefully. He could hear the growing howl of the wind over the pitch-dark sea and smell its cleansing salty air, his senses fully alert, but the pinging was gone. The sonar was dead.

Quickly Scotty grabbed the mike, turning the frequency dial to exactly 9.5 kilohertz. "*Petrel* to Frank, *Petrel* to Frank. Do you read me?" He released the mike's Talk button, waiting anxiously to receive. There was nothing but sizzling static. He tried again, even though he knew the communications line was out. Quickly recradling the mike and grabbing the lookout's flashlight, he ran past Tate, who had immediately turned to the steering console, checking that the automatic navigation system was functioning. Within ten seconds, swiftly navigating his way through radio, radar masts, lifeboat and emergency Beaufort life raft drums, Scotty was at the stern rail of the wheelhouse deck. He shone the flashlight, which sliced through the salty air, bringing its beam to bear on the articulated hydraulic arm craning over the starboard side like some huge bird's neck, holding the block through which the hydrographic wire ran that tethered Frank's AD suit to the *Petrel*. The beam picked up a glint of wire, but this wasn't proof positive that the wire and communication cord about it were still tethered to the AD suit. Even if they were broken, the weight of water would be sufficient to keep the wire running taut up from the water, through the block and down to the winch.

His hands sliding down the rail while still holding the flashlight, his feet not touching steel until they hit the stern deck,

Scotty made for the stern's hydraulic arm. Ignoring the heavy roll, he took hold of the wire between winch and block with both hands and hooked his feet about it like a trapeze artist. It was a better test than having the winch haul in a foot or two, for there was a certain feel to a cable that still had a specific weight attached to it in addition to the weight of water that could hold a snapped cable down and make it look as if nothing was wrong. The bosun shifted the spotlight above him, watching the block. The cable not only felt taut to Scotty but had that "hard against" feel that told him it was still attached to the AD suit— to Frank. He waited till the ship's stern was at the apogee of the next roll and let go, dropping several feet to the deck. A crewman helped him to his feet.

"Is he still attached?" the bosun called.

"Yes," answered Scotty. "Communications cord and transponder would have been a pushover for the sharks, but the cable—it's a different matter. The bastards can't bite that off. We've still got Frank tethered, even if we can't talk to him."

"Amen to that," added Tate, coming onto the ship's intercom. "I've checked the navigation system. We're exactly where we should be. Frank should be right over the sub now."

"Well, at least he can see with that wrist light on the suit," said Scotty. "How long's it good for, Bosun? Six hours?"

"It's an eight-hour battery."

The sea was becoming rougher. Looking at his watch in the soft light of the bridge, a veritable island in the storm, Scotty said, "It's 2310 now. He's got till after dawn to do what he has to do."

"Maybe the *Karpaty* or *Leningrad* have him on their sonar trace," the bosun suggested. They called the ships, but it was the same story. Total sonar blackout or badly scrambled signals, due either to the daily falling of the scattering layer or to malfunction of the transponder caused by sharks. Or, as the Soviet captain said, passing on the suggestion of some of his crew members, perhaps the swarms of squid attracted by the ships' lights were responsible. They'd seen it happen often enough before. And, indeed, wherever light was hitting the water, squid could be seen swarming to the surface.

"Then we're both in the dark," said Tate.

"Sorry to say, yes," said the Russian captain. "We will be telling you if there is improvement."

"Thanks. Appreciate that," said Tate, signing off.

CAPTAIN PETERS on the *Boise* was shaking his head in sheer frustration. "Goddamn it, I wish we had the side scan that the *Petrel* does. Then maybe we could get into this act."

"We'd have the same problem as they're having, sir," said the first officer.

"Maybe, maybe not, but I'd send over our divers and blow those goddamn sharks, squid, whatever, to kingdom come."

The first officer didn't bother to mention that that would blow the divers to bits, too. Of course the old man was merely letting off steam, but a spear gun was the best way to handle sharks—either that or concussion sticks.

GENERAL KORNON, aboard the *Leningrad*, lit another acrid-smelling Turkish cigarette as he sipped fresh coffee and watched the flickering black-and-white television pictures coming up from the DSRV from the camera mounted atop it. They also showed the American off to the left of the screen. The *Leningrad* not only continued to get relatively good video pictures from the DSRV, her sonar was pinging along nicely, too.

"Are they all back?" asked Kornon. He meant the twelve members of the Spetsnaz team.

"Eleven of them, sir. One man was lost. He got tangled in the *Petrel*'s props. The ship swung too sharply, probably on an automatic adjustment from its navigational system. They were following your orders to the letter, General, using only pencil-thin lights so as not to show any reflection at the ship's side. As it happened, the *Petrel* was well lit, anyway, so they didn't have to worry too much about that. It had quite an apron of light. The man was just unlucky that—"

Kornon sat up straight, cigarette in midair. "But he'll float to the surface. They could see—"

"No, no, sir," the captain assured him quickly. "Spetsnaz teams are better trained than that. They weighted him. He won't come to the surface. He's gone."

"Good," said Kornon. "Give the men my congratulations. Extra shore leave when we return to Vladivostok."

"Very good, sir." But before the captain could leave, the general, wreathed in thick, bluish-gray smoke, pointed at the flickering black-and-white picture. "Can you correct the vertical?" he asked. "It gives me a headache, all that flickering."

"No, sir. It's the best we can do."

Kornon shrugged and sat back again, one hand massaging his forehead while the other held the cigarette. He watched the outline of the sub getting closer. About now the fairing, the only raised flat area on the entire sub, aft of the sail, where the missiles were, should be coming into view. "Who is our English speaker?" Kornon asked an aide.

"Lieutenant Saburov, sir. He's the nephew of Colonel Saburov, who I believe was on Eagle Island, and . . ."

"Yes, yes," said Kornon impatiently, waving his cigarette. "But is his English good?"

"I can't tell him from an American, sir."

"We'll see."

The *Lenin I* was now about ten to twelve feet above where the fairing should be. In the blackness, it and Frank Hall were no more than twenty yards apart; the lone American in his AD suit with the wrist light was approaching the forward section, while in the DSRV in a blaze of six lights, the three Russians—pilot, copilot and the *Amur*'s torpedo lieutenant—were approaching the sail from above the sub's after section. On Kornon's screen the *Lenin I* was identifiable by the two clusters of lights fore and aft of the vehicle as it proceeded slowly, and it was obvious that all the Russians and lone American could see of one another were their lights approaching in the artificial graying around the sub's tilted sail.

Kornon ground out his half-lit cigarette. Immediately another was offered him and lit. He said nothing, drawing the smoke in deeply without taking his eyes off the flickering bluish screen.

## 36

HALL REACTED to the sudden shutdown of the sled light that had afforded some illumination over the sub and to his loss of communication with the surface as coolly as any professional can with two thousand feet of water above him. At least he was still tethered to the *Petrel*, he thought. Immediately switching to the halogen filament wrist light on his left arm, he slid it farther along its thin, tubular wrist track, reducing the glare back on his acrylic helmet. He could withdraw his arms completely from the suit's arms into its body section, so that if necessary, the left arm could be shifted backward as well as forward into a number of positions that would be physiologically impossible for anyone but a contortionist. His eyes followed the wrist light's cone, which extended twenty feet ahead, the end of the cone covering an area six feet in diameter, its circle of light beginning to fold over a small forward section of the sub's outline. To his right he saw the two clusters of eyes, fore and aft, of the DSRV, the bubbles issuing upward in a bluish-white stream. The noise reached him a split second later, like soft rain falling on the white aluminum skin of the bulbous-jointed AD suit, as Frank kept moving slowly farther into his cone of light, his progress delayed by the thick, gelatinous ooze of mud built up over aeons.

Then quite suddenly he saw that he was only a few feet from the outline of what they were all sure was the *New York*.

Hall was aware of his labored breathing. The outline of the sub was lost in a cloud of mud that he kicked up as he dragged his way through what seemed to be dead seaweed buried in the mud. Less than twenty yards away the DSRV was motionless. Its four propellers, two mounted high forward and two astern in protective O-shields, were so angled that the Russian craft was hovering over what Hall guessed must be the fairing—the only raised, flattened part along the whole of the sub's elongated tear shape.

But if it was the fairing, he couldn't make out any of the two parallel rows of semispherical bumps, or lids, that he knew capped each of the twenty-four missiles on a Trident. And anyway, what were the Russians doing above the fairing? The nearest escape hatch was either the one in the sail or the one forward of the sail at a point five to six feet directly in front of Hall. If they were trying to get at one of the missiles, they must be mad, for short of blowing off one of the caps, which he still couldn't see, they'd never get away with it. The *Boise* and the *Petrel* or one of the other U.S. picket ships now gathering would surely pick up the explosion. In any event, what the hell would a DSRV do with a missile more than ten times longer than itself, especially when the DSRV's maximum speed was only three to four knots. Or perhaps they were simply as perplexed as he was by the absence of hatches.

Then, high up on the sail in the penumbra of the DSRV's lights, Hall dimly but definitely made out the numbers *921*. The submarine was the *New York*.

Inside the windowless DSRV sitting in front of the integrated control and display panels that completely surrounded them, the pilot and copilot carefully watched the main power monitor to their left, the sonar monitor panel beside it, the overhead alarm panel and television monitor, and to the right of them the life-support gauges and film control. Behind them sat the *Amur*'s torpedo officer, surrounded by banks of lights monitoring the central control panel and emergency jettison equipment.

The pilot and copilot and Malik's torpedo officer now knew why the sub outlines was so indistinct and why they couldn't see any of the missile tube covers. They weren't getting a clear echo from the metal surface of the sub because the active signal they were sending out was being distorted by the heavy mineral content of the thick, gelatinous ooze—ooze that Frank Hall, only yards away, was measuring with his thin telescopic steel probe and discovering to be more than four feet thick.

The problem was at once stunningly simple yet devastating, equally, for the American and the Russians. The USS *New York* had been driven into the primeval ooze of a conduit or channel leading from a high plateau a thousand feet above to the very edge of a precipice that plunged ten thousand feet, forming the abyss of the Aleutian Trench. The channel, which millions of years ago might have been the bed of an oceanic stream or river, had long since been filled with the sedimentary deposits of tens of thousands of years; having filled the ancient depression of the stream bed or whatever, the ooze was now spilling over the precipice's edge. The towering wall of mud that Hall and the DSRV could see on the sub's far side was, in reality, an enormous rock cliff thrown up in one of the many volcanic convulsions of the Aleutian Trench, now acting as a catchment wall piled high and thick with mud. The sub had plowed sideways into its base in a skidding motion, as it had slithered its way along the bottom deeper and deeper into the sucking clay. Its forward section had come to rest only six yards from the abyss where the light from Hall's lamp abruptly ended. Tilting hard right into the mud base of the cliff, the sub had there buried the top of its sail and its starboard plane. This explained both the foreshortened sonar images of the sail and the fact, of which both Hall and the Russians were now aware, that the escape hatch in the sail was buried under tons of mud, as was the rest of the submarine, inclined, Frank estimated, at an angle of at least twenty degrees to starboard. The cliff itself towered high above toward the plateau, forming, in effect, a dividing line a thousand feet beneath the surface of the sea, separating the Russian ships in the shallower water above the plateau from the American ships on the near or deeper side directly above the *New York*.

Now that the *Lenin I* was closing in, Kornon and his colleagues in the *Leningrad*'s combat center could see the bestirred mud clouding the cameras, demonstrating what the DSRV pilot was reporting on the radio phone, namely that no hatches or fairing could be found because they were buried under more than a meter of dense mud.

To Hall the mud, or rather its thickness, immediately explained why it had taken so long for them to find the submarine—why no flare had been sighted, no messenger sonobuoy, only the oil managing to slowly seep through, to rise above the enormous weight of what his rapierlike probe told him was a gelatinous brownish-green ooze of peatlike consistency. He felt a strange mixture of alarm and relief: alarm because none of the escape hatches was as yet accessible, yet relief because the Russian DSRV was useless in the situation, its flared skirting midway along its belly unable to lock onto any of the escape hatches. In fact, the DSRV was in danger of sinking into the mud itself and of becoming trapped should it attempt to settle on the sub or the bottom. In any event, the DSRV's skirting extended for no more than two feet below the vehicle's hull, and the mud was at least a meter thick.

Inside the *Lenin I* there was rank disappointment at being unable to fulfil Kornon's immediate order to gain access to the submarine by pretending to rescue its crew.

Aboard the *Leningrad* they saw it, too.

"It's a Mexican standoff," said Litov. "Of course it will make great propaganda for the press, General. The Soviet Union and the United States trying their best to rescue their fellow seamen."

Kornon wasn't interested in Mexican standoffs or good stories for the press. With the Americans' cameras cut off—and, as far as the press had been told, the Russians', too—Kornon knew he could tell the press whatever he wanted. They would be a problem only when they could see what was happening near or on the surface.

"What do you think our unorthodox American will do now?" asked Litov in a noticeably self-congratulatory tone.

"What will the *Lenin I* do?" asked Kornon, without shifting his gaze from the flickering screen.

The rapidly changing light made it difficult for Litov to interpret from the general's facial expression just what his reaction to the situation was. "I think," he began, "we should recall the DSRV and send down our Spets in it to start digging away some of that mud."

"Yes," said the general evenly. "And you think Hall hasn't already thought of doing that himself?" Kornon turned to face Litov.

"I don't know, General, perhaps he—"

"I do. You see, Admiral, I *do* know about Hall. I've had occasion to study his file. He's the best they have. He'll think of a way."

"But what can he do down there? One man—with nothing much more than a flashlight and a silly-looking walking stick."

"I don't know exactly what's on his mind," answered Kornon, returning his gaze to the flickering screen, "but I know he won't give up."

"Then kill him," said Litov "and have the Spets team we send down in the DSRV implode the sub. Just as you suggested—a time-delay mine. Only instead of taking it aboard and getting what we wanted from inside the sub as we hoped to do when the DSRV interlocked with the escape hatch, we'll now simply dig a hole in the mud and attach it to the sub's outer hull." Litov was clearly becoming more and more excited by his idea. "We'll tell the media exactly the same story we planned to—an explosion caused by leaking propellant in the missile bays. We've already planted that speculation among them. They're like cattle. One gets the idea and the rest are too lazy to think of anything different."

"Who," asked Kornon, "have you got speculating on it?"

"The networks, both European and U.S. *Everybody*."

"That's correct," added Ustenko, who had been quiet until now. "The American network, ABC—its *Nightline* has been talking about the danger of a propellant leak or ruptured diesel tanks exploding."

"I hate," said Kornon with a passion he hadn't so far displayed, "to have come all this way not to get the whole thing intact. I don't want to have to sift through trawl dredges full of scrap metal to piece together superior American technology, Comrades. I want the *submarine*. *Intact*. Understand? *Intact!*"

What Kornon meant but didn't say was that only *intact* would resurrect him fully in the eyes of the Politburo. Anything less would place him halfway between Ulan Ude and Moscow, when he wanted only Moscow. He got up, lit another cigarette and walked around the *Leningrad*'s bridge, his tired body buffeted by the roll and pitch, yet strangely oblivious to it, as if the only thing that was operating was his mind.

Suddenly he stopped, the glow of his cigarette bright in the semidarkness. "No," he informed his subalterns and Admiral Litov, "if there is one thing that exile has taught me, gentlemen, it is not to be proud. Oh, pride, yes—enough to survive. *Essential* to survive, but never too much. Too much will drive you to starvation. Too much will kill you. No, let us not be too proud, Comrades. Let us permit Mr. Hall to show us what American technology can do, to show us whether it is possible to raise this monster from the deep." He drew heavily again on his cigarette, the glow illuminating the faint smile spreading across his face. He hadn't shaved since the beginning of the

mission. "*Then* we will kill him—while far above we are enter-
taining the ladies and gentlemen of the press. Admiral."

"Yes, General?"

"Tell the Spets team I want them resuited immediately. And
then order the *Lenin I* to stand by. Ustenko's English is good,
so I want him to give the order to the DSRV—on the open
channel so that the *Boise* and the *Petrel* will hear—explaining
that insofar as the submarine is covered in mud we can do no
more but wait and possibly assist our American comrades in
whatever way we might make ourselves useful to them."

"Yes, General," said Litov, full of admiration. "Should I
release that last bit—about 'helping our American comrades'—to the media?"

"By all means. By all means. By the way, how are the media
faring? Not too drunk, I hope."

"Very well." Litov beamed. "Most of them are so seasick
they wouldn't care what we told them. We have them, as I think
our American friends say, in the palm of our hand."

"Good. Keep them well fed and—"

"General…" Ustenko was pointing to the video screen. They
all watched as Hall approached the sail, his AD suit a ghostly
image in the backwash of the wrist light. The lone American
was like an astronaut during a space walk, except that the wire
that tethered him to the ship more than two thousand feet
above looked less like the umbilical cord of an astronaut and
more like the slack curvature of the old-fashioned air hoses
used by an earlier generation of deep-sea divers.

"What the hell is he up to?" asked Admiral Litov. "The sail
is inaccessible. The escape hatch inside it is surely covered with
mud. Look at how it leans right into the mud cliff."

"Not all of it is covered in mud," said Ustenko. "Where their
number is printed there is still—"

"Yes, yes, I know that," cut in Kornon. "I'm not blind,
Colonel. But as the admiral has said, what good is it going near
the sail if he can't enter through it?"

"Perhaps he wants to make sure of the number, sir."

"He can see the number from where he is," said Kornon.
"What the hell is he up to?"

Before anyone could reply, they saw the American aquanaut thrown back from the sail, his body tumbling out of con-

trol over the mud bottom. To the Russians watching him in the combat center of the *Leningrad*, he looked like an astronaut spinning away from the mother spacecraft. His tether was now limp, snagging about his legs like some huge snake and entangling him as he kept somersaulting as if under the impact of some invisible force punching him back from the submarine.

APPROACHING THE SAIL in the condition of neutral buoyancy, Hall did feel like a spacewalker, except for the clouds of mud obscuring his view of the *Lenin I*. Then he felt the impact, not so much as a direct blow but as a kind of sideswipe that caught him on the right side and sent him reeling back in a roiling cloud of greenish-brown sediment. He was sure it was a bottom current, but its strength surprised him. He had no idea whether it was locally induced or a particularly dense subflow of the surface Japanese Current that, because of its density or heaviness compared to the main current flow, had plummeted over the edge of the plateau to the two-thousand-foot level where the Trident lay. Then, in a flash, he understood, or rather thought he understood, what had caused the sub to sink. It had been caught in the high-density water column and had dropped like a stone.

Except that if the sub and its crew, its sensors and the crew's training had been up to par, the captain, provided he realized quickly enough what was happening, should have been able to get the planes into an up angle before the downward speed had passed the point of no return and the vessel had literally driven itself farther down.

Having recovered his equilibrium, Hall approached the sail again, his thin, yard-long telescopic probe extended before him.

The DSRV, meanwhile, was still hovering, twenty-five feet to the right of the sail, waiting, and watching through its array of sensors, which looked like so many different-size barnacles and outgrowths on its fat, cigar-shaped body.

About twelve feet away from the sail, Hall felt rather than saw the probe rising up as quickly as a branch lifted in a sudden updraft. Then he was aware of something else; in his AD suit he felt as if he were inside a sauna. For a moment in the swirling, greenish-brown cone of light that now penetrated no farther than fifteen feet, he couldn't see the watch-size temperature dial clipped to the wrist light. Then the mud cloud cleared enough for him to see that the pointer on the dial had gone out of the fan-shaped green section through the yellow into the red. The temperature had reached over eighty-five degrees Fahrenheit.

Now Hall understood why one part of the sail, that between the buried top and outer hull of the submarine, had remained mud-free. This clear section that he had been approaching must have been cleaned by a superheated column of water jetting out of a hydrothermal crack or fissure at the cliff's base—a column that he ascertained, by moving around the sail in a semicircle, extended out from the sail no more than twelve feet. But its jet of superheated water was so powerful that it had created an invisible wall in the blackness that a man could not hope to penetrate.

Waiting a few minutes for the mud to settle, he glimpsed the shimmering of the column against the exposed metal of the sail as one sees the rising wall of a mirage. This upwelling wouldn't act as a support for the submarine, as Hall knew most people might suppose, but rather as a trap. Being a hot plume from the suboceanic crust and therefore less dense than the colder saltwater above it, the plume would act on the submarine, riding at neutral buoyancy, like a vacuum. The sub *must* have dropped. Even so, the diving planes, one of which on the port side he could see in the apron of the *Lenin I*'s spotlights, seemed to be covered with a great clump of seaweed of the kind that had tripped him earlier as he had approached the sub along the ocean's muddy floor.

But as the mud cloud continued to settle, he saw that the clump wasn't seaweed but a mass of tangled fishing net. The diving planes had obviously been enmeshed in netting, which somehow or other had also been sucked down, floats and all. Or perhaps the sub had become entangled like a whale in one of the thousands of miles of drift nets that stretched out over the North Pacific and Bering Sea, trapping all in their path.

It was eerie for Hall, seeing the DSRV hovering there no more than fifty feet from him, an inanimate, eyeless thing that sensed all about it, current flow, temperature, density, salinity, oxygen content, and yet couldn't or wouldn't communicate with him, even though it obviously knew what he knew, by observing him then drawing the same conclusions. Meanwhile, he knew, the world press up above were busy feeding their voracious news agencies with stories of mutual cooperation between the superpowers, whereas in fact, two thousand feet below them, the men in the *Lenin I* and the American were in a game of shadowboxing that, once the sub became accessible, would suddenly become deadly.

KORNON SMILED for the first time in several hours. "Ah," he said, "our hero cannot get near the sail." He lit another cigarette with his prized Dunhill lighter, while using the other hand to hold up an earphone that connected him with the DSRV. "I still don't know..."

"General!" Ustenko was pointing at the video screen. The pinpoint of light that had been the American was gone.

WRIST LIGHT OFF, Hall hit his belt release buckle. The lead weights dropped, and he ascended in the darkness at over a hundred feet a minute. He would break surface in plus or minus twenty minutes, depending on salinity/temperature variations throughout the different layers. Rising with a sensation of weightlessness through the pitch blackness, he could nevertheless feel the increasing temperature in the AD suit. Sweat poured off him as he passed through the margins of the vent that was causing the temperature inversion that, he knew, must be turning the sub into a gigantic steam bath. The added effect of bad air would be pushing the crew to their limit, some no doubt already past it.

He knew, too, that the Russian DSRV would be useless in the mud. The thick peatlike ooze would have to be removed before the DSRV could be effective. The only way was to dig through the mud. To try blasting the mud out, no matter how small the charge, would be to risk the *New York*'s implosion. To try to do it with the *Lenin I* might be possible, but it would be extraordinarily slow and cumbersome with the vehicle's articulated arms. While the arms had the delicate touch to pick up shrimp and galatheid crabs without injuring them, they didn't have the ability to dig a hole like a child in the sand and to compensate for the sides constantly caving in on what had already been dug. This needed human intelligence and agility on the spot.

But for Hall to have stayed and started digging without a proper tool would have been to do the Russians' work for them, so that they would need only to move in onto the hatch as he finished. The sheer weight of the four-prop *Lenin I* would be able to knock him aside and lock onto the hatch to gain entry to the sub. But by ascending before the DSRV did and returning quickly with the proper tools, he would have a head start on them—especially in the heavy seas at the surface where the *Petrel*'s job of hauling in a lone man, while difficult, would be much less time-consuming than for the *Karpaty II* to secure the *Lenin I*. Like all submersibles, the DSRV, sleek and efficient when submerged, was an unstable wallower in any surface chop over two feet. In what Hall saw as the ultimate battle of the individual against the collective, he was gratified to see the DSRV far below, still hovering over the submarine, while every moment added to his lead.

KORNON WAS WEARING a self-satisfied grin. As he was the only one present who had been in action against Hall before, on Eagle Island, he was confident that he enjoyed a distinct advantage in being able to predict what the American would do.

"He wanted," said Kornon shrewdly, "to reach that part of the sail not buried in mud in order to tap out a message to its crew. To let them know that help had arrived."

Despite static, Kornon remained in contact with the DSRV, which he could see as a glowworm at the bottom of the video screen. His order to its pilot was simple and instantly obeyed. Despite its four propellers running at maximum revolutions, the DSRV moved slowly forward toward the sail through the shimmering curtain of the twelve-foot-diameter plume that had made it impossible for the American to get near the clear area of the sail. The *Lenin I* extended one of its powerful steel arms, which didn't rise as Hall's probe had, nor even vibrate, but began tapping out delicately yet firmly a message in Morse and in English: "*Boise* to *New York*. Will enter to bring you out twenty-four at a time. Russians nearby. Do not open hatch until we tap New York Mets. Repeat New York Mets.''

No more than five minutes later, a message came back from inside the *New York*: ''God bless Mets and Yankees.''

''What does it mean?'' asked Colonel Ustenko when the *Lenin I* completed a report to Kornon. '' 'And Yankees'?''

''It means,'' Kornon explained with undisguised relish, ''that they are dead. The Trident is mine.''

# 37

WHEN HALL CAME to the surface, he was a mile away from the *Petrel* and the *Boise* and the quarter-mile ring of flashing-light-topped Day-Glo buoys the *Petrel* had dropped, to mark out the search area. In the turbulence of the surface waters he only caught water-teared images of the oceanographic vessel between heavy swells, the latter causing his AD suit to slosh about in precisely the same way astronauts do when emerging from a capsule at sea. Though feeling cumbersome and seasick in the violent buffeting of the huge swells and troughs, Hall nevertheless managed to reach over with his right claw to pull the pin from the location flare affixed to his left leg. Immediately the sea around him was a stuttering then vibrant sheet of vermilion, undulating over the waves. Within a minute the *Boise* answered with a flare, turning and making haste to pick him up. Unfortunately, however, as the *Boise*, leaving her mast salvage lights on, began her run toward him, so did Kornon's cruiser, five other Russian warships and seven assorted AGIs.

''SHALL WE RUN HIM DOWN?'' an elderly officer asked Kornon matter-of-factly. He was one of Litov's old cronies, along for the ride—listed as one of the admiral's ''maritime'' advisers.

Oh, thought Kornon, isn't it wonderful? Isn't it terrifying? You get so close to victory, and an old clown in officer's uniform wants, in front of the entire world press, to ''accidentally'' run down the American aquanaut. ''Are you quite mad?'' shot back Kornon. ''Or have you been drinking? Or both? We can finish him off down there, where no one will see what is happening. The press know how terrible the sharks are in this area.''

"But he'll be in contact with the *Boise*, Comrade," returned the "adviser," smarting from Kornon's sneering retort. "Have you thought of that? Don't you think he'll go down again tethered to the *Petrel*? It will only take them minutes to coil a communications wire down with the new tether."

Kornon could have wept. The old sailor, no doubt a good one in his time, with a great deal of experience, perhaps in the Persian Gulf, maybe even in the Great Patriotic War, was nevertheless a tactical idiot in complex operations such as this. Little wonder, Kornon thought, that Litov was attempting to disown the old man, turning away from him, obviously embarrassed, to fake preoccupation with the *Leningrad*'s radar.

"Oh, bring me tea," said Kornon in exasperation. "Bring me tea."

"Well?" the old adviser challenged petulantly, tendentiously. "They won't let him down again from the *Petrel* without a tether. I'm telling you, if there's a communication cord with it the press will hear everything. They poke their noses in everywhere. Am I right there, Comrade?"

"Oh," said Kornon, biting hard on a cube of sugar before gulping the tea, "explain it to him, Ustenko. I can't bear it."

The colonel looked across at the adviser with equanimity. He had no grudge against the man and thought Kornon was behaving abominably, given the man's age. But then again, he mused, most men do behave abominably when, after days of unrelenting tension, one mistake could ruin it all—when they are so close to victory that a kind of deliriousness gets hold of them.

"Yes, they'll tether him again," Ustenko told the old man. "And if there's a communication cord, yes, it'll provide a direct feed to the journalists. You're correct."

Kornon cut in, irritated by Ustenko's mollycoddling of the old man. "Our Spets commando team is all ready on the stern deck—ten of them to be exact—standing by, of course, as the press has been briefed, to assist in the event that our American friend runs into 'difficulty' trying to raise the sub. Actually, they'll cut his lines the moment he's out of sight, and they'll do it without him or the press seeing a thing. Now, do you understand why we don't have to run him down like some Beijing taxi?''

"And you think the American will sit still for this?" asked the old man, looking about for support.

"Yes," said Kornon, "if they wait to do it until he's deep enough. No one will be able to prove it wasn't an accident. We know there are many sharks in the area, or the lines could get twisted around a prop—think of all the ships on the scene, as well. The lines don't go straight down, you know. They bend and curve. Anyway, do you think the American has time to come up again to get *another* tether line? We all know this is a race against time."

"You mean," pressed the adviser, "that the Americans don't think we're out to trick them?"

Kornon's eyes closed in disgust. "Comrade, what the enemy thinks we might do and what it can prove are two entirely different things."

UPON BEING PICKED UP and taken on board the *Petrel* by means of the wire basket chair, Hall contacted Captain Peters aboard the *Boise* and rudely told him to prepare his heavy five-eighths-inch cable on the stern deck.

"You going to use spreader bars, Frank?" asked Bryce over the intercom.

"Couldn't you tell on the sonar? No, I guess you couldn't."

"Our sonar's on the blink—sharks, apparently."

"Even without sharks that sonar's not much good. Anyway, the sub's bow is too close to a precipice to use spreader bars. There's not enough room to approach and slide them under. Just stand by with that heavy haul cable and do as I tell you."

As the *Petrel*'s bosun removed the tinted hemispherical helmet from Hall's aquanaut suit, he was as oblivious to everything else as Hall was to him, sticking his head into Hall's stomach, poking his flashlight down into the suit. The action struck the crowd of American and Canadian reporters as hilariously funny, as if the bosun were some kind of maritime Peeping Tom about to disappear like a joey kangaroo into its mother's pouch—the rest of his white boiler suit standing headless on the heaving deck.

"Looks good and dry," said the bosun with approval.

"Dry?" commented Hall, gulping ice-cold water from the after lab's water hose, with which he was still flushing off some of the extraordinarily sticky mud that had adhered to the elbow and knee joints of the AD suit. "It was like a furnace coming up. I hit a vent."

"What's that?" A CBS correspondent pushed in, shoving a microphone forward.

Hall explained in snatches, between the rapid-fire instructions he had to give for his next descent. "The sub's not crushed, so I'll try Cox bolts. I'll take the air box down with me. Let's see—better give me half a dozen mags."

"Three cartridges in each mag," said the bosun, meaning three Cox bolts in each magazine. "That means eighteen in all. Think that'll be enough?"

"Jesus Christ, I'm not bringing up the *Queen Mary*."

"Better take some weights off your belt then," said the *Petrel*'s bosun, about to strap it around Hall.

"No," said Hall. "Leave them on."

"Man, you're going to travel down a lot faster with that tank of compressed air and the Cox bolts."

"Put the bolts and the Cox gun in a bag and attach it to a Styrofoam marker. If I'm going down too fast, I'll drop them below me and pick 'em up when I get down there."

"Well," said the bosun, "mind you don't hit a Russian on the head."

Hall saw that the CBS reporter had them on an open mike. "No worry," said Hall. "Lots of room down there for all of us."

"Can the Russian DSRV assist you, Mr. Hall?" It was the Canadian TV outfit.

"Oh, yes," said Hall. "Oh, yes, definitely. Once I manage to clear the mud from that forward escape hatch, the *Lenin I* is ideal to lock on and take the men out."

"Are you aware, Mr. Hall," an ABC reporter interjected, yelling to drown out his rivals, "that our own DSRV in the Bahamas is now reported ready and is being flown up here? It should arrive in the next forty-eight to seventy-six hours. A team of Navy divers will be accompanying it. Shouldn't you—''

"Too late," said Hall, chewing one of the glucose tablets the bosun had handed him and wedging himself more comfortably in the stern deck's starboard corner where the pitch and roll of the bright island of light was least punishing.

"Have you made contact with the sub, Mr. Hall?" came another reporter's question.

"No."

"Tass reports the *Lenin I* has."

"Well, then." Hall smiled as if he were the first nightly guest on the *Tonight Show*, the same show on which he'd heard that a joke had been made about him being used to "clear beaches." "That's great," he continued. "If the crewmen aboard have already been contacted by the *Lenin I*, then it will save all of us time. We could have those boys up before dawn."

"Will it take that long?" asked an NBC reporter.

"The DSRV can only bring up twenty-four at a time. Besides, every move is dangerous down there—particularly with the hot-water plume we have to contend with. We don't know how big an area that covers up closer to the surface."

Ever since he was assigned the job, Hall had known he had to get the submarine up in the hours of darkness. Unless he could, his method wouldn't work. But there was no way any reporter was going to get *that* out of him.

Then one reporter who hadn't yet asked a question came up with the most intelligent one of all. "Will you be able to find it again—even with the *Petrel*'s sonar and the marker buoys that have been dropped?"

"I think so," said Hall, "but I'll take some TDSSs—time-delayed sound sources—down with me. If Captain Wain and his crew respond to them—sound travels much faster in water than in air—I might get a response. Even though we've lost all radio contact with them, they can still thump on the hull."

"What's a time delayed sound source?" asked the ABC reporter.

"A grenade," said Hall, grinning.

The bosun joined in the general laughter as he attached a canvas bag containing a short-handled shovel, several balloon floats the size of squash balls and some other tools to a three-foot-diameter polyethylene ball. He handed the bag, now quite heavy, to Hall.

"Holy Toledo, Frank, you look like Santa Claus going down with all this stuff. You better remember that at two thousand feet you're around a thousand pounds psi. If you have to use the Cox bolts, put 'em in straight on to the hull. You know what happens when you hit a nail at a bad angle."

"Yes, Daddy."

"I—" The bosun's reply was lost to a deep stuttering noise overhead, and then a bluish pall of light swept over the *Petrel*'s stern and stayed there in a wide disk that spilled over the stern onto the sea. It was a Russian chopper, its outline lit up by the reflections of the *Boise*'s and the *Petrel*'s lights, the two ships only two hundred yards apart. The Russian helicopter's dramatic arrival was made for the television crews, which Lebdev had clearly known, and all the TV crews were now swinging their cameras upward toward the red-starred Hind. Over the cacophony of sound, a booming megaphone-amplified voice descended like that of God from on high—in Russian. Tate's angry curses at the grandstand play, which posed a danger to the high communication masts clustered about aft of the *Petrel*'s wheelhouse, weren't heard by anyone as the booming voice continued, followed by that of a translator, the disembodied voices descending with an authority that impressed almost everyone on the stern deck—except Hall, who announced to the *Petrel*'s bosun, "A hot-air vent from above."

The booming Russian speaker was Kornon, translated by Lebdev. He announced that he, General Kornon himself, had come to wish Mr. Hall and the American on-scene ships all good wishes, and to inform the American newsmen that the *Lenin I* was already descending with special mud removal equipment aboard to help effect the rescue of the "brave American submariners." Actually, the Spets team hadn't yet made the gut-wrenching transfer from the *Karpaty*'s stern to the DSRV, which Kornon had ordered up shortly after seeing the American ascend.

For a fleeting moment, a few people saw Kornon waving from the chopper's cabin. Hall didn't see him, his line of sight blocked by a phalanx of big, soft, foam rubber-sheathed mikes and their overhead booms.

"Anything in reply, Mr. Hall?" someone shouted. A mike came dangerously close to his eye as the ship slid then lifted into a wave, taking the full impact amidships.

"I, too, wish my Russian friends Godspeed." Hall smiled and waved up at the helicopter as the mike boom shifted away from him, then confided to the bosun, "This is my one and only performance as a politician."

The network crews were delighted. This was marvelous stuff for the late newscasts. What more could you ask for? A Soviet military chopper thundering in, red star emblazoned beautifully in focus, swept by gusty rain, and the Russian wishing the lone American, Hall, the best of luck. Such good material left the correspondents scrambling for metaphors. The American would clear the hatch of the sunken sub, and the Russian ship would bring the men out. Even a few hard-bitten cynics amid the network crews were moved to wax sentimental in taped overlays for the videos. Not bothering to move inside to the lab, they preferred to be photographed on the heaving stern of the *Petrel*, adding even more windblown drama to the pictures that millions of Americans would be watching in their living rooms:

> "This tragedy might yet have a happy ending—not the happy ending of fairy tales but the successful struggle of brave men on the high seas. The common nationality out here tonight is not Russian or American but Seaman—the only concern of all being the rescue of their fellow men. All those predictions of gloom and doom that we so often hear pervade the relationship between the superpowers are not in evidence now. We are privileged to witness an example of men—men not of this country or of that country but men of the planet earth, men of the sea—helping one another in the most crucial of all tasks—survival."

"Got your shovel?" asked the bosun.

"Yeah," said Hall. "I'll need it after that."

"Now, be nice," said the bosun, checking over the four replacement oxygen bottles. "And remember, those Cox bolts are to go in at right angles."

"You already told me that," said Hall.

"What happens," interrupted the CBS reporter, "if for some reason you can't open the hatch—or if the *Lenin I* has problems?"

"We don't anticipate any problems," Hall lied.

"Yes, but if you can't open the hatch?"

"You don't rush a thing like this," Hall answered. Now all the microphones were spearing toward him. "If you hurry, you're more likely to make mistakes, and one mistake down there is disaster. Slow and careful, that's the ticket."

"But what will happen," shouted the ABC journalist, "if something goes wrong with the DSRV or you fail to reach the hatch?"

Hall wanted to respond that that was the dumbest question he'd ever heard, but he thought of all the parents and families of the men in the *New York* and answered calmly, "Then the men inside the *New York* will have to wait until we can organize—"

"Frank." It was Bryce, who had come over from the *Boise*. He handed Hall a soft, rubberized bag, the size of a small backpack. It, like Bryce in his heavy-weather gear, was dripping with water.

"About time," Hall snapped.

The *Petrel*'s bosun and Bryce glanced at each other, acutely embarrassed, not knowing what to say.

"What's that?" asked the ABC journalist, indicating the bag.

"The time-delayed sound source," replied Hall grumpily. "In case I do have trouble relocating her."

"You might have," said Bryce. "You were at least a half mile from us when you came up. The bottom currents must be pretty fierce, I guess."

"The problem was, Bryce, you guys on the *Boise* couldn't stay on base if you made a seven-point moor," Hall retorted, referring to the Navy maneuver where seven sea anchors are used to secure an on-scene ship during salvage operations.

"I guess the plume's the problem," said Bryce, ignoring Hall's rudeness. "It probably washed you off course."

"I'll try not to inconvenience you," said Hall. "I sure as hell don't want to end up like Bremmer." The two men stared at each other, the hostility palpable. Some of the reporters were letting their tape run, hoping to record further acrimony.

Tate's voice crackled on the intercom. "Clear the stern. Clear the stern." Through his binoculars he could see the DSRV, its light ablaze, off the starboard beam of the *Karpaty II* about half a mile away. It was going down.

Before he began his descent Hall got on the open line to Peters. "You better get some of your shallow-water scuba guys overboard and check out your transponder. If we can't get those guys out and have to bring the sub up, you've got the heavy-gauge wire for the haul, so you'll need to see just where the sub is. How many qualified divers have you got aboard?"

"Six men qualified for scuba, and Bryce."

"Well, have two down every half hour, or an hour if they're up to it. Keep them at it all night if you have to."

"Will it take that long? Six men aren't many to rotate right through the—"

"Listen, Peters, in case you've forgotten, I have overall authority here. Directly from CNO. Right?"

"Yes." Peters's voice was barely audible, restrained; he was about to blow.

"Then don't argue with me. I don't want any more screwups from the *Boise*. If you didn't have the heavy wire, I wouldn't use your outfit at all. But you happen to be here, so if it isn't too much trouble, just try to do what you're told."

On the *Petrel*'s stern, then, nothing could be heard except the continuing howling rage of the sea. Finally a reporter, who hadn't gone inside and was eavesdropping well back by the winch where Hall couldn't hear him, muttered to another, "Can we use this stuff? It's dynamite."

His colleague shook his head. "Maybe *60 Minutes* would run it—a war between the civilian, Hall, and the Navy. They love that sort of stuff. But the news reports wouldn't go for it. Besides, the Navy wouldn't give us squat for the next ten years."

IN THE COMBAT CONTROL center aboard the *Leningrad* they were watching the videos that had been played by the American networks, showing scenes of the communities where many of the *New York*'s crewmen lived, of their families, who had messages for their loved ones, and of prayer services in churches, asking God for the safe deliverance of the downed American sailors.

Kornon shook his head, looking across at Litov in the semi-darkness. "They must always bring their God into it. It's our DSRV that will get them out—not God. Besides," Kornon added, glancing around the combat center with a smirk that he simply couldn't help now that his exile was all but ended, now that the Kremlin again would be his, "they're not going to heaven." There was a ripple of laughter from the Russians on watch.

"Maybe they're going to hell, General," said a sonar operator with unusual presumption. "It's quite hot down there."

Kornon was so struck by the joke he almost choked on his cigarette. "And," he replied to the young crewman, "it's going to get even hotter. *Da?*" The room erupted in laughter.

Litov, however, didn't laugh. He had no love for Americans, but he'd served many years ago as a midshipman aboard submarines; he knew the strain, the sheer terror that the trapped men must be feeling. But he pushed away the memory. These were the rules of the game—or rather, there were no rules, except for the one that said you must win. He looked up at the clock. Within four hours at most, he guessed—even before dawn perhaps—the Trident would be theirs. He turned around to Kornon. "We must get into the sub as soon as possible, General. As soon as the American clears that hatch, we should send in the Spets."

"Don't fret," advised Kornon. "As soon as the hatch is open, we cut his tether and communications cord and kill him. His weights will keep him down till he rots."

"It will be a slow death," Litov said. "Unless we puncture his suit."

"We can't do that. Whatever was left of him would float up, parts of him and the suit, anyway. Don't worry, though. Young Saburov, the Spets leader, has everything well in hand. They'll simply cut the tether and communications cord first, and then the others will go and seize the American and tie him up in that fish net on the plane. He'll last as long as the oxygen—six to eight hours. Saburov's men'll use a jagged cutter so that it won't look as if the tether and cord were simply snipped. They're terrible, those great whites.''

As he watched the *Lenin I* diving, Kornon was pleased that the *Leningrad* alone of all the ships had been successful in tethering a sled light and camera in neutral buoyancy at eighteen hundred feet. It meant that while the Americans on the *Boise* and even the *Petrel*, with its state-of-the-art side scan, were in effect blind to what was going on in the deep below, he had, as it were, a ringside seat.

He knew that on their sonar screens the *Boise* and the *Petrel* wouldn't have images of the shape of the DSRV or of the American, but simply blips. Once the *Lenin I* and Hall neared the submarine any signals would be lost, reflected from the great hulk of the mineral-mud-covered sub. The signals would be further jumbled by the scattering layer, the planktonic swarms that rose with sunset and descended at sunrise; the present scattering layer at seven hundred feet was already causing what the Americans called "fly dirt" or meaningless traces where the bottom of the sea was registered on the traces as being at the depth of the scattering layer reflecting the signals.

Outside on the vast, heaving sea, the rain was decreasing and in its place great banks of fog were rolling in. Kornon took the fog as a good omen, for it would make it easier for the Russian AGIs—intelligence-gathering trawlers—to move in closer, to monitor radio transmissions, while making it as difficult for the Americans to carry out surface observations of the smaller trawlers as it was for them to follow the DSRV on a sonar trace.

While the fog worried some of the captains, including some of the Russian fleet, who weren't used to the Aleutians where fog was more normal than not, it didn't worry Joe Cherco's *Amlia*, which felt very much at home.

HALL DESCENDED, giving minute-by-minute reports because of the increased danger of the upwelling. The tether and communications cord had sufficient slack so as not to either hinder his progress downward or strain the tether line's connection to his AD suit. At fifteen hundred feet he spotted two pinpoints of light—the forward and after spotlights of the *Lenin I*. The meteorological-balloon-size float was now no larger than a cantaloupe.

TATE HAD SUGGESTED to Kornon on the open channel that he put several hard-hat, deep-water-suited scuba divers aboard the *Lenin I* to help Hall at the hatch, for it would be a long and exhausting job at that depth to dig through the thick peatlike mud. Tate said he realized that this would necessitate a day or more of recompression for the divers afterward, but it would mean getting into the sub sooner.

Kornon had declined gracefully, assuring Tate that he had thought of this possibility, but with the extra number of scuba divers, fewer Americans could be taken out of the *New York* because of the extra weight aboard the DSRV during ascent. Tate saw his point and thanked him for his consideration, mentioning to the lookouts and Scotty on the *Petrel*'s bridge that he thought it was magnanimous of the Russian to think of the Americans.

Scotty grunted. "He wasn't bloody magnanimous at Eagle Island."

"Men change," said Tate. "Situations change."

"Aye," said Scotty. "As the Frenchies say—everything changes and everything stays the same." It made Scotty increasingly nervous that he couldn't tell what was going on at the bottom since they'd lost their sled light and camera. The occasional blip from the *Lenin I* and what might be Hall, or could be a fish, a small mud fall or any number of things, actually made him more anxious, he said, than if the screen was blank, as it had been earlier before the shallow-water divers from the *Boise* had repaired the lacerated cable. He would feel much better, he told Tate, when it was dawn and the damn scattering layer would "piss off below to the bottom where it belonged."

"Oh, stop your bellyaching," said Tate. "It'll be fine, Scotty. You'll see."

"Aye."

KORNON WATCHED the oceanographer moving toward the submarine, putting down some kind of bag and extracting a smaller black sack of some kind and then starting to shovel off the mud above the hatch. There were only six inches of the four-foot layer of mud left, but it was so thick and he was down so deep that Ustenko, who had been watching him digging all along, said he estimated that it would take the American another ten minutes to reach the bare metal.

Even though he knew the communication between him and the *Lenin I* was secure, Kornon lowered his voice to communicate with it, for they were now approaching the point of no return. "Spets ready?" he asked quietly.

The DSRV pilot confirmed that they were.

HALL STOPPED to catch his breath, the sound of his breathing inside his suit like that of a trapped animal.

"You all right down there, laddie?" asked Scotty.

"Fine," said Hall, adopting the mate's inflection. "A wee bit knackered, that's all. It's been a long day."

"Well, take it easy, laddie. We don't want to lose you, too."

"Who else have we lost?" Tate asked Scotty.

"That young Bremmer. And maybe a few of the *New York*'s crewmen, as well."

Tate didn't bother responding. Scotty was a born worrier, and that was all there was to it.

# 38

KORNON RANG Captain Peters on the *Boise*, using the open channel, to suggest they warn Mr. Hall "that the *Lenin I* reports sharks in the area."

The message was passed on to Hall, but beyond the small cone of light concentrated on the outline of the hatch, on the few inches of mud remaining and beyond the moat no wider than twenty feet that surrounded the DSRV, Hall could see nothing. Still, for a moment he stopped work and glanced about, remembering the sudden attack on the *Serena I*.

Looking back down at the hatch, he decided that although it could be opened now, he might as well get all the mud off it. It would make for clearer resonance through this tiny part of the mud-free hull, through which he could tap his message telling the crew to stand by to assist him in whatever way they might in his attempts to raise the sub. It was possible, for example, that if he managed to raise the sub even a foot or so out of the mud, she could jettison the heavy lead shot ballast that the Tridents carried so that they could at any later date install new equipment without altering the operational weight and therefore performance of the sub.

As he began the final dig, he moved to his right around the hatch using the shovel to tap out the message: "Stand by for instructions. Am trying to raise sub with USS *Boise* to assist. Will contact later." He waited for a minute, but there was no response, no tapping from the submarine. In the deep chill of the ocean at two thousand feet, it struck him that because of some accident within the sub there might be no one left to tap out a reply.

"WHAT'S HE DOING?" demanded Kornon, his head darting from side to side, trying to get a better view. It was no use; the American's AD suit was obscuring the hatch.

"Can't see, either, sir," answered the DSRV pilot.

"Well, move your vehicle, damn it! Get your cameras on him. See what he's up to. Quickly."

INSIDE THE DYING SUB, Sloane and Wain for the first time in their careers aboard the *New York* had no idea what to do.

"Maybe it's those goddamn Russians the guys from the *Boise* warned us about," whispered Wain.

"Then where the hell are our guys?"

"Ask whoever's outside a question," someone suggested.

"Brilliant," said a mechanic's mate. "What kind of question?"

"I dunno—anything. About the States. You know, capital cities, that kind of stuff."

"All right," said Chief Ryman, "what's the capital of California?"

"San Francisco . . . no, wait a minute—L.A."

"Sacramento."

"Shit!"

"For fuck's sake," griped an oiler, "what the hell is this—*Wheel of Fortune*?"

"Got any better ideas?"

"Yeah, wait till our guys come from the *Boise*."

"Stupid! They *said* they were from the *Boise*."

"Okay!" said Sloane. "If the Russians wanted to fool you, what would they do? Pick the name of a real American ship, right? Say, the *Boise*."

"How about them knowing about the Mets?" asked the senior electrician's mate.

"Hell," said the chief, "the *Japanese* know more about the New York Mets."

"Yeah," added a quartermaster. "Anyone could—"

"Listen!" cut in Sloane.

The tapping was starting again: "Acknowledge. Do you read me?"

Dyer pushed through the crowd. "Sir! Sir!"

Wain turned about. He felt weak, dizzy. He had difficulty focusing on Dyer; the civilian seeming nothing more than a shadow approaching.

"Sound signature!" said Dyer. "Whoever it is out there mentioned the *Boise*, Right?"

"Yes, but so did that other outfit—whoever *they* are."

"That's just the point," continued Dyer excitedly. "Ask whoever's outside now to have the *Boise* run at flank speed. We can do a matchup."

"Hey, Doc, way to go!"

"He's right," added Sloane. "The Russians couldn't duplicate the sound signature, if it *is* the Russians."

Sloane tapped out the request.

Hall was about to tap back "Roger" when he stopped, thinking about the *Boise*'s motion, how he had recognized he was aboard her even while in the chamber with Elga and the dour Russian doctor. Part of the *Boise*'s motion—her violent jerking to port and the smoother slide to starboard—was a definite pattern, all right, a direct result of the way her prop turned; but it was a pattern that had only come into existence after the *Boise* spent time for repairs to her prop in Attu dry dock. That meant that her sound signature now wouldn't be the

same as the one the *New York* would have for matchup. But
maybe they had matchup for the *Petrel!* That was the answer.

KORNON COULD STAND it no longer. The American was up to
something. The code the *Lenin I* had given the men on the *New
York* should be used now that the hatch was cleared of mud.
Hall had served his purpose.

"Let them out!" he ordered the DSRV.

HALL BEGAN TAPPING out his message: "Can arrange matchup with *Petrel*. Repairs to *Boise* prevent—"

Suddenly he dropped the shovel, retracting his arms from the
AD suit's metal limbs. The roaring in his ears was almost un-
believable. Then, as suddenly as it had begun, the sound
stopped. His communications cord had been cut.

Seventy feet away, coming directly toward him out of the rear
of the DSRV, like baby sharks from a mother, he saw four
black figures in commando scuba suits with hard hats. They
were joined by a fifth from the darkness above the *Lenin I*—no
doubt the one who had cut the communications cord. For a
moment he lost sight of them in the glare of the lights from the
DSRV, but he picked them up again in the thick grayish gloom
separating his thin cone of light from theirs.

They were coming at him from his right. Their weapons
looked like high-compression underwater Uzi machine guns,
with an effective range around twenty feet in deep water.

As quickly as he could, he snatched the bag, extended the
probe and headed quickly in moonwalkerlike hops toward the
sail until he felt the probe rising again. Then, shifting quickly
to his left, tracing the outer wall of the invisible plume, he made
for the mud cliff six feet away. There he turned, his back
against the cliff, and switched off his wrist light, watching in the
pitch-dark. His attackers were coming for him on his right to
avoid the plume barrier to his left, which rose straight up
against the cliff face. Hall's maneuver meant they'd have to
come at him head-on or risk being sideswiped and sent tumbling by the plume. Bending down in the blackness at the base
of the cliff, Hall reached into the bag, never taking his eyes off
the five Spets.

As soon as he heard the rush of static then dead silence, Scotty, aboard the *Petrel*, knew the communications cord had been cut. Within two minutes he was at the stern, hooking his legs and arms around the tether cable, its "soft" feeling confirming his worst fear—not only had Hall's communications cord been severed but also the tether line. Hall was alone.

"Sharks!" said Tate.

"Sharks, my ass!" retorted Scotty.

"Don't just sit there!" Kornon shouted through the mouthpiece to the pilot of the *Lenin I*. "It's not a hockey game. Get moving over to that hatch and put me on to young Saburov."

As the DSRV's stern props started up, spinning at their maximum of six knots, streams of bubbles trailed through its sphere of light into the blackness, and the vehicle's nose turned toward the cleared hatch seventy feet away. Lieutenant Saburov, the English-speaking Spets in charge of the remaining four commando divers in the DSRV's after section, heard the pilot's commands piped through from the forward watertight cabin.

"Saburov? General Kornon says under no conditions are you to use the mine until you get everything he wants from the sub—code books, K-47 machine, reactor layout and sound baffle sample. The lot. Leave the mine in the interlock section, as you'll be the last man out."

Saburov, breathing evenly and unhurriedly, long trained for such underwater commando work, rapped twice on the bulkhead to show he understood. The final check he ran through before they reached the hovering position twenty feet above the giant Trident's hatch was to look around at the other four Spets divers, making absolutely sure all insignias were correct.

From the darkness, Hall was able to see the DSRV's slow approach toward the sub. Withdrawing his arm from the arm of his suit, he wiped off some condensation on his small window to the underwater world. "You're really something, Kornon," he said to himself. "You don't miss a trick." The insignia the Spets were wearing were those of the U.S. SEALS—the

American Navy's underwater commandos—so that when the crewmen aboard the *New York* opened the hatch the first thing they were going to see coming down from the *Lenin I* was good old U.S.A. uniforms. "Beautiful!"

Hall was holding the ten-pound Cox gun in the right claw of the AD suit, the left grip resting on the five-inch-square metal frame that projected an inch and a half from the barrel; the square was a combination safety-accuracy feature, the gun firing the sealed but internally hollow-nosed bullet bolt only when the square, like a stapler gun, was pressed against a resisting surface. But you could cheat by releasing the gun's safety catch and pulling the metal frame back with one hand, faking the push of a hard surface.

Hall moved the gun so that its metal square framed the first diver coming at him, only fifteen feet away, and fired. The recoil sent a shiver through the AD suit, and from inside the tinted helmet Hall could see a trail of silvery bubbles so small that they looked like flecks of foil.

The next instant he saw a piece of a diver's black hard hat rising fast into the blue like a wafer of soot from a chimney, then disappearing into the darkness above. On the ocean floor a thick billow of mud spread like dense green smoke between the American and his attackers. Bringing another bullet bolt up from the Cox gun's three-bolt magazine, Hall moved along the cliff face another six paces. He went down on one knee and waited; it was a standoff until the cloud from the fallen diver cleared. Or so he expected—until the DSRV's two spotlights began sweeping over the sub into the plume, close to where he had just been. The beams of its lights penetrated the churning clouds that were now turning from dark olive to a light bottle-green.

He pulled the pin from a grenade—the time-delayed sound source he had joked about with a reporter—and threw it hard to his left where he'd been. Then, holding the Cox gun with both hands, he went forward into the mud cloud as rapidly as the suit would allow. The grenade's crash reverberated through the suit like someone hitting him with a hammer, and his ears began to ring; the cloud of mud where the grenade had gone off thickened to a chocolate mousse.

In front of him, where the cloud had been thinning, Hall spotted two of the Spets barely ten feet away, their attention drawn for a moment to the explosion. They were giving hand signals to each other to go in toward the cliff around the point of the explosion in a V-shaped outflanking movement. Hall fired once, moved the square to his left and fired again. The first man sagged, and a lot of blood spurted, obscuring the other diver on the offside.

Immediately Hall shoved another three-bolt magazine into the Cox gun as his eyes searched rapidly for the three remaining divers. He spotted two of them over the hatch, bodies horizontal and opposite each other like two long bottom fish waiting for surface prey to sink, ignoring what was happening beyond the hot plume behind and off to their right. All their attention was absorbed by their attempt to guide the DSRV's skirting down to the hatch for lock-on. The two divers were pushing and pulling the skirting's flange with obvious effort as the *Lenin I*, in neutral buoyancy, was using one prop and then the other in order to counteract the turbulence created around the general area of the plume.

Hall finally found the remaining diver, the dark shadow reminding him of a shark, more than forty feet above him. The commando, having apparently come too close to the plume in an effort to surprise Hall with a tight turn around the jet of water, had miscalculated and, caught by the plume, had been forced high above the sub. Seeing Hall, he fired his weapon, but at that distance, under the pressure of thousands of pounds per square inch, the bullets dropped harmlessly after twenty feet, some of them slowed further in the eddies of the plume and tinkling ineffectually on the DSRV like gravel. The diver had by then been taken so high by the plume that he was having difficulty regaining negative buoyancy to come back down to the bottom.

Keeping one eye on the two men by the hatch fifty feet away, Hall took out one of the small balloon floats, snapping its elastic stem about the striker level of a grenade. He pulled the pin from the grenade, counted three seconds and then threw it as high as he could into the plume. The balloon immediately began to expand, rising fast. At four seconds it blew. The diver, kicking spasmodically like a stunned fish, dropped the marine gun, which made him lighter and caused him to rise even farther. The slipstream effect of the vent took him up faster and faster, like a piece of paper near a fire, his lungs bursting in the upper layers.

Hall turned toward the *Lenin I*, the sub's hatch only a few feet below it now. The mud stirred up by the vehicle's props enveloped it and the divers in clouds of mud.

"Got a problem," Hall told himself. He realized now why the two divers by the hatch, their priority being to lock onto the DSRV, had seemed so cool in ignoring him. They knew they would be protected shortly by the screen of mud around them.

The Cox gun had a longer range than the pneumatic automatics of the Soviet commandos, so that Hall had had the kind of advantage that a rifle, with fewer bullets, has against a submachine gun. But now the comparison worked against him. If he stayed back beyond the range of the two Spets' machine guns, he would be safe, but unless he got closer to them, well within their range, he wouldn't be able to stop the interlock between the sub and DSRV. He thought of firing at the DSRV but dismissed the idea, for though the Cox bullet could kill or at least badly injure a man at a distance of forty feet, it couldn't penetrate the DSRV's steel skin, and the DSRV was too far away from him for grenades to be of any use. But he had to stop the interlock. Once that was made, the Americans inside the sub would be doomed.

INSIDE THE *Lenin I* the *Amur*'s torpedo lieutenant was terrified. He'd never been under enemy fire, and the noise of grenades, marine machine guns and what had sounded like rifle shots, so much louder and more immediate because the fighting was underwater where the sound traveled so much faster than in air, shook him up badly. This, together with the DSRV's being windowless, the TV cameras useless in mud clouds and the DSRV infinitely more claustrophobic than his submarine, made the experience in the confined space that much more horrifying. Over and over he wished the American dead.

IN THE REDDED-OUT control room in the *New York* Chief Ryman was looking up, trying to imagine what was going on outside, as was everyone else aboard the sub, the men grouping
together, not in their sleeping quarters or in any of the leisure
compartments but at their battle stations. From torpedo room
through control to the auxiliary engine room these were the
places they preferred to be, from habit and from deep affec-
tion for their boat, if they were to die.

The heat had finally overcome Wain. He was prostrate on his
bunk, gasping for breath, resting, trying to regain enough
strength to resume command. Until then, Sloane was effectively in charge.

"Those Russian bastards," said Yeoman Smythe. "They
must be trying everything short of depth-charging us to stop
our guys on the DSRV. Jesus, I wish I had a—"

"Hey! Shut up!" It was Dyer, his outburst as unexpected as
his excitement. "Listen!"

There was the unmistakable clunk of metal upon metal.

"Thank God!" said Sloane, the noise just forward of control.

"Bang over the escape hatch!" whooped Smythe.

"I'm going to name my boy," began Dyer, now wanting to
celebrate the fact that, if everything had gone well with his wife,
he was now a father, "I'm going to name him Boise."

In the delirium of excitement and silly jokes, no one heard
the attempts of the boat's hospital corpsman to say something, until Sloane shouted with what little strength he had remaining for everyone to hush, and waved the corpsman
forward.

"Knead's in bad shape," announced the medic. "I don't
know whether he'll make it. He's got no chance at all unless we
give him a blood transfusion and quickly. Type O negative.
Anyone?"

The corpsman had a list of the O negatives on board, but he
was waiting for someone to volunteer—otherwise Knead would
die.

MOVING TOWARD the *Lenin I* Hall could now and then see its
spotlights the faint color of distant suns, but the weak light

failed to reveal either the hatch or the divers, who he suspected were cunningly using the mud stirred up by the vehicle's props as protection until they had secured the interlock. Then they'd come for him. He took out two grenades and threw them toward the sub, knowing he'd never hit it but that the explosions would further churn up the mud on the port side around the *New York*'s escape hatch and the DSRV. Moving parallel to the long body of the submarine, Hall made for its rudder, then once he drew level with the DSRV's stern, he turned sharp left, heading straight for the *Lenin I*. He turned left again around its stern.

There were the two black figures at point-blank range, kneeling by the inverted V of the DSRV's skirting. One of them rose, lifting something. Hall fired, shifted his aim and fired twice more at the remaining figure. There was a dull thump as the second man fell into the mud. Hall clipped in another cartridge before he walked over to them and knelt, his wrist light on, the Cox gun steady. Both were dead.

There was no other noise now, but the occasional banging of the skirting around the hatch as the *Lenin I*, its TV cameras still blinded by the mud, rose and fell a few inches. Hall took two of the seven remaining grenades out of the bag, secured them in the left claw but dropped one in the mud and cursed. He hooked the drawstring of the bag around one of the *Lenin I*'s sensors—whether it was for salinity or temperature he didn't know and didn't care. Pulling the pin with his left claw, he dropped the grenade into the bag, moved across the sub's fairing, or rather the mud lying over the fairing and dived into the gap between the sub's starboard side and the cliff face.

Even when the seven grenades went off, the DSRV's steel was thick enough that only a ragged hole the size of a dime punctured its hull. But that was enough. A roaring torrent filled the pilot's cabin in less than a minute under the enormous pressure. The *Lenin I* rolled off the sub, mortally wounded, into the mud.

Hall got up as the shock wave passed him, sweating profusely, his heart beating fast, and walked toward the DSRV. He knew there might still be some Spets divers in its after section, sent down to take over the sub, either by machine-gunning all the Americans or blowing up the Trident after they finished ransacking it for its secrets. His muscles were now so tired that he felt the trapezius tightening again, which made him think of Elga and Kornon and how they hadn't cared a whit about killing a hundred and fifty Americans in cold blood.

The DSRV was sliding around on its side, its midsection crushed like some huge caved-in can, two of its props still turning. Soon they, too, stopped, and only then did Hall see the first of the five remaining Spets coming out. As each one emerged, he shot him before he could swing into action. The fifth man, Saburov, appeared. Hall pulled the trigger, simultaneously realizing that the cartridge in the Cox gun was finished. Saburov was bringing up his machine gun, when Hall gave him the telescopic probe in the stomach. By then the mud had thinned out considerably, its greenish ooze becoming tan-colored, suffused with blood. The DSRV's lights went out.

KORNON WAS STUNNED. He was seeing the death of his career—the end of his life. He would be lucky if they sent him back to Ulan Ude, unless... Unless. Suddenly he rose up in front of the shocked audience in the *Leningrad*'s combat center, reminding them that they all shared responsibility for the operation, for what had happened to the Spets and the DSRV. "No one," he said, his voice trembling, "no one saw this. Understand? If I fall, you fall with me. We bear *collective* responsibility."

Ustenko rose to the occasion. "General, we sent down our DSRV and it imploded. That's all we know."

There was murmured assent.

"But," someone said tremulously, "what will the American say?"

"Yes," added Litov's old adviser. "He's still the problem. And the press."

Kornon had to sit down. Ustenko handed him a cigarette. He sat there immobile with it until Ustenko lit it. The cigarette went out, for Kornon could hardly breathe. He stared again at the TV screen, seeing his nemesis calmly getting ready to shoot more cartridges. This time Hall was using them for what they were made for; he shot them into the sub's external hull, into its ballast tanks, preparing to do what the sub could no longer do. Using air from a compressor on either the *Boise* or the *Petrel*, the *New York* would once again attain positive buoyancy. Watching Hall calmly move from tank to tank after he had demolished Kornon's Spets team angered the general beyond endurance. The bastard was even using the light afforded by their sled to work by, saving the bright dart of his wrist light for the close-in work.

"The cheeky bastard," Kornon said. "The utter gall! He kills ten of my best men—"

"Thirteen," corrected Admiral Litov.

"What?" snapped Kornon.

"Thirteen," Litov repeated. "There were three in the pilot's compartment, also."

"Yes," said Kornon, "and now he's using the light from our—"

"Twelve," said Ustenko. "Look!" It was difficult to see much on the TV screen now with the bright DSRV lights gone but Ustenko had thought he saw something moving. "Yes," he went on, "one of our Spets is moving toward the hatch. He must only be wounded."

"Zoom in," ordered Kornon. "Quickly!"

But they still couldn't tell what the wounded man was doing, heading for the hatch. Hall was walking, or rather dragging his feet through the mud toward the forward ballast tank closest to the precipice that fell off into the trench—at least two hundred feet away from the lone Spets inching his way toward the hatch.

*"Bozhe moy!* My God!" said the *Leningrad*'s first officer. "He must be going to tap out the message. Get the Americans to open the hatch." Someone cheered.

"Shut up, you fool!" shouted Kornon. "They can't open the hatch at that depth unless there's an interlock. That's why we sent the DSRV down there."

"Then what's he going to do?" pressed Litov.

"I don't know," growled Kornon. "He can't do anything, as far as I can see."

Then everything changed in Kornon's mood, as a dark cloud passes the sun. He decided to launch his ultimate strategy, against which there was no known defense. "Colonel!"

"Yes, sir?"

"I want you to get a launch over and go to the trawler *Amlia*."

"Yes, sir," answered Ustenko, looking nonplussed, wondering, quite frankly, whether the general had lost his grip.

Kornon looked down at the fading image of Frank Hall as he moved toward the precipice beyond the dim light still provided by the sled. "I'm not finished with you yet, you bastard. I'll hit you on two fronts."

One front would be the surprise he would send to Hall through the *Amlia*. The other was a message via satellite to Zurich, Switzerland, to an old friend of Kornon, a supposed "neutral" who did business with both the Soviet Union and the West—a man who had already fulfilled part of Kornon's general plan. Though the plan now seemed so close to collapse, Kornon, with marked and growing confidence, believed it was fully retrievable, and all the sweeter for that.

The message was addressed to Herr Klaus, head of SRP, Swiss Rhine Petrochemicals, one of the world's largest multinationals: "Pacific Ocean Department invites bids on new deep-sea rescue vehicle. Final specifications will be forwarded within twenty-four hours. Sincerely, Skolensky."

"Skolensky won't like that," Litov put in.

"I don't care a shit what Skolensky likes. It must appear to come from his department."

Kornon turned back to the screen. "Now we will see, you whore's turd!" he said vehemently to Hall, who, having finished shooting in the Cox valves to which the air hose would be attached, had now moved over to the sail, where he proceeded to cut and slash at the tangle of net, to free the sub's planes.

"Colonel, before you go."

Ustenko turned. "Yes, General."

"The *Amlia*," Kornon continued, "is ideally suited for fast maneuvering in these seas. I want her to be the first to pick up Hall when he surfaces. And give him this message." He wrote quickly and handed the slip to the colonel.

Ustenko read the message, biting his bottom lip as its full import struck him. He looked across at the general with a mixture of fear and admiration in his eyes. "Do you think he'll yield, General?"

"Colonel, it's his one great weakness."

Ustenko nodded in full agreement. "Yes, it's every man's weakness, General."

*"Exactly!"*

The general walked with Ustenko from the cruiser's combat center to the launch that would take the colonel to the *Amlia*. They stopped off at Kornon's stateroom to pick up a large manila envelope, containing all the relevant details, which the colonel would take with him.

# 39

IN ZURICH THE SUN was shining. The lake was caressed by gentle zephyrs, the interplay of shadows over the water a never-ending study in contrasts for a painter who had set up his easel on the walkway beside the Limmat River, where his view included part of the Bauschantzli, the island at the confluence of the lake and river. Herr Klaus, head of Swiss Rhine Petrochemicals, tall, distinguished and impeccably dressed, was sitting in a Bauschantzli café sipping a cappuccino while reading the *New York Times*, its European edition now composed electronically via satellite in Zurich. The shares of SRP were doing well, for Klaus had bought out some American companies at rock-bottom prices, including a deep-sea research company that had left South Africa in protest against apartheid. Klaus didn't care about blacks in South Africa or anybody anywhere, providing he was making a profit.

He had first met Kornon, whom he'd done business with as head of Soviet fisheries and deep-sea strategic mineral research, when they had both clashed with the American oceanographer Frank Hall who was, inconveniently, also interested in deep-sea mineral deposits. Klaus hated Hall deeply because of their past battles over sea gold. He was hoping that the Russians would be successful in raising the American submarine or, better still, that Hall would fail—hopefully die. Either way, Klaus didn't worry; through its shadowy, ostensibly "state-controlled" import subsidiaries in Eastern Europe and through his American companies, SRP supplied both the Soviets and Americans with a wide range of petrochemical products, especially computer-controlled Swiss precision lathes, which were essential for the extreme accuracy in machining the all-important quiet props for submarines.

And so it was no surprise when what he was pleased to call one of his "runners," a young man in his early twenties, entered the Bauschantzli café with a message from Kornon about bids for building a DSRV. In accordance with their previous agreement, Kornon had signed his name "Skolensky." The runner was flustered, not knowing whether to dare interrupt Klaus's after-lunch cappuccino and *Rübelikuchen*, the local carrot cake, or wait until Klaus returned to his office on the Bahnhofstrasse, only a short walk from the Bauschantzli.

"I thought," began the runner apologetically, unconsciously checking his necktie—Klaus detested any sign of slovenliness—"I thought you would—"

"Be quiet," said Klaus, taking a pair of gold-rimmed bifocals from a florentine leather case. The runner, acutely aware of several other customers half hidden by the vines and Chinese lanterns twirling in the gentle breeze, felt so conspicuous standing that he drew out the chair opposite Klaus.

"Stay!" Klaus ordered. He rarely sat with anyone whose net worth was less than a million Swiss francs a year or who was not highly influential. The runner was neither—though one or both was his goal, which was why he literally stood still for insults.

A small notepad with gold pencil attached suddenly appeared in Klaus's hands as if by some form of legerdemain—Klaus simply would not countenance a notebook that did otherwise. Peering over his bifocals with an air of serene contempt, he wrote a message to be telephoned immediately to America; his handwriting, like his dark suit, was immaculate and to the point, devoid of any flourish except for the *s* of his signature, at the end of "Klaus" which possessed a tail that swept back like a panther's. He handed the paper to the runner who, torn between fear and common sense, nevertheless felt compelled to point out that it would be now quite late on America's West Coast.

"Have Stein ring," replied Klaus, returning to the stock columns of the *New York Times*. "He's American."

"HELLO?" Gloria Bernadi's voice was heavy with sleep, apprehensive. No one except the FBI office in Portland was supposed to have the cottage's telephone number. She saw that the light in the living room was still on, a sliver of it forming a sharp triangle beneath her bedroom door. She was dimly aware of someone on the phone asking for her.

Suddenly she sat up, holding her forehead as if in pain, noting the time was 4:10 in the morning. "Yes," she said, "I'm Gloria Bernadi." The call being so late, she was sure that something had happened to Frank. "Who is this?" she asked, sitting farther upright in bed. She switched on the bedside lamp, hearing the crashing sound of the Oregon surf and static simultaneously.

"Sorry to bother you at such a late hour, Miss Bernadi. It's the Portland FBI officer here. It's important I speak to Agent Burroughs or Morley."

"What's wrong?" she asked. "Is something wrong with Frank?"

"No, no, I'm afraid it's the press. We'll have to move you."

"Oh," she groaned. She loved it at Cannon Beach. Given the circumstances, she couldn't think of anywhere else she'd rather be hiding from the press. "All right, hold on," she said. "I'll get them for you."

"Only one'll do," said the caller half jokingly, but she had trouble hearing him because of the static. "Hold on," she repeated, donning her robe.

When she opened her bedroom door, she started in fright. One hand darted to her chest, pulling at the robe, while her other hand was still on the doorknob. Burroughs was waiting right outside the door.

"Sorry," he said, looking weary, unshaved, his breath foul. "I thought it might be a reporter. I told Portland twice to get you a place where *we* could answer the phone for you." Morley, the younger agent, was sitting on the plaid couch still in his blue suit pants and white shirt, his head cocked to one side like a parrot, reading *Bawdy* magazine.

"The Portland office," said Gloria. "For you."

"Thanks."

As Burroughs went into the bedroom, she sat on the edge of a rattan chair, smiling at the other agent, listening to Burroughs.

Burroughs said, "Uh-huh. Right. No problem. Okay. Thanks," then put down the phone. He came out, looking down at her apologetically and stifling a yawn. "We have to move," he said.

"Not now?" she pleaded.

"No. Not till morning. One of the newspapers has somehow found out we're down on the coast, but they're not sure just where. Still, Portland thinks it's better if we move into another area altogether."

Gloria slumped back in the rattan. "Where?"

"Don't know yet, but they'll call us back in the morning. Sorry you were woken up. Good night."

"Night."

When Gloria had closed the door, Burroughs looked across at Morley and his girlie magazine. "Degenerate!"

"What? Lots of good articles in this."

"Yeah," said Burroughs. "Body language. I could see pussy from her bedroom."

"Got to pass the time somehow," answered Morley.

"All right, Mr. Hoover. Wake me at six."

# 40

HALL WAS SORE AND EXHAUSTED, despite the fact that he was working at one atmosphere, as he would have been if working at the surface. The AD suit was a marvel, and eighty-percent mobility in the darkness of two thousand feet was a stunning engineering feat. Still, eighty percent wasn't a hundred, and doing hard physical labor—cutting the tangle of fish net—while lacking twenty percent mobility, made him feel as if he were toiling in thick winter clothes, including an overcoat. He was having more and more difficulty, too, seeing in the wrist light's cone, which in the vastness of the deep Pacific was a mere pinpoint of light in unending night. Drenched in perspiration, every muscle aching, Hall felt his waste bag sloshing with every move and bumping the calves of his legs until it started to leak. Adding to the discomfort, he had to climb back up the sail three times after minor mud slides knocked him off balance, forcing him to hang on to the fish netting until the slide passed over him. So much, he thought, for the thrill of working underwater.

When he first heard the tapping, it reminded him of a woodpecker making a few exploratory whacks on a knot of dry timber. Then the sound slowed, stopped altogether for a few minutes, began again but, it seemed, in a different place. Hall stopped cutting the net, which he figured he'd just about beaten; he'd loosened several clumps of it in the past half hour and had sent them falling into the gap between the sub and the cliff.

He was torn between going to investigate the tapping, and staying on the sail. It was probably one of the crew moving about the sub, trying to make contact to find out what had happened. Hall knew that despite the crew's understandable anxiety, there was nothing more he could do right now except free the planes' surface. He'd have to come down again with the high-compression air hose and inflate the tanks, hoping this would be enough to give the *New York* adequate buoyancy and up angle, once she could move the planes to start an ascent. The other reason he held off from investigating the tapping, which sounded as if it was coming fifty feet below and about twenty feet forward of the sail, was that it was imperative, if he was to outwit Kornon, to be finished before 4:00 a.m. At first light the scattering layer seven hundred feet below the surface, consisting of thick swarms of plankton devoured by millions of shrimp and other tiny invertebrates, began to descend to the lower depths. There, below two thousand feet, the layer waited during the daylight until sunset began, and then rose again. The essential part of Hall's plan, the only way he could see of beating the Russians, was for the sub to be hidden beneath the sonar-impenetrable scattering layer, so named because of its ability, first noted in World War II, to scatter sonar signals, giving a "false bottom" bounce-back. It provided a veritable curtain and was the reason for his reluctant but—as he saw it— necessary and deliberate rudeness to Peters and Bryce, whose ship would be helping to haul the sub up. After first light all would be lost, the scattering layer would descend, revealing the ascending sub—if it did ascend—to sonar signals; its profile would show on the sonar trace paper instead of the fly-dirt false bottom previously reflected by the layer.

It was now 2:17.

As WAIN, through sheer will, dragged his limp body back to control, he and the crew of the *New York* could hear faint tapping.

"What do you think?" Wain asked Sloane.

"It's a weak signal," replied Sloane, "but I thought I could make out *Boise* now and then."

"I dunno," said the chief, tired from the fetid air. The plume had raised the temperature in the sub to over one hundred and five degrees Fahrenheit. It was even an effort to talk. Wain was leaning for support on the rail around the attack center, the same way the elderly use a walker. "There's something screwy about it," continued the chief. "It seems to be saying *Boise* in Morse, but then it sounds like it's moving away from us. I mean, it sounds like a kind of bumping on the port side." He wiped his face with an oilcloth. The cloth had become so drenched that he had to go to the head to wring it out. The stench there was nauseating because of the inability to flush against the mud.

Wain waited until he came back. "I've been thinking about what you were saying, Chief. It does seem to move away from the hatch, then all you can hear is a few bumps."

"Yeah. Why aren't they giving us the whole message?"

"Because," said Yeoman Smythe, in no better shape than the others but naturally suspicious, "it's a goddamn Russian who only knows how to spell *Boise*—because he's seen it on a U.S. frigate. He doesn't have to understand English to tap that out in Morse."

"I think it's another outfit altogether," said Sloane, sitting in one of the planesmen's seats, his sodden shirt stuck to its leather back. "A vessel of some kind was smack over our escape hatch, then the next thing we know there's this godawful crash and tumbling, like we were coming apart at the seams, and then the sound of something like a . . . I don't know."

"A whip cracking," said someone.

"Yeah," interjected an oiler. He was sitting on the floor, battle stations long since abandoned. "A whip and a lady in black leather and—"

"Shut up!"

"You shut up, Smythe! If you're so friggin' smart, you tell us what it was."

"A shark stick. The kind they have on ships for divers to use. You know, like a cattle prod, with a shotgun cartridge inside the end of the stick. One push on the shark and blam! End of shark."

"So it was a shark stick. We're still stuck in here, and we ain't never gonna—"

Wain cut in. "Could be some diver out there giving his all, the pilot and copilot of some rescue submersible, safe and dry inside their chamber up forward, with a passenger section all dry and waiting for us behind them, but the diver is the only one who can communicate with us. He could be hurt, maybe in that roll we heard, but maybe the DSRV made it back and he managed to guide it over the hatch."

"That's a long shot," said Sloane.

"Long shots are all we have left," said someone.

"How about those whacks on our side?" asked Smythe. "Could be someone *is* trying to raise us."

"Yeah, could be they're trying to flood us so we never get off."

"Jesus Christ!" exploded a planesman, who until then had kept his desperate terror bottled up. "Let's find out, for Christ's sake!"

"Steady on, sailor," Wain cautioned authoritatively. But he knew morale had hit rock bottom, and the air supply was so poisonous they had only a few hours remaining. He had to do something. He moved forward of control to the ladder leading to the interlock chamber.

"Captain!" It was Sloane.

Wain paused and looked down just as he was about to open the lower hatch into the empty interlock chamber. "What is it?"

"Take care up there. We don't know what's outside."

"Don't worry. Unless I'm sure there's a DSRV up there—one of ours—I won't be opening any hatch. And if there isn't a DSRV latched on, you know I won't be able to open the hatch anyway, because of the water pressure."

He gave them a brave smile, opened the hatch to the interlock chamber and entered it, his footsteps a muffled echo in its emptiness. Below, the men huddled around Sloane at the base of the ladder. Waiting.

The hatch slammed shut, and they saw the locking wheel turn.

AFTER CUTTING THE LAST PIECE of net free from the sail's plane, Hall made his way carefully down from the sail and the base of the cliff, using his light and probe, careful to avoid the plume. Now he could hear more of the bumping sounds that he'd heard earlier while working on the sail. They appeared to be coming from across the forward deck of the submarine on the port side. As his light couldn't reach that far, he first made his way to the hatch, using it as a reference point, and only when he reached the port side, moving softly in the mud, did he stop and shine the thin cone down toward the bumping sound. The beam caught a bubble of effervescence, and a metal tube the size of a small sledgehammer.

For a fleeting moment he saw the wounded Spets turn slowly like a slug, his hard hat still intact, his right hand lifting the heavy metal tube from the wreckage of the *Lenin I* and bringing it down hard on the protruding half of a Cox bolt. The commando dropped the tube when he saw Hall and reached for the pneumatic machine gun nearby, but Hall had already jumped down from the side of the sub, driving the exhausted Spets into the mud. He reached down almost lethargically with his knife and cut the hose leading to the Spets's mixed gas pack. The man's final sound erupted, the helium in the mixed gas making his outcry a loud Mickey Mouse scream.

The Spets's head rose briefly, then fell limply with a dull thud onto Hall's boot as the oceanographer turned away, conscious of time pressing. He began working his way around the sub, making sure that none of the other vital Cox bolts had been tampered with. Relieved that they were all intact and that no disastrous leak had occurred, he looked at his watch.

He had to hurry. A lot depended on how quickly the *Boise* or the *Petrel* picked him up so that he could take down the air hose and whatever other equipment he might need to raise the sub far enough out of the mud. If that didn't happen, he'd have to use the *Boise*'s winch cable alone. Hauling on just one cable made him nervous, even though he knew that, just as in the analogy of the child's bath toy that he'd given to the sailors on the *Boise*, all the sub probably needed was a nudge into positive buoyancy. The pull up, then, wouldn't be a pull on a deadweight, that is, not a pull on the sub's whole weight, but only on the few hundred pounds that made up the borderline between the sub's negative and positive buoyancy, between her sinking or rising.

From the starboard plane, three feet of which was still sticking into the mud cliff, he started up the cliff to double-check that the top of the sail was free of any obstruction other than mud. It was. Hall pushed himself off from the top of the sail, away from the plume and out over the submarine, his light unable to illuminate any part of its hull in the void forty feet below. He jettisoned his weights, switched off the wrist light and began to ascend. Even if Kornon had Spets teams waiting in the upper subsurface layers—which he doubted, for the press would surely see them—it would do the Spets no good if they couldn't see him. And once on the surface he knew he was halfway home.

Or so he thought.

# 41

HALL CAME OUT FAST like a cork, popping at least four feet into the air, then crashing back into the ocean. He pulled the tab on the leg flare as soon as he saw the distorted moons of the lighted marker buoys. He found the buoys a welcome sight, but also an ominous one; he'd seen a colleague killed off Long Island by coming up too fast, through a thermocline right under a metal

buoy. The concussion hadn't killed him, but the sharp edge of
a ring bolt with which the buoy was tethered had pierced his
helmet, his AD suit flooding in a second, and he'd drowned
before they could get him out. This time Hall saw he was closer
to the ships than on his last ascent, but his sense of relief was
short-lived when he realized the flare was fizzing away under a
canopy of heavy fog. He could hear the mournful sounds of
foghorns, so many, in fact, that he didn't hear the trawler
bearing down on him until she was only a hundred feet or so
from the flare.

AT FIRST HALL THANKED the skipper of the *Tuna Star* for the
fast pickup. Joe Cherco, wearing a balaclava against the cold
fog, shook hands, his eyes crinkling. He patted Frank on the
back and told him to "have some bourbon down below, the real
stuff...not that cheap horse piss they try to sell you in Attu."
Hall declined, though he would have loved a shot of rye. It was
2:24 and there was work to be done before 4:00 a.m.

It was when he climbed out of the suit and went below for
coffee during the bumpy ride to the *Petrel* that his mood suddenly plunged from the high he was usually in after a deep dive
to the chill he felt when he saw the smiling face beneath the
military cap with its red star.

"Colonel Ustenko," said the Russian in very good English,
handing the oceanographer a mug of coffee and indicating he
take a seat opposite him at the chipped, fake marble Formica
mess table. "I hired the *Tuna Star* to be the first to pick up a
brave man."

"Why?" asked Hall. There had been no handshake, no false
civilities. Despite his handing Hall the coffee, the Russian was
all business, his friendly expression and tone clearly forced.

"Oh," said Ustenko, his face angular and sallow in the cabin
light. "Why did we hire the *Tuna Star*? Because she's fast."

"No, why did *you* pick me up? After what happened down
there, Comrade, I would have thought you bastards would be
on your way home."

"After what happened?" asked Ustenko, feigning puzzlement.

"You know damn well. It's been like a goddamn butcher's shop around that sub—and that *was* your TV light and camera sled, wasn't it?"

"Yes. You shouldn't have cut the TV cable before you came up. It made General Kornon very annoyed."

Hall started to make an appropriately rude reply when Ustenko held up his hand. "Please, Mr. Hall. I'm here to offer you what you Americans call a deal. Let's not argue over trifles."

"Thirteen dead men are trifles to you?" he asked Ustenko angrily.

Ustenko shrugged. He was being sincere. "After the purges? Yes. Besides, they were soldiers."

Hall started to sip the coffee, but hesitated, staring down at the steaming black liquid.

"There's nothing in it," Ustenko assured him.

Hall reached over and poured it into the sink.

Ustenko shrugged again. He enjoyed being top dog for once, talking as he knew the general might but free now of the inhibitions of being junior in rank to Kornon.

"Get on with it," said Hall. "What deal? I've got work to do."

"Very well. I would have preferred to talk like two gentlemen and take my time and—"

"I don't see any gentlemen," said Hall.

Ustenko sighed. Didn't the Americans understand it was impossible to insult a colonel who'd worked for the KGB, who had fallen from grace like Kornon, and so was capable of doing anything and *would* do anything to be on top of the pile rather than at the bottom?

"All right, Mr. Hall. Let us talk like men of the world. Short and—how do you Americans say?—sweet."

"Get *on* with it," said Hall, wishing now he hadn't thrown out the coffee. He could drink the whole damn pot.

"I think you'll have an accident," said Ustenko, "in raising—or I should say in trying to raise—the *New York*."

"That's what you hope," said Hall.

"No. That's what will happen. Now that we've..." The colonel hesitated. "I might as well be frank—" Ustenko thought the pun amusing. Hall didn't. Ustenko continued, his hands clasped benignly around his coffee. "We don't care how it happens, Mr. Hall, but the *New York* is not to be rescued. Arrange any accident you like—so long as she goes to the bottom."

Hall leaned forward. "Look, you shit—"

Ustenko was holding up his hand again like a traffic policeman in Red Square. "No, *you* listen. You must surely understand, Mr. Hall, that as we have failed to recover it there is no way Moscow will allow America's most powerful weapon to be raised from waters it considers its own, militarily, in the first place. Moscow will settle for nothing less than a draw, Mr. Hall. Understand, please—it's not the general's policy but Moscow's. Moscow will not permit you to take the Trident out of Soviet waters. Either she is ours or she is no one's. Moscow rules. Surely you're not so naive as to think we can afford such a massive loss of face in front of our Warsaw Pact allies. Besides—" Ustenko sat back, his head resting against the trawler's bulkhead, the red star catching a sickly yellow light, "—the world media are already speculating about all the things that could go wrong. Leaking propellant in the missile bay—"

"Who told them that?"

"We did," said Ustenko. "But even your American networks are talking about this possibility . . . among others." He paused, then added, "I can promise you Moscow will express great sorrow for the loss of the *New York* and the hundred and fifty gallant Americans."

Hall started to laugh. "You've got gall, you bastards, I'll give you that. What are you going to do? Pay me a million dollars?" Frank got up from the table. "So long, Colonel. It's time I got a little fresh air before I get ready to go back—"

"If you don't, we'll kill your woman."

The trawler lunged in a wave, and Hall, staring at the Russian, was thrown hard against the stove guard, the glass coffeepot spilling its contents over the element.

"Moscow is playing what you Americans call hardball, Mr. Hall. And never mind detente, *glasnost*, arms reduction treaties. You're a big boy. You know there's only one question in the equation—the one Comrade Stalin asked the pope: 'How many divisions have you got?' Well, we have the divisions."

Ustenko slid a photo across the table, a very grainy black-and-white. Gloria, near Haystack Rock, Ecola State Park in the background. On either side of her two very well-dressed young men. "It was sent via fax machine," said Ustenko, casually adding more sugar to his coffee. "I have no idea who they are— I mean their real names. We work through an intermediary in Europe. But they're professionals. Your Gloria—" Ustenko paused. "I've always liked that name, so dramatically Italian, *da*? Anyway, your Gloria thinks they're FBI agents protecting her, and *you* indirectly, from being hounded by the press."

Hall had slid back down onto the mess bench.

"Anyway, as I say," continued Ustenko, "they're professionals. They'll make it look like an accident, too. A fall down a cliff track, or some such thing."

Hall picked up the picture. If he knew anything in his life, he knew the Russian wasn't bluffing, and Ustenko knew he knew, but nevertheless seemed to enjoy the exercise of naked power. The colonel pointed to the photograph again. "The one on the left, the taller man—imagine wearing a necktie and suit on the beach! Hoover would have approved. Well, anyway, he's using the name Burroughs. Turn the photo over."

Frank did as he was told, as obediently as a schoolboy serving a detention. There was a phone number on the back—area code 503. Oregon. It was the number of Gloria's dorm at the university.

"You can ring," said the colonel. "You'll find she's no longer there. She won't be at Cannon Beach, either. She's to be moved. The phone number will keep changing, of course. But when our intermediary in Europe calls this evening he will leave one of two messages at that number. One message and the two men simply walk away. The other—"

Hall knew what the other message would mean.

"Of course," added Ustenko, draining his coffee mug as the man with the balaclava called down that they were approaching the *Petrel*, "you could tell the FBI, CIA, whoever you like. We would deny this conversation ever took place, and she, I can assure you, would be dead." Ustenko grunted, lifting a small, heavy case the size of a laptop portable computer. "You can have it hauled across in your empty AD suit."

"What—" Hall began. But he couldn't go on. His throat was so parched he couldn't speak. He swallowed hard. "What's in it?"

"Don't be stupid," said Ustenko. "An explosion is the best way. It's very simple—set the timer, push the button. A child could do it. Anywhere on the pressure hull—it doesn't matter."

"Anywhere?" Hall was holding the case, staring numbly at it.

"The sooner the better," said Ustenko. "The ladies and gentlemen of the media are tiring of caviar. To be truthful, most of them are seasick, and there are problems with our satellite communication. There's a lot of pressure on the general to leave for the Komandorsky Islands where the journalists can better file their reports. But don't let that give you any ideas about delaying, Mr. Hall, because I can assure you the general won't leave until he knows the *New York* is finished. So my advice is to do it quickly."

"Who needs your advice?" said Hall quietly. But there seemed to be no fight left in him.

"You do," Ustenko said mercilessly. The more he used his power the more he was enjoying it. "You look very confused."

Hall held on to the towel rack on the bulkhead and forlornly lifted the mine, wrapping it in his foul-smelling suit, which had been crammed into an oilskin closet halfway down the stairs. "It could cause an enormous explosion," said Hall. "The missiles, torpedoes—"

"All the better. The missiles' nuclear warheads aren't armed, so only the propellant will explode."

*"Only,"* Hall said.

"Good luck," said the colonel. "For obvious reasons I won't come on deck with you. Oh—one more thing." Hall turned like a whipped dog. "Make the explosion sound convincing to your press contingents on the *Boise* and the *Petrel*. The general insists on that."

The irony of it all, Hall realized as the *Tuna Star* carried him to the *Petrel*, was so terrible that he could hardly bear to think about it. He had been carefully preparing to deceive Kornon, right from his first calculated words of abuse to Peters and

Bryce. He'd planned to pretend to lose the sub under the protection of the scattering layer and then to rage at Peters that he'd bungled it all, to say that a hundred and fifty men had died because of a bungled rescue attempt, like the rescue of Bremmer. Hall had prepared this deception to mislead the Russians, knowing Peters would respond to his raging accusations that the *Boise* had lost the sub, and betting that the Russians, convinced the *New York* had been lost, would move off—while all the time she would have been raised, he'd hoped, and lying safe below the protective shield of the scattering layer. To know that he had thought it all out so carefully, so meticulously, only to see his plan now in shambles—it was too much to endure. He was sure they would kill Gloria unless he did what they wanted. How could anyone make a decision like that—whether to save the life of the person he loved most in the world, or the lives of a hundred and fifty men he'd never seen but who were equally loved by others. It was the worst, the most torturous decision, he had ever faced.

# 42

THE MOMENT HALL and his suit were hoisted aboard, the *Petrel*'s bosun knew something was wrong. Hall's face was ashen, beyond mere exhaustion. He gave the instructions for his next dive in a flat monotone, so inaudible at times that he had to be asked to repeat them. "Air hose, communications cord and tether all in one—clipped together. Hauling cable'll have to come down from the *Boise*. I'll pick it up down there."

"If we *can* haul, Frank, you watch yourself. That's dangerous business."

"Everything's dangerous. Don't start the haul until I say so.... If something goes wrong and the communications cord fails, I'll send up a float flare. Strap three of them on me," he continued somberly. "Steady pull. No jerking on the haul."

Somebody thrust a mug of hot chocolate toward him. Several seconds passed before he realized he was holding it; he was looking down at it as if wondering how it had gotten there. "I'll be riding up on the sub's deck if I get her off the bottom," he told Tate and Peters on the open channel. "So make sure when you're hauling—"

"Riding up on the sub? What for?" asked Peters. "If the haul happens at all, it happens. You don't need to ride her. You might as well be up here and lend a hand with—"

"I can give instructions to the men inside the sub," said Hall, his voice still subdued.

Then off the port side Hall saw the trawler *Tuna Star*—if that was her real name—lit up like a Christmas tree. The balaclava man was watching the *Petrel* through binoculars. "So?" continued Peters over the communications line. "How are you going to give them instructions?"

"In Morse."

"What do you know about a Trident that its crews doesn't? Anyway, all they can do is just sit there and—"

"Shut your mouth," said Hall, not loudly but with such an icy tone that everyone on the heaving deck of the *Petrel*, including the press, fell quiet.

The bosun was the first to speak again. "Hey, Frank—what's wrong, man?" he asked.

"Haven't time to tell you now."

"But, Christ, man, why do you have to ride the sub?"

"Personal," said Hall. "Bring me the hose, will you? I want to flush out this suit. It smells like an outhouse."

"I'll do it for you," said the bosun.

"Goddamn it! I'll do it!" Hall shouted, grabbing the hose. He reached in and unclipped the waste bag, emptying it through the scuppers, and hosed out the suit so that its neck was facing away from everyone and flush up against the scuppers as he continued hosing. He put fewer weights on the waist belt than was usual for two thousand feet. In the rocking, gut-wrenching motion of the *Petrel* and the swirling dampness of the fog, only the bosun noticed the weights, telling Hall he'd need more.

"No, I won't."

The bosun pulled over the rubber-footed ladder for Hall to climb up and into the suit, which was wedged between the *Petrel*'s davit and railing to keep it steady in the roll. Hall felt seasick. He wanted to eat one of the chocolate bars he had, but knew if he did he'd throw up.

"You got something in there, Frank?" asked the bosun straight out. "Extra weight?"

"Screw the helmet on and tether me. I want it played out fast, so whoever's in charge of the air hose and communications cord better not foul up. I want them all going down at the same time."

"Frank," said the bosun. "You look like death. You're exhausted, man. Rest for a while—even an hour or—"

"Screw on the damn helmet!"

As Hall disappeared in the final descent for this mission, the bosun thought about the way the oceanographer had acted. Hall was his friend, but there were a hundred and fifty lives at stake, quite apart from the submarine. He went to warn Tate. "Something's got into Frank. I don't like it."

"You don't say?" Scotty said. "Working continuously for hours on end in bloody mud up to his armpits? Mon, who wouldn't be cranky?"

"I don't just mean he's tired, Scotty," replied the bosun. "I'm saying there's something queer about it all. He seems...I think he's cracking up."

"Oh, balls," said Scotty. "He's dead worried about those poor bastards in that steel coffin doon there. If he gets them up, he'll be the biggest hero in the world. You'll all be cheering him."

"And if he doesn't?" pressed the bosun.

"Ach, then he'll be in it good and proper. A congressional bloody inquiry it'll be and *Nightline* with Dan Rather."

"Ted Koppel," Tate put in.

"And all the newspapers," said Scotty, ignoring Tate's correction. "After that sex thing on the beach he was accused of, he'll have to leave the country."

"What do you think, Scotty?" asked the bosun. "Think he'll get 'em up?"

"Fifty-fifty, laddie. But if I was a betting man, which I'm not, I'd pass."

"By God, you're a cheerful fellow," said Tate, looking haggard and drawn himself.

STARTING ON THE STARBOARD cliff face side, Hall worked his
way around the sub, the air hose fitting snugly onto each Cox
valve. But as he moved he had the feeling of a man walking in
a nightmare in a black void that by itself could drive some men
mad. So worried was he about the terrible choice he had to
make, caught between the devil on the *Leningrad* and the deep
blue sea, that it was several seconds before he noticed, in part
because of the narrowness of the wrist light's beam, that the
starboard side of the huge submarine had moved an inch or
two. Once he realized what was happening he gave each of the
valve's nipples on the tanks on the starboard side, closest the
cliff, an extra surge of air.

There was a terrifying groan as the entire Trident seemed to
come alive like some great leviathan, causing the mud on top
of the sub's outer hull, particularly that on the fairing above the
missile tubes, to shift across to the far port side away from the
cliff. This freed the sail from the cliff, though it was still not
perpendicular to the ocean's bottom. The movement was slow
at first but ended with the roar of a freight train, the mud
clouds boiling hundreds of feet into the pitch-dark above the
port side. The clouds were so dense that Hall thought his wrist
light had stopped working, until he heard the mud raining on
his helmet. He realized it would be several minutes before he'd
be able to see anything with the light. He could use one of the
signal flares strapped to the left leg of the AD suit, but they
were too precious to use, in case something went wrong with his
communication cord.


WHEN THE STARBOARD SIDE of the *New York* began to rise, the
crew was alarmed, thinking they might be sliding into the
oblivion of the trench ten thousand feet below. It took Wain
only a split second to realize they were on the verge of positive
buoyancy.

"All right," he said, "we're going up. Man your stations!"
Then he had second thoughts. Maybe his was just one last
frantic hope after all the disappointments. But the sub rose
some more.

Then they heard a noise like a thin metallic snake rapidly
uncoiling, rushing upward against the sail. It stopped. No one

knew what it was until Yeoman Smythe remembered, from years ago on one of the last diesel electrics he'd served on.

"Goldarn! It's the message buoy taking up the haul cable."

"Holy Mother!" said a planesman. "*Now* it's gonna tell everyone where we are."

"'Bout fucking time."

"Steady!" Sloane ordered with what little energy he could muster. "This is a submarine, not a bar."

"Wish the hell it *was* a bar."

"I said steady. Depth reading?"

"Says two thousand feet, sir. We're still on the bottom."

As there was hardly ever a sense of motion aboard a nuclear submarine except during the dive and the rapid ascent, most of the men didn't know whether they were regaining positive buoyancy. But they knew there had been some movement, and at the report of two thousand feet a sudden depression swept through the boat again. Little was said, however, and soon they could hear more air hissing into the starboard tanks. It was having no effect in at least one of the forward tanks, which had been gashed during the slide along the bottom. All the crew could hear was the loud, futile bubbling of air passing through water without expelling it from the tank.

The *New York* was still heeling to starboard but not as much—about ten degrees. There was no noticeable movement for a while as air kept hissing into the tanks, but when the sub did move it was with such a sudden and violent shift to port that three men in the galley and Captain Wain in the control room were thrown hard into the steel bulkhead, and seriously injured.

Outside, Hall was almost killed by scattered debris from the shattered DSRV, which flew up as a shower of shrapnel in the sub's down draft. Loose wiring from the DSRV whipped against his helmet. Still, despite the danger he had to go back, working in close to the Cox valves to put in more air.

Finally Hall was able to report to the *Petrel*, "Looks like she's going into positive buoyancy. If we can get a hard rise on the planes, I think she'll come up under her own steam, but I'll try to attach the *Boise*'s cable underneath her midsection so that we'll have a loop around her. Maybe use two Cox valves as lift points."

"What's their pullout limit?" asked the bosun, his voice extremely clear.

"Eighty tons pullout," answered Hall.

"You okay?"

"Has *Petrel* got the messenger buoy aboard yet?"

"Christ, Frank!" said the bosun excitedly. "You mean it's loose?"

Hall looked at his watch. "Yeah, it should surface in about ten minutes."

"Way to go, Frank."

Normally Hall would have been on a high with the job he'd done so far, but the sensation of enormous weight was pressing in on him again—the realization that the more successful he was with the submarine the more certain it was they'd kill Gloria. "Oh, Christ!" he muttered, feeling such turmoil that he could hardly breathe.

He was now at the base of the sail, standing only feet above the men in the *New York*'s control room. He decided he'd have to use a flare after all, to get a better idea of just what was happening. He could afford the flare now that the messenger buoy, trailing cable behind it, was on its way up. His wrist light picked up a glint of the cable, the downed sub's lifeline—or was it to be its deathline? And if it was, how could he stop it? How could he live with either terrible decision?


"HEY, SIR . . ." It was the operator manning the *New York*'s depth gauges.

Sloane turned around. "Yes?"

"We're rising, sir. Nineteen hundred fifty feet." The operator found it difficult to speak in the foul, oxygen-starved air. "Nineteen hundred forty feet."

There was a cheer so faint that Sloane started to laugh. They were near hysteria. It was always the most dangerous time, with the exhilaration of hope in what had so recently seemed a lost cause.

Then Sloane saw Wain's cap on the floor by the attack island, and the sight silenced his laughter. The captain had died five minutes earlier from the severe concussion.

LISTENING ON THE OPEN CHANNEL to the growing excitement and expectation on the American ships, Kornon wasn't amused. The *Boise*'s commander was ordering all foreign ships to keep well clear of the salvage area as the *Boise*'s launch dropped more flashing orange glow buoys to mark a two-mile-diameter circle over the *New York*. The media people aboard the *Karpaty II* had been urging its captain to move in for a closer look, and had also relayed their request to Kornon aboard the *Leningrad*. But Peters was insistent that the last thing he wanted was a sub coming up—if it did come up—and colliding with another vessel.

Kornon didn't want to move back beyond the circle. He started making noises about the Soviet security zone into which the Americans never should have ventured in the first place. But Ustenko quickly stepped in, afraid that the general's fatigue was undoing his normal common sense. He advised Kornon to show restraint; Moscow didn't want anything to damage its meticulously orchestrated propaganda offensive, which had been so successfully maintained ever since the open press conference at the Foreign Ministry.

Kornon, the ghost of Ulan Ude hard upon him, then addressed the press on the *Karpaty II* and those who had followed him onto the *Leningrad*. "Ladies and gentlemen, I realize you are as anxious as I am to see the successful conclusion of the rescue, but in due deference to our American colleagues we must withdraw from the salvage area. If the rescue is successful—and this, of course, is still, I'm sorry to say, in much doubt—we do not want to endanger either the American rescue ships or the submarine."

The general was absolutely stony-faced about the fate of the *Lenin I*, clearly embarrassed, more than concerned, about what had happened to the men aboard. By his studied military reserve, he encouraged the press to treat his attitude to the tragedy as merely another example of Soviet resoluteness and ability to withstand misfortune without complaint.

Some of the Eastern press asked to be taken to the *Boise*. Kornon quickly agreed to this, for they would serve, in effect, as his observers by proxy and would provide more good footage of how cooperative the Russians were—in what was really, from their point of view, Soviet territory.

HALL'S MAIN WORRY NOW was that as the sub rose she wouldn't need any more hauling but would start to rise too fast. Even with full plane control returned she might not have enough power to work the valves that opened the vents in order to flood the ballast tanks, and so reduce or brake her rate of ascent. But his fears were unfounded, for some of the tanks he'd "blown," expelling the water by air hose, had minor leaks from the *New York*'s initial impact on the bottom; even though the submarine was slowly gaining buoyancy and started to rise faster for a while, with less pressure on her the higher she went, the leaks now acted as brakes, controlling her ascent at fifty feet per minute.

Hall contacted the *Petrel*. "Bosun?"

"Yes, Frank?"

"I'm riding the sub. It's a bit tricky weaving in and around these cables with the communications cord and air hose so I'll have to disengage the communications cord and tether. I'll clip them together with the air hose on the haul wire. The point is, I'll be out of communication with you for a while."

"Hey, Frank—Frank!"

He was lying about its being tricky for him to move around with the communications cord. The truth was, he didn't want anyone to hear his instructions to the submariners. After their experience with the Spets though, he didn't know what signal might convince them that he was not an enemy. Finally he simply tapped in code: "Frank Hall. Oceanographer for CNO Washington, Imperative you follow my instructions. Will you do this? Acknowledge Immediate."

Sloane looked around at the crew. He knew he'd have to make the decision, but the faces of the men told him clearly enough what they wanted. Somebody had gotten them off the bottom and they were on their way up.

"It's a gamble," said Sloane.

They heard more tapping. "How many Cox bolts did I fire in?"

"Twelve," said two men. Sloane, too, knew it had been twelve. Most of the crew had made a point of counting the shots.

Sloane tapped back, "Fourteen."

"Twelve," came the answer.

"Will follow your instructions," Sloane tapped out.

They were the most unorthodox instructions Sloane and the crew of the *New York*—or any other ship in the U.S. Navy—had ever received, and the orders Sloane would have to give would be equally so.

# 43

"WHERE IS IT?" growled Kornon.

"Can't say, General. Not until it breaks the scattering layer."

"Let's hope it doesn't," said Ustenko. "Everybody would see it then on the sonar traces—those that have been repaired." He looked across at the general. "By then we couldn't expect an accident, General."

"Well, I wish he'd hurry and blow it."

"You mean blow ballast tanks," said Admiral Litov's old aide. "But that would only make it rise more."

"Blow it up, you idiot!" thundered Kornon. "Blow it up!" He could see Ulan Ude as clear as day. "You said he understood?" Kornon pressed Ustenko.

"I gave him her picture, General. I tell you he was devastated."

"Well, there's hope then."

"I'm confident," answered Ustenko.

"Oh, yes, you can afford to be."

"No," said Ustenko evenly, his voice bordering on insubordination. "As you said, General, if you fall we all fall."

"Yes," said the general in a more positive tone. "Yes, exactly."

IN THE FETID redded-out control room of the *New York* the depth gauge now read thirteen hundred feet. The higher they went the less pull the *Boise* would have to exert on the cable sling. The *Boise* pulling in the sling and the *Petrel* winching in the haul-up cable from the messenger buoy would be able to keep her reasonably steady at a thousand feet. If she started to rise any higher than that, the oceanographer had instructed

Sloane to flood a tank. That would keep the sub below the scattering layer long enough to keep her image off any sonar trace.

"How long do we hold at one thousand," Sloane tapped out.

"One hour."

Sloane looked at his watch. It was almost 3:00 a.m. The scattering layer would come down at first light. He had to be ready to do everything Hall had told him by 3:20 and no later.

"Ask him," Chief Ryman said to Sloane, "what happens if we can't stay beneath the layer for an hour."

"Say your prayers," was the answer.

AT 3:00 A.M. FRANK knocked hard three times above the control room. In two minutes he would have to jettison almost half his weights. His ascent to the surface approximately one thousand feet above would take ten minutes.

Inside the sub Sloane began to do what Hall had told him, to follow what he hoped would be the road of salvation.

"Torpedo officer!" he said as he stood by the attack island, headset on, lip mike up.

"Sir?"

"Bleed anything you've got. I want all the compression this baby's got left put in those tubes."

"We're ready, sir."

"Very well. Depth, Sonar?"

The sonar man sent out an active pulse, the first one he'd been able to send since the sub had gotten out of the mud. "One thousand feet to bottom—one thousand feet from surface."

"Torpedo tube report?"

"One, three and four loaded with Mark 48s. Tube two loaded with one MOSS 70."

"Very well. Set range on Mark 48s for two thousand feet below surface. Repeat, below surface."

"Range set on Mark 48s two thousand below surface. Short fuses and impact."

"Very well," Sloane acknowledged. "Set MOSS for level running at four hundred feet below surface. Maximum speed ten knots for five minutes, then arcing to two thousand feet."

"MOSS set for level running four hundred feet below surface, speed ten knots for five minutes. Arcing to two thousand."

"Check MOSS is in tube two."

"Affirmative."

"Hold the trim steady."

"Steady she is."

"Fire number two," Sloane ordered.

"Fire number two."

A slight tremor passed through the *New York*.

"Dive angle fifteen degrees."

"Diving angle fifteen degrees."

They all felt the sub slowly tilting until the needle hit fifteen degrees.

"Check tubes one and three and four loaded with Mark 48s."

"Affirmative."

"Fire one, three and four."

"Fire one, three and four. One, three and four fired and running, sir."

"Very well. Sonar, switch echoes to speakers."

"Echoes to speakers, sir."

There was a moment of alarm in the sub as the Trident, lightened by the exit of the three Mark 48 torpedoes and the mobile submarine simulator, or MOSS, rolled slightly and lifted her bow. Sloane was on the verge of opening a ballast tank when she steadied out.


A SAILOR ON THE *Leningrad* burst into the wardroom. "Where's the general? He's wanted on the bridge."

The stewards, two sullen women from Turkestan, shrugged. They didn't know, they didn't care. The East German TV crew was lounging about, sipping coffee and smoking. "He's probably in the head," said one of them. "What's up?"

The sailor said nothing and opened the wardroom door. As he stepped out into the corridor, he crashed into the general, knocking him back against the fire alarm box. Kornon glowered down, but the sailor quickly saluted, telling him he was wanted on the bridge immediately.

Entering the cruiser's bridge, Kornon heard the sonar operator calling off depth and speed.

"General! He's brought it above the scattering layer."

Kornon's body stiffened with excitement and apprehension as Ustenko pointed to the sonar trace—a very definite line running above the scattering layer at five hundred feet, moving slowly, around ten knots. The *Leningrad*'s oscilloscope-computer consoles quickly interpreted the incoming sine wave patterns as being definitely those of a Trident—Class K. USS-SLBM 921. *New York*.

"She must be on auxiliary power," said Ustenko. "Litov's been telling me they apparently have two props in the stern for what they call 'bring home capability' and—"

"Range two thousand yards," continued the sonar operator. "Depth steady at five hundred feet. Range nineteen hundred yards, steady at five hundred feet..."

About two minutes later the trace vanished, both on the sonar and oscilloscope-computers.

"Vessel off screen," continued the operator in a steady monotone.

"She's going down?" asked Kornon, his voice taut with emotion.

"Yes, General," the first lieutenant confirmed, one eye on the steering console, trying to keep the cruiser as steady as he could in the chop. All around him there was elation on the bridge. Then suddenly the sonar operator shot back in his chair, yanking off his earphones. At the same time the sonar trace needle reached its "throw limit," the stylus stuck against the guide bar, the paper burning with a strange smell of singed flesh, the amplifiers giving off sounds like crashing thunder, one crescendo rolling into another, then another, creating an enormous rumbling, reminding the general of rapidly advancing artillery.

"He's done it!" Ustenko shouted. "Aha, General, he's done it!" A warm smile was spreading over the general's face as he straightened to full height, exhaling slowly, quietly savoring his victory, while those about him broke into applause.

Apart from Kornon, one of the most jubilant was Admiral Litov, even while he gave orders that the battle group would have to get under way immediately, given the great danger of radioactive contamination from the destroyed sub. The post-Chernobyl East Bloc press would be quick to report that it was the Americans who bore full responsibility for the contamination, and so it should be they who stayed in the area doing what they could to prevent the complete wiping out of the fishery in the area and, worse still, the contamination of the entire North Pacific food chain.

As the sonar traces on the *Boise* and the *Petrel*, too, were wiped out by the deep water explosions, Hall was being hauled onto the *Petrel*'s deck in the davit's recovery basket operated by the bosun. The moment he was on deck Hall began screaming hysterically, out of control, at the *Boise*. He didn't realize it, but he was already on Polish and American videotape, for the news crews, alerted by the explosions, had spilled out onto deck. Taking off his helmet, he threw it, all three thousand dollars' worth, onto the deck. Once out of the suit, he took the steps three at a time up to the *Petrel*'s bridge and shoved Tate aside, still screaming and yelling at Peters on the open channel. "You bastard! You goddamn incompetent bastard! You've just killed a hundred and fifty men. I told you not to jerk the goddamn wire—"

Peters tried to get a word in, to say he'd been hauling steadily, but Hall's hysteria was such that even Peters's outraged defense was drowned in the continuing stream of oaths—all being picked up, unbeknownst to the oceanographer, by every network that could get a mike either on the *Petrel* or the *Boise*, or by the *Leningrad*'s bridge, where the Russians were enjoying Hall's tirade enormously.

"He's quite an actor," Kornon said, laughing with Ustenko.

"Well, wouldn't you want to sound convincing, General? I expect the U.S. Navy—not to mention the American public—will want a head or two for losing a Trident."

At her flank speed of thirty knots, spray enveloping her two forward turrets of three 125 mm guns each, the *Leningrad*, with the rest of her battle group following, headed toward the Komandorskys in triumph. No one aboard who had come in contact with him could remember the general ever having been in such high spirits. He even made the two morose stewards actually smile, but no one was sure whether they did so at his jokes, mainly about Mongolians and Ulan Ude, or because of the vodka he allowed, with Admiral Litov's consent, to flow so freely in contravention of normal naval rules and regulations. The only disgruntled ones aboard the entire cruiser were those on watch, who weren't allowed to celebrate the occasion with anything stronger than tea.

The general was having such a good time that it took three reminders from Colonel Ustenko before he finally sent a message that all was well, relayed via Klaus's Zurich office to Klaus's two operatives—or, more accurately, his two free-lance professionals—in Oregon.

GLORIA HAD OVERSLEPT. When she awoke, the bedroom was flooded with sunlight. She wouldn't have awakened then except that the phone was ringing. Expecting it to be the Portland FBI office again, she was startled to find that both agents were gone and to hear, on a very bad line, Hall's voice, croaky with fatigue but calm.

Outside it was a wonderfully clear day, the gulls squawking and gliding high above Haystack Rock, the Pacific crashing in, sending sparkling silver mist high into the glorious blue summer air, its tangy smell the most invigorating she could remember.

Gloria hung up the phone, ecstatic. Hall was coming home.

# EPILOGUE

THE MONUMENTAL BLOWUP between Captain Peters of the USS *Boise* and Frank Hall, the oceanographer, was aired by every major American and European network, especially by those who had been actually filming on the *Boise* and the *Petrel* at the time. They had scooped their Soviet and Eastern Bloc counterparts by appealing to Peters's pride in his ship, so that he delivered them to Attu's superior video satellite hookup before the Russian battle group reached the Komandorskys.

A U.S. Naval Board of Inquiry was subsequently convened under the authority of Admiral Clayton, Commander of Submarines Pacific. At first the inquiry named Captain Peters of the USS *Boise* and his executive officer, Lieutenant Bryce, as "interested parties," an innocent-sounding term that was often an ominous death knell to Navy careers. The board, however, ultimately found both officers blameless for the loss of SSBN 921 during the rescue attempt off the Aleutian Trench. The bulk of the blame, the board concluded, lay with oceanographer Frank Hall of Sea Gold, Inc. The board specifically cited, as the cause of the loss of the sub, Hall's failure to take "all due precaution" against sudden temperature inversions of the kind believed to have been a major cause of the submarine's sinking in the first place, and his failure to pay "sufficient attention" to the ever-present danger of haul-line slippage in the rough sea conditions present at the time. Experts testified that an already crippled sub plummeting in such a temperature inversion would implode at two thousand feet with a speed in excess of one hundred miles per hour, the accompanying explosions no doubt originating in the missile bays.

In his defense, Frank Hall, with Gloria Bernardi by his side, pointed out that as time was a crucial factor in the attempted rescue operation, he had had little alternative but to rush the hookup of the haul cables and risk the *New York*'s breaking free in the subsurface turbulence caused by the vent.

The Soviet press ate it up or, as the Chief of Naval Operations described it to the President, "swallowed it hook, line and sinker," especially when, after the weather over the area had abated, *Pravda* published Bear reconnaissance aircraft photos of an oil slick showing several telltale yellow plastic reactor bootees and "quiet" cork baffling unique to nuclear submarines. In the same way, the CNO pointed out to the President, the Soviets, years before, had fallen for the more intricate U.S. cover story surrounding the activities of Howard Hughes's *Glomar Explorer*, a ship specifically designed to retrieve a sunken Golf class Russian sub but believed by all the world, including the KGB and avid readers of *National Geographic*, to be a deep-sea mining vessel.

General Alexander Androvich Kornon was reinstated, not as a full member of the Politburo—after all, he hadn't retrieved any secrets from the Trident—but as an alternate member, and was awarded the Order of Lenin for having destroyed one of the enemy's most dangerous weapons in "Soviet home waters." In Red Tass, editor-in-chief Lebdev, commenting on a story by his newly hired East German correspondent Elga Kirche, reported that attending the ceremony in the Kremlin were Colonel Ustenko, retired General Borgach, Ustenko's old boss, and Kornon's wife, Natasha, who had recently returned from vacationing in Ulan Ude. Mrs. Kornon regretted that their daughter, Tanya, couldn't be present at the award ceremony but explained that her daughter was required to attend a Bolshoi rehearsal. The story also informed readers of Red Tass *and* Green Tass that Colonel Ustenko had been assigned as Kornon's aide in the general's new position of Director of Security, Pacific Ocean Department. Lebdev was at pains to point out that Kornon's appointment in no way indicated demotion for Director Skolensky but was merely the creation of a new position in the department in light of new developments: the South Pacific offered the Soviet Union new initiatives in the years following Colonel Rabuka's coup d'état in Fiji through the increased pressure in the region for "nuclear-free zones" in the interest of world peace.

The *New York* crew taken aboard the *Boise* and the *Petrel* in the heavy fog were transported to Dutch Harbor in the eastern Aleutians for medical examinations, then returned to the United States for assignment to another submarine.

The towing of the USS *New York* SSBN 921—now the USS *ALASKA* SSBN 926—was taken up by another fast missile-guided frigate. Martin Knead survived his suicide attempt, due in large part to blood donated by Yeoman Smythe. During the tow Knead, along with other crew members, was shown the videos of crew members' families talking to reporters—the same videos that Kornon had been so contemptuous of when they were first broadcast. One of the brief interviews was with Joanne Knead of Bremerton, Washington State. It wasn't much different from the others, except that she commented, "You know, it's when something like this happens that you really appreciate what you have in this life," and ended by saying that she was looking forward "to seeing Marty again." Knead was astonished and confused, and had to be assured by Sloane and Chief Ryman that the interview was genuine.

Dr. Dyer was informed that during his ordeal on the *New York*, his wife had given birth to a healthy eight-pound baby boy.

The *Tuna Star*, alias the *Amlia*, was confiscated by the U.S. government for fisheries violations, its owner held by "executive order" until the *New York* reached Kiska—rather than Attu—dry dock. Joe Cherco couldn't buy another trawler for no bank would extend the necessary loans, which forced him to live in a dugout hut on Attu and work for a local Japanese-owned canning company.

Over a beer at the seaside cottage that Hall and Gloria rented for the remainder of the summer, Hall and Captain Peters, a frequent visitor, made a bet over how long the cover story would last. Peters, with more faith in the power of officialdom, thought it would run longer than the one used to hide the activities of Howard Hughes's *Glomar Explorer*. Hall, on the other hand, was more skeptical. His experience made him doubt that the Navy's cover would survive more than a few months, even though Peters reminded him of how the U.S. government had managed to keep the secret of the six American hostages in the Canadian embassy in Iran for more than a year.

In any event, the length of time didn't matter; Hall's plan and his execution of it had enabled the U.S. to retrieve the costly Trident and to rescue most of its crew.

But on one thing Hall and Peters both agreed—if and when the Soviets discovered the ruse, the potential international embarrassment it could cause them, particularly in front of their Warsaw Pact allies, would be so acute, they would say nothing. And something else was even more certain than that: Kornon in the Kremlin and Herr Klaus in Zurich would go absolutely *beshenstvo*—"ape."

From Scott Stone, the award-winning author of *The Dragon's Eye* and *Song of the Wolf*, a blistering new thriller of revenge

# SCOTT STONE

# SCIMITAR

Richard Casski is a lone CIA agent primed for revenge and prepared to stalk the world's four most ruthless killers. From Tahiti to Hong Kong to a secluded cabin in Idaho, Casski and the beautiful woman he's forced to use as bait play hardball in the most dangerous game of their lives!

---

# The Catapult Ultimatum
## Peter Leslie

1940. French North Africa. As French military command resists
Churchill's protection, as Hitler secretly moves closer to striking,
as America anxiously watches and waits, the world's most
cunning secret agents clash in a head-on collision that will alter
the course of World War II.

# Blistering new thrillers of intrigue, suspense and adventure

# Exciting novels of international intrigue, adventure and suspense

# Thrilling adventures of espionage, suspense and revenge . . .